Praise for Lexi Blake and Masters and Mercenaries...

"I can always trust Lexi Blake's Dominants to leave me breathless...and in love. If you want sensual, exciting BDSM wrapped in an awesome love story, then look for a Lexi Blake book."
~Cherise Sinclair USA Today Bestselling author

"Lexi Blake's MASTERS AND MERCENARIES series is beautifully written and deliciously hot. She's got a real way with both action and sex. I also love the way Blake writes her gorgeous Dom heroes--they make me want to do bad, bad things. Her heroines are intelligent and gutsy ladies whose taste for submission definitely does not make them dish rags. Can't wait for the next book!"
~Angela Knight, New York Times Bestselling author

"A Dom is Forever is action packed, both in the bedroom and out. Expect agents, spies, guns, killing and lots of kink as Liam goes after the mysterious Mr. Black and finds his past and his future... The action and espionage keep this story moving along quickly while the sex and kink provides a totally different type of interest. Everything is very well balanced and flows together wonderfully."
~A Night Owl "Top Pick", Terri, Night Owl Erotica

"A Dom Is Forever is everything that is good in erotic romance. The story was fast-paced and suspenseful, the characters were flawed but made me root for them every step of the way, and the hotness factor was off the charts mostly due to a bad boy Dom with a penchant for dirty talk."
~Rho, The Romance Reviews

"A good read that kept me on my toes, guessing until the big reveal, and thinking survival skills should be a must for all men."
~Chris, Night Owl Reviews

No Love Lost

Other Books by Lexi Blake

ROMANTIC SUSPENSE

Masters and Mercenaries
The Dom Who Loved Me
The Men With The Golden Cuffs
A Dom is Forever
On Her Master's Secret Service
Sanctum: A Masters and Mercenaries Novella
Love and Let Die
Unconditional: A Masters and Mercenaries Novella
Dungeon Royale
Dungeon Games: A Masters and Mercenaries Novella
A View to a Thrill
Cherished: A Masters and Mercenaries Novella
You Only Love Twice
Luscious: Masters and Mercenaries~Topped
Adored: A Masters and Mercenaries Novella
Master No
Just One Taste: Masters and Mercenaries~Topped 2
From Sanctum with Love
Devoted: A Masters and Mercenaries Novella
Dominance Never Dies
Submission is Not Enough
Master Bits and Mercenary Bites~The Secret Recipes of Topped
Perfectly Paired: Masters and Mercenaries~Topped 3
For His Eyes Only
Arranged: A Masters and Mercenaries Novella
Love Another Day
At Your Service: Masters and Mercenaries~Topped 4
Master Bits and Mercenary Bites~Girls Night
Nobody Does It Better
Close Cover
Protected: A Masters and Mercenaries Novella
Enchanted: A Masters and Mercenaries Novella
Charmed: A Masters and Mercenaries Novella
Treasured: A Masters and Mercenaries Novella, Coming June 29, 2021

Masters and Mercenaries: The Forgotten
Lost Hearts (Memento Mori)
Lost and Found
Lost in You
Long Lost
No Love Lost

Masters and Mercenaries: Reloaded
Submission Impossible
The Dom Identity, Coming September 14, 2021

Butterfly Bayou
Butterfly Bayou
Bayou Baby
Bayou Dreaming
Bayou Beauty, Coming July 27, 2021

Lawless
Ruthless
Satisfaction
Revenge

Courting Justice
Order of Protection
Evidence of Desire

Masters Of Ménage (by Shayla Black and Lexi Blake)
Their Virgin Captive
Their Virgin's Secret
Their Virgin Concubine
Their Virgin Princess
Their Virgin Hostage
Their Virgin Secretary
Their Virgin Mistress

The Perfect Gentlemen (by Shayla Black and Lexi Blake)
Scandal Never Sleeps
Seduction in Session
Big Easy Temptation

Smoke and Sin
At the Pleasure of the President

URBAN FANTASY

Thieves
Steal the Light
Steal the Day
Steal the Moon
Steal the Sun
Steal the Night
Ripper
Addict
Sleeper
Outcast
Stealing Summer

LEXI BLAKE WRITING AS SOPHIE OAK

Texas Sirens
Small Town Siren
Siren in the City
Siren Enslaved
Siren Beloved
Siren in Waiting
Siren in Bloom
Siren Unleashed
Siren Reborn

Nights in Bliss, Colorado
Three to Ride
Two to Love
One to Keep
Lost in Bliss
Found in Bliss
Pure Bliss
Chasing Bliss
Once Upon a Time in Bliss
Back in Bliss
Sirens in Bliss
Happily Ever After in Bliss

Far From Bliss, Coming 2021

A Faery Story
Bound
Beast
Beauty

Standalone
Away From Me
Snowed In

No Love Lost

Masters and Mercenaries
The Forgotten, Book 5

Lexi Blake

No Love Lost
Masters and Mercenaries: The Forgotten, Book 5
Lexi Blake

Published by DLZ Entertainment LLC
Copyright 2020 DLZ Entertainment LLC
Edited by Chloe Vale
ISBN: 978-1-942297-33-8

Sign up for Lexi Blake's newsletter
and be entered to win a $25 gift certificate
to the bookseller of your choice.

Join us for news, fun, and exclusive content
including free Thieves short stories.

There's a new contest every month!

Go to www.LexiBlake.net to subscribe.

Acknowledgments

It feels like forever ago that I started this little offshoot of the Masters and Mercenaries series. It all began when Theo Taggart took a couple of bullets. It should have ended with Theo's book, but as so often happens, my characters had other ideas. So here we are five books later and I'm going to miss this bunch of misfits so much. It's been good to watch them achieve their happily ever afters when joy seemed so far away from each. These books have been soaked in memory and time and how precious each of those things are in our lives. It's made me reflect on the importance of both in my own life and how building a trove of memories is one of life's great achievements. As I write this, the world seems to have changed in so many ways, but this truth will always hold true. No matter what happens we are made of memory, each precious moment stamped indelibly on our souls. Each hard time is yet another brick in our foundations, something we overcome that makes the structure of love stronger. I thank the Lost Boys for giving me that revelation. So here's to one last mission with Theo, Jax, Owen, Rob, Tucker, and their leader, Ezra/Beck. And when this book is through, know that the missions will continue, a younger generation taking over. Thank you so much for sticking with me.

Thanks to everyone who helped make this book come to life. To my team – Chloe Vale, Maria Monroy, Stormy Pate, Riane Holt, Kori Smith. Thanks to the amazing marketing brains of Liz Berry, Jillian Stein, Jenn Watson and the team at Social Butterfly. Thank you to Denise Lacavalla for her help with the Italian translations in this book, and to Marie-laure Bellon for the French.

This book is dedicated to Rich for reasons that will only be obvious to him.

Part One

Chapter One

London, England

Kimberly Solomon stood outside the door that led to the tidy offices of MI6 and wished she was back in DC. Something was wrong. She could feel it in her gut, the deep instinct of a long-term operative who'd seen an op go south more than once.

She couldn't go back to the States because she was weak, because she'd always been weak in one specific part of her life. If she'd had a lick of sense she never would have gotten involved in this op, but no, she was the idiot who offered herself up. A masochist. That's what she was.

But then maybe Beck was a sadist deep down, and wasn't she interested in seeing how hanging around a bunch of Doms had changed him? He'd been alpha in bed before, in every part of their life, really, but how had studying at clubs, under Ian Taggart and Damon Knight, transformed him?

She needed to let go of that thought because she wasn't welcome in those clubs. Neither of those men trusted her as far as they could throw her, and she couldn't even blame them. She'd had a job to do, and it hadn't always been to their betterment. She'd shared what information she could, protected them as much as she was able, but in the end she would always be the bad guy for Beckett Kent and the men he worked with. She was Agency, after all.

Once Beck had been Agency, too. Once he'd understood what it meant to be an operative, to have to make the hard calls.

Now she worried that she wouldn't even be able to protect them at all.

She stared at the door in front of her and thought seriously about walking away. Just walking away from all of it. Maybe it was time.

The cell in her hand buzzed and she was thrilled to have a reason to put off making that decision. She'd watched her ex-husband walk through with Damon Knight mere moments before and had stood there, trying to figure out why she couldn't simply walk away.

Because you love him. Because you've always loved him, and you won't ever love another man the way you love Beck.

Because you betrayed him, and he won't ever love you back again.

She slid her finger across the screen to accept the call.

"Are you actually going to go in or are you simply going to stand around? You know they usually frown on that here," a familiar feminine voice said. "If you're going to have to deal with MI6 and the Agency, at least let me buy you lunch."

She loved the sound of that lady's voice. Ariel Adisa. Once she'd been the baddest assassin to ever work for an intelligence agency. She'd also been one of the few people on the planet Solo could call friend. Then she'd hung up her guns and used her brain for good, and ended up all married and happy and working for the very man who'd so recently walked into that conference room with Beck. She looked around, trying to figure out where Ari was hiding. "You're here? I thought you were spending a couple of weeks in Wyoming. Did the big family reunion go bad?"

She didn't like the thought of something going wrong between Ariel and her husband, Robert. They'd made it through a storm and seemed so solid.

"I got back yesterday, but Rob's staying on for the rest of the week," Ariel replied in her crisp British accent. "And it was perfect. My new mother-in-law is lovely. Tucker and Roni are staying on for a time. I'm going to miss them terribly. I came home because I'm consulting on a case and they've had a bit of a breakthrough. I came up to read through some confidential files they couldn't send over to me. I thought avoiding the Tube would be a good idea. It wasn't. Ezra is even more morose than usual."

She moved away from the door and saw Ari down the hall. Her friend waved and slid her cell into her fashionable bag. She was dressed in a lovely pink sheath and smoking hot white stilettos. Ariel was gorgeous, and now she glowed in the way only a woman who was well loved ever managed.

The way she used to glow when he'd loved her. Before she'd taken his brother from him.

Sometimes she hated Ezra Fain. After all, it had been Ezra's death that had been the final nail in the coffin of her marriage. The fact that her husband now went by the name was simply another way to twist the knife.

She strode toward Ari and wondered if it wasn't fate that had brought her here. Ari, that was. It hadn't been fate that brought Solo. It had been an order from her boss to stay in London and finish the job she'd started. "Well, I'm sure he's upset because he knows I'll be here today. He's been good at freezing me out since Paris."

They worked together on her last mission. It had been the mission that brought Tucker and the rest of the remaining Lost Boys out of the shadows. She'd started the job because she'd wanted to see if she and Beck could try one last time. She'd ended up staying because she'd believed in those men, wanted what was best for them. They'd been through a lot of shit and all because an evil doctor had decided to treat them like guinea pigs. Although now that she thought about it, she didn't like people who treated guinea pigs like test subjects either.

Now she wanted to know who'd supported Dr. Hope McDonald with money and assistance. She wanted the names of everyone McDonald worked with. It had been the whole point of her being in Europe. She'd worked with McKay-Taggart and Knight to get the list of McDonald's consortia from the pharmaceutical company who'd backed her in the beginning.

Ariel's expression turned serious. "Why aren't you back in the States? The Agency took the data. I assumed you would go with it."

19

Yes, she'd assumed that, too. "The boss wanted me to wait here in England and liaise with MI6 and German intelligence. Not to mention I've had to deal with DGSE."

"Well, you had to know the French would want in on whatever you found," Ariel pointed out.

The French intelligence agency had been key in trapping the man who'd tried to trade Roni Croft's life for the data Tucker had hidden all those years ago. "Yes, and they've been perfectly reasonable. It's Beck who isn't. He thinks I'm hiding something from him."

She was hiding so many things from her ex, but this wasn't one of them.

"I think it's hard for him to trust anyone from an intelligence agency," Ariel replied with sympathy. "Kim, I have to ask you what you're doing. Not with work, but with Ezra. It's been years since you divorced. Don't you think it's time to move on?"

Her heart clenched at the thought, but she knew her friend was right. "When I found out he was getting involved with McKay-Taggart, I knew he would be in danger because of who they were investigating. I'd stayed away for years, Ari. I gave him space. He was grieving and he needed a place to put it all. Then he was angry because he found out about the mistake I made with Levi."

The biggest mistake of her life, and she'd made so many. She'd been divorced and she'd gone out with a man she'd thought was her friend, and he'd taken such advantage of her. She didn't even remember the night. She was a deadly CIA operative and that night had proven she was still a woman and still fucking vulnerable.

"I don't know that he's in a place where he can forgive," Ari said slowly, as if she knew the words would be a blow. "I'm not sure he ever will be. Obviously I didn't know him before his brother was killed, but I know the man he is now. He's perfectly reasonable until it comes to you. Normally I would say that means he's still got feelings for you and as long as there's an emotional connection, the relationship isn't truly dead."

"But his feelings for me are hurting him." It was the conclusion she'd come to after long hours of self-reflection.

Ariel reached out, putting a hand on her shoulder. "They're hurting you, too. I don't like saying this, Kim, but he's not in a place where he can find any peace with you around. And I don't think you'll find any either. Do you want to go have lunch? We can talk. I'll wait around if your meeting takes longer than mine."

The last thing she wanted to do was cry to her gorgeous, happily married friend who would likely start having babies and raising a gorgeous family with her loving husband. She hated the jealousy that gnawed at her. It wasn't Ariel's fault she'd done everything right.

But Kim had thought she would have a family by now. She'd thought she and Beck would have had their two point five kids and retired to the country where they would raise them, and she would sell homemade jam or some shit.

Instead she was thirty-four and had nothing but a bunch of medals she couldn't bring out at parties to show for it. She'd tried dating over the years, tried to forget him, but the minute she'd found a way to work herself into his world she'd taken it.

"Come on, Kim. Please have lunch with me. We don't have to turn it into a session," Ari prompted. "I'll stay at your place tonight and we can order in and drink as much as we like and watch ridiculous movies. I won't say a thing to upset you."

God, it was nice to have a friend. She was going to miss Ari because when she was back at the Agency, she would go deep this time. She would take an assignment that would last years and lose herself in it. She would start over again, and this time she wouldn't let herself ever get pulled back in.

"I can't tonight." It would be too hard to keep from talking to Ari. Ari had a way of dragging the truth out of her, and there were some things she couldn't admit to anyone. Some secrets that had to stay hidden or the world would crash in again.

She had promises to keep. Even if they cost her everything.

Ari nodded. "All right, but I won't let you mope forever. Call me sometime this week. I want to get together before you go back to the States."

She nodded, though it was another lie. Hopefully she would go back to the States as soon as this meeting was over. "Sure. I should go in. I'll think about everything you said."

She wouldn't be able to do anything but think. That was why she needed to get out of Europe, away from him. Maybe then she could finally move on.

She watched as Ari took the stairs and then forced herself to walk into that office. She stopped at the reception desk and showed the badge she'd been given downstairs at the security check and then let herself be led down the hall to the conference room.

Solo felt every eye on her. It wasn't that being looked at bothered her. She hadn't worn the Louboutin boots that came up over her knees to be ignored. But this felt different. Had Damon Knight warned his old crew not to trust her?

Or had it been Beck?

She strode in, her Prada bag over her shoulder. What had her mother told her? Use clothes and makeup and looks like a shield.

No hate can get through a Prada bag, my darling.

Her mother had been wrong, of course.

Her mother had hated Beck. She loathed his middle-class background, and the fact that he hadn't gone to an Ivy league school. Her mother had cheered on their divorce. Not that it had helped her mother's cause. She'd died hating her daughter for not following in the family traditions and marrying the wealthiest man she could find.

"Hello, Beck." She picked the chair furthest from him because his eyes were already staring a hole through her. He was dressed in what she thought of as his uniform. Dark shirt, pressed slacks. She couldn't see his feet, but she knew he would be wearing comfortable loafers. No brand names. He didn't care about anything but functionality. His new boss, on the other hand, was quite fashionable. Damon Knight looked like he could be in a James Bond film. He was wearing a dapper three-piece suit, his hair slicked back, and when his arm moved she caught sight of a Cartier watch. "Damon, it's good to see you."

"And you, Solo." Damon sat back as though waiting for the sparks to fly. "I want to say thank you for everything you did for the lads. I suspect you're the only reason we're here today, too. I appreciate it all."

At least one person appreciated her. No. That wasn't fair, and she wasn't going to give into pessimism. Ian Taggart had called her, too. He'd thanked her and told her if she ever needed a job, she would be welcome in Dallas. It was a tempting offer, but she couldn't do it.

"I'm glad it worked out. But I've got to admit they've been stonewalling me about that drive. I tried to go back to DC to help analyze the data and I was told to stay here in London to liaise with MI6. I think someone convinced the big bosses that I'm too close to the subject. I have to wonder if that was you, Beck."

She called him Beck because he'd told her it didn't sound right when she called him Ezra. They'd been in the English countryside, and for a moment she'd thought that they might still have a spark between them.

Then he'd chosen his job over her. Like she'd been forced to do. She didn't blame him. He'd needed to get Tucker and Levi Green to Paris, and she would never have allowed him to do that. So he'd started a fight knowing damn well as long as he was paying her any kind of attention she wouldn't notice Tucker slipping away with the prisoner she'd vowed to guard.

Everything Ari had said sat on her chest. Being around her hurt him, hurt her. He wasn't ever going to forgive her, and if he found out the truth, well, he might take their fight to an actual physical level.

At this point, they'd been divorced for far longer than they'd been married. Why couldn't she move on?

He frowned her way. "No. Why would I try to put you on the outside? We kind of need you on the inside. Are you telling me you haven't seen the report?"

He had needed her. She should remember that. She'd gone into this mission working for very powerful people—the president and his closest advisors. President Zack Hayes had been working around certain forces in the CIA, and that had given her leeway the Lost Boys had needed quite badly.

It was the only reason Beck had been willing to put up with her. Now that she'd done her job, those same CIA bosses who would have made things hard had taken over the case. At least she thought they had. She'd been sidelined, and that worried her.

Not that she would show Beck and Damon.

Damon's focus lasered in on her. "Who is running the op now?"

She shrugged. "No idea. I suppose it's one of the big guys. I'll find out when they walk through the door."

Then she would know where her place was. She would know if

she'd traded every bit of her position at the Agency to help a man who couldn't stand to be in the same room with her. She'd known the big bosses would be upset that she'd gone straight to the president, but she'd hoped once they got the real data, the true story, she'd be vindicated.

The truth was she'd started down this path to get closer to Beck, but she'd continued because she'd come to care about those men—Jax, Owen, Robert, Tucker, and Sasha. She'd done the best she could, and she feared she was about to be demoted for it.

"Kim, whose name is on that list?" Beck's voice had gone low and he glanced back at the door like he was afraid of who would walk through it.

She knew that tone. It was the tone Beck used right before the bullets started flying. It was his instincts kicking in. "What do you mean?"

She was watching Beck's ridiculously handsome face when she heard the doors open and saw his eyes flare in obvious shock. Her gut tightened and she turned. Her breath caught in her chest because the last person she'd expected to see strode confidently through the door.

Of course the reason he was the last person she'd expected was the fact that the last time she'd seen Levi Green he'd been in custody. He was supposed to be in a holding cell somewhere until the bosses decided how to punish him.

Levi Green. He'd been her "friend" once. He'd been someone she'd trusted, and he'd turned on her. He'd become obsessed with her. She was a possession in his eyes, a trophy to be claimed, and he didn't like the fact that she'd rejected his romantic interest.

Her mind started to whirl with the possibilities. He was leading the small group. She recognized some of them, and they were strictly muscle. Levi was obviously in charge, so things had changed, and this was exactly why she'd been sidelined.

Levi was dressed in a dark, three-piece suit, his hair tumbling over his brow in a way that looked casual but had likely taken him an hour and plenty of hair gel to achieve. He was wearing thousand-dollar loafers and a tie that probably cost more than everything Beck was wearing combined.

He was dressed to be seen, dressed to impress. She'd seen him dress for a date less carefully than he was now. Levi was all about image, and that suit screamed power. He wasn't in a cell anymore.

He was in charge and something had gone so very wrong.

Oh, god. Her brain went over everything that had happened in the last few weeks. They'd discovered Levi had been working with Tucker all those years ago, that he'd been attempting to find out who was in league with McDonald even before they'd known how bad her experiments were. He'd connected McDonald to the shadowy group known as The Collective and used Tucker's need to find his brother to convince him to go undercover and get him the data he needed to prove his theories. Tucker had lost the data and they hadn't found it until a few weeks before. Solo had been the one to turn it over, but she hadn't been able to look at what was on the thumb drive.

What was on that drive? What had she turned over?

God, had she betrayed Beck again?

Levi stopped at the head of the conference table, the arrogant look on his face telling her he was about to do something terrible. "Hello, all. It's so good to be back."

Had Levi set up a long line of dominoes all those years ago? Was this why he hadn't admitted he knew Tucker? She could see him putting Beck's name on that list. It would be a plant. It would be why he'd done everything he'd done. So he could take down the man he hated. So he could punish her for not being able to love him. "What are you doing here? Why have you been released?"

He should be sitting in a cell at Langley, answering question after question about the things he'd done, the missions he'd fucked with for his own ambition.

"My darling, not only have I been released, I'm back to my full duties, and unfortunately the first is a bit distasteful." Each word that came from his mouth was a silky threat. He was enjoying every minute of this. His head turned slightly to speak to the armed guard he'd brought with him. This had all been a setup, and MI6 had been in on it. "Gentlemen, it's time."

Beck was on his feet, his shoulders squared, and for a moment she wondered if this was how he died. Would she watch him get gunned down here and now because he wasn't about to let Levi take him into custody? Her whole body tensed.

If he went down, she would go, too. She saw it so clearly in her head. She wouldn't let these men take Beck in. Levi would do cruel things to him, would try to break him before ending his life, and she couldn't stand the thought of Beck being broken. Not again. She would do whatever she could. Whatever the outcome.

Levi turned his attention to Damon as four of the guards stepped up. "Mr. Knight, I invited you here because someone should be a witness. Don't make me regret it. You'll have full access to the data after I do what needs to be done."

Her breath caught in her chest and she got ready to move. She'd turned over her gun to security when she'd entered the building. But that didn't mean she was unarmed. She was never unarmed. If she could get them out of here, she would. Adrenaline started to flow as she prepared to defend the man she loved.

"Kimberly Solomon, I'm placing you under arrest for treason."

For a second the words didn't mean anything. She was too concerned with Beck for the words to sink in. A strong hand snaked around her arm and she realized it hadn't been Beck's name that had come out of Levi's mouth.

Her name. It had been her name Levi had planted in that data years before. The revenge wasn't on Beck. Beck couldn't care less what happened to her. Beck would likely giggle at the thought of her in Levi's custody. Or would think it wouldn't be so bad since she'd fallen prey to him once before.

She heard a shuffle to her left like Beck or Damon had moved, but when she glanced over they were still, Damon's hand on Beck's arm.

"What's happening?" She tried to pull away, but the room was too tight, and she found herself completely surrounded by burly guards who likely wouldn't mind roughing her up a bit.

"Be careful with her." Levi pointed to his guard. "I told you I'll kill the first person who hurts her. She's an important prisoner."

"Levi, I swear if you take her, I'm going to kill you."

Beck. Beck had said that. Why would he say that? Still, the fact that he had settled something inside her. She didn't truly expect him to save her. Once, she would have believed those words had come from a place of love, of protection. Now she had to consider that this was more about Levi than herself. She was the bone two dogs fought over.

And it looked like she was about to get torn apart.

"I'm sure you'll try." A faint smile crossed Levi's face as though he was truly satisfied. "Damon, I wish you hadn't stopped him. I wouldn't mind shooting him right here. Solo, your name was on the list. We know you were working with McDonald. What a pity."

For the first time in years she felt truly vulnerable. Not merely her heart. That was always vulnerable to Beck, but now her body and soul were on the line. "That's not true. You're lying."

Damon was whispering something Beck's way, likely a plea to not cause a fight. Any impulse in Beck to help her was merely the remnants of another life. Or perhaps the desperate need to fight Levi. It was good Damon was there. He would convince Beck to take a breath and realize he didn't want to save her.

When Beck thought about it for a few moments, after the shock of seeing Levi had fled, he would very likely come to the conclusion that she was guilty. After all, wasn't she guilty of everything in his eyes? Including the death of his brother. At some point he would determine that this was pure justice, and maybe he would sleep again at night. Maybe then he would be able to move on.

She squared her shoulders. There was no fighting her way out of this. Not now. She would have to bide her time, wait until the right moment.

Then she would make sure Levi Green paid for treating her like a piece of property he could do with as he liked.

She needed to remember that she was alone. She was the only one she could count on.

She walked out the door and didn't look back.

* * * *

Ezra Fain watched as his wife was walked out of the conference room, four men surrounding her like she was some kind of prisoner.

Levi Green let them escort her out, watched her with deep satisfaction in his gaze. He was taking the prize in the game they'd started long ago. The queen in their chess match.

Ezra's queen. No. Beck's. The man he used to be before all of this had started. Before he'd let that fucker ruin everything. Kim Solomon didn't belong to Ezra Fain. She'd been directly involved in his brother's death. She'd lied to him, wouldn't listen to him when he'd begged her not to send Ezra on that mission that had proven to be his brother's last.

Levi turned and gave him a wink before the door closed behind him.

"I'm going to kill that man," Ezra vowed.

"I'm going to help you," Damon promised, his voice low.

In that moment he knew it was about more than the game Levi kept dragging him back into. It was about her. It was about the Kim who'd smiled up at him the day after they'd eloped. The sun had hit her hair and she'd looked like some sunny goddess who'd wound up in his bed, and he'd felt like the king of the world.

He couldn't let her go, couldn't leave her in Levi's hands. Even if it was only to honor the vows they'd made so long ago, he had to save her.

"You have to get that wild look off your face because any second now the head of MI6 is going to walk in, and we need to look good. Shaken, not stirred, if you know what I mean," Damon whispered. "If they haven't changed things, the security cameras are to our backs. It's why I insisted we sit here. But the director will come in to brief us, and he'll report back to his Agency counterparts. You have to keep your cool. Trust me. I'm not going to let you down, brother."

Ezra took a deep breath because his boss was right. Damon knew these people because Damon had been MI6 for years. But his impulse was to chase Levi and his men down, throw Kim over his shoulder, and run. Run and never look back. His impulse was to take her away and hide with her. They could find a place where none of the Agency stuff could touch them and start over again. It had always been work that came between them. This time they would be away from the politics and power. This time it would just be them.

It was a stupid thought since Kim thrived on intrigue, but it's what was going through his head.

The door came open again and sure enough, there was the head of this particular MI6 division looking all professional and very

British in his tailored suit. He couldn't forget the fact that this was the man who'd raided Damon's club. He'd stormed The Garden looking for Tucker, and he'd taken Jax as leverage to get what he'd wanted.

Rupert Milbern was in his mid-fifties and had the arrogance of a man who knew he controlled as much of his world as he possibly could. His salt and pepper hair was cut in a fashionable style, and there was an expectant look on his face as he entered. "Knight. Mr. Fain, it's good to see you again, though I must apologize for the circumstances."

Damon slid his cell phone into his jacket pocket. Ezra hadn't even realized he'd had it out. If Damon was at all upset, he didn't show it as he looked to the man who'd taken over the section he'd worked in for years. "Yes, that was a bit of a shock. I thought Mr. Green was still in Agency custody. I didn't realize he'd been returned to the field. Or did I miss the memo?"

Rupert's expression turned distinctly superior as he took the seat at the head of the table. He was followed by several men and women who entered and took their places as if getting ready for a long meeting.

He couldn't fucking sit here. She was being taken away. She was moving further and further from him with every second and they wanted to have a fucking debrief?

This was all part of Levi's plan.

"You don't get any memos at all, Damon," Rupert was saying. "You left. You are a private citizen and lucky we didn't choose to press charges against you and all your friends for what happened a few weeks ago."

Damon leaned forward, his eyes narrowing. "And you're lucky I don't talk to the press about the fact that MI6 knew for years what Hope McDonald was doing and kept their distance because at the end of the day you wanted to know how those experiments worked out."

A rosy flush went over Rupert's face. "That's not true and you know it."

"Do I? I only know what it looks like to this private citizen. I only know that MI6 raided private property on British soil without any kind of warrant," Damon shot back. "So I would like for you to explain to me why we're here, except that little prick of an Agency operative wanted to see if he could get a rise out of my friend. Ezra Fain has been very helpful to British intelligence over the years, so I would like to know why you thought it was a good idea to arrest his wife in front of him."

Rupert frowned. "I thought they were divorced and had been for a long time."

"But they were married at one point," Damon replied. "You've got an ex. Would you feel absolutely nothing if you had to watch her be arrested? It doesn't matter how acrimonious the relationship was. She was someone he cared about once and you forced him to sit through something traumatic."

They continued arguing and Ezra realized what Damon was doing. He was giving him cover. Damon was giving him time to think. They couldn't run off after her. They couldn't make a scene and start fighting. They needed to look like they accepted the situation, like they weren't about to start a high-speed chase through the streets of London.

They had to be subtle. They also had to figure out exactly what they were up against.

"I need to see it." Ezra sat up, his hands on the table like he wasn't about to draw down on anyone. Because he wasn't. He couldn't put a gun to the head of MI6 and force him to turn over Kim's whereabouts. Levi wouldn't have told the man the truth anyway. "I need to see the evidence against my ex-wife. A whole lot of the trouble we had was over work, but not the way you think. It was because she always picked work over our marriage. She was an excellent operative, far better than me. I find it very difficult to believe she would commit treason."

Rupert sighed. "It's odd. Mr. Green seemed to think you would be satisfied with this outcome. He said you and Ms. Solomon had been at war for years."

"My war was always with Levi." His marriage had simply been one of the casualties. He couldn't forget how she'd listened to Levi, gone over her own husband's head to send his brother on the mission that had cost him his life. She'd chosen Levi time and time again, and it was finally going to cost her.

So let it. Let her go with him. He won't really hurt her. He won't do anything he hasn't already done to her.

His hands fisted because that was the dark bastard inside him talking, the one every man had somewhere deep down. The one every good man managed to shut up.

If Levi put his hands on her this time, it would be assault. It would be rape, and he wasn't going to let that happen to any human being, much less one he'd loved more than life itself at one point.

"We're prepared to give you a briefing on the subject," Rupert allowed. "But only Mr. Knight. I'm sorry. You no longer work for the Agency, and they've been a bit intransigent on this. I believe it might be Mr. Green's influence. However, given the fact that you have helped us on numerous occasions, if Mr. Knight leaves his notes somewhere on his desk, well, despite our personality clash, I do trust him to a point. I'm sorry things have come to this. We were quite happy with the outcome of the Paris operation."

He bet they were. And he knew what was happening. Levi had a plan and it included cutting Ezra off from Damon. Damon would stay here and that would leave Ezra alone to chase Levi down, and wouldn't Levi love that when he had a whole crew with him.

Or he would sit his ass down in the lobby and wait for Damon. Ezra was sure there would be video of him casually sitting while Kim was taken god knew where, and Levi would make sure she saw it. It would be one more way to hurt her, to show her that her ex-husband didn't care what happened to her. The fucker likely meant to Stockholm syndrome her.

Or he would cut her into little pieces and send them to you.

He had to do something. He couldn't fucking sit here. He had to get out. Maybe it didn't matter if he got mowed down by Levi's army. Maybe that was what he'd been waiting for all these years.

"Ezra, perhaps you'll wait for me in the lobby," Damon said gently. "I apologize for dragging you out here. I wouldn't have if I'd known what was going on. I'm sure Ariel will be done with her meeting soon and she can join you."

Ariel. He'd forgotten about Ariel. Ariel, who was Kim's closest friend in the world. Ari, who had never forgotten how to assassinate an asshole.

"This could be a while. Feel free to take the Benz." Damon

handed him the car keys. "I'll take the Tube back. And then we'll talk about what to do next. If you don't mind, could you update my partners on the situation? Let Ian know I'll call him tonight. And I'm sorry about Solo."

Damon was telling him what to do next. Call Ian. Take the Benz and the former MI6 sharpshooter and go get his…go get Kim. Not his girl. Not anymore. But she damn straight wasn't going to be Levi's victim.

He remembered how to play this game. He sighed and took the keys and gave Damon what he hoped was a sad-sack smile. "Thanks. We'll see you back at The Garden. I'll let your wife know you might be late."

He stood and nodded to Rupert before leaving the conference room. It took everything he had to not run. They might still be in the building. Levi had probably taken her down to the secure parking garage and prepared her for transport.

His heart was racing as he forced himself to casually walk past the reception desk and out into the hall.

He started to move toward the bank of elevators. His security badge wouldn't get him to the secure garage. He would have to bet on which exit they would take. And he needed to get Ari.

"Hello, Ez," a cultured British voice said. Ariel stepped up beside him, a smile on her face. "I got a text from Damon. We should go back to The Garden. I'm sure there are a lot of feelings you need to process."

Though her tone was casual, he could hear the bite beneath it. Ariel was well aware they were still on camera and that ears might be listening.

"Yeah, though I want a beer more than a session." The elevator doors opened, and they walked in. Luckily they were alone. "I'm shocked. I hope I can spend some time with my friends tonight."

He hoped the rest of the team was already on it. Not that there was a whole lot of team left since the Lost Boys had gone. Owen was in Scotland with Rebecca, and Tucker and Jax had left with their families for the States. Rob would be back, but he was with his brother, Tucker, for now.

He'd come to think of those men as family, and he hated the

thought that he was losing them.

Ariel's eyes were on the floor indicator as it began the descent down to the garage. "I hope so, too. It would be good to have a family dinner, though you should know Nick's probably going to be late. He's on a surveillance assignment with Brody. But Walt is back at The Garden. He's running one of his crazy experiments. You know the mad professor. He thinks he can find a solution to everything."

Walt Bennett was a brilliant doctor who'd gotten off his original path when he came up against The Collective. He'd worked for McKay-Taggart and Knight since then, and his focus wasn't merely on medicine. He'd learned a lot about tech over the years.

So if he was reading Ari right, Damon had texted her then she'd put a plan in motion, one that included putting Nick Markovic and Brody Carter on the streets, with Walt using all the tech he had to figure out where they were taking Kim.

"Maybe I should find some place to hole up and drink for a couple of days," he said, knowing someone was listening. "It's not every day you find out your ex-wife is a traitor."

A soft gasp let him know Ariel hadn't been told that part. Damon's text had likely been brief and to the point. She hadn't known how Levi had taken her.

"I find it hard to believe," Ari said as the doors came open.

"Her name was on the list." He would tell her as much as he could.

She bit her lip and nodded as they came up to the security station.

The guard smiled at her. He was an older man who'd probably been manning the desk for years. "Ms. Adisa, back so soon? I thought you were going to be a while."

She returned her pass and gave the man a smile that could charm the most ill-tempered of men. "It was a quick meeting, and I have to get my friend back home. He's had a bit of bad news. I was wondering if you could tell me the best exit to take. I heard there's a VIP group going out of the high-security lot, and I would prefer to avoid getting caught in that traffic. You know how the Americans can be."

It was such a good play since some of his Agency coworkers had made scenes over the years, and it made them all look like assholes.

Nothing could connect people like having to deal with assholes.

"I would go west if you're heading back to Chelsea, my dear," the guard said with a fond smile. "Though you should be good, if you get my meaning."

Then they were already on the road.

She reached out and shook the man's hand. "Excellent. Thank you, George. I'll be back in a few days, I suspect. Please send my love to your wife."

He wanted to hurry her along, but she was playing this perfectly. She'd gotten the guard to admit that Levi's group was already gone, and they'd left through the southernmost exit that would block traffic to the east. Now they knew what road they would most likely be on, and they could watch the traffic cameras.

The guard buzzed them through and they were in the parking garage, Ariel's heels echoing with each step she took.

"I need to get my bag from the boot," Ariel said with that placid expression on her face.

He'd been completely unaware she'd put a bag in the trunk of the sleek Mercedes, but he opened it for her anyway. She reached in and came back with what appeared to be a gym bag.

"You drive, please." Ari slammed the trunk door down and moved to the passenger side. "I'm not good in traffic."

He'd spent a lot of time in London and knew how to drive in the city. He wanted to be the one with his hands free, but if one of them was going to take a shot, she was the better choice.

Like Kim was better. Kim had killer instincts and always knew when something was going down. Only once had she…he wasn't going there. He needed to focus on getting her back. Then he could let his rage take over. Anything was better than this complete sense of hopelessness he felt at the thought of never seeing her again.

He slid into the driver's side, and the minute he closed the door he was finally able to breathe. "I want you to take that asshole out if you can."

He wanted to be the one to do it, but he wouldn't argue at this point. He wanted to know Levi fucking Green was dead.

Ariel clicked her seat belt in place and opened the bag as Ezra backed the car out of the space. "Play it cool until we get to the street.

They've still got cameras on us for a couple of blocks. What the bloody hell happened? I saw Kim not twenty minutes ago and she was fine."

"Levi Green happened." He drove in a careful manner, well aware they had one more guard to get through.

Ariel reached over and activated the touch screen on the dashboard. It seemed Damon had some extras on this vehicle because the touchscreen didn't merely bring up the car's systems. It connected to a video call. Walt's face came up on the screen. "Walter, we're about to leave the building. What have you got for us?"

Walt was a lanky American in his mid-thirties. He was staring at another screen, his face illuminated by the greenish light. "I'm in the CCTV around the building. I don't dare hack MI6. Do we have any idea what kind of vehicle I'm looking for? He's Agency, right? They usually like their nondescript black SUVs. I've got several of them coming out at the right time."

"Only pay attention to the southernmost high-security exit," he instructed as he approached the checkpoint. "And he'll be in a limo."

Walter snorted. "Sure he will be. Oh, wait. Are you serious? Shit. I've got a limo that would have come in the right direction stopped at a light right now. You need to take a left when you get to the street. It looks like they're heading out of the city."

The guard stepped up but waved them through when he saw Ariel.

The minute they hit the sunshine, Ari pulled a semiautomatic out of the bag. "Damon keeps a go-bag in this car. They'll head to a private airfield. Walt, I need you to figure out where they're going and get Nick and Brody there as fast as possible."

"Will do," Walt said. "I'll come back as soon as I know anything."

The screen went dead.

Ezra turned onto the road and sped up.

He had to catch them. He had to get her back. What he would do with her then, he had no idea.

Chapter Two

Solo sat back in the ridiculously over-the-top limo. Only Levi Green would bring a stretch limo to pick up a so-called traitor. She tried the door but naturally it was locked. Child locks worked. She could get through a lot of tech, but she couldn't take apart the door and get that lock to pop up.

Sometimes simpler was better.

She glanced down at her hands in her lap. One of the guards had zip tied them together in the elevator. She could have told them she wasn't foolish enough to try to get away in the building, but that was a lie. If she'd seen any chance to run, she would have taken it. She'd barely managed to force herself to walk out of the conference room. She'd wanted to fight, but sometimes it was better to be patient. Especially when surrounded by a whole lot of people with guns.

The door came open and the devil himself slid onto the seat beside her.

Levi had taken off his jacket and laid it across the seat in front of him. The limo was top of the line and had space for at least six people, but Levi had made sure it was only the two of them. "Hello, Solo. We didn't get a real chance to talk, but don't worry. We've got all the time in the world now. Champagne? I believe this is your favorite."

He reached over and opened the small fridge.

Dear god, was he going to try to make this into a date? "Have you lost your damn mind? You know I had nothing to do with Hope McDonald."

He pulled out a bottle of Dom Pérignon. "Look, I didn't even poison it. The label is still on and everything." He proved he was well aware of how to handle the bottle. He had it opened with nothing more than a quiet pop. "And I was as surprised as everyone else to find your name and dossier on that list. There was also a detailed calendar of your movements and the jobs you did for The Collective. What happened, sweetheart? Did you lose all that money? It's the only reason I can think of. Unless Beck made you do it. You always did have an unhealthy affection for him."

"He was my husband," Solo seethed. He'd been the love of her life. He'd barely looked her way. Was he sitting in his meeting believing everything they said about her? Had he already written her off? Or worse, was he satisfied that she wouldn't cause trouble in his life anymore?

"Yes, and you saw how much those vows meant to him," Levi said quietly as he poured a glass. "Do you want some? I promise it's not poisoned."

"Sure. Release my hands and I'll take a glass." She would punch him in the face and find a way out of this car.

Levi sighed. "You know I can't do that because you would punch me in the face and try to kick your way out of the limo."

At least he knew her well. "What do you think you're going to get out of this? Because you know who I've been working for. Did you even run this by the director?"

He sat back as the limo stopped at the checkpoint and then moved through and out onto the street. "Of course I did. You think the president is going to save you, but he's got other things to deal with right now. He's on his way out. He's got a couple of months left and he's trying to push his agenda through before the election. After that he's a lame duck and no one will listen to him. Do you honestly think he's going to spend the rest of his capital on a CIA operative who worked for The Collective?"

"Now I worked directly for The Collective? Why don't you tell me the whole story? I would love to hear this fiction you've crafted."

He touched his chest with a wounded look on his face. "*Moi?*

You hurt me with your suspicions. And there's time enough for you to answer my questions. After all, I answered yours and you weren't very nice to me."

"You lied about everything, Levi. You're the one who's been working against Agency interests. Are you planning on paying me back?"

"Do I plan on paying you back for months of interrogation? For not trusting me? For years of refusing to see what's standing right in front of you?" His lips tugged up. "No, sweetheart. I'm not going to torture you. We're going to sit down and have a long talk and I'm going to get you out of this the only way I can. Make no mistake. The evidence is against you."

"The evidence you planted."

"We'll have to agree to disagree on that." He sighed as they made another turn. "I don't understand why you have to be so stubborn. We always made sense. When you met me, you immediately liked me. You practically clung to me while we were in training."

"I obviously have terrible taste in friends." She'd spent those weeks wondering if she was doing the right thing and Levi had been there. They'd had a lot in common. They'd both come from extremely wealthy families, but neither had sheltered childhoods. She'd watched her parents rip through the world not caring about anything but making more cash. His father had been cold and distant. Levi had seemed sympathetic back then. "I thought we were friends."

Sometimes she missed that Levi. Training had been rough, and he'd been someone she could talk to. Everyone else assumed she was in the program because her parents had bought her way in. The minute they realized she had a trust fund worth more than the gross national product of some small countries, they assumed she was in to be immediately promoted to a power position and dismissed her. Levi had been the only one who understood she wanted to be an operative, to do some good.

"We *were* friends," he said quietly. "I am more your friend than anyone in your life. You simply can't see it. I've stood by you even when you left me, even when you chose that bastard over me, even when you turned your back on me, I was faithful."

"Faithful?"

He shrugged slightly. "Well, not in a physical sense, of course. A man has needs. But I've never cared about anyone the way I do you. Who saved you when you were in trouble in Hong Kong?"

"I didn't ask you to do that." He'd been the last person she would have called. By then they'd already had their falling out and she'd seen Levi in a different light.

"It certainly wasn't Beck. He didn't care. He was far too busy tanking his own career by assassinating an asset."

"You can't prove that." Beck had been assigned to deal with the leader of a small nation with resources the US had needed at the time. Unfortunately, the leader had been a brutal dictator who killed and raped his way through his nation. Beck had been the one to pull the trigger and set off a revolution that had led to the birth of a new democracy.

But it had cost Beck a lot. He'd lost his golden boy status within the Agency and he'd never gotten it back. It had been that mission that led him to McKay-Taggart and the Lost Boys.

She'd found that trying to do good in the world was complex when working for the Agency. She'd been naïve. Not that she hadn't understood there would be shades of gray. But it was all the red that really bothered her.

"Everyone knows it was Beck," Levi said as though they were talking about a prank or something casual. "The fact that they couldn't prove it merely means he's good at covering his tracks. The point is while Beck was indulging his own bourgeois sense of morality, you were in MSS hands."

"I was on the run from MSS," she corrected. "Don't make it sound like you rescued me from enemy forces."

"I did rescue you from a dank basement where you'd been hiding for weeks," he pointed out. "I got you out and you didn't even thank me. Nor did you thank me for saving your life in Colorado."

She really wished she could punch him. "You're the reason I was shot."

He waved that off. "It wasn't me. It was a bad hire. Civilians. We really shouldn't work with them. Give me a Special Ops team. I love those flag huggers. Well, most of the time. Every now and then you get that one bad apple."

She didn't mistake him for a second. "Don't say his name."

"Why not?" Levi asked in that smooth as silk voice of his. "After all, Beck makes everyone say it. Do you think Beck would go around calling himself by his dead half-brother's name if he knew how many drugs the real Ezra Fain had run? If he knew that his sainted medic brother was a drug addict who used his position to help drug lords?"

She turned Levi's way, pointing a finger at him. Well, all her fingers really since her hands were bound together. "You promised you would never tell him."

It was one of the things that kept her awake at night. It was one of the secrets Levi held over her head. If Beck ever found out, he might kill her himself.

"And I've kept it. I've kept it despite the fact that I hate Beck and it would be so satisfying to let him know, to send him my report on his precious brother. Do you think I don't sit up at night and imagine the look on his face? Only the fact that the fucker died kept me from parading him in front of the press."

"But Ezra did, and Beck's paid enough for that." She'd paid. God, how she'd paid.

He sat back and sipped his champagne. "If you say so." He was quiet for a moment, that hard truth sitting between them. "I think Beck took your arrest well."

"Did you think he would try to rescue me and then you could kill him in the chaos?" She could break the zip tie, but they were in close quarters. She needed space to have enough force to bust out.

"I knew I won either way," he admitted with a smug smile. "Any way, really. I'm actually surprised at how it went down. He barely looked up. I rather thought he would go the defiant route and I would get to shoot him. I have to say, it was the one I hoped for. I shot the fucker in Mexico but he didn't stay down. Damn vests. I know to go for a headshot this time."

"You pathetic piece of trash." How had she ever liked this man? Called him her friend? She remembered crying on his shoulder and feeling comfort from him. He'd hidden his inner sociopath well. Or she'd simply refused to see it because she'd needed one person in the world who seemed to understand her.

His eyes narrowed. "And I was hoping we could keep this civil.

After all, once I get you to a secure facility, you're all mine. I will make all the decisions concerning you. I'll decide what you wear, what you drink, when you sleep, what you eat. I think you should be a little more willing to play ball. My patience is only going to go so far."

The laughter that bubbled up was far from humorous. It was damn near hysterical. "You're finally going to do it, aren't you? You're going to try to make me into a doll. Your fuck toy."

"Well, I can't have you the way I want you so I shall have to make do," he conceded. "One does what one must."

Frustration welled up inside her. How could this be her life? "I told you I can't love you. I won't ever love you. I love Beck."

He was silent for a moment, the only sound the tires turning against the pavement. "Then we'll start over again. Don't you ever wonder what your life would be like—what our lives could be like— if Beck never existed? If he hadn't shown up and wrecked everything? Look at the misery he's caused. What would it be like if you could forget it all and start over again?"

A cold chill went across her skin at the words. "What are you talking about?"

He gave her a tight smile. "I don't want to hurt you. I don't have the stomach for it. And honestly, if I really ask myself the question, I don't truly want the you I see now. I don't want Beckett Kent's leavings. I want the woman I knew when we first started training together. I can't have her, so I'll settle for the next best thing. Solo two point 0."

She was going to be sick. She knew exactly what he was talking about, had seen the damage it could do. "You have McDonald's drug."

"Of course I do. Or rather I have the formulary, and it's being worked on right now." He set his glass down. "You can't go on like this. He's never going to love you. He isn't capable of loving you the way I do."

"You are a fucking sociopath."

"But I'm *your* sociopath."

She felt a scream strangle in her throat. He was crazy enough that he would do it. There was something deeply deranged inside Levi

Green, something that had responded to her all those years ago, and it had ruined her life. His obsession was a weed with roots that strangled out anything good she tried to grow there.

"You were the one working with McDonald."

"Not at all. I really was spying on her. I started the mission with the man you know as Tucker long before she was on the Agency's radar. I saw her for what she was early on, and I knew beyond a shadow of a doubt that the work she was doing was important." He always managed to sound so reasonable. It was his greatest skill, to hide the psycho behind a veneer of respectability. "I knew if she managed to perfect her drug, she would likely sell it. Shouldn't our country be the one to benefit?"

"There's no benefit to taking a person's memories."

"Oh, I disagree. It's going to be to both of our benefits." He looked at her with a sick resolve on his face. "When I'm done, you will be unburdened by the past. You'll be free of him. We'll start over and I'll treat you like a queen. You won't know a moment's despair. You'll forget that your parents ignored you. You'll forget that you were nothing but a prop for them. You'll forget how hard it was for you to get through high school and how lonely you were. And the wreckage Beck wrought on your soul will be gone. You'll be left with nothing but a husband who puts you first. I do promise that. I'll always fight for you."

She'd only thought she'd seen the depths of his madness. "Even when I've made it plain that I don't want you?"

"Isn't that the stuff of epic love stories? I'm the man who won't give up, who'll have you no matter what. Because I know I'm what's best for you." He turned in his seat. "I've known I had to do something about the situation for a long time, but I needed two things. I needed that formulary, which I picked up from the data we found in Colorado."

He was so good at rewriting history. "You mean the data Jax Seaborne found and you stole."

"That data was taken from a secure CIA site, so who was stealing?" Levi asked. "I originally planned to get the formulary from Tucker's mission. It was precisely why I hired a hacker to add your crimes to Kronberg's files. This was supposed to go down over three years ago. Never let it be said I'm not patient."

He'd been planning to steal her memory for a long time. "Why not have the hacker give you the files?"

"They had to come from an op the Agency would approve of. Otherwise I couldn't use the data the way I wanted to," Levi admitted. "Do you think I don't know there are people who watch me constantly? Any data I brought in would be suspect—especially anything concerning you. Unless that data came from a secure place, say, directly from the head of Kronberg's computer. The fact that my operative sacrificed so much to get the intel out is merely the cherry on top. I mean I had to wait because Tucker was dumb enough to get caught, but it's really worked out."

What a tangled fucking web. "So you admit you did this to me. You admit you know damn well I didn't commit treason."

"Of course. Sweetheart, this was meant to put you under my control. That's all. I promise I'll clear it all up later. I know you would never betray your country. You're an excellent operative. It's one of the things I admire about you. You're brave and strong. Sometimes you're too queasy to really get things done, but that's why I'm around. It's why we make a good team."

The enormity of what he'd done slammed into her. "You've been planning this for years. You meant to do this to me over three years ago."

"I think I've been planning it since I truly understood you were going to marry Beck. I thought he was nothing more than a passing crush. He's broody and rough and you were rebelling, but I always knew you would come back to me."

"We never dated," she said between gritted teeth.

"People like us rarely date." Levi took another sip. "We form relationships. For that first year we ate most of our meals together, studied together, when you went for a run, I would go along. It came as a shock when I realized you were attracted to that dull moron, but I got it. I knew he would bore the hell out of you and you would come back to me."

"I never felt that way about you." She glanced out the back, trying to figure out where they were going. How long did she have before he would put her on a plane and she wouldn't see freedom again? How long before he took the most precious thing she owned—her memories?

She saw a black Benz driving behind her. There was something familiar about that sedan, but then there were lots of black Benzes on the road. It was pure wishful thinking that someone would come for her.

"I'm sure that's what you tell yourself," Levi replied. "But I know the truth."

There was no talking to him about this. She glanced out the tinted windows. They were leaving the city. She could see far more green than concrete now. How was she going to get away? If she got on that plane with him, she would disappear, and by the time anyone saw her again she would be some Stepford wife for Levi to show off. Of course there were other reasons he could want her. "I suppose you'll have my accounts transferred to you."

She was worth roughly sixty million. That was a lot of attraction for some men.

"I have my own money." It was the first time he'd looked anything but perfectly satisfied.

She'd made a direct hit. "But nothing like mine."

"No. I had a small trust that my father managed to not lose when he blew every bit of our family money." Levi sat up a bit straighter. "When I'm married to the heir to the Solomon fortune, with ties that go across the globe, I'll be back to my proper place. I'll show my father that I'm better than him when I bring our family back to some sort of honor. Or maybe I'll crush him like he tried to crush me. I don't know. I haven't decided yet."

He was an angry child with far too much power. She needed to find a way out or she would become another toy he broke. "You can't possibly think you're going to get away with this."

"Of course I will," he said like it was a foregone conclusion, like the game was already over. "I'm back in the director's good graces. The data we recovered from Paris ensured that. It's the gift that keeps right on giving. Have you ever heard of a company called Fitzgerald Inc?"

Everyone had heard of them. "They're a multinational, one of those mega corporations with their fingers in every pie from agricultural to Hollywood."

"Including a majority share in a small pharmaceutical company that worked with Kronberg, and more specifically funded Hope McDonald in a direct fashion."

She wasn't sure where he was going with this. "I suspect a lot of companies did that."

"Ah, but did the daughter of a presidential candidate sit on the board of one of those companies? Did she sign off on backroom plans to use McDonald's research?"

Levi Green had always been the luckiest fucker in the history of time. "You're planning an October surprise?"

"No, though I assure you we thought about it," he admitted. "Look, the last thing we need is another Zack Hayes. We've had eight years where we couldn't work the way we need to because it would offend the president's delicate sensibilities."

She rolled her eyes. "You mean he took human and civil rights seriously. That must have been very tough on you."

He completely ignored her and continued on. "Since Hayes can't run again, we're left with two candidates. One of them is reasonable and the other is all Captain America huggy. Now we have a way to force the Captain America guy to bow out. Or we'll arrest his daughter and bring down his whole family. He'll claim he can't handle the pressure or some shit and our guy will breeze in."

Then Levi Green would be in power. And she would be completely fucked.

"Sir, I believe we have a tail," a deep voice said over the intercom.

Levi sat up and turned. "How long have they been on us?"

"That Benz has been behind us for ten minutes. They caught up when we hit the M25," the man said. "I didn't think anything of it until they followed us off. There's nothing but the airfield going this way. It's why we selected this spot. No one should be following us. We're the only departure for hours."

Her heart rate ticked up and she strained to see the vehicle again. That Benz looked an awful lot like Damon's.

"Lose him," Levi commanded. "Or better yet, get us to the airfield as fast as you can. If he wants to follow me in, I'll shoot the fucker, and I won't miss this time."

Levi reached to his side, pulling the SIG Sauer out of its place in the shoulder holster he wore.

It was time to cause some chaos. If she could break free, she was running for that car the minute she could. They would have to kill her before they would get her body on that plane. He was about to find out she wasn't going gently into that medicated night.

She brought her hands up over her head.

"Don't do it, Solo," Levi said between clenched teeth.

She brought her hands down with all the force she could muster and dragged them apart, splitting the plastic of the zip ties. He really should have used cuffs.

Adrenaline started to pour through her system as she readied for the fight of her life.

That was the moment she heard the shot and felt the limo careen out of control. Levi cursed as the limo started to roll. She held on and prepared to make her escape.

* * * *

Ezra's heart was in his throat as he punched the gas. The limo had turned off the M25 exactly where Nick said it would. They'd been following the fucking douchebag limo for the last half hour, and every single mile had been nauseating.

What had Levi already done to her? Had he drugged her to make sure she couldn't fight back?

"He made the turn?" Walt's voice had been steady over the line. He was playing the Overwatch position, and it was something he seemed to do well.

"Yes." Ariel had spent the drive preparing for her role. The go-bag she'd pulled out of the trunk seemed to contain everything she would need, including a couple of guns. One for her. One for him. "They're going for the airfield. He's in a limousine but there's an SUV in front of him. I believe he's got at least four men with him. They'll be armed. Should we expect the police?"

"You will find the police around here are currently dealing with a situation at a local shopping center," Walt explained. "I don't have any vehicles within a five-kilometer radius, but you have to be quick. A prolonged firefight is going to catch someone's attention, even out there. I know the airfield is private and they only have one departure scheduled in the next few hours, but there are at least five employees working. They'll likely be able to hear gunfire."

"Are we a go?" Ezra asked, his voice sounding tight even to himself. That wasn't surprising since his whole fucking body felt like a live wire ready to go off. He hadn't been this wound up in...he didn't get wound up. Being emotional during a mission got an operative killed. Even when he'd been angry as hell, he'd been able to turn that emotion to ice in his veins.

"We're in place." Nick's voice came over the system. "Brody and I are outside the airfield. There's some security. I suspect they're hired guards and not military in any way. Mr. Green has gotten arrogant."

No. Mr. Green thought he wouldn't have any resistance at all. "He didn't think we would care."

"Or he wanted a fight and he couldn't have witnesses to it," Ariel offered. "You need to stay calm, Ezra. You cannot let him bait you into doing something you shouldn't."

"Like stopping the Agency from arresting one of their own?" He was well aware that what they were about to do would kick up a hornet's nest that could sting them all.

"I meant like putting a bullet between his eyes. He's got a team with him and they likely believe everything he's told them. We can't kill a bunch of Agency employees. If we keep things clean, we might get away with it."

"You don't think he'll bring the bosses down on me?" He said *me* because he fully intended to take all the responsibility for tilting at this particular windmill.

"I would bet anything that he's doing this under the table. He would have to or Kim would have gotten notification." Ariel worked a long-sleeve jacket over her arms and shoulders. It was dark and would camouflage the brightly colored dress she'd worn today because she'd had no idea she would be taking on the Agency. "Otherwise he would have shown up with an actual warrant. He didn't produce one, did he?"

Why hadn't he thought of that? Kim had been working for some heavy hitters lately—including the president and his closest advisors. Somehow he didn't think Connor Sparks would have let this hit his desk without asking some questions. "No, but that doesn't mean he doesn't have a deal with British intelligence. The director knew what was going down."

"Still, they won't make an international incident out of it," Ariel assured him. "They can't because too many questions would be asked. If we can extract her without too much trouble...well, we'll still have questions to answer."

"Blame it all on me," Ezra replied.

"Big Tag has already been informed," Brody Carter said, his Aussie accent thick over the line. "Beyond listening to him shout every curse word he knows, he's firmly behind us extracting Solo. He's already putting a plan in place. We've got a safe house ready for you. And don't worry about the rest of us. Nick and I are back in Soho on assignment. There's CCTV of us. Thanks, Walt."

"Glad to help out, partner," Walt replied cheerily. "And Ezra, you dropped Ariel off for her lunch date. Hayley says you're really enjoying the fish and chips at Meg's this afternoon."

They had put together alibis very quickly. He would be the only one to take the fall, and that was how he wanted it. He would take Kim and they would figure out how to bring that fucker down. All that mattered was not leaving her in Levi's hands.

He would be alone with her for the first time in years. He would have to work with her, stay with her, protect her.

It might be the most dangerous thing he'd ever done.

"All right, according to your GPS, you're on the road that leads to the airfield. It should be flat without any structures on either side. I would take the limo out here," Walt said.

Ariel pulled a ski mask over her head and brought her gun up. "I'm ready. I'm going to blow a tire. It's a risky move, but I know Kim. She would rather I took the chance than allow her to go with him. God only knows what he'll do with her. I doubt he's taking her back to Langley. But this is your call."

The limo could roll. A car accident could kill her.

She would want him to take the chance. He knew damn well he

would want her to. If Levi got her on that plane, she would disappear and he would never see her again, never know what happened to her.

He couldn't live with that outcome.

"Do it."

Ariel slid the passenger-side window down and moved her graceful body out, balancing against the windowsill. She showed zero hesitation to put herself in harm's way. If he lost control, she would be flung out of the vehicle, and there was no way she survived.

So he wouldn't lose control. He let a cold professionalism settle over him. He was retrieving an asset, that was all. He'd done it a hundred times.

The trouble was the asset he was usually attempting to liberate hadn't held him late at night, hadn't wrapped her body around his in perfect communion, hadn't made his whole world spin.

Hadn't wrecked his soul with her betrayal. Hadn't turned to the enemy for comfort.

His hands tightened on the wheel as Ariel took her shot. She only needed one. She took out one of the back tires with the precision of a true artist. A loud screech seemed to bend the air around him, and Ariel slid back into her seat.

The minute her belt clicked on, he slammed on the brakes as the limo swerved and the driver tried to regain control. The back of the limo fishtailed and the sparks flashed from where metal met concrete. Up ahead, he could see the second vehicle slowing down, but Nick and Brody were there. Before the car could stop, they had weapons trained on the men inside.

Nick and Brody had their faces covered. He was the only one who wasn't going to bother. He didn't care if they all knew. If he got caught, he would tell them he hired a group of mercenaries and no, he couldn't quite remember their names.

The limo spun off the road and seemed to hit something that sent it lurching to its side.

He threw the Benz in park and got out of the car. She had to be in that limo. Levi wouldn't have put her anywhere else. Levi had always said Kim was the queen, and he'd made sure to bring a car fit for one.

Ezra would have brought a car fit for a woman who tended to blow everything up. To him, Kim wasn't a queen. She was a goddess who controlled so much of his world. Who brought pleasure and pain. Order and chaos.

"Ezra, no bodies." Ariel was out of the car, moving around to the driver's side. "We get her and we leave. If we have bodies, we have press."

And if they had press, they had trouble.

The door came open and he saw the most beautiful sight he'd ever seen. Kim crawled from the wreckage, her blonde hair out of its tidy bun and wild around her face. He started to move to help her as the driver door came open and a burly man started to climb out.

Ezra planted his feet and took aim. She couldn't get across the road if that asshole got between them. "Get your hands up and don't move if you want to live."

His gut twisted because this could go south so fucking fast. If the bullets started flying, they would be outnumbered. Where was Levi?

The driver's hands came up as Kim swung a leg over and managed to drop to the ground. He could see the zip ties on her wrists, but it looked like she'd busted them apart. She had both hands free as she got to her feet. She immediately went for the small holster she kept at her ankle when she wore slacks. She would have a backup there, likely a single-use gun she'd printed. It would be made of resin so it wouldn't set off metal detectors. Despite the fact that he hadn't lived with her in years, he still knew her habits. She kept a 3D printer with some super illegal files in most of her safe houses. It would only give her one shot, but sometimes that was all she needed.

The Benz pulled up beside him. Ariel had taken over driving. She'd opened the back seat passenger door so they could both slide in. "Let's go."

But Kim seemed to have other ideas. She had that gun in her hand and she turned back to the limo.

He wanted so badly to let her do it, end the threat. But they were sitting on a powder keg, and it could go off any second. "Kim, get in the car. Now."

She faced him, her expression going stubborn. "He's right there. He's knocked out and vulnerable."

And didn't that sound perfect? Maybe they did have enough time. Maybe it would be worth it. If he got taken in and Levi was dead, he could handle that particular outcome.

But Brody Carter had a son and a wife, and Nick's wife had recently given birth to their first, a daughter. Ariel had recently gotten married.

Then the questioning was over because the driver decided to take his shot. The driver moved a hand and came up with a gun pointed right at him. Ezra dropped to the pavement and rolled as Kim turned and fired on the driver.

"Now, Kim," he shouted. They were out of time. Like they always seemed to be with Levi. Ariel was right. Levi was likely trying some shady shit, and he would want to cover it up. But if there was a body...

She cursed and ran for the car as the driver took another shot. Ezra gave her some cover but felt a bullet graze his left shoulder. It burned but he managed to fire again, sending the driver back into his hidey-hole.

"She's in," Ariel shouted. "And Walt says the police received a call about an accident. We need to move."

He backed toward the car, firing off another couple of shots to keep the driver at bay before sliding in the open door. Before he could even slam it shut, Ariel was taking off.

He leaned over and covered Kim's head, getting them both below the windows. Sure enough someone was firing as Ariel sped away.

"Nick and Brody are off," she said in a low voice. "The other car isn't following. They're back trying to help the limo, which means they've been ordered not to follow."

"Police are coming from your east," Walt announced. "I'll send you the best route to get to Damon's garage. He's got a car stored there. I'll meet you and give you the address for the safe house. Ari, drop them off and then get to that restaurant. It's the one by the Tate. Hayley's waiting for you. I want you on CCTV asap. Nick and Brody are going back to their surveillance job, and I'll send a car for Damon."

Kim was quiet underneath him, perfectly still as he covered her. He'd expected she'd fight him, not let him protect her. She could be fierce.

"Will do," Ari said. "Keep your heads down. Kim, it's good to have you back."

"It's good to not be kidnapped and taken to a bunker somewhere," Kim replied quietly.

He stayed where he was, covering her with his body. They couldn't get up until they were well past that airfield. Levi might have men waiting there, men who would try to take her back. "Are you all right?"

He wanted to hold her, but now that he was here with her, everything that sat between them rustled around in his head again. She was trouble. She'd always been trouble. Even when she was trying to love him, she somehow managed to hurt him.

What the hell was he doing? He should send her to Tag and let him figure this all out. Even as he thought the words, he knew he wouldn't do it.

"I am now," she replied. "Thank you for coming for me."

He went silent as they drove back into the city, wondering if he hadn't made a terrible mistake.

Chapter Three

W hen the door to the storage unit closed, Solo was finally able to take a deep breath. "Thank you so much for helping extract me."

She turned to Walt, a lanky, unassuming genius of a man. She'd met him during her brief stay at The Garden a few weeks before.

Had that really only been weeks ago? It felt like she'd aged a decade in that time. It hadn't been so long since she'd been forced to run with Beck and the others when The Garden had been raided. They'd used the secret exit that had taken them into underground London to an apartment not far from this garage of Damon's. They'd taken this same sedate sedan and fled north to a country home.

She knew that for Tucker and his now wife Roni it had been a harrowing time, but for her it had been something different. For her it had meant spending time with Beck, having a few moments where he didn't look at her like she was some kind of demon sent to steal his soul. For those few days, they'd relied on each other again.

"Hey, I'm happy to help. I was working on a couple of experiments. This totally livened up the day." Walt gave her a broad smile and gestured to the woman who'd come with him. "Steph came along to make sure no one needed a stitch up. Apparently she's way better with a suture than I am."

Stephanie Carter was a pretty woman with shoulder-length brown hair and big, kind eyes. She was a physician, one who still worked as a GP. The Garden had a plethora of medical professionals. "Well, you're an epidemiologist, not a general practitioner. I brought my kit. Ezra, looks like you got hit."

He'd been grazed. She'd checked it out in the car when they'd felt safe enough to sit up. While she'd been laid out on the back seat, Beck's big body covering hers, she'd felt safe. She'd felt like he still loved her.

It was time to wake up and face the truth.

Beck took off his shirt. "It's already stopped bleeding. I don't think it needs stitches. Burned like hell though. Did Brody and Nick make it back all right?"

Steph opened the bag she'd been carrying and pulled out a first aid kit. "They're both good, and I think this was exactly what they needed. They've been feeling so dad-like these days. It's good to get the old adrenaline up over something that isn't baby related."

Her gut knotted. She hadn't thought about the fact that Brody and Nick had kids. "I'm sorry I dragged them into this."

"They wouldn't have come along if they hadn't wanted to." Beck hopped on the stool that sat by the table. Damon had completely replenished this way station since they'd used it all those weeks before. He'd replaced the water and food and weapons they'd taken with them while they'd hid from British intelligence.

Now she would hide from her own agency.

"Well, please let them know how much I appreciate it." She didn't know when she would be able to repay them. Likely never. In fact, she might not be able to .pay for anything. She hadn't even thought about it. "I need a computer. I need to figure out if he froze my accounts."

Walt nodded. "There's an encrypted laptop on the table. I thought you might need it. It's set to ping around the globe a couple of times to mask its location. Feel free to use it. You can take it with you, and I've also included several burner phones. Expect a call from Big Tag at some point. He's in a crabby mood, by the way. But then he usually is."

Steph flashed a smile as she dabbed at the burn mark on Beck's left arm. "He's quite charming when he wants to be. Though it's super early back in the States, so I don't think he's going to turn the charm on. Maybe he'll take a nap or something."

She seriously doubted it. The good news was she would thank him, ask him for any updates he had, and then let him off the hook. It wasn't Big Tag's job to save her. She'd actually burned the man a couple of times, though she hadn't meant to. She'd done it because it was her job.

She didn't have one of those anymore.

She stepped up to the laptop. She would be able to tell a lot about what was going on based on whether or not she could get into her accounts.

"Tell me you still keep money stashed across the globe." Beck winced as Steph applied a topical to his burn.

"Of course." She had accounts and then she had shadow accounts, money stored in business accounts that couldn't be traced back to her easily. Then there was the cash she had in various safes. "I'm sure Levi knows where most of my safe houses are. I don't suppose I could sneak back into my London flat."

"No," Beck said with a frown. "I assure you he has someone watching it. He probably has for a long time. I'm surprised you would suggest it."

"My e-reader is there." A lot of things were there, and she would have to leave them all behind. All her ID, her phone, everything in her handbag was still in Levi's hands. God, she should have killed that fucker but she'd had to use her only bullet to scare away the driver. "I was enjoying my book. I bet that asshole will shut down my account for that, too."

She tried her main account, the one she was sure the Agency knew about.

Beck moved in behind her. He hadn't bothered to put a shirt on. His cut chest was on display. "What's the verdict?"

She gritted her teeth as the message came up. "This one's frozen. I can assume most of them are." She wanted to throw the laptop across the garage, but that wouldn't help her. "Levi might want to do this quietly, but at least someone at the Agency knows. He couldn't have frozen my accounts without permission."

"Can you call the president?" Beck asked. "He put you on this mission in the first place."

She wished it was that easy. "Yes, he did, privately. Technically the Agency doesn't know I was working for POTUS. Realistically everyone knew, but as it's been pointed out to me so recently, Hayes is only going to be in office for a few more months. Whatever's going on, he won't be around long enough to fix it."

"He could pardon you," Steph pointed out.

"For a crime that won't ever be on the books?" It was the conundrum she was in. No one would acknowledge McDonald had been a problem, therefore technically there was no crime. But the Agency wouldn't forgive or forget, and she knew there would be a whole lot of her coworkers who bought what Levi was selling. There would be a bunch of assholes who would glory in her downfall. "Look, I knew when I took the job that Hayes wouldn't be able to get me out of trouble if I fell into it. He and Connor Sparks did as much as they could, and now I'm on my own."

"That sucks," Walt said.

She appreciated the fact that he didn't try to find a way out of the situation for her. He simply stated the obvious. "It does. Do we know if Levi survived?"

She brought up a secondary account. Same message.

Behind her Beck cursed under his breath, obviously understanding the state she was in. "Please tell me he died in the accident. Also, are the police looking for us?"

Steph handed him a fresh T-shirt. "I was listening to the radio and they dispatched an ambulance. Two men were treated at the scene—one for scrapes and cuts and the other was listed as a possible concussion, but no one was taken in."

"And the police were called away long before they should have been," Walt added. "I think we can bet there won't be a report. He's cleaning up as we speak."

She made it to the third account, got the same message, and gave up. She closed the laptop. "Well, he's likely got access to roughly forty million now. He'll use it to try to find me."

Beck gingerly pulled the shirt over his head, wincing when he moved his arm. "We'll see about that. I know some pretty good hackers. And some lawyers, if it comes to that."

She didn't want to pull him in any further than he already was. "It's cool. I know some, too. I'll see what I can do about it."

She wasn't going to cry. She had to suck it up because she couldn't let Beck see how weak she felt, how much she wanted to beg him to help her, to stay with her. She needed to acknowledge that she had to face this alone.

Beck turned back to Walt. "You think it's safe for us to be on the streets? I'd like to get to the safe house as soon as possible. How far away is it?"

"Oh, it's a drive," Walt replied. "I've programmed the route into the computer. I'll monitor you the whole way and let you know if we need to change course. You're going to take the Chunnel across to France and then make your way to Paris. That's where the safe house is."

She could handle Paris. She had a small flat there, but she wouldn't be visiting it. Levi definitely knew about that place. She would take a couple of days and figure out where to go from there.

Then she would disappear until she could clear her name.

She turned to Beck. "Thanks for the save. I can take it from here."

A single brow arched over his heavenly eyes. "Oh, you can take it from here? I'm supposed to hang around and wait to be arrested?"

She didn't see that happening. Beck was far more protected than she was. Damon Knight had serious pull in Europe, and Big Tag could work miracles in the States. Neither of those men owed her anything. Beyond that, Levi had shown his true hand today. "Levi's not coming after you."

"He's always looking for an excuse. Every time I've come up against the man in the last few years, he's tried to kill me."

"Killing you would cause him problems." She wasn't sure what Beck's point was. It would be far better for him in the long run if he wasn't in the middle of this war she found herself in. "I think it's best you stay here in London and work on the problem with Damon. I'll find a way to contact you when I land somewhere."

Beck stared at her, his gaze predatory. "I don't think that's a good idea. You shouldn't be out there alone. Unless I'm mistaken. Maybe I'm looking at this the wrong way. I assumed you wanted to be rescued. Or do I find myself in the middle of a lover's spat?"

Her heart rate was right back up. "What did you say?"

"Maybe we should get back to The Garden." Steph packed up her kit, a forced smile on her face.

Walt nodded, obviously feeling their bad vibes, too. "Yeah, that's a good idea. Look, when you get to Paris, a man named Rene will be waiting for you. He's a friend of Big Tag's. Used to be French intelligence, but Tag said he's solid. He's going to arrange everything. Call if you get in trouble." Walt started for the door and stopped. "Like real actual mission trouble. Not the marital kind. I'm not good at that. Ariel is, though. I could try getting her on the phone."

Beck smiled, a predatory expression. "We don't need therapy. Go on, Walt. We'll head out in thirty minutes. I don't want to leave until I know you're watching."

Walt was right. This was a fight they should have in private. "I'm going to leave sooner than that. And thanks for everything, both of you. Please let Nick and Brody know how much I appreciate what they did for me today."

Walt frowned. "What should I tell Damon? That you're splitting up? He's going to want to know what's happening. I think Big Tag told Rene to expect two of you."

"And there will be two of us," Beck announced with arrogant finality. "Go on, Walt. I promise she's safe. I didn't wreck my life to turn around and let her fuck this mission up. We'll be fine."

She felt her fists clench. That hadn't taken long. She should have known this was some weird impulse of Beck's that he would regret as soon as the bullets stopped flying. She watched as Steph and Walt left, the door closing behind them with an audible click.

"You want to explain to me what this crap is about?" Beck asked, turning on her like she was some teen caught after curfew. "You almost got taken by that fucker. You want to give him another shot? Is there something I'm missing? I know you like it rough sometimes, but this is taking it too far."

She couldn't help it. Her hand came out and she slapped the fuck out of him. Not a punch. A punch would mean a fight. This wasn't a fight. She open-palm slapped him because he was being small and petty. Because this was the way he treated her now. "Fuck you, Beck.

And no, I do not need you. If accepting all this help means listening to you call me a whore, then I'll make my own way."

She started for the door. She would have to risk going to her place. In her mind she was already thinking about how to sneak in. Levi would have someone watching, but without a car or her purse or a single weapon, she didn't see another way to go.

"Kim, stop." Beck sighed, an exhausted sound. "Please."

It was the *please* that did it. He was so rarely polite to her. She took a deep breath and turned to him. They needed to ratchet down the emotion. It was what always tripped them up. "I don't think we can work together."

"We certainly can't if I continue to be a massive asshole." He moved toward her, putting his hands on her shoulders. "I'm sorry. You're still a touchy subject for me."

She nodded, unable to say a word for fear of unleashing a tidal wave. Not seconds before she'd told herself to tamp down the emotion, but here it was, threatening to overwhelm her and all he'd had to do was touch her.

"How about we agree that Levi Green is a problem for both of us and we work together to solve it," he offered. "Kim, we've been going in circles for years. Maybe it's time we find a way to move on. I know I'm tired of hating you."

She stepped back. She couldn't have his hands on her when he used that word. It was wrong when all she'd ever done was love him. "Ariel pointed out that it would be easier on both of us if I stopped showing up in your life."

His gaze softened. "Would it? I didn't see you for a couple of years and it didn't feel any easier."

She let a moment pass. How was it she felt even more vulnerable than she had when she was with Levi? "I know. I've tried to move on. I don't seem to be able to."

His hands moved as if he wanted to touch her, but he seemed to rethink the idea. "So maybe we should go about this another way. Maybe we should take this time and do what we didn't do before. Talk. Try to find a way to get through this. I'm sorry I said what I did about you and Levi. It still hurts and I'm lashing out. All I know is when I thought you were in danger, I knew I couldn't sit on my hands and let it happen. I can't do it now either. Let me come with you. Let me help fix this."

No. It was the only word she should say to him, and then she should turn and walk out and never look back. If she let him in, he would hurt her no matter how good his intentions were. Beck had always had a well of rage inside him that he wouldn't deal with, wouldn't acknowledge even existed. He hadn't changed.

"Okay." She hadn't changed either. She was still helpless when it came to this man. She was still in love with him and likely always would be.

He let go of a heavy breath. "Good." He was silent for a moment, looking her over. "Did he hurt you? Are your wrists okay?"

She'd managed to get what was left of the zip ties off in the car. She had some red marks on her wrists. "They're sore, but all right. He didn't slap me around this time."

She watched as Beck's hands formed fists and wished she hadn't said that. His rage was always simmering under the surface when she was around.

He seemed to let it go. "All right. We should get on the road. Can you grab some water and protein bars? I don't know what we'll find when we get to Paris."

She kind of thought she did know. She'd done a lot of homework on Big Tag, and if Rene was who she thought he was, then Beck would feel right at home.

Still, she grabbed the water bottles and bars and stuffed them in the duffel Steph had provided for her. There were a couple of T-shirts and a pair of sweatpants that would likely be too short, but beggars couldn't be choosers.

This was all she had in the world. It was odd. She would have said possessions were meaningless, but now that she had no access to any of the things that brought her comfort, she missed them with all her heart.

She had one thing. She reached up and found some peace knowing her ring was still there. All these years and she still had her wedding ring. It hung low around her neck, and she always hid it under her shirt when Beck was around.

It was all she had left of her marriage.

"You ready?" Beck fitted a cap to his head and passed her another. "You might want to put your hair up. I know if I was looking for you, all that hair would be the first thing to catch my eye."

How many nights had he tangled his fingers in her hair and gently tugged, had he told her how beautiful it was and that he never wanted her to cut it? "Yeah. I'm ready."

He stepped in front of her and placed the cap on her head, his gorgeous eyes staring down at her. "I really am sorry I said what I did. Can you forgive me?"

Her whole soul threatened to melt. She nodded.

"Can I hug you? I want to. I want to reassure myself that you're really okay."

She nodded again and then she was in his arms for the first time in years.

"Promise me he didn't get a chance to hurt you," Beck whispered.

He sounded like he actually cared. His arms around her made her feel safer than she had in forever. "He threatened me with a bunch of stuff, but I don't want to talk about it. I will, but not now."

"Okay."

They stood there for the longest time, the sound of his heartbeat the only thing she could hear.

* * * *

Ezra glanced around the club and sighed. He should have known. "It's a BDSM club."

Of course Big Tag would send them here. There was no sign outside the building, but he'd noted the discreet placard in the lobby. *Le Collier de Velours.*

French wasn't his best language, but he was pretty sure that translated to The Velvet Collar.

Yep. It was Big Tag's world, and everyone else just played in it.

"You'll only be here for a few days," Rene said as he gestured them through. "Tag is going to move you to Dallas as soon as possible. The only reason you're here now is the fact that Tag's got business in Europe. He'll be here in the morning."

"I thought Charlotte had a baby recently. He's leaving her alone?" That didn't sound like Big Tag. He could be a sarcastic son of a bitch, but he was a good husband and father.

A brilliant smile came over Kim's face. "Did they find her? Is that why he's coming?"

"Find her?" He tried not to think about how that smile warmed his whole body, and it wasn't merely about the fact that she was still the sexiest woman he'd ever seen. When she smiled like that, the world felt right.

"Big Tag and Charlotte have been searching for a girl named Natasha Federova," Kim explained, looking more animated than she had in hours. She'd spent the long car ride mostly silent, staring out the window even when they made the crossing under the English Channel. "The second company has been working pretty much nonstop to try to figure out who Sasha was."

He wasn't sure how the founding members of Miles-Dean, Weston and Murdoch would feel about being called a second team. The former members of McKay-Taggart had formed their own company specializing in missing persons. He felt his eyes widen at the implications. "They think they found Sasha's daughter?"

"I found her. Or at least I found records of her birth. See, we always thought Sasha was probably SVR or something like it. I have some contacts who are experts and I managed to find his real name. He was a higher-up analyst who worked for SVR, but he got involved in a case that threatened to implicate some bigwigs at the Kremlin, so no one was surprised when he turned up dead. Although now we know whatever body they pulled out of the Moskva wasn't actually his. We think someone sold him out to McDonald for cash when she was looking for men with his physical training. His real name was Oleg Federov."

He had no idea she'd been working on finding Sasha's daughter. "You tracked her down?"

"I only found the name," she replied. "Adam and his team did the rest. I don't know much about the project. I handed them the name and then got back to my own business."

How hard had that been? Kim liked a good mystery, liked to pull on a thread and follow it to the end. It had been her downfall many times, but it looked like she'd known when to hand over this mission to the right team. "That's great. But why is Tag coming here? Shouldn't he send someone to check up on her?"

Rene held up his hands. "I don't know why Tag does what he does, but he will be here tomorrow morning and he's going to want an update on what's happening. I've already gotten in touch with some of my old colleagues and you should know the Agency has briefed French intelligence. They've put the word out about you. You're to be brought in at all costs. Ms. Solomon, that is. You're considered disposable, Mr. Fain."

Of course he was. He was sure Levi would be thrilled if the Agency brought him home in a body bag. "What do you know about Levi's position at the Agency?"

Rene shrugged. "Nothing except he's obviously got the ear of someone important. It's why I have to do something I normally wouldn't do. Could you follow me?"

The smile on her face fled. "If it's dangerous for us to be here, I'll find someplace else to go. I know what happened the last time one of Big Tag's friends helped out."

Rene's face went grim. "Peter. Yes. He was a good man, but this situation is different. Unless one of you two plans on murdering me. I'm not worried about this Mr. Green showing up to shoot me. I'm worried about what happens when he shows up at this club looking for you. I need for him to not find you here and look elsewhere. There's a reason Big Tag chose this location. He knows sometimes the best place to hide is in plain sight."

"I hope that's a euphemism because I was planning to hide in some place hideyer," Kim said with a frown.

He was concerned, too. "I assure you, Levi's got a full dossier on Big Tag. You've got connections to Damon, too. He'll know all about those. He will absolutely show up here, or he'll send someone to watch the place. There's no question of that. Maybe we should hit the road."

"And go where?" Rene asked. "Neither of you has alternate identification. Truly good ID takes more than half a day to construct. I know it's easy to move around Europe, but you still need ID."

"We'll stay in the Schengen Area." They were in France, a part of twenty-six countries known as the Schengen Area. They were a loose alliance that didn't require passports to move across borders.

"Even in the Schengen countries you'll need some kind of identification, and you'll definitely need money," Rene pointed out.

"I can get money." Kim's hand clutched the duffel she carried. "I need some time to move things into place."

He should have known Kim would have a plan. He did, too. "I can access some funds. After the Agency burned me, I made arrangements. But he's right about the ID. Can you get it for us?"

"I've already got a friend working on your cover. We should have it in a few days, but we need some time to get a handle on what's going on." Rene moved deeper into the club. It was different from any of the clubs he'd been to. This was pure *Moulin Rouge* decadence done up with tons of red and gold. "We think we can move you out of here in a week or so. We have to ensure Mr. Green is occupied in other ways. He will no doubt send someone to check here. When he finds nothing, he'll move on. Big Tag intends to open the doors to Sanctum and welcome the Agency inside. I think he's looking forward to whatever Agency hack shows up. He's planning an all anal play night for them."

Kim snorted but her eyes were wide as she looked around the place. "That should be interesting. So we hide out in the back room until Levi's satisfied we're not here?"

"Oh, I have a much better hiding place than some back room," Rene said. "This building has been standing for three hundred years. It's been in my family for the last hundred. Like many older buildings in Europe, it has its secrets."

He stopped in front of a wall and moved his hand over the wainscoting.

Beck heard a click but saw nothing. "I don't get it."

Rene gestured to his left. "The door is three panels down. From what we can tell, the rooms were first used to move around noble families hiding from the mob during the revolution. My great-grandfather was a talented architect. He made some improvements to the secret rooms during the occupation. Originally the latching mechanism was attached to the door, and it would come open even if someone accidently tripped it. Now you have to unlock the mechanism in one place and then push in the door to get it to open. It was how he kept our Jewish neighbors safe from the Nazis."

Rene walked to another panel and pressed it in, the door revealing itself.

They would be stuck in there together for days. Days alone with her. Days where they had nothing to do.

What the hell was he going to do? How was he going to keep his hands off her?

Should he even try? Fate seemed to be pressing him to finally work things out with her so they could be done.

What if the real solution had always been to spend one last night together?

He shook the thought off as he followed her up the narrow stairs lit by a single flickering bulb.

"Sorry about the lighting. Like I said, the building is old." Rene moved up behind him. "But you'll find everything works in the apartments. There are three rooms. There is a living area and a rudimentary kitchen. We connected it to the water and electricity lines forty years ago. I've stocked the refrigerator and the pantry. There's a small bathroom and one bed. There is a security system as well. There are security cameras in the lobby, and several around the outside of the building. There is one in the dungeon, but it only protects the door to these rooms. You'll be able to see anyone coming up."

He sincerely hoped there was a comfortable couch. He doubted they would find some massive king-sized bed where they could put up a wall of pillows and find a way to share.

He was going to sleep close to Kim and there wouldn't be anyone there to keep him from giving in to the urge to climb in beside her, to rest his head on her breast and listen to her heartbeat again.

The stairs were narrow and winding, and he had the best view of her backside.

Fuck, he should be thinking about how to get out of the conundrum they found themselves in and all he could think about was how gorgeous that ass was, how good it felt to cup her cheeks and hold her tight against him.

He was in trouble.

"I've made sure you've got Internet access with a secure

connection," Rene continued. "You'll need it to investigate. If you need to call anyone, use the communications protocols on the laptop. They were developed by one of Tag's hackers, and I've found it's impossible to track it down. You also have access to the CCTV cameras I talked about. You can monitor them all from this system. I'm going to leave you here and get back downstairs so I can open the club for the evening. We don't want anything to look unusual."

"How many people know about these rooms?" He followed Kim inside the small apartment. Yes, they were going to be in very close quarters.

"Myself and my wife and a few trusted friends," Rene replied. "Tag knows about it, obviously, and Charlotte. They stayed here once before her unfortunate death."

Charlotte's death hadn't been real, and he needed to start thinking about that option for Kim if they couldn't find a way to prove her innocence. The Agency wouldn't treat her like they'd treated him. They would come after her. He looked around the little room. "Seems so vanilla for Tag."

A mysterious smile crossed Rene's face. "There's always the club downstairs. You should understand the dungeon has no windows. If, say, after the building is secured, you want to come down and use the amenities, feel free. Simply clean up after yourself and make sure you're back in the safe room before dawn. There's a light by the door to the safe room. When it's lit that means the security system is activated and you're alone here. Use the secure line if you need anything. Good night."

Rene closed the door behind him and he was left with the one woman in the world he shouldn't be alone with, the one woman in the world who could wreck him. And there was a whole dungeon down there they could play in.

No. He wasn't going there. Not even if she wanted to. Which she wouldn't because Kim wasn't into the lifestyle. She was vanilla.

Except hadn't she always been open to anything he wanted to try? Hadn't she been the one to push him to keep things sexy between the two of them?

She set her duffel down on the bistro table and moved to the small pantry. "Are you hungry? I can probably put something together. Oh, thank god we're in France." She pulled out a bottle of wine. "It's a Pinot. I know you prefer beer."

"I'll drink anything right now." He shouldn't, but if there had been a bottle of Scotch, he might have sucked it down like water. "It's been a day. You know we're going to have to talk about it."

He'd given her time, but they would have to go over what Levi had done to her, what he'd said. He knew that fucker, and Levi liked to talk, so he had likely discussed his plans with her.

"Talk about what?" She opened a drawer and came back with a corkscrew. "I mean we probably have a lot to talk about. It's been ten years, after all."

"We've talked since the divorce." It might have been one of their problems.

"We've argued. You've yelled and I reacted. That's not a discussion."

"Well, I didn't think there was anything to discuss after you got my brother killed."

She stopped, going still as though she needed a moment to absorb the blow.

His anger was his greatest flaw. He knew, but he couldn't quite tamp it down. "I didn't mean to say that."

"But you still believe it. That's good to know. We were halfway civil in England. I almost hoped you'd forgiven me."

His jaw actually clenched to keep the words in. How could he forgive her?

Her eyes came up. "You might as well say it. You know you want to. You'll feel better if you get it off your chest."

But he wouldn't. That had been their problem. He'd raged at her time and time again and it never seemed to quell his anger. He shoved down the need to rehash their old issues. Why should he bother when they had so many new issues to get through? "I would rather talk about what happened today."

She pulled the cork and went to work finding glasses. "I'll write up a report. I think it's safe to say Levi is back in good with the big bosses."

He took a long breath and forced himself to sit on the couch.

It wasn't comfortable. It was kind of lumpy.

"Yes. I think we can safely say whatever was on the files we picked up here in Paris was enough to get them to overlook everything Levi's done in the last couple of years." Like work with drug dealing generals and shoot operatives who didn't agree with him. The Agency had picked teams and it looked like everything had come up Levi's way.

She poured two glasses of the wine. "I know what he has. The question is will the Agency admit they have it."

"What is that?"

She put the glass in front of him, moved her duffel to the floor, and sat down across from him. "There was a ton of information about who McDonald worked with. Some real. Some placed in there for blackmail purposes, like me. But the other thing you need to understand is that Levi has the formulary for McDonald's drug."

He felt the hairs on his arm stand up. That drug had taken everything from the Lost Boys, and he'd prayed they'd destroyed it utterly. "Tell me it's not the final formulary."

"No, but I worry that's out there somewhere."

He happened to know otherwise. "I'm going to tell you something that I hope you don't feel necessary to share with the Agency when you get back."

Her eyes widened. "Get back? I don't think my job will be waiting for me at the end of this. Once you get burned it's very hard to rejoin, and I wouldn't ever move up again. You know that. They offered to let you return but you walked away. I always wondered if that was more about giving me the finger than not wanting your job back."

"It wasn't about you." Seeing her had been the only reason to remain at the Agency, even though he'd known how unhealthy it was to stay around her. "It was about...everything. It was about what happened in Africa. It was about what happened in Mexico. It was about my brother."

"If it was about your brother then it was about me. You can't separate the two of us in your head anymore." She stared at the wall behind him, her eyes a bit glassy. She suddenly shook her head and her eyes cleared. "I won't be going back to the Agency. I don't know what I'll do, but even if I managed to get rid of Levi, there will always be people there who hate me. After what happened this morning, I don't think I can trust anyone there. So you can tell me anything. Despite our trouble, I've always been on your side."

She'd worked hard to try to get his job back. He knew she was one of the reasons the Agency hadn't come after him harder when he'd left. Big Tag had been another, but Kim had actively worked to keep him safe. He could trust her in this. "I helped Big Tag destroy the final formulary. We found it at the secondary base here in France. I came in a few hours after they freed Theo. Big Tag thought it would be good to have an Agency operative there so he would have accountability. He picked me because he knew I would do what he wanted. He knew I would help destroy that woman's work and I would cover for him. Not even the rest of the group knew I was there until later. It's all gone."

"Well, the first versions of it are now in Levi's hands, and I assure you, he means to perfect it all over again." She sighed and took a sip. "Like I said, I'll write it up tonight."

"I would rather you told me. I was surprised. The fucker finally managed to shock me. When I realized something was going wrong, I thought it would be me he arrested."

"Only because you fundamentally misunderstand what Levi wants out of this war we're in."

"Oh, I understand. He wants you. He wants to be able to say he took you from me."

She laughed, though the sound held not an ounce of true amusement. "You genuinely think he's doing this to prove he's better than you? That's why you were surprised?"

"He hates me."

"No, babe. He hates me and that's why he fucks with you. You think this war is between you and Levi and that I'm some pathetic prize one of you gets at the end, but you're wrong. I'm not blaming you for thinking that way. I did for a long time, too. But I hate to burst your bubble. You're incidental to this war because it would have happened whether or not you showed up."

His first instinct was to argue with her. This was obviously something between himself and Levi. After all, he'd been shot by the fucker and left for dead, not her. But arguing wouldn't solve anything.

"Why do you think that? You know he's hated me pretty much from the moment we met."

"You were a prick to him, but then he was annoying and trying to show off for me," she replied. "Though I didn't realize it at the time."

He'd met Kim when she was in training. She and Levi had been members of the same class. They'd been in a seminar that Ezra hadn't intended to teach. He'd only been working for a few years longer than their training class. "He didn't understand geopolitics the way he thought he did. He was a showoff, and I put him in his place. It was the incident that proved to the instructors I wasn't cut out to be one of them."

But he'd noticed her. He'd taken over three days of lectures on the political situations in smaller, often overlooked countries. Levi had been an ass, but he'd noticed the woman with all the blonde hair and the smile like sunshine. He hadn't been able to stop thinking about her and when he'd found out she frequented a bar in Foggy Bottom, he'd found himself hanging out there more and more. It had been before he'd gone into the field, when he'd been an analyst.

"See, he's always wanted to get back at me for that," he replied. "You don't understand the male psyche. I wounded his pride that day."

"And I wounded it when I wouldn't love him back."

He felt his spine straighten. He didn't want to hear about what she'd done with Levi before she'd met him. Sometimes he thought half their fights had been about that fucker. If she needed to believe she was the center of the universe, then he was going to let her. "There's no point in discussing ancient history."

She sat back. "Of course there isn't. I'm going to pull up the laptop. I'll stay on the couch tonight."

"I can handle the couch."

She stood up and grabbed the sleek computer and brought it back to the table. "I'm going to check my messages. I want to see if he called."

"By *he*, you mean Levi?" She wanted to know if he'd left her a damn message? "You so desperate to hear his voice?"

She didn't look up at him, merely stared at the screen. "The door is that way, Beck. You should feel free to use it." She sighed and looked up at him. "If you won't talk about the past with me, could you at least not accuse me of things you don't understand? That man has ruined my life in numerous ways. You don't want to hear about it? I get it, but you can keep your mouth shut about things you don't understand."

But he did understand. Didn't he? Levi had always been a touchy subject. "I told you he was trouble."

"Of course you did. Look, you were always right about everything and I was always wrong. We have to be here for a couple of days and then you don't have to see me ever again. I promise. I'll go my way and you'll go yours and I'll respect your wishes and stay far, far away from anywhere you might be."

He hated the fact that she wouldn't look at him. "I didn't say I was always right."

"You don't have to. It's implied in pretty much everything you do."

"What is that supposed to mean?"

She shook her head. "Sorry, we weren't supposed to talk about ancient history."

He was about to reply that he really wanted to know what she meant, but a frown crossed her face. "What is it?"

"It's a message from him. He didn't even use a burner. He wanted his name to come up."

"Play it." He wanted to hear it. He needed to hear that fucker's voice. His gut twisted because he'd accused her of the same thing, though he'd put an awful spin on it.

She touched a button and a beep came over the line.

"Hello, Solo." Levi's voice sounded smooth over the computer's speakers. "I'm going to assume it was Ezra who saved you today. It won't work. I'll find you and then I'll deal with him. If you want him to live, you'll turn yourself in. Make no mistake, I'm in charge now. I have control of your case, and when I bring you in I'll have complete control of you. The fact that you'll be in my charge is a foregone conclusion. How I bring you in now is up to you. I played nice, Solo. I won't next time. Next time we meet I'll show you my other side. The truth is the dark side of me loves you every bit as much as the light side. The dark side simply wants to hurt you more. I look forward to unleashing that part of myself. And tell Beck that he might have saved you briefly, but you'll be in my bed before the end of the week. Just like you were the first time."

Rage rose inside him hard and fast, and before he knew what he was doing, the glass in his hand exploded.

He heard a gasp and looked up at Kim. There was a drop of blood on her cheek. That speck of red was the only color on her face because her skin had gone a pasty white. She looked down at his hand and stood.

"I'll get the first aid kit. Don't move. You'll spread the glass around if you move." Her every word was dull and rote.

He'd cut her. He hadn't meant to, but wasn't that what they did when they were together? They were volcanic, and even when they started with the best of intentions, one of them ended up hurt.

He looked down at the red wine he'd spilled all over the table and his clothes. It looked like blood.

How much would he spill before they got out of this situation?

How much would he give? How much of hers would he take?

When she came back into the room, he was silent and allowed her to clean up the mess he'd made. He wondered if there was any way they got out of this whole.

Chapter Four

There were no windows in this small space, but Ezra knew it was night outside. He didn't need to look at a clock to know it was late. He stood in the bathroom, his hair still wet from the shower he'd taken, and wondered why he even cared about time. Somehow the realization that it was dark outside and they were alone in the building made his heart thud in his chest.

She was no more than a few feet away. All he would have to do was open the two doors that separated them and he could be in the same room. She would have changed into the pajamas provided for her and she would look soft and sweet, and her breasts would press against the T-shirt, her nipples outlined by the thin cotton.

Not that it would matter. Not that she would look at him.

It had been more than an hour since the light had come on above the door, letting them know the club had closed for the evening and Rene had locked the place up. Nothing was stopping them from going downstairs, picking an apparatus, and testing it out.

Nothing except the fact that he was a massive ass who couldn't control his anger. He stared at himself in the mirror and wondered if his brother would even recognize him now. The real Ezra Fain had been better. He would never have dismissed his wife, would have found some way to forgive her. His brother had been the generous one, the one who could find a reason to like everyone he met. Beck had been the hard-ass, stubborn one, the righteous, judgmental one.

He'd taken on his brother's name in an attempt to find some of his brother's grace, but he was failing at that, too.

The burner phone that had been in his go-bag buzzed against the small sink where he was supposed to be shaving. The scruff would have to wait. He picked up the cell and answered it. "Yes?"

He wasn't giving a name or asking for one. If he didn't recognize the voice on the other end, he would hang up and destroy the phone.

"Are you settled in?" Ian Taggart's voice came over the line.

He'd thought it would be Damon. "Yes. I'm surprised to hear from you. I thought you would be on a plane. Rene told me you would be here in the morning."

"I am on a plane. I borrowed it from Mia. I'll be there in the morning and I'll be cranky as fuck because the time difference sucks, but I need to get in and get out as soon as possible. It's freaking eight p.m. my time. If I get a couple of hours of sleep, I'll count it a win. At least the girls are sleeping."

"You're bringing the girls? You're bringing your six-year-old girls to a Parisian BDSM club when the Agency is likely to be all over this place?"

"I have my reasons. The girls can totally handle it, and I wasn't about to leave them home to help their mother who is currently taking care of their newest brother. I'd have Seth with me if Mia and Case hadn't offered to take care of him. The good news is I'm bringing Chelsea, too. If anyone knows how to deal with Agency dickheads, it's my sister-in-law. Look, I'm coming in on a different project, but it'll be good cover. I wanted to warn you that Levi's already looking. Chelsea's been on the Deep Web."

Kim had been on the web all night, barely looking up from the laptop. "If you're talking about the bounty on her head, we know."

The fact that she'd barely registered an emotion on finding out Levi had put her in the crosshairs of all kinds of unethical hunters was a real problem. She'd shut down. Kim was an emotional woman and she'd always needed an outlet.

He was worried she wouldn't cry in front of him.

"Good, then you understand that he's not playing around this time," Big Tag replied. "Solo's in serious trouble. Damon sent me a copy of his report. Tell me you understand this is all bullshit and that

Levi plays a long, very convincing game. And again, it's all bullshit."

"I know she didn't betray her country. But we have to prove it."

A snort came over the line. "Did you not understand the word *convincing*? I'm already trying to give her an alibi, but the very nature of her job is working against us. I've got about two hours tomorrow, and Chelsea and I will go over all of this with Solo. If we can prove even one of his claims is false, we can likely bring the whole house of cards down."

At least someone was working on the problem from the outside. Big Tag still had some Agency contacts. "Good. The faster we clear her name, the faster I get to kill Levi Green."

Big Tag sighed. "Yeah, I was worried that was what you would be focused on. How is Solo? Not that I care because I barely know the woman, but Charlie worries about everybody and she's going to ask."

Sure. Only Charlotte wanted to know how Kim was. Big Tag was a notorious busybody. "Solo's solo. Her name is more than a nickname. It's a very good description of who she is."

But not of who she'd been. It was odd to think about it now. When he'd met her, she'd seemed to fall so easily into his life. She'd been a flower drinking up water and blooming under his affection. She'd been a lonely child, and as an adult she'd desperately wanted to fit in, wanted to build some kind of family since her own had been cold and distant.

They had not approved of him. And yet it hadn't mattered to Kim one bit that he hadn't fit in with her parents' fancy lifestyle. She was the only ridiculously wealthy person he'd ever met who he believed genuinely could have done without the money. Some of the best times they'd had were simple. A picnic in the park. Staying in and ordering sweet and sour chicken and watching TV.

She'd loved Bliss, Colorado. There was nothing fancy about the place, yet it had been plain how much she'd wanted to fit in there.

"Well, I'm sure she's feeling pretty alone now," Tag pointed out. "Unless you've gotten your head out of your ass."

He rolled his eyes even though Tag couldn't see him. "My head is exactly where I want it to be. Look, I got her out. I'm staying with her and protecting her. We're fine."

"I seriously doubt she's fine. She understands that you hate her on an intellectual level, but living in close quarters with a man who despises you is another story."

"I don't despise her." He'd had to come to that conclusion weeks ago. It was easy to hate her when she wasn't sitting in front of him. He could shove out all the good memories they'd made together when she wasn't smiling and lighting up the room. Somehow when she walked in, the world seemed more vibrant than it had been before.

"You put on a good front."

He sighed. "Yeah, and the second she's in danger I toss out my whole life to rescue her."

"Ah, see, your brain does work. And what does that mean?" Tag asked.

"It means I have complex feelings when it comes to her."

Tag chuckled. "Excellent. Explore those feelings, especially the ones concerning your dick. Now I know I talk a lot about how dicks are dumb, but sometimes dicks are so dumb they're smart. Dicks don't let the past get in the way of something they really want."

"Tag, I'm not one of your projects." The last thing he wanted was for Tag to treat him like one of the Lost Boys.

"I don't have projects, brother," Tag shot back. "I merely impart knowledge, and if anyone understands your position, it's me."

He'd heard this lecture before. Charlotte had done Big Tag wrong by faking her own death and blowing up Tag's life. She'd cost him his career with the Agency, and he'd mourned her for years before she'd shown back up in his life. To hear Big Tag tell it, he'd been a saint, welcoming his wife back with loving arms. To hear Charlotte tell it was a whole other story.

It wasn't the same. Charlotte had been trying to save her sister. She hadn't sent Sean Taggart on a mission that got him killed—after Big Tag begged her not to do it.

It wasn't the same.

"Do you have anything else you need from me? I'd like to read that report."

Big Tag was quiet for a moment. "I've got a printout and Chelsea's got a report for you, too. We'll be landing in Paris early in the morning. My package is being delivered in the afternoon, and then we'll be heading back to the States if everything is in order. You should know Levi's still in London. He demanded to be let into The Garden, and Damon gave him a tour."

So their plan was already in motion. "You expect he'll show up in Paris."

"Oh, I think he'll come sometime tomorrow, and I'll be there waiting for him," Tag promised. "You will stay in that hidey-hole of Rene's. I know the bed looks small, but you can actually do some pretty nasty stuff on it. See, there was this time Charlie and I had to hide from a whole bunch of groups because she'd assassinated the head of a syndicate. Got stuck there for five days. Best days of my life, man."

He did not want to hear about how the man got his nasty on for five days. "We will definitely stay inside. Rene explained the way the place is set up. I might go downstairs for a while. Hopefully they have a hamster wheel like Sanctum. I could use a run."

"Unless he's gotten all modern and shit, I wouldn't look for that in Rene's club. He's pretty old school," Tag replied. "Have you thought about the fact that Solo is very likely sexually submissive?"

Only every minute of every day since he'd understood what D/s was really about. He'd sat in the classes at Sanctum and a couple at The Garden and finally realized what had been missing from most of his sexual encounters.

He'd finally realized why sex was so much better with Kim.

"Somehow I don't think she's going to be up for a session."

"I think after the day she's had, a good long session ending with a screaming orgasm would be exactly what the doctor ordered," Tag suggested. "But what do I know? Anyway, you might think about it. It could do you both good. Unless you're willing to let me take her back to Dallas when it's safe and have you go your own way."

He didn't like the sound of that. "I'm not leaving her until I know she's safe."

"That could be a while."

"It's not like I'm doing anything else with my time." When he thought about it, he'd been drifting since the divorce. He'd blamed it on his brother's death, but pushing Kim away had been a big part of him losing his direction. He hadn't thought about the future in anything more than a vague way in years. Not since he and Kim had sat up in bed and talked about having a couple of kids, eventually moving into the private sector so they could have a normal family life.

"All right, then you should think about calling a truce since you're going to be together for at least a few weeks, maybe longer. Better to spend that time working out your shit than fighting. See you tomorrow. And do I have to say it?"

Ezra hung up because he didn't need Big Tag to tell him to wear a freaking condom. Like he was fifteen and couldn't control himself. Besides, he hadn't had sex in a very long time, and Kim was on birth control. All operatives with working ovaries were.

He wasn't going to have sex with his ex. Not that she would. Except she'd spent the last several months saving his ass as often as she could. He could tell himself it was guilt, but she was as alone as he was. Neither of them had been able to move forward with their lives.

Maybe it was time to figure out why.

He dragged on a pair of flannel pajama bottoms and a T-shirt. What would it hurt to talk to her? To try to end the day better than they'd begun?

He'd felt uncomfortable with some of the things she'd pointed out to him, and he was old enough to know that if he felt uncomfortable about it then she was probably right.

He stood in front of the door to the bedroom and wondered if she would welcome him inside. Or punch him in the face. He would take either because either meant they were communicating.

But what if they could find a better way to work through the pain? Tag was right. Kim was a deeply independent woman who needed to submit sexually to feel free to enjoy the pleasure sex could bring her. He was a man who needed control in order to truly unleash a part of himself he didn't indulge in his daily life. It was why they'd been so good together back then.

It's why you can be good together now. All you have to do is stop being so fucking angry.

Or he could talk to her. He could start there. He knocked on the door and waited.

After a moment he opened the door and realized she was gone.

Ezra shoved his feet in shoes and vowed to not let her get away.

* * * *

Solo wandered around the dungeon, letting her hands brush against the leather-covered furniture that probably wasn't meant for seating. She was pretty sure she was looking at a spanking bench. The dungeon floor was a pretty red and black stained concrete, but the walls were mostly decorated with heavy velvet drapes that would mask the sounds coming out of here, trapping all those moans and groans and shouts of pleasure/pain in this space.

She had to wonder how many times Beck had walked the floor of The Garden. The dungeon at Damon Knight's London club was totally different from this, but it was every bit as decadent and beautiful.

Of course she hadn't been allowed to play. She'd been allowed to use one of the privacy rooms, specifically the one that contained a sauna, but only because she'd requested it for medical reasons.

All of her life she'd looked for a place where she could be accepted. It sucked that Beck—the one who'd kind of had a stick in his ass when it came to sex—had been the one to find it. It would have been cool, but he was the very reason she was left out in the cold.

I'm sorry. Normally I welcome a submissive who wants to explore, but I think having you in the dungeon would make Ezra...uncomfortable.

She could still hear Damon's words when he'd turned her down. It had taken a lot of her pride and courage to ask him. It wasn't easy to admit what she wanted. Of course she'd heard the words he hadn't said—everyone would be uncomfortable. Even Ari.

She'd gotten used to the fact that even her friend didn't completely trust her. No one did.

She groaned as the pain shot down her right leg, and she was reminded why she'd come down here in the first place.

Pain.

"Is it bugging you?" Beck asked.

She nearly jumped out of her skin but managed to stay cool. "I didn't hear you behind me."

"I thought we should still be quiet even though the light tells me we're alone. You snuck out while I was in the shower."

"I didn't think you would notice since you wouldn't take the bed. Did I forget to close the door?" She'd snuck out because she'd needed a place to stretch. The bedroom was far too small, and she hadn't wanted to bother Beck. They'd pretty much been silent for hours. She'd sat at the laptop searching the Deep Web for anyone who had information they would share with her. He'd been on the phone with Damon. She'd made them both sandwiches that she'd forced herself to eat in silence.

"I opened it to check on you," he admitted.

Of course he had. He didn't even trust her to sleep properly. "I wasn't trying to leave if that's what you're worried about."

"I know, but I did check to make sure your bag was still there. I know you think it would be easier to do this on your own."

She shook her head. "No, I don't. Not in any way. But I do think it would be easier to have a partner who trusted me, who wanted to be with me."

His hands went to his hips, a sure sign all that silence from him was threatening to explode. "I came for you."

"I know, and I have to wonder why." She winced as the pain shot through her again.

"Lie down on the table. The one to your left."

"I'm fine but I need to stretch." She'd managed to go hours without talking to him. She didn't intend to start now.

He wasn't ready to move past what they'd been through. He might never be ready. When his brother had died, something had broken inside Beck and she wasn't sure it could be healed. At least not by her.

She would walk a bit and stretch and get through the pain.

He moved in and she suddenly found herself swept up into his arms.

"Hey," she said even as she held on.

"I'm sorry I'm being an ass," he said quietly as he moved toward the table he'd pointed out. "I can't seem to help myself with you."

"A good reason for you to go back to The Garden as soon as it's safe." In so many ways it would be easier to be on her own. Simply being around him broke her heart.

He laid her gently on the big table. "Roll on your stomach. I still remember how to do this."

Because in the beginning, he'd been the one to deal with the pain left from her time with an unfriendly government. In their defense, she had been spying at the time, but it didn't help the shooting pains she still got or the aches she suffered from the broken femur.

Beck had been the one to come for her. Her husband. They'd only been married a few weeks when she'd gotten in trouble. He'd been the one standing at the opposite end of the tunnel at the prisoner exchange. He'd been the one to pick her up and hold her. He hadn't let go of her hand until they'd wheeled her back for surgery.

And Beck had been the one to hug her and kiss her and not give her a second's grief when she went on her next assignment. He'd understood the job, known she was competent.

She rolled on her stomach, giving him the access he needed. "I think eight hours in the car probably did it."

He put one big hand on the small of her back and heat flooded her system. "Really? You think it was the drive and not the fact that you were in a horrific car accident?"

The minute he pressed down in exactly the right place she sighed. Sometimes the absence of pain was pure pleasure. "Can you call it an accident? I think that was pretty much what Ari intended to do. I'm not complaining. I was never happier to get out of a limo in my life. God, that feels good."

He started to work the muscle in easy strokes. "I would have done pretty much anything to get you out of that car. I know I was an ass earlier. I'm sorry. I do want to be here with you. It's complicated. Ever since I saw you again in Colorado, I can't stop thinking about you, about our marriage. I thought I was over it all."

"I don't think our marriage is the kind of thing you get over. I know I haven't, and I know why, but I don't think we have the same reasons."

"Because you still love me."

She hated how vulnerable that made her, but it was true. "Yes."

"Why do you think that can't be my reason, too?" Beck asked.

She shook her head. "I don't want to fight. Anything I say right now is going to push you over the edge and I just can't."

He was quiet for a moment, his strong hands easing her pain. She wished she wasn't wearing the pajama bottoms she'd found, wished she'd had a gown on instead so she could feel those hands on her skin.

"That's what I do, isn't it? I argue with anything you say. Even if I agree with it, I fight. Do you wonder why that is?" Beck's voice was as soothing as his hands.

"Because you hate me."

"Because if I don't, if I let my guard down for a single second, I'll remember everything I ever loved about you and I'll give in. But lately I've wondered if I'm not punishing myself as much as I am you. And I'm wondering why I'm punishing you at all."

She needed to remind him or they would both be in a bad position. She pushed up off the table so she could look him in the eyes. "Because you blame me for what happened to your brother. Please don't forget that. I say it because I know if you forget, it won't be long before something reminds you and we're right back to you hating me again."

He stood where he was, dangerously close to her. "Tell me why you took the Colorado job."

Her chest felt too tight. It always did when she thought about the time she'd spent in Bliss. It had been a place she'd almost managed to think of as home. "It was Colorado. It's beautiful. It's peaceful. I got to spend months and months surrounded by those mountains and those crazy people. It's the best job I've had and all I had to do was watch John Bishop."

"Tell me why you really took the job."

She kind of wished she'd taken the pain and stayed in bed. Telling him the truth would likely be far more uncomfortable than her leg had been. "Because you were involved with Ian Taggart, and I knew there was no way you didn't end up in that town. Because John Bishop was one of Ian's mentors. Because by then you had gotten involved in the Lost Boys lives, and it was a good bet someone was going to go for The Ranch."

The Ranch had been a research site funded by some of the darker elements of the CIA. It was a secret site deep in the Sangre de Cristo mountains. It was where Hope McDonald had done much of her early work. The site had been closed down suddenly and without notice, so all the research and data that had been inside had gotten trapped. She'd known the Lost Boys would someday come for that knowledge because they'd been a big part of those experiments.

Beck stared down at her. "You wanted to work your way into my life again?"

"No, asshole. I wanted to make sure you survived." She started to move off the table. He was so fucking arrogant.

He put his hands on her shoulders. "Hey, I was asking. That's all."

He was also forgetting a few very important facts about that time. "I didn't exactly announce I was there, you know."

His lips kicked up in the sweetest grin. "No, you made damn sure you were never in the same room with me. I thought River's friend Heather was a figment of everyone's imagination. Especially Tucker's."

She winced. "He was definitely interested in female companionship. And he wasn't picky about it at the time. We're never telling his wife that story."

Roni was one of the only people in their world who didn't look at her with suspicion. Roni had made her feel like one of the girls. She would do a lot to avoid hurting Roni Croft-Seeger.

A single brow cocked over his eyes. "Yeah, you're the one the less picky guys go for." He studied her for a moment. "You're still the most gorgeous woman I've ever met."

She rolled her eyes at that. "Yeah, you followed Mia Lawless around for a good six months. I'm sure I'm still the most gorgeous."

His hand moved to the ponytail at the back of her head and he tugged gently. "I said what I meant, Kimberly." He seemed to realize what he was doing and let go of her hair, backing off slightly. "I'm sorry. We're in a dungeon and I'm acting like a Dom."

Her heart had started racing the minute his voice had taken on the deep timbre she remembered so vividly. "You were always a Dom. I just didn't know what to call you."

She'd been all of twenty-two years old when she'd met him, and he'd been twenty-five. So freaking young, and they hadn't even truly begun to explore their sexuality. She'd thought she would have decades with him, decades to learn with him, grow with him.

She'd barely gotten two years with him from when they started dating to their divorce. It was funny that she'd been divorced from him for far longer than she'd been married, but those precious months were the most important of her life.

"Yeah, I figured that out, too." He moved so he was leaning on the table next to her, their hips almost touching. "Big Tag pointed out a lot of things to me. The man's an ass but he's an observant ass. He might have pointed out how much Mia looks like you. She was a safe version of you to follow around for a while. I didn't even realize I was doing it at the time. I thought she was pretty and nice, and I had a job to do. She was also madly in love with Case Taggart. I never touched her. We became friendly, but I wouldn't even say we were friends."

Somehow hearing he hadn't gone to bed with the gorgeous, do-gooder reporter made her feel a bit better. "One of the things I liked about Bliss was that I didn't get hit on very often. Most of the men around town are married, and the others are super respectful. Being there, it was the most free I'd felt in forever."

He shook his head. "I would never have said you would be happy in a small town. You like the city too much."

"I probably wouldn't have dreamed it either. Then I found one I liked. That's the funny thing about change. It doesn't happen until we let it. I took that job because I was worried about you, and I ended up loving the people there. Of course, now they all hate me. That's the story of my life." Once they'd figured out she'd lied to them for months, that she'd been watching one of their own, they hadn't been so welcoming.

"It's the nature of the job. I had the same problems at first. No one at McKay-Taggart and Knight trusted me with anything until I sacrificed for them. For a long time I was the Agency dude they hated the least." He sighed and seemed to relax a bit. "They didn't really trust me until they realized I wasn't ever going back to the Agency."

"I don't know. I think it's more than that. I've felt it all my life—that distance from other people. When your parents are the not-so-kind overlords of all they survey it's hard." From an early age she'd realized her playmates were carefully cultivated. It hadn't been until she'd entered the ultra-exclusive boarding school her parents selected for high school that she realized almost everyone she knew was afraid of her because all it would take was a whisper from her mother to ruin their family in their society.

"Well, that's how he got to you," Beck pointed out. "Levi, that is. I've been thinking about it all night. You were lonely and he was willing to be your friend. He should have been upfront with you. He should have told you what he wanted and let you make the decision."

Some memories were sweeter than others. Some pushed out the darkness. A vision of Beck sitting on a barstool beside her, telling her exactly what he wanted, haunted her in the best way possible. "Like you did?"

His smile deepened, finally revealing the dimples that only showed up when he was genuinely amused. "Hey, I was very open and honest that I was trying to get into your pretty panties."

Their attraction had been out of control. He hadn't approached her until he was no longer teaching her class, but she'd had some ridiculously over-the-top fantasies about the man. "Yeah, well, I didn't make you wait long. If I remember correctly we were going at it in a motel because neither of us wanted to wait to get back across town."

"The Kingsman. I remember that motel fondly."

She wrinkled her nose. "It was not nice in the cold light of day. There was a definite layer of grime in that bathroom."

His expression went serious. "There was nothing cold about that day."

No. It had been a sunny, gorgeous summer day, and they'd laughed as they decided to not use that shower. They'd held hands on the metro and bought bagels and gone back to her place where they'd spent all Saturday in bed. She'd known she was madly in love with him that day.

That day seemed so far away now.

"Are you all right?" Beck asked.

She wanted to break the intimacy between them. The moment felt too warm. It was a falsehood, and she would end up hurting again. "Yeah, you got the exact pressure point. I'll be fine as long as I move."

"I wasn't talking about that. That call from Levi… He's stalking you."

He'd been stalking her for years, but no one called it that when the man stalking her used to be a friend, still pretended to be one. She was the bitch who couldn't see how much he cared about her. "He is."

"Tell me what he did. Not that sanitized report. I want to know how he made you feel."

"If I do that, you'll get angry again."

He shook his head. "No. I promise I won't make this about me. I heard you. I've let those words sit with me, and I realized I was doing exactly what you said I was. I'm marginalizing what happened because I can't stand the thought that this wasn't about me, that I was incidental in this story. It's hard to think that all this pain I've felt didn't have any real meaning."

"That's not what I said. Of course it has meaning."

He shrugged. "But oddly it feels worse that the pain wasn't intentional."

He had some toxic masculinity to work through, but then she'd always known it. He had anger issues that he'd never turned her way before the incident with his brother. What did she owe him? In her rational moments she knew she owed him nothing. But her stupid heart kept wanting more. "He told me he was going to use the drug on me. He told me he's got a dose with my name on it."

Beck went still and she knew she'd made a mistake. There was a reason she'd left that specific part out of the report. She'd thought someone like Taggart would understand the underpinnings of the threat without putting it baldly out there to taunt Beck.

Or maybe she'd been worried Beck wouldn't care.

It seemed one way or the other when it came to this man. He either went over the top with rage or he was cold. There was none of the in between she needed from him.

He pushed off the table. "I'm going to kill him."

She should have known. "Good. Way to make it not about you, babe."

He turned on her, his jaw clenched tight so every word came out peppered with tension. "How am I supposed to act? Am I supposed to be perfectly fine with the fact that he means to drug you and put you through everything McDonald put my men through? You expect me to be okay with that?"

She'd wanted to avoid more masculine bullshit. "This is why I didn't put the specific threat in the report. And I seriously doubt he was going to train me to commit crimes for him. He was interested in other things. He wanted a good little wife who would submit to him."

There was a fine flush to Beck's face. "Don't you bring that into it. That is not what submission is about."

Why did she love him? Why did it have to be this one stubborn, obnoxious man? She bit back a wince as she got to her feet. "Fine. I didn't use the right words to describe what he was going to do to me. Maybe you can write up my next report so I get it right."

She was done with this, done with the seesaw of emotions this man brought out in her. Maybe Ari was right and it would genuinely be better for both of them if she walked away and was never heard from again. She would take her secrets with her and leave Levi and Beck to fight this out on their own. Or Levi would leave Beck alone once he realized she wasn't trying to get close to him anymore. She could find a deserted island and *Survivor* the crap out of the rest of her life.

A big hand gripped her elbow and whirled her around. "Hey, where are you going?"

She was out of his hold in two seconds. One more and she was the one with hands on him. She wrenched his arm behind his back and had him on his toes. "I think I've been manhandled enough for one day."

He went still. "I don't know what I did wrong. I'm mad because he threatened to hurt you. You can't expect me to not care that he's planning to dose you with that drug. I've spent the last few months of my life trying to fix the results of that fucking drug. Tell me you wouldn't be upset if he'd done the same to me."

She sighed and let go of his arm. "I wouldn't let anger take away from comforting you. You would be my first priority. The way I used to be yours."

He ran a hand through his hair, pressing it back as he began to pace. "All this time and we lose it to him. To fucking Levi Green."

She understood his frustration. "Levi always wins. It's why the next time I have a shot at killing him, let me take it. No matter the cost."

His jaw went tight. "What is that supposed to mean?"

"It means I want this over with. All of it. If it means I go down then I go down, but I will take him with me." This could all be over with if he'd simply allowed her to get back in the limo. Yes, she would have probably been taken out, but Levi would be done.

She could have done one good thing before she died.

"I couldn't stand there and let you die." He moved in behind her, his hands coming to her shoulders. "I'm fucking everything up again. I swear I came down here to make sure you were okay."

"I thought you came down here to make sure I hadn't run."

"I walked out of that shower and damn near panicked," Beck admitted. "It's because I know if you run this time, you won't come back. My feelings for you are so complicated, but I knew I couldn't sit there and let him take you. You're right. I'm not putting you first. I haven't in a very long time, but I don't know if that's my place anymore. I worry if I put you first, I'll disappear."

"No, you're worried if you put me first, if you let go of the anger you still feel, you'll be betraying your brother," she corrected.

He gave her a slow nod. "Yeah. I guess that's what it comes down to."

"The funny thing is, the real Ezra wouldn't have blamed me and you know it."

He sighed. "I don't want to talk about him. I want to talk about you. I'm sorry. Not that I got mad, but that I didn't control it. You haven't cried. Not the whole time. Your life fell apart and you haven't cried."

"Well, it wasn't much of a life."

"That's something to cry about, too," he said. "Talk to me. Tell me what you felt while you were in that limo. I want to hear it because you need to say it, because under all that toughness, I know there's a soft heart. You need to cry and let it out or it's going to fester."

"You're one to talk."

"Yes, I've let things fester for a very long time and I'm a walking wound." He drew her back against him. "I'm feeling helpless. I don't handle that well. Maybe we both need to deal with the day. I'm not going to sleep tonight if I don't try to take care of you. You can talk to me or we can try something else."

She let her head drift back and then she was surrounded by him. Despite the fact that she knew it couldn't work out in the long term, she wanted this moment, needed it so badly. It would be better to run back to her room and lock herself in, but she couldn't do it. He was a drug and she'd never stopped craving him. The temptation to find out how this Beckett Kent could take care of her was far too much to turn away. "What do you want to try?"

"You are one big ball of stress and you don't trust me."

"Beck," she began.

"No. It's true and I understand it. I have trouble with trust, too. So let's work on it. Let's take this time and see if we can figure out a better way to deal with each other. Let's start with brutal honesty." He took a shaky breath behind her. "I've missed you."

She closed her eyes and let the words sink in. "I missed you, too."

"I'm still angry with you, but I don't think that matters now. I think what matters is that my instinct is to protect you. I need to follow my instincts."

Yes, she should definitely run because there was still so much he didn't know, so many other reasons to be angry with her. But they didn't matter because she couldn't talk about them. Those promises had been made to someone else and she couldn't break them. Not even to save her marriage.

"Can you trust me enough to let me touch you? I know I did that when I helped with your leg, but you know damn well it would feel better if you didn't have clothes on, if it was my hand on your skin. Let me touch you."

There was nothing she wanted more, but she couldn't say it. All she could do was step out and turn to face him. She held up her arms and let him pull the T-shirt she was wearing off. She'd been ready for bed so she'd taken her bra off, and now cool air whispered across her skin. But it was the fact that his eyes were on her that made her nipples tighten.

"I've been with other women," he said carefully.

They'd been divorced for years. She hadn't thought he would be faithful. "I've dated some. Not much. Two guys. Not…"

He shook his head. "No. He wasn't a date. I know that. He was a mistake you made, and Levi likely manipulated you."

She suddenly felt so vulnerable. "If we're going to actually talk about this, I should be dressed."

"No. That's been our problem all along." He reached down and pulled his shirt over his head and tossed it to the side. "Every single time we've talked in the last ten years, we've put on our armor and gone into battle. This isn't a battle. It doesn't have to be. It can be something more."

Like once, they'd been something more. "I'm afraid to be vulnerable with you."

He kicked off his shoes. It was obvious he'd shoved them on his feet when he'd come down to look for her because he wasn't wearing socks. How odd that the sight of his feet made her heart clench. She'd seen his chest, his arms and legs. But it had been so many years since she'd seen his feet, brushed hers against them when they were in bed.

"I've never loved a woman the way I loved you. I put it in the past tense, but we both know there's still something here." Beck shoved the pajama bottoms he'd been wearing down and revealed he wasn't wearing any boxers. "I don't know where we're going, but I know as long as we're stuck here together, I won't be able to keep my hands off you. I'm sick of being angry with you."

She was so sick of his anger, though she knew there was some justification to it. "You want honesty? You want to know what I felt when I was in that limo with him?"

He moved in, his body on glorious display. The man was even more lovely than he'd been all those years before. Though he bore a few new scars. She did, too. It was funny because they were almost in the same place. He reached out and touched the place where she'd been shot in Colorado. It was a few inches under her collar bone. She waited for his anger to rise, but he merely touched the spot. "Yes. I want to know. I want to know how you felt so I can try to fix it."

He couldn't fix it, but he might be able to make her feel something. She'd been numb for so long, forcing herself to not want anything. The few times she'd allowed herself to hope, she'd found the depths of despair. It felt good to want even though she knew it wouldn't last more than a night or two.

"When I realized he'd come for me, I was scared at first, but then I felt so fucking lost because you wouldn't look at me. Because you didn't say anything. I wondered if you thought I was guilty and I was getting what I deserved."

"Damon stopped me," he admitted. "Damon begged me to stay calm. He knew we could get you back, but we couldn't stop him from taking you. I wasn't calm or cool in that moment. I was white-hot raging angry, and there was a part of me that was angry with you."

Just like that she was done. She couldn't handle another second of his anger. Not when they'd gotten so close to something else. He couldn't help himself. He was made of rage and he'd found a place to put it all. On her.

This had been a terrible mistake. She shouldn't ever be vulnerable with him because for all his sweet words, they were still at war. He wanted the chance to really wreck her this time.

"Hey, don't," he began. "I promised I would be honest and that anger was there, too."

She nodded. "Of course it was. You're always angry. I would bet you sat there and wondered if it wasn't some sex game between me and Levi. Or if I was doing it to get your attention. Like a kid who acts out because she can't get love any other way."

His gaze went hard. "I was worried we might have to do it this way."

"What way? It's your way. It's always your way." It had been for years. The divorce had been his way. The anger had been his way. The inflexibility was his way.

"I assure you losing my brother wasn't my way." His hands clenched. "I didn't mean to upset you. I meant to get you talking."

"About what? About Levi? Are you trying to trick me into telling you I did it? Is that why you came after me? Did you think you could get the truth out of me better than he could?"

"I never once thought you were guilty," he replied. "This is why we have to talk. You're a bundle of emotions but you won't let them out. If we're going to get through this, we've got to do it together."

Hearing the word come out of his mouth made her ache inside because that word was a lie coming from him. "Together? We haven't been together in years, and maybe we never were."

"I assure you we were together once. I still dream about it at night. It's the reason I can't have another relationship."

She couldn't do this with him. She'd been stupid to think they could have some sex and she would feel better. There was too much between them. God, the day had been too much. It all threatened to crash in on her. She'd lost it all, and now she was stuck with a man who actively hated her. He might be able to hide it for brief periods of time, but he hated her with as much passion as he'd ever loved her. He would turn on her and she wouldn't survive it this time.

She tried to move to grab her shirt but he was right there, getting in her space.

He loomed over her, his face gorgeous in the low light of the dungeon. "No. We're going to talk. I'm not leaving you like this."

He was in his element. Somehow even without a stitch of clothing on, there was nothing vulnerable about Beckett Kent. He stood there, his stupid attractive feet planted on the ground, his gorgeous cock hard. He belonged here. Like he seemed to belong everywhere. This was his place of power. She didn't have one. "Fuck you, Beck."

"Yeah, I'd intended for this to end that way, but if you need to rage a little more, go on. I assure you I can take it."

He'd already taken so much. She wanted to have it out with him, to let him know the truth about all things, but she couldn't. So instead she gave him some truth of her own. He wanted honesty? She could give it to him. She moved in, needing him to understand that he couldn't intimidate her. "You know what I thought when Levi told me he had the drug?"

"No. What did you think?"

He was infuriatingly calm now. It bothered her because she felt white hot. Like a live wire that was twitching and jumping, looking for something to send all that energy through.

"When he told me he had that drug and that he planned to use it on me, I was afraid at first. Then he pointed out that all my pain would go away because I wouldn't remember who you were. I wouldn't remember how easy it was to break me because I wouldn't remember meeting the man who'd done it."

His eyes flared, the first sign of his emotion. "You think you can forget me? You think some drug can make either of us forget?"

"I think I might like to try." She didn't mean it. She would never give up her memories of him. For a brief time he'd been everything to her. He'd been her future, and while they'd been together the world had been a better place. She would cling to that memory until the day she died.

His hand came up, gripping her hair and forcing her head back. "Then maybe I should remind you."

His mouth came down on hers and all thoughts of leaving fled.

She knew she should be fighting him, but how long had she wanted this? How long had she waited for those gorgeous lips of his to be on hers again? All these years and she'd had a few encounters, one she didn't remember at all, the one that cost her any hope of a reconciliation—but no one ever moved her the way Beckett Kent did.

She brought her arms up to circle his shoulder and bumped against the bandage on his arm. He hissed. She tried to pull away, but he tugged hard enough on her hair to make her gasp.

"No. Don't stop me."

She shook her head. "You're hurt."

"I'm always hurt around you. Make me feel better. You're the only fucking person in the world who can make me feel better."

She couldn't resist him, couldn't say no, though she worried there was a stark undertone to his words. All that mattered was taking this moment. She might never see him again. This might finally be the end, and she wanted something sweet, something to hold on to, something that she would fight to remember even if Levi caught her again.

She wanted one more moment with Beck.

He devoured her mouth, kissing her with a hunger she matched with her own.

"This is what you need, what we both need," he whispered against her mouth. "Take off those pants and those fucking panties and let me touch you. Let me help clear some of this poison. Let's get it all out of our systems, and then I'll beg you to not make me sleep on the couch tonight."

This was such a dangerous place to be. "You can't make me

forget. You've been an asshole to me for years."

"I can. Give me a chance. You don't have to love me again. You only have to want me. You have to trust me to get you through this. Let me start by getting you through the night. Tell me you don't want this. Tell me you don't want to know what I can do to you now and I'll walk away. I'll sleep on that couch and we can go right back to being polite in the morning."

"You are never polite."

"Because you don't need polite. That's not what you want in bed. You want me to take charge. You want to be able to close your eyes and focus on the pleasure. You want to shut your brain off and know that you can relax. I promise you won't be thinking about anything but the way I can make you feel. Let me show you what I've learned over the years we've spent apart. Let me show you how much better I can take care of you now. Give me the power."

She wanted to, but there needed to be boundaries. "I can't make love to you."

His hands tightened in her hair, lighting up her scalp and making her skin tingle. "Who said anything about making love? I want to fuck you. I want to spank you and make you cry for me. I want to hurt you but in the best way, in the way that unleashes your pain and makes me feel like I can do something good with all the bad inside me."

If he'd offered her something tender, she couldn't have even considered it. There was no tenderness between them, but there was need. The need to find out if he could do all the things he promised, if he could take her out of herself, if he could make her forget even for a few moments that she was alone in the world.

She nodded.

"No, you have to say it," Beck commanded. "You have to give me the power, but with the understanding that you can take it back at any time. You can stop me. But I have to hear the words. There's no shame in it. There's no shame in this dungeon. It might coat the world outside, but it has no place here."

She wanted to believe it, needed at least to try this with him. She shoved away every single reason to run from him.

"Please hurt me, Beck."

Chapter Five

She couldn't believe she'd said the words, but they were true. She wanted what he was offering. How long had this need been inside her, unfilled, unresolved?

Beck's hand came up to grip her neck, to force her to look up at him. "You obey me in this room. You will do what I tell you, take what I give you here. If I scare you or tell you to do something you don't want to do, say the word *red* and I'll stop. I mean anything, Kim. You can stop this at any time."

She could take everything he had to give and stop him before actual sex. He was telling her she didn't have to pay him back with intercourse.

But the sex would be for her, too. "I'm not going to stop you."

His fingers tightened slightly, bringing her up on her toes. "You always have a choice, but sometimes it's fun to pretend you don't. I need to hear you tell me you understand that you do."

He was offering her a fantasy but needed her to understand consent was everything or the fantasy didn't work. "I can tell you no if that makes it hotter for me, but all I have to do to stop it is say the word *red*. You need to understand that I want you. I want everything you promised me, but I'm afraid that you'll hold back because you know how much I want it."

"I promise, I'm not trying to punish you, but in the end you'll have to trust me. If you can do that, take the rest of your clothes off and then I want you to go to the table where I rubbed your legs and I want you to put your hands on top and spread your legs wide with that pretty ass of yours up in the air."

"You're going to spank me."

"I am. I'm going to make your ass red and your pussy wet. I'm going to touch you everywhere I want because for these moments your body belongs to me and you don't have to think about anything but following my commands and taking my discipline. If that doesn't work for you, we can try something else, but I want to be in bed with you tonight and I want to be the reason you can sleep. Tell me if the idea of me disciplining you is frightening or arousing."

"You know it's arousing."

"I do, but unless you're willing to admit it, this can't work."

She stepped back slightly and he let go of his hold. He didn't scare her on any physical level. He wouldn't hurt her like that. Emotionally he could wreck her, but she couldn't let this chance go. If there was any way to connect with him again, she would take it because she was an idiot and she was still so in love with this man.

Maybe tomorrow she could fool herself again, shove those emotions deep, but tonight she wasn't going to lie to herself.

She hooked her thumbs under the plain cotton undies she was wearing and eased them over her hips, her heart starting to thud in her chest in a mix of excitement and dread. It was an intoxicating cocktail because she'd been numb for so long.

"You are so fucking gorgeous." He stopped her before she could do what he'd asked, and his eyes were back on the scar from the bullet wound she'd gotten in Colorado.

"Don't, Beck. Please don't bring him into this." She couldn't have Levi here with them. It felt like Levi was always there between them, pushing them apart.

His jaw tightened but he nodded. "Then do as I told you."

She breathed a sigh of relief and moved across the floor to the table he'd indicated. She placed her hands on the padded top palms down and spread her legs outward. The position made her incredibly vulnerable, putting almost every inch of her skin on display for the man who was about to discipline her.

His hand came down on her ass with a resounding whack. The pain hit her system and she gasped, forcing air into her lungs. He held his hand there as if he could force the heat into her skin. After a moment that same hand stroked down to her thigh and back up again.

The wait was killing her. She would rather he'd gone fast and gotten through this part so she could feel his arms around her, his body moving inside hers.

Another hard smack and tears pierced her eyes. The pain was jarring, and he coupled it with the sweet sensation of his hand stroking her skin. It reminded her of how good it felt to have him touch her. Not merely anyone, but this man.

"I've dreamed of doing this to you, of being here with you. In my dreams you're always naked." He spanked her again, a sharp smack against the underside of her ass. "You always start out unsure about whether or not you like this."

"Your dreams are my reality," she admitted as he spanked her again. "Is it always so slow?"

His big palm cupped her, and he gave her a squeeze that made her heart rate tick up. "Not at all. Sometimes I'll pull you over my lap and spank you hard and fast. You won't have a chance to breathe, it'll be so shocking."

"And this is supposed to do something for me?" Even as she asked the question she knew the answer because she could feel heat flooding her system and she was deeply aware of how close his hand was to her pussy. The brief pain she'd felt was working to sensitize her.

He was right. This was what she needed. She needed the pain to give her permission to feel the pleasure. She was sure a therapist would tell her she needed to spend some time on a couch, but she didn't care. She would take any moment of respite she could find.

She lost track of how many times he slapped her ass and then eased the ache with the touch of his hand.

"Still wonder if it's doing something for you?" His voice had gone deep and she felt his hand slide between her legs. He slid a finger through her pussy. "Yes, I dream about this, too. I dream about how fucking wet you get every time I touch you. I dream about how good you smell, and I fucking can't wait to taste you again. Tell me how you feel right now."

She didn't want to talk. She wanted that finger inside her, but he was skimming over her flesh, teasing her.

He slapped her pussy, sending a jarring wave of pleasure/pain through her. "I asked a question. I expect an answer. Now."

She wished she didn't love it when he took charge. Her life would be so much easier if she didn't feel that tug inside her the minute Beck's tone went all commanding. "It hurts but not so much I want you to stop. I want you to touch me. I'm getting antsy."

"You're getting impatient, but I'm going to show you how good it can be to go slow," he replied as he gently fucked a single finger into her pussy.

It wasn't enough but she tilted her hips to try to get him to that spot he always found so quickly.

His hand was suddenly gone, and he peppered her ass with sharp, short slaps.

She groaned and sucked in air, letting the pain flare before the wave of heat rolled over her.

"You don't get to control this." He wrapped his hand around the nape of her neck and gently eased her up. He moved in behind her, so close she could feel his cock against her tender ass. "I control this. Do I make myself clear?"

"Yes." She needed to give this a shot because not being in control sounded so fucking good. She was always in control, always had the heavy burden of responsibility on her shoulders, and she had for years.

His hands moved to her waist and then he brushed them up her torso to cup her breasts. "Excellent. I want you to be a very good girl because I would hate to stop when you're so close to an orgasm. I want to watch you come. I want to feel you shake when I suck your clit between my lips. Would you like that?"

Her spine felt like it was going to melt. No one in her whole history had ever eaten her pussy the way Beck had. He could do it for what felt like hours, bringing her pleasure again and again until she couldn't take another orgasm and he finally gave in and gave her his cock and proved that she could. "Yes. You know I would."

"How do I know?"

"Because I used to love it when you would eat my pussy."

His teeth scraped the shell of her ear, making her shiver and wish he would bite down just a little. "I love that you're willing to talk dirty. I don't have to pull it out of you. Tell me what you want. Let me hear every dirty, glorious word out of that sweet mouth of yours."

It was funny because it put other men off. Never Beck. He liked her dirty and hot. He was the only man she'd ever felt fit her sexually. "I want you to eat my pussy, and then I want you to fuck me hard. I want that cock of yours inside me, and I don't want you to stop until neither one of us can stay awake a moment longer. Then do it again in the morning."

"I'm clean. I've had a physical recently. You would be surprised how quick Tag is with tests."

He didn't want to wear a condom. She didn't want one either. "I haven't had sex in over a year and I passed my last physical. Fuck me, Beck. Please. Don't make me beg."

"I like to hear you beg," he admitted as his fingers found her nipples and she arched her back. "I like every single noise you make when I'm fucking you. I'm definitely going to like the sounds you make when I use a violet wand on you. I'm going to tie you down and light up these nipples until you scream."

"I might scream soon if you don't stop teasing me."

He pinched her nipples. Hard. The pain shot through her like lightning going straight to her pussy where she felt a surge of fresh arousal. She was soaking wet. She might have been embarrassed by it, but not with him. He would love it. He would revel in it and lick it all up. When he kissed her she would be able to taste her own arousal on his lips.

"I'll stop teasing you when I want to." He licked her ear and then kissed his way down her neck. "I should do what I said I would. I should push you until you cry."

She reached around and put her hands on his waist. "Please. I don't need to. I need this. I need you."

She didn't want to get emotional. It could spark a fight, and all she wanted was some peace. She could find that but only if they didn't talk about the past. This was a moment in time that suspended past and future. She wanted to stay in it.

He turned her and she found herself up and on the table in an instant. "Lie down. Spread your legs."

She breathed a sigh of relief because she knew that look in his eyes. He was done playing. He was ready to move on to the main event, and she had avoided the one thing she didn't want to do with him.

Get really emotional. Open up. She could take his affection without offering up her soul, and that would be best for both of them. She wasn't a fool. He would leave again at some point. They'd passed the moment when they could have had forever. So she would take these hours and hold them close.

Beck stood at the end of the table and stared at her. He slowly brought his hand down to grip his own cock.

Maybe he wasn't done playing yet.

She stared right back at him, memorizing the way his body looked now, including the new scars. She'd loved and worshipped every inch of his gorgeous body, from his silky dark hair to those ridiculously large feet. But she adored his cock. It was long and thick, and a pearl of creamy fluid pulsed at the slit as he stroked from the head all the way down to those heavy balls she loved to cup. She could spend a long time licking and sucking that cock and working his balls into her mouth.

"While we're stuck here, every night we'll come down here after hours and play. That will be my time. You'll serve me down here, and all day I'll do whatever you need me to do on this investigation. You're in charge of that. I'm in charge of this."

She could handle those rules. She wanted to explore this part of his life, to see how it could bring them closer together for the time they had. The last thing she wanted to do was waste a moment of it. "Yes, Sir."

He stopped and shook his head. "No. I want to hear my name."

She felt those words in her heart and knew she was going to lose the whole don't-give-your-soul-to-him game. If he could get back to being Beck, they might have a shot. For so many years he'd used Ezra's name as a shield to protect himself. "Beck. Yes, Beck. In this room, you're the king and I am your happy sub."

She might be happy if they could break through the walls.

He gripped her ankles and dragged her down the table so her pussy was right on the edge. He spread her ankles wide, and she was utterly vulnerable to him.

The table seemed to be at the perfect height. Beck dropped to his knees and she watched as he breathed in her scent. The decadent look on his face made her breath catch. Then he leaned down and licked her, and then she wasn't breathing at all. Then her eyes were rolling back and her whole body focused on one thing, that soft feeling at her core.

Beck's tongue worked her over, spearing her again and again. She could feel a pleasant ache where he'd spanked her. The ache coupled with the soft stroke of his tongue, drowning her in sensation. He pushed her higher and higher as he settled his mouth over her clit, and that big finger pressed inside her pussy. She brought her head up so she could see him. His eyes were staring right at her, connecting them and tearing down any shield that might have protected her from him.

This was how sex had always been between them. They couldn't hold back, couldn't pretend there was anything but need between them—a need only the other could fill.

She held his gaze and gave him everything as he stroked inside and his tongue laved her clit in the perfect rhythm. She wanted the moment to last, to stay in this place forever, but she finally couldn't hold out a second longer.

The orgasm rushed over her and her whole body tightened and released, relief flooding through her.

Her head fell back as Beck gave her one last lick and rose to his feet. She watched as he moved between her legs and knew it was his time.

She forced herself to sit up and open her arms.

* * * *

Beck's whole body was alive for the first time in years. It didn't matter what he'd told her. Fucking Kim Solomon was making love. It always was. Every single time. Even when they came together in anger, it was making love.

No other woman in the world could make him feel the way she did. He could try to fool himself, but he knew deep down he'd never really let her go.

She came up off the table, moving gracefully and opening her arms to him. He reached for her, drawing her close and lowering his mouth down to hers. Kissing her felt so perfect, and he worried he wouldn't be able to stop. It was good that they had hours and hours before Tag was scheduled to show up because it was going to take all that time to even begin to feed the hunger he felt for her.

He could still taste her. All these years later and he'd thought he could remember, but she tasted better than memory. Sweet and tangy. She coated his lips and tongue, and he would never get enough of her.

Her legs wrapped around his waist, and he felt the heat of her pussy rubbing against his cock. He was surrounded by her, and it made him feel safer than he had in forever.

Even as he had the thought, he knew how dangerous it was. Kim was his kryptonite. She was the person who could lift him up, and she was the only one in the whole world who could drag him right back down to hell. He'd spent ten years on the wagon, but it looked like he was falling off tonight.

And every night until he had to give her up again.

His tongue plunged deep, dancing with hers. Over and over they stroked together, building his need higher than he'd thought he would ever go again.

Did he have to give her up? What if the problem the first time around was that he'd been too indulgent? He hadn't insisted that she stay away from Levi. He'd listened to her when she said he was harmless. Maybe she'd learned her lesson now.

He let the thought float away. He was living this minute by minute. He wasn't going to let himself think of some dreamy future with her.

Except he already had. He was damn good at fooling himself these days.

What wasn't a trick was how wet she was. She was soaking wet, and it was all for him. He'd been the one to make her cry out his name as she came. He was the one who'd made her shake and shiver. The whole time he'd spanked her, he'd promised himself he wouldn't stop until she'd cried. But this was what she'd needed. She needed this more than anything.

He thrust his hands in her hair, feeling the soft silk against his fingers. He'd missed all that honey. Her hair was long and thick, and he'd always loved to control her with it. They might be more formal this evening, but he'd always topped her in the bedroom. From that first night when he'd taken control and she'd screamed out his name, he'd been her dominant partner.

He kissed her, tangling their tongues together as he rubbed his dick against all her softness. His cock was so hard he could barely breathe, but he wasn't about to rush this. He wanted this to last all night. He was going to sleep with her, going to wrap his body around her and wake up with her in his arms.

"God, I missed you," she breathed against his mouth.

He'd missed her so much, felt her absence like an ache in his soul. It had been so long that he'd gotten used to that hole inside him, but now that it was full again, he realized how empty his life had been without her.

He gripped the globes of her ass and started to force her onto his dick. He'd thought he would turn her over and drive into her from behind, but he wanted this intimacy. He wanted to fuck her while he kissed her, while their mouths mingled and hands clutched.

"I want to try everything with you," she said, her eyes wide and guileless as she looked up at him.

"Everything," he promised. They would be like two kids in a candy store. Every night they were here he would bring her down and they would have hours to play. "Sanctum is even better. Sanctum has everything."

Everything he would need to train her, to train himself. To discover what made her purr and what made her howl. He would learn her all over again.

But first he would revel in how good it felt to fuck her.

He pressed his cock inside, the heat surrounding him and making him grit his teeth. There was nothing like the feel of her pussy tight around him, her nails digging into his back as she accepted him. He felt her breasts pressed against his chest and the way she shuddered the deeper he went.

"You feel so good. Your cock feels so good."

He loved that she never held back during sex. She might shut down outside of it, but while they were making love she was open and completely honest with him. "You're the one who feels good. You're the one who feels right and perfect."

She'd always felt that way. Until the minute she hadn't.

He kissed her like she was something precious. Maybe he'd been wrong. He hadn't known how to process his feelings back then, and now he worried he'd thrown his anger at her. He still wasn't great at it. This was what they needed. Holding her, loving her, would let him see past his own rage. If he let her in, they might be able to move on. They had to find a way because he wasn't certain he could survive losing her twice.

She tightened around him and he lost control. He gave over to the magnificent feel of her wound around him, of their bodies combined. He fucked into her, the rhythm of his hips becoming primal. He lost the need to do anything but come inside her. He managed to hold off until her head fell back and he felt her tighten around him.

Then he let go and pounded into her, holding her up because he wouldn't let go of that connection. He kissed her as his orgasm hit, breathing in and out with her.

"Move up and lie down on your side." The order came out a bit harsher than he'd meant, but then he was way more emotional than he'd thought he would be. Blood pounded through him, but there was more. He felt for her.

She moved back and laid down. He followed her. The table was wide enough, but he still had to cuddle. He spooned her, dragging her back against his body.

"Lie here with me for a minute."

She cuddled back against him and for a moment he felt like the world was right again.

Chapter Six

"Levi Green is now the head of his own department." Chelsea Weston sat down at the tiny table made even smaller with the addition of Big Tag's enormous body. They'd shown up at their door only moments before, the sound of the knock a shock to Ezra's system.

The morning had been peaceful, and hearing that fucker's name reminded him of everything that was wrong with the world. "How did he go from being interrogated for treasonous acts to head of his own freaking team in the course of a couple of weeks?"

"I should have known something had gone wrong when they didn't want me to come back to Langley." Kim had a mug of coffee in front of her. She'd puttered around the tiny kitchen after they'd gotten up, and he'd had a sweet sense of domesticity that he'd been missing for years.

"He's a cockroach," Tag said with a humorless chuckle.

Chelsea nodded her agreement. "I don't know the whole story, but I can confirm that he has the authority to arrest Solo and take her to a place of his choosing for interrogation."

He sat next to Kim, their legs brushing against each other. He wanted to reach out and hold her hand.

So he did. He drew her palm against his. He had the right and the duty to comfort her. She'd given herself to him last night and they were starting something this morning, something softer than they'd had before. "He wants to use the drug on her."

Big Tag had shown up bright and early along with his twin daughters and sister-in-law. The girls were currently at Rene's apartment, the club owner and his wife watching over them. Ezra had been told they only had a brief time to go over everything they needed to before Tag intended to be back at the airport. He still didn't fully understand what Tag was here to do, but the most important thing was ensuring they all knew what Levi was capable of.

"I've talked to a couple of people at the Agency who owe me some favors." Chelsea yawned behind her hand. If he was correct, she'd recently had a baby, too. The McKay-Taggart team bred like rabbits. "I believe the formulary he has is one of the older ones. It's not as devastating as the final drug, the one she used on Tucker and Jax. Though from what I understand even they're getting some of their memories back. In Tucker's case, I think being in his hometown and with his family has helped enormously."

"So he'll only take part of my brain. Good to know. And I don't have any close family. I guess I could walk around my childhood home and maybe remember my parents didn't care about much except money." The words sounded bitter coming out of Kim's mouth, but her hand squeezed his.

"He won't take anything at all." Tag glanced down at his phone. The man was utterly preoccupied. "Chelsea and I have been talking and we need to do a timeline of where you were and what you were doing during the six-month period when Levi is accusing you of working with McDonald."

It was good to have a finite period of time to work with. They could focus in and find the crack in Levi's plan. There had to be one.

"I can tell you that I was definitely in Europe during most of that time," Kim replied. "I was working on tying a couple of organizations to arms dealers. Surprisingly enough, some of my best leads came from Levi. So I would suspect he can place me in some suspicious places."

No one said the fucker wasn't smart. "Still, there has to be proof."

"We'll find it," Tag promised. "But we need to figure out how fucked she is, and that means asking some uncomfortable questions."

Kim's shoulders straightened as she obviously braced herself for the worst. "It's fine."

"Were you aware that one of the companies your family owns had connections to Kronberg Pharmaceutical?" Chelsea asked.

Kim pulled her hand away, seeming to draw into herself. Her family was a sore point for her. She rarely talked about them and when she did, she tended to get emotional. "No. I don't pay much attention to what the corporation does. I didn't have any interest in it when my parents were alive. I have even less now. My cousins handle all the business. I don't even make decisions for the charities anymore."

He didn't like the fact that it was one more thing connecting her to McDonald. "When did the company get in bed with Kronberg?"

Tag sighed and sat back. "A few months before Solo's so-called work began. I've got someone looking into whether or not Levi had been in contact with anyone from the company. It's a neat way to set Solo up to take a bad fall. We've got the additional problem of the plane crash that killed your parents."

Kim's eyes went wide. "I thought it was mechanical failure."

"It's awfully coincidental that all these dominoes fell at the precise right time to put Levi in a position of extreme power. The plane crash happened a few weeks before all of this was set to go down," Chelsea said.

"Okay, let me make sure I understand this." Ezra was putting it all together in his head, the plot of Levi's forming like a spider's web. "He set Tucker in motion. Tucker works for McDonald, and anything he gets his hands on will be considered above suspicion. Somehow Levi gets your name in the records that are smuggled out on the data drive."

"The same one that was lost in Paris when McDonald caught him," Tag continued. "But Green couldn't have known that would happen. He assumed his plan would work and that he would have the data, including the shit he falsified. When he's sure he's got everything in place, he sets it all in motion."

Kim stared down at the table. "He likely had my parents killed."

Chelsea's expression had gone distinctly sympathetic. "Tell me what would have happened if you'd been arrested shortly after your parents died. Before you had a chance to settle things."

"Everything would have come to me. Because he didn't, I divested myself of a lot of the responsibilities that came with inheriting," Kim explained. "If he'd arrested me back then and he'd managed to dose me and convince me to marry him, legally he could have done a lot with those shares. Honestly, he still could. There's no permanent legal document giving my cousins my shares. All I would have to do is show up and the vote would be mine."

"So this might be a play to take over the company your family runs." Tag nodded to Chelsea. "Can you have Phoebe put together an overview? I'd like to know all the financial dealings of the company."

"It'll take a while." That company had multiple arms and they went into a whole lot of pies. "So Levi wants power, and he set himself up to be the head of Kim's family."

"It probably would have worked, too, if Tucker hadn't lost the data," Tag pointed out. "He could have had you swept away quietly. Ezra was working in Africa at the time."

"I wouldn't have even known she'd been arrested." Levi had planned carefully, and he'd been incredibly patient. He wouldn't have heard a thing until he'd gotten back to the States, and then likely he would have been told that Levi and Solo had gotten married. He wouldn't have looked in on her. He wouldn't have made sure she was okay. He would have quit and walked away and been a bitter fucking drunk the rest of his life. "But once the data was lost, he couldn't fake it again. He'd placed his bet and if he'd come up with proof in another way, it wouldn't have worked. I bet he really talked up this project, and its failure in the beginning is why he got moved to less than stellar ops."

"It must have killed him knowing that shot was gone." Kim sounded a bit hollow and he wished she hadn't needed to hear these hard truths.

He wished they were still in bed and she was clinging to him the way she had this morning. They'd been in complete darkness, but he'd woken with the knowledge that she was right beside him. He'd rolled her over and kissed her awake. When her arms had come around him, the world had felt right for the first time in forever.

"And it must have thrilled him when he realized Tucker wasn't dead. So that's where we are right now. I'm moving cautiously on this one. Solo, I know you want your name cleared," Tag began.

She shook her head. "Of course I do, but I understand it could take a while."

Tag paused for a moment as though he wasn't quite sure how to handle her. "If it's at all meaningful, Connor Sparks reached out to me and asked to be kept up to date. I've put him in our loop."

"The president could shut all this down." It bugged him that he hadn't already.

"No, he can't." Chelsea closed her laptop. "Not unless he wants to start congressional hearings on his overreach and put the guy he recently endorsed in the crosshairs, too."

"Does the president know Levi's planning on forcing the competition out? I put it in my report," Kim said.

"Yes, I talked to him this morning and he's looking into it. The situation is delicate," Tag explained. "Apparently that was something Levi didn't have to fake. I don't want you to worry about it. The president can handle the political stuff. Our job is to prove Levi's data wrong, and that begins with you documenting every job you did during that time. I need all the information you can give me. Damon will hunt down people who can support your alibi in Europe."

Kim groaned. "I don't suppose you can get into my place in DC and get my calendars? I don't put my schedule on my phone because it can be hacked, but I do keep detailed journals. The old ones would be in DC."

"I assure you, he's already got them," Chelsea replied. "From what I've been able to gather in the short time I've had, he's already been inside your DC apartment, your Manhattan brownstone, and the London flat. He'll take everything he can and either burn it or use it to his own gain. I'm sorry. I know how much it sucks. Charlotte and I spent years on the run, and every time we had to leave a place, I felt like I'd lost some piece of me."

How much had Kim lost in the last two days? "I want to see the warrants."

"You know he doesn't really need them." Kim sounded weary. "He'll have legal documents to show my property managers, but he can also easily make something up. How long do we need to be here in Paris?"

"A few more days. I'm working on moving you to Italy," Tag explained. "Chelsea and Si have a place in Venice. From there we'll get you back to the States. Sanctum is the perfect place. You can work and live there, and you won't have to hide out on club nights, so you'll have some company."

"Is there any way I could go to Colorado?" There was a wistful quality to Kim's question.

He felt his heart threaten to seize at the hope in her voice. And actually it wasn't a terrible idea. "They don't have CCTV there. We could find a quiet cabin and have a little freedom."

Kim liked to hike and take long walks. Being stuck in one place would be difficult for her.

"I would have to talk to John...I mean Henry." Tag fiddled with his phone again, typing something in. "But I don't know if it's a good idea."

Kim sat back. "Of course. Dallas it is. And thank you so much, Chelsea. Please thank your husband for me, too. I appreciate you letting me stay at your place. I know it's risky."

Chelsea shrugged. "Nah. I know what it means to be on both sides of this. I've worked for the Agency and pretty much been hunted by them. It all sucks. I should also let you know that I'm trying to run down the hacker Green used. He's honestly our best bet at proving this data is forged. If he or she has half a brain, they likely kept a record. It's like a before and after shot. I would do it in case I needed to prove something."

Tag sent his sister-in-law a glare. "You did it so you could blackmail your clients."

"I..." Chelsea began and then gave up. "It was a different world, and most of my clients were assholes. I haven't blackmailed anyone in years. I kind of miss it."

"Yeah, we desperately need to get you back in the game," Tag said under his breath before looking to Ezra. "Look, we're going to find a way to fix this. You've got two teams on your side, and we won't let you down. Solo, I owe you for what's happening today, and I don't forget to pay my debts. Chelsea and I have to go get the girls.

Our package is being delivered shortly, and I suspect it's going to coincide with Levi's arrival. How's that for perfect timing?"

"Well, you are Satan," Chelsea said with a grin. "You do have the devil's luck."

"What I have is a kid on the inside. At least I hope I do. We're about to find out." Tag pocketed his cell and stood up. "Rene showed you how to work the security cameras, right? You might find this interesting. I kind of like the idea that you'll be watching the fucker while he's trying to figure out where you're hiding. You two stick together. And Ezra, I'm glad you followed my advice. Now don't fuck it up."

Chelsea picked up her bag. "This is going to be the fastest trip to Europe ever. The good news is I sleep well on that Lawless jet. Most sleep I've had since Sophy was born."

"And I don't sleep at all so I'm cranky," Tag shot back. "Let's go. I want to get this over with and make Levi feel like a massive asshole."

"Is she okay?" Kim asked.

He was curious about Sasha's daughter, too.

Chelsea stopped at the top of the stairs. "She's spent the last two years in an orphanage in Siberia because her mother died under mysterious circumstances. We think she was looking for her husband and someone silenced her and then dumped her daughter far, far from home."

"But we're going to take care of her, right?" He owed Sasha. They all did.

Tag's brow rose over his eyes. "You're kidding, right? You honestly believe my Charlie could find a seven-year-old girl who's been abandoned and not bring her home? I'm not here to check up on Tasha. I'm here to pick up my daughter because that's what she'll be in a few months."

"I thought one of the Lost Boys would take her if she needed a home." He knew Robert and Tucker had talked about it.

"She only speaks Russian," Chelsea explained. "That's why I'm here, and the girls. Ian's Russian is shit."

"It is not." Tag's hands were on his hips. "My Russian is excellent. I talk to the kids in Russian all the time."

"Yes, and they laugh at you behind your back," Chelsea retorted as she started down the stairs.

Big Tag grimaced. "They don't bother. They laugh to my front. The word for *fact* in Russian is pronounced a whole lot like *fuck*. So naturally my girls point out a lot of fucks to me. It's a whole thing at school. You two stay safe. We won't come back after the meeting. We've got to get home."

"Thanks for this," Kim said.

Tag nodded and descended the stairs. Ezra closed the door behind him and turned to his ex-wife. His new sub. "Are you all right? He's going to be here, inside this building. Do you want to watch it or pretend it's not happening?"

He could think of a million different ways to distract her. They didn't need to be down in the club.

"I want to see Tasha. I want to make sure she's all right. And I think it's better for me to see that he's here in the building than to let my imagination go wild. Besides, I'm super interested in who he brought with him." She moved back to the table and opened the laptop.

He sat down beside her. "I'm sorry we can't go to Colorado."

"Me, too," she said, her eyes on the screen. "They don't trust me, and I would likely bring more danger into their lives, so I don't blame them."

"I could reach out to Henry Flanders." He would point out that yes, Kim had lied about who she was, but she'd done it to protect Henry as well. She'd been the one to tell the Agency he wasn't a threat.

She shook her head. "No. He's got enough on his hands. It's okay. I'm worried we shouldn't go to Dallas, either. I can't stand the thought of bringing the Agency down on their heads. They've got families. I shouldn't put them in danger. I've got a couple of places no one at the Agency knows about. I've built a few more nests since we broke up."

Nests. That was what she called those little apartments or homes she kept in foreign countries. He'd kept a few himself. "I think we should trust our friends."

She went quiet as she pulled up the security cameras.

"Kim, what's wrong?"

"They're not our friends," she said quietly. "They're your friends. I know Big Tag says he owes me, but he owes you more."

"Then he'll help us more."

She was silent for a moment. "Why did you hold my hand? And what did he mean by advice?"

"I held your hand because I wanted to," he explained. "He called last night. You know Big Tag. He's the world's worst busybody."

"Really? I don't know him except for the few times I've worked with him. He's pretty standoffish with me."

"Well, as Adam Miles has said on many occasions, beneath all the meathead muscles lies the beating heart of an eighty-year-old grandma who wants all her kids to get married."

"So he gave you advice about me?"

"He told me I should give you a break." He wasn't going into all the crap Big Tag had said. "He pointed out that time only heals wounds if you don't continually rip them back open."

A slight smile crossed her face. "He's a smart old lady."

Ezra chuckled as Tag closed the door on the screen. The big guy stared at the wall as though trying to make damn sure no one could see the seam of the door. It reminded him that this wasn't a game. "If anything goes wrong, I want you to barricade yourself in the bathroom and don't open the door until you hear from me or Tag."

She slid him what he liked to think of as her "dumbass said what" stare. "So I can run where? Because we're pretty much in a cage here. Don't get me wrong. I'm happy for the cage, but we've got nowhere to go if Levi figures out where we are. If that happens, you have to promise that you'll let him take me."

Now it was his turn for the dumbass stare. "I'm not doing that."

"So we're going to go down like Bonnie and Clyde?" She turned her attention back to the screen. She switched to the lobby camera where Big Tag and Chelsea greeted twin girls racing down the stairs. They were going on and on about how hot chocolate was better here.

"I don't know. I need some kind of plan. I feel helpless without one."

"We can't plan this out, Beck. We *are* helpless in this case, and the best way to handle it is to let me go and try to get me back later.

That's what Tag would tell you to do. You should be the one hiding in the bathroom and I'll talk Levi out of murdering you. I couldn't handle that."

He wasn't about to agree to letting her go. "Well, let's hope Tag is as smart as he says he is. Wow. That's her. She looks so much like Sasha. Can you turn up the volume? You know a little Russian, right?"

She smiled as she stared at the screen. A thin girl was led into the lobby of the club. She was carrying a small suitcase and wearing a plain dress and black shoes. She had her father's eyes and that frown of his.

The woman who was traveling with Tasha said something and nodded toward Big Tag.

"She's telling Tasha that this is her new family and she needs to go with them now," Kim translated.

Tasha shrank back and Kenzie and Kala stared at her.

Big Tag stayed where he was and let Chelsea take the lead.

Chelsea got down on one knee and addressed the child in Russian.

"She's telling her not to be afraid. She says she knows what it's like to lose her mom and end up going to a strange country." She glanced his way. "She was only nine when she went to Russia?"

He nodded. "That was when her mobster dad killed her mom and kidnapped Chelsea and Charlotte."

Kim laughed suddenly. "She told Tasha that Big Tag looks scary but he's a marshmallow and that she'll quickly learn how to manipulate him."

Tasha set her pitiful suitcase down and walked over to Tag. She looked up at him and asked a quiet question.

"She asked if he knew her papa."

Big Tag got to his knee and he still loomed over her.

"He's says that yes, he knew her father, and he knows lots of people who knew her dad. He wants to honor her father by taking care of her and making sure she has a good life. He says he knows she's scared but he's going to make sure no one hurts her again." Tasha's nose wrinkled and one of the twins said something. "His Russian isn't as good as he thinks it is. That's what Kenzie pointed out. Or Kala. I can't tell the difference."

Tasha looked back to Tag, her face so serious. "I will be going with you then."

Tag looked as soft as a man that big could. "I'm glad. We're going to take care of you. These are my little monsters. They speak better Russian than me so you can plot with them. Kenzie and Kala. If you can't tell them apart, use a marker in their sleep. It's what I do."

"Dad!" they managed to say in one voice.

Then the girls were off, talking in a mix of Russian and English, and he understood why Tag had dragged his daughters halfway across the globe. Because he was kind and knew Tasha would be far more comfortable with other kids around. Tag stood back and watched the girls while Chelsea had a conversation with the woman who'd brought Tasha to the club.

"She's telling Chelsea that all the paperwork is in order." Kim bit her bottom lip as she listened. "She's got a passport, and everything is done on her end for the adoption. Apparently someone named Dusan greased those wheels. Is she talking about Dusan Denisovitch? The head of the syndicate?"

"He's Charlotte's cousin." A flutter went through him when he realized someone was at the door. A shadow had crossed the frosted glass of the windows. "Someone's here. Switch to the outside camera."

Her spine went stiff and she stared at the screen as Rene went to open the door.

"We don't have to. He'll be inside in a minute. This was all part of Tag's plan." Kim's words were proven true as Levi stepped into the lobby.

"Taggart, I'm not surprised you're here." Levi was dressed in all black, a hat on his head. It was one of those hats worn by college dudes who only listened to vinyl and liked things in an ironic fashion.

He was joined by another man, one he hadn't met before. He was younger, looked barely twenty, though he dressed down in black slacks and a collared shirt. He definitely didn't look like the typical CIA employee. He had boy-band hair. "Who is that kid?"

Kim whistled as though she really hadn't expected that. "Drake Radcliffe. He's a wunderkind brought in by one of the big bosses.

He's a genius at finding patterns. I think he's connected on the political side, but I haven't figured it out yet. He's only been on the scene for the last six months, and I've spent most of that time either in Colorado or Europe. I haven't been in the office much. If he's here then Levi's pulled some strings."

"He makes you nervous?"

Kim shrugged. "Like I said, he's known for being able to see patterns, for his incredible deductive powers. Some people at Langley call him Sherlock."

On the screen Taggart was watching as the girls headed up the stairs. "Don't get comfortable. We leave for the airport in thirty minutes." He turned back to Levi. "Well, I'm not so happy to see you. If you've come to try to stop me from taking Sasha's daughter home with me, you better have brought the big guns."

Levi actually seemed taken aback, and Ezra realized that was all part of Tag's plan. "No. That was Sasha's daughter? You found her?"

"I did, and I'm taking her back to Dallas with me. So if you're not here to fuck with those plans, why *are* you here?" Tag asked.

Chelsea leaned against the reception desk. "He thinks you're hiding Solo. He tried to arrest her yesterday and she got away."

"Got away?" Levi zeroed in on Chelsea. "She didn't get away. The London team freed her from a lawful arrest and nearly killed me in the process."

"If it was a lawful arrest, she would have been taken in by the London metro police or Scotland Yard." Chelsea didn't back down at all. "She would have had a trial to determine whether her extradition was legal under British law. I don't think you were taking her to the police station, right? You know the funny thing is I haven't heard an outcry in the media."

"You know we do things differently. It wasn't so long ago you were one of us." Levi was talking to Chelsea, who had worked as a data analyst and all-around walking computer for the Agency until she'd quit to start a company with Adam Miles.

"Yeah, and I thought you were all assholes then, too," Chelsea shot back. "Now, why are you here in Paris if you're not trying to fuck up a little girl's adoption? She was in Siberia, you know. First they took her father and sold him to McDonald, and then they killed her mother and shipped Tasha to somewhere cold and quiet so they didn't have to look at her. You here to send her back?"

Levi threw up his hands in obvious disgust. "Why would I care about some kid? Tag wants another one, good on him. I'm here because this is one of the spots I suspect you might hide Solo in."

Tag proved he could have been an actor because the surprise on his face seemed totally real. "Why the hell would I hide Solo? I don't know if you've noticed but I don't hang out with a bunch of Agency fuckwits. I left a long time ago and I haven't looked back. Solo's been a pain in my ass for over a year and you're welcome to her."

He turned to Kim. "He doesn't mean that."

Kim rolled her eyes his way. "He can't exactly proclaim his deep affection. He's not going to be nice about you either if he's smart."

Levi turned his attention to Tag. "Okay, I'll give you that my girl can be troublesome, but I know you're loyal to Beck…Ezra Fain. He's been working with you for over a year."

"And he did what I needed him to do," Tag replied simply. "Now he's a pain in my ass, too. I assure you I didn't give him a thumbs-up to do anything. If I see him again, I'll fire his ass. Do you honestly think I want the Agency all over me right now?"

"You've got friends at the Agency. You've always got someone willing to cover for you," Levi pointed out.

Drake was walking around the room, studying it. "He's adopting a kid from a country that no longer allows foreign adoptions. He's basically smuggling her into the US. Where do her papers say she's from?"

Chelsea crossed her arms over her chest. "Her papers are from the Ukraine. They'll hold up under scrutiny. You're not taking her back. She was in an orphanage and she was never getting out. She wasn't getting a proper schooling, and I don't think they were feeding her enough."

Drake didn't bother to look at her, merely kept staring at the walls like he could see through them. "I wasn't suggesting we take some kid away from her newfound Daddy Warbucks. I was simply explaining Mr. Taggart's problem to my colleague. It's not a good time for him to have the Agency looking into his activities, so I can see where he might be upset about what Mr. Fain did. Is there a dungeon? I assume this is a BDSM club."

Levi frowned. "Yes, but how did you know that? I didn't tell you anything about it because I wanted you to come in cold."

"Don't be surprised that the guy you brought in for his deductive reasoning powers deduces things correctly." Drake seemed to find the walls fascinating.

"You'll have to forgive my friend, Taggart." Levi was frowning Drake's way. "Mr. Brown is a bit of a savant when it comes to finding things."

"Mr. Brown?" Tag asked, a suspicious brow arched. "Really?"

"No, of course not," Drake replied. "But it's better than Magenta."

"I like magenta," a voice said.

Tag turned and his face tilted up. "Girls. When I said upstairs, I meant all the way."

"Okay, but Magenta's a cool name," the voice said and then there was much giggling.

Chelsea sighed. "I think you can handle the rest of this on your own. I'll go make sure the girls stay out of trouble. And maybe I can find a cup of coffee."

Chelsea strode up the stairs.

Drake turned to Levi. "Can I look through the dungeon?"

Rene had been standing in the back, but he came forward. "Of course. I don't want trouble with the Agency either. Are you old enough to be in a club? You look like you're thirteen."

Drake frowned. "I'm twenty-three. You can't shock me. I've had some kink in my life recently, I assure you. I'm not looking to join. Can you tell me about the building? Some of these older buildings have interesting architectural elements, I hear."

"Fuck. How good is this kid?" Ezra stood and went to the small table where he'd set the Beretta he'd brought along.

Kim was bringing up the camera that was focused on the wall that hid their door. Rene had explained that there was only one camera in the dungeon, and it was only pointed at the hidden door. It was a small micro camera camouflaged in one of the light fixtures. Kim adjusted the feed so she had a split screen of the lobby and the camera that was there to help protect whoever was hiding behind the walls.

"Don't tell me." Drake's voice came over as a whisper. "I want to see if I can find it."

He knew. He knew something was here. Ezra felt every muscle in his body flood with adrenaline. "I'm going to be waiting for him at the bottom of the stairs."

"No. You're going to stay right here. He can't hear us moving around if we're still," Kim said, her voice low. "Sit down, Beck. You have to be patient. You have to trust Tag."

He didn't want to be patient. He didn't want to trust anyone. Over the last year he'd come to depend on the men they'd called the Lost Boys, but they were off on their own now, living their own lives.

Drake came into view after agonizing moments. He walked past the camera and Ezra breathed a sigh of relief. It didn't last long because Drake moved into frame again, his back to the camera. He stayed there for a moment, still as a ghost.

He eased the safety off the gun.

"Don't, Beck," Kim whispered. "You can't kill him. If he opens that door, I'm going in."

He wasn't sure he could allow that, but he snapped the safety back on and held his breath as Drake stepped up to the panel that hid the door and put a hand on it.

"Tag said you were good." Rene's voice was barely above a whisper.

Kim's shoulders sagged. "Oh, thank god."

Drake turned, and as though he knew exactly where the camera was and who was watching, he gave a wink and walked away. "I'll need to inspect the kitchen, too. I want to be able to say I was thorough. And your office."

"Of course," Rene said. "The Velvet Collar is completely open."

"Tag knows him." He sank back onto the chair and reached for her hand, tugging on it.

She let herself be pulled onto his lap, and after a brief moment of awkwardness, cuddled against him. "I told you to trust him."

"No, *I* told you to trust him." He loved the feel of her against him. He let himself really breathe for the first time since Levi had entered the building. He wanted to walk downstairs and kill the fucker, but she needed more than that. Eliminating Levi wouldn't solve all of their problems. "And it's all good now."

"He's still not out of the building," she said with her head on his shoulder. "I won't feel safe until then. And safe is a relative term."

Didn't he know it? They wouldn't be safe for a very long time, but at least he knew Levi wouldn't come storming up the stairs. They had a shot, and after the night before, that shot wasn't all about surviving.

He'd felt more the night before than in the last decade without her. Maybe it was time to start talking about what happened, to start thinking about forgiveness. Being angry with her had done nothing but cost them years, and god he'd missed this soft feeling. He'd missed giving her the things she needed, being a part of her world. It was easy to fall back into old habits, and sitting with her, just breathing her in, was a habit he remembered so well.

"Damon had to have given Ezra the go-ahead," Levi was saying. "I suspect some of the London team was there, too."

"Take that up with Damon," Tag shot back. "Man, I am running on very little sleep. I've got a newborn at home and now I have to figure out what that girl upstairs has been through and how to help her. I do not give a flying fuck about Agency games. As far as I'm concerned, Ezra Fain is on his own."

"I suppose you'll let me into Sanctum, then."

"If that's what it takes to get the Agency off my back, but you need to understand that there will be no more favors. You feel free to fly in and inspect my private property and then we'll be done, and I'm not talking about you and me," Tag explained. "You mean less than nothing to me. I'm talking about your bosses who love to come whining to me that they need help. My door will be closed."

"I suppose that goes for Miles and Dean, too. It must be handy to have that ax to wield," Levi complained.

"Is he talking about Adam Miles?" Kim asked, not looking up. She had her face buried in the crook of his neck.

Big Tag was making a power play. "Adam's facial identification software is something the Agency is very interested in, but he's smart. He's kept most of the really innovative programming completely private. He's got a server that no one can touch, and I'm sure they've tried."

"That is smart because the Agency would steal it and use it however they want."

Well at least she was willing to admit the Agency had a dark side.

"Adam makes his own decisions," Tag replied with a weary sigh. He obviously wasn't faking his tiredness. "You'll have to talk to him."

Levi snorted. "You know damn well he won't take my calls. And when he won't take my boss's calls, I wonder who they're going to blame. So that's your play."

Even through the screen Ezra could feel the weight of Tag's stare as the man replied. "I'm not playing. That's what you need to understand. I don't know why Ezra did what he did. I don't know if Damon had anything to do with it. I don't care right now. All I care about is my family and getting home to them. So if you want to push me, you'll find out what happens when I do play."

"He's very intimidating when he wants to be," Kim murmured.

Ezra stared at the screen, watching every move Levi made. He still didn't completely trust that this was over. It wouldn't be until Levi was on another continent, and even then they would still have problems.

"I didn't see anything out of the ordinary," Drake said as he reentered the lobby, coming down the stairs. "Mr. DuBois was very forthcoming. As far as I can tell there's nowhere to have hidden them. I inspected every room and saw no evidence that anyone is living here. Like I tried to tell you before, I think they're still in England. I would like to take a look at Knight's country home."

"I told you Knight isn't being very forthcoming," Levi replied through clenched teeth.

"Have you thought about the fact that Solo has multiple homes and likely still has plenty of cash?" Drake asked. "My profile of her was pretty plain. She's got several places she would be able to go, and bank accounts I think she would hide from everyone. She's got the resources to go to ground for years. I think we've seen the last of her."

"Absolutely not. She won't go away," Levi insisted.

Drake turned to him. "Why? Criminals usually run and hide

when they're caught. Criminals with Solo's resources are generally never heard from again if they're smart, and I believe Solo's smart. I still don't fully understand why she would work with a person like McDonald unless she was undercover."

"I told you, I know Solo better than anyone." Levi stood in front of the kid. "I don't need you to profile her. The evidence against her is unassailable."

Drake merely shrugged one lanky shoulder. "I still think she's not going to resurface for a long time. Like I said, she's highly intelligent, and if she believes she's been caught, she'll hide."

"She's very dumb if she thinks she can get away from me," Levi replied. "But I can see I'm going to get nowhere with Tag. I'll deal with this on my own. There's more than one way to handle this. I can see I'll have to use some finesse." He looked to Tag. "Tell Solo when you see her—and I don't believe for a second you won't—that this is far from over."

He turned on his ridiculously expensive loafer and strode out.

"He'll likely still be watching," Kim said, and he noticed she wasn't as relaxed as she had been.

"I don't know. He won't have much manpower." He knew how the Agency worked. Levi had his one real shot at bringing her in. He wouldn't be allowed to keep ten operatives working at all times. He might get an analyst or two watching the web for any evidence of her whereabouts, but that would be it. If Drake really could convince him to go back to England, they would be safe. They could wait a week or two here and then begin the slow move to Dallas. "We'll have to wait and see."

"Thank you for your hospitality, Mr. DuBois." Drake nodded the club owner's way. "Your building is lovely. Mr. Taggart, I wish you luck with your family. I think we'll be going back to England, and then perhaps looking at some other places where Solo might have hidden. I doubt we'll bother you for a while."

Drake turned and walked out.

Ezra reached over and flipped the laptop lid down. "Excellent, now we can take a breath and relax for a few minutes. Kiss me."

She sat up. "Are you sure this is a good idea? Maybe we should talk."

He didn't want to talk. He wanted to find a way to use all the adrenaline that had coursed through his body. "We've had a stressful morning. If we talk, we'll likely argue. I know we're due a really good argument and we'll have it, but can we have some peace for now?"

Her hand came up to brush his jaw and she stared in his eyes for a moment as though trying to figure out what to say. Or how honest to be. "I don't want to fall in love with you again."

When she looked at him like that he remembered what it felt like to like himself. "You never fell out."

She'd chased after him and he'd treated her like crap. He'd been angry and felt betrayed, but hadn't he owed her more?

"But I wish I had because I think you'll break my heart again. I worry I won't be able to put it back together. If you break it this time, it'll die."

He seriously doubted that. Her heart was a mighty thing. "If it helps, I don't think I ever truly fell out of love with you."

"You did a good job of convincing everyone."

He actually chuckled at the thought. Maybe he'd convinced her, but he hadn't convinced a lot of the people who knew him. Now that he was here with her, he had to wonder how much he'd fooled himself. "Did I? I think I was good at focusing my anger on you. I know we need to talk about it, but I'm tired. I don't want to hash it out. I want to pretend like it didn't happen for one afternoon."

"But it did happen, and what do I do if you can't forgive me?"

He asked the only question he could. "Did you mean to get my brother killed?"

She frowned up at him. "Of course not."

"You were young and arrogant." He'd had years to think about it and he'd come to this conclusion. "You thought you could prove you knew more than I did."

She'd always been competitive. Even with him when it came to the job. She could be reckless. At least she had been back then. And she'd had a deep desire to prove that she wasn't merely the rich girl in the group. She'd wanted to belong, and that had led to a tragedy. Did he have to be angry with her for the rest of his life?

She sighed. "You're right. I don't want to fight either."

She would probably never admit why she hadn't followed his advice that day, and he might have to live with it. He didn't know what was going to happen when they got out of this place, but he knew what he wanted while they were here. He wanted her. He needed this time with her without the influence of anyone else. It was the two of them for now, and maybe that was what it would take to rebuild their relationship. "Then kiss me."

She only hesitated for a moment and then she raised her lips to his.

He stood up, lifted her into his arms, and carried her to the bedroom. Levi wasn't going to occupy another second of his time.

But later that night, after he'd finished spending the whole afternoon with her, Levi showed him that he would not be denied.

* * * *

Kim glanced at the clock and wondered how long it would be before the light came on and they could go downstairs and play. The club wasn't open this evening according to Rene, but he worked out of an office upstairs and had a late call. Outside it would already be dark and the city would be bustling with couples going out to dinner and workers heading home. Her own apartment wasn't far from here, and the lights would have come on. They were on a timer connected to the security system. The soft lights would be on and anyone who didn't know better would think there was a family inside.

She wanted to walk outside with Beck's hand in hers. The last time they'd been in Paris together they'd only been married for a few weeks. They'd taken a long weekend and stayed at the tiny flat she kept near the Louvre. They'd walked the length of the Tuileries Garden and talked about the future.

It was fitting they were here again. Starting again.

She moved out of the bedroom where she'd been making some notes about dates and places she could remember. Putting together her schedule from years before would be a hard task, but she was determined in a way she hadn't been before. Being with Beck made her want a future more than she had in years. She realized now that she'd been drifting. It was good to want again.

He sat at the tiny table, his face illuminated by the light from the laptop. He was staring intently at whatever was on the screen.

He'd done the few dishes she'd used to heat up the soup they'd had for dinner, and the tiny kitchen was neat and clean. The wall beside the little stove, however, was covered in sticky notes they'd worked on all afternoon. He'd been completely true to his word about allowing her to lead the investigation. He'd been helpful, taking notes on everything she could remember about that time and then placing them on the wall where they could sort them into a rough calendar. While they'd been working together, she'd actually felt a sense of hope that they might be able to figure this thing out.

That they might actually have a shot at being together after this.

"Hey, you look serious," she said quietly. "I thought you were closing up shop for the evening."

He didn't look her way, merely kept his eyes on the computer. "I got a couple of emails I need to deal with."

She could understand that. He'd dropped his whole life for her. She glanced up as the light over the door came on and she felt her body shift. "I hope it doesn't take you too long. It looks like Rene's locked up for the night."

That meant it was his time. Beck's. She'd worked with him all day on the case, and now she would serve her Dom. She would pay him back for everything he'd given her. Would he force her down on her knees, command her to take his cock in her mouth and swallow him down?

He stood and turned on the overhead light. "It was from Levi."

A chill went down her spine. She'd managed to forget Levi much of the day even though she'd been working on the problem he presented. Somehow she'd found a way to pretend it was just her and Beck working together again. "Is he coming back here?"

Beck's eyes were lasers staring through her. "I don't think so. I think Tag's plan worked, but remember when Levi promised he would find another way to get to us?"

She nodded. What had Levi done?

"He meant me. He had a way to get to me. Tell me how long you knew he was investigating my brother."

Her heart dropped, gut tightening. This was the moment she'd feared for years, even more than she'd feared telling him Ezra was dead. "Beck, you can't believe everything in that report."

She'd worked so hard to hide this from him, to keep the promise she'd made to his brother. She'd promised the real Ezra Fain she'd go to her grave with this secret, a last plea from a desperate man.

"Believe it?" Beck pointed to the laptop. "You think I honestly believe my brother would run drugs? Would dishonor himself and our family in that fashion? He wouldn't be my brother if he'd done that."

Yes, there it was. That was exactly why Ezra had been so desperate. Beck had placed his brother on a pedestal. He could be so judgmental about certain things, and this was one of them. She kept her mouth shut because she'd promised there wouldn't be lies between them again. Unfortunately, this might be a lie she couldn't avoid.

His gaze pierced through her. "Levi was setting my brother up and you knew."

Yes, she remembered this feeling well. This was exactly how she'd felt when he'd accused her of sending his brother to his death. His righteous nature was taking over. "I knew he was investigating Ezra's unit."

"And you didn't bother to mention that fact to me?"

Her gut was in knots. She wasn't sure she could do this again. "I went to Ezra about it."

"But not to me."

Did he remember anything about what had happened back then? "You weren't in the country at the time. Not when I found out he was being investigated. You were on an assignment. I didn't even talk to you for two months."

"And then I was home for three before my brother was killed. Not once did you mention to me that he was in trouble."

"Because he'd asked me not to." She was treading a fine line. "You have to listen to me. It was such a weird time. Ezra was desperate and he was trying to find a way out. He got stuck in something he couldn't handle, but the last thing he wanted was for you to know how low he'd gotten."

"What are you trying to tell me?"

How much could she say now? What did she still owe the real Ezra Fain? She'd given up her marriage because she'd promised him she wouldn't tell his secrets.

Was that true? Maybe her marriage had been doomed either way because she wasn't sure Beck would ever have been able to handle the truth about his brother, and that rage would have needed a place to go. It would have always fallen on her because Beck refused to believe he had a problem. When she thought about it, both of the brothers had an addiction problem. "Ezra got addicted to pain killers after he broke his leg. Like really addicted. He would go on missions high."

"That's complete bullshit," he replied. "Who told you that? Levi?"

"Ezra." If she was going to tell him, she would at least be honest about what happened before that last mission. Maybe they would have a chance then. "He changed teams and the one he ended up on…well, the CO had been doing shady shit for a long time."

"But he specifically asked to be on that team."

"Yes, because he knew he could get the drugs he needed and no one would bat an eye as long as he did his part."

"His part being helping to run drugs in the area. My do-gooder, go-to-mass-every-week brother did this." His hands were on his hips, a look of utter disbelief on his face.

She wasn't sure how to make him believe her. "Why would I lie to you at this point?"

"That's a very good question and I can think of a couple of answers. One is that you got caught. You got caught working with Levi. Again. And you were working against my best interest."

She started to reply but he held up a hand.

"No, I get to finish. Two. Levi was the one running drugs and he was your friend, so you helped him cover it up and you made my brother the scapegoat." He started moving toward her, ice in his eyes where a mere hour before he'd looked at her with such tenderness.

But this was the nature of Beck's beast. He was the sweetest man until his anger took over, and then he could brutalize her with words.

"Did you send my brother in to die to protect Levi? I know he

127

was your close friend back then. Did you have to choose between your friend and my brother?"

"No, but I won't be able to convince you. You're judge, jury, and executioner, and you always have been." He hadn't even given her a chance to try to explain. Three days after his brother's death, he'd moved out, and she hadn't heard from him again until he'd sent her divorce papers. He hadn't fought for their marriage. He'd decided she wasn't worth fighting for and he'd moved on.

He pointed to the computer. "How else am I supposed to make sense of this? You hid an entire investigation from me."

"We knew we would have to keep secrets when we got married. We both worked for the Agency and that meant putting a wall up when it came to certain missions. It was classified and beyond that, Ezra didn't want you to know he was using drugs. He begged me. I was worried if I told you, he would hurt himself. He couldn't deal with the shame you would have heaped on him." She felt every bit as helpless now as she had then.

His jaw went tight and he started to pace like a lion in a cage. "So now this is my fault? I'm the bad guy here? Apparently I was the only one who wasn't doing something criminal. If you knew my brother was doing drugs and you didn't pull him off of his team, you're just as bad as him. He was the fucking medic."

She was screwed. It didn't matter which way she went. This was always how they ended. "I was trying to protect him the only way I could. By that time there were some bad people after him."

"So you took his team on an op and decided it would be better to let him die?" His face was an angry mask.

"I'm done, Beck." If she talked much more the real truth would come out, and she suddenly realized it wouldn't save her. It would bury her deeper, and she would have given up a piece of her soul.

"You're not done. This is now an investigation of you, and if you don't want me to turn you over to Levi, you'll comply with everything I tell you to do. And no, I'm not going to touch you again, so you can get that straight out of your head. You're the same snake I always knew you were. The stupid thing is I'd convinced myself we had a chance. That pretty pussy of yours made me think you could do no wrong and I was the one who fucked up. I was actually thinking about a future with you, about kids and a house."

"Well, it's good that you know the truth then."

"Yeah, because wouldn't you make a hell of a mother. You'd be exactly like your own. You'd use that kid to make yourself look respectable, but you wouldn't give a shit."

Something inside her died in that moment, some light that had started to flicker back to life.

He went quiet as though he realized he'd gone too far, but the damage had been done.

She turned away. "I'm going to bed."

"I shouldn't have said that," he said on a sigh. "I'm mad and I'm struggling to understand."

She nodded. "You'll figure it out. You always do."

She would be the bad guy. It was the role she played in his life and she was done.

"I'm not joking about the investigation," he said, his tone back to commanding. "I'm going to find out what happened then, and you are going to tell me everything you know."

Sure she would. He thought that because for the most part she'd been indulgent with him. She'd dealt with his anger because she'd loved him, and she'd thought somewhere deep down that she could fix him. In some ways he was every bit as bad as Levi. He thought he loved her when what he mostly did was hurt her.

She'd done things she wasn't proud of, done things she deserved his scorn for, but she'd loved him. She'd wanted the best for him even if it meant sacrificing.

"Of course." She would agree to anything to get away from him. She needed to plan because she couldn't stay with him. She had no one who would help her. Well, no one she could call. There was one person in all the world who couldn't deny her aid.

"I'm going down for a run," he said. "There's a treadmill on the second floor. I shouldn't talk to you when I'm this angry. I need to burn some of this off and then maybe I can look at you and be somewhat civil."

He wouldn't have to look at her ever again. Drake had been very correct in what he'd said. She had resources Beck didn't know about.

She stood and watched him walk away from her and planned her escape.

In the end, it was easy. She packed a small bag, put a hoodie on, and walked out the door. The security system gave her a full minute before the alarm went off, and that was more than enough time to get lost on the streets of Paris.

She made her way to the apartment she kept and took the chance to enter. It took her exactly five minutes to get to the safe, get the cash, gun, and passport she kept there. She was hiding in the tree in the back of the building when Beck got there. She waited until he'd strode out, yelling at someone on his cell.

When she was sure he was gone, she walked to the road and hitched a ride out of town. From there she took a train to the south of France and chartered a small plane to take her into Italy. Every now and then she would feel eyes on her and change direction. She knew Beck had found her once when she recognized one of the McKay-Taggart guys at a train station in Turin, but she managed to elude him.

Two weeks after she'd left Paris she felt comfortable enough to take the ferry from Catania, Sicily, to her final destination, the tiny island nation of Malta. The ferry landed in Valletta and she took a cab to the Birgu waterfront and walked to the base of Fort Saint Angelo. It was late and she jumped the fence that barred her access to the long winding path that led to the top of the fort.

The sun was slipping into the Mediterranean as she made it to the top. A lone figure stood, blocking her path.

"Kim?" a familiar voice asked. "Is that you?"

She stood in front of the man who owed her everything. "Yes. It's me. I need some help."

He stepped toward her and she could see the collar around his neck that denoted he was a priest. The real Ezra Fain held his arms open. "Of course. What's my brother done now? He's the only one who could put that look on your face."

She hugged the man who had been her brother-in-law and let the tears fall.

She knew in that moment that she would never love another man.

She was wrong.

Part Two

Seven Years Later

Chapter Seven

Dallas, TX

Beckett Kent sat back in the comfy chair Kai kept in his office and briefly wondered how many sad sacks like himself had sat in this very chair. How many had come through this peaceful office and found a way to move forward with their lives? "Am I your oldest patient?"

Kai frowned, looking at him over the glasses he wore when he was working. "Absolutely not. I've got a couple of patients in their seventies. You know the need for mental health doesn't go away just because you age."

He chuckled. "I meant who else has been coming here every week for seven years."

"Ah." Kai closed his notebook, a sure sign that their time was almost up. Kai often spent the last ten minutes of their sessions simply talking. "No. You don't win that contest either. I've got a couple of guys I've been seeing for ten years. There's no shame in it."

He knew that deep down. He'd worked hard, harder than he'd ever worked to get past that volcanic rage that had blown up his world not once but twice.

"Are you thinking about her today?" Kai asked quietly.

Beck nodded. "Yeah. I mean I think about her every day, but it's been rough this week. You would think after seven years she wouldn't be the first thing I think of in the morning and the last thought I have before I go to sleep, but there it is."

"You lost her," Kai pointed out. "That's hard to get over."

"No. I pushed her away. I threw her away." There was the real shame, but he'd come to realize that shame could be productive. Shame had driven him to come to Dallas, to show up on Kai's doorstep after he'd realized he wasn't going to find her. She'd run and hid from him as much as she'd hidden from Levi Green.

"Did you just think his name?" Kai had a knowing smile on his face.

Beck sighed. He'd managed to deal with a lot of his anger issues, but Levi Green still had the ability to make him see red. It didn't help that the fucker was living the good life in DC, moving up steadily through the ranks at the Agency. He wouldn't be surprised if Green was one day moved into a directorate position. Now, from what he'd been told, the fucker was planning a wedding. "Yes. Sorry. I know it was my fault Kim ran. It's my fault she's been in hiding for seven years. But I can't help but hate that man. I'm the one who let him come between Kim and myself, but I can't let go of my anger toward him."

He would never let go of that.

"Some therapists would tell you to work on that," Kai pointed out. "But you know how I feel. Anger can be healthy. Anger can be productive. What we've always been doing here is working on giving you control over your anger. I often think some people are born with a well of rage inside them, and it's like a fire. It can burn out of control and wreck everything around it. Or it can bring warmth and light where there was none. Human rights, justice, these are all things that were made possible by anger properly directed to bring about change."

Confronting his own anger had changed him in numerous ways, but it hadn't changed the fact that his wife was still out there, still hiding. It hadn't changed the fact that he hadn't found the evidence he needed to acquit her and give her back her life.

Kai leaned forward, taking off his glasses and putting them on the table beside his chair. In the years since Beck had joined McKay-

Taggart there had been many changes, but the only age he could see on his therapist was a bit of gray at his temples. "Do you have any idea how far you've come, Beck?"

"Not far enough," he said wistfully. "Although I suppose going by my real name again is a step in the right direction."

He didn't even think of himself as Ezra anymore. For a long time, he'd fooled himself into playing the part, even in his head. But Kai had helped him realize how destructive it was.

"The anniversary of your brother's death is coming up. How are you feeling about that?" Kai asked softly.

He still hated it when Kai put him in a corner and made him want to fight his way out. He didn't want to talk about these particular feelings, but he knew if he didn't they would bottle up again. "Angry. Sad. Weary. I still feel anger when I think of my brother, and that makes me understand fully why Kim kept that secret. She knew how I would respond. But I'm still mad at my brother for asking her to keep the secret in the first place."

"He was desperate."

On this point, he would not be moved. "She should never have been placed in that position. He should have come to me. I know I can be self-righteous and judgmental, but I never would have told my brother I wouldn't help him."

"Addicts do awful things to protect their addiction."

It was still so hard to think of his brother that way, but he'd come to understand that Kim had been telling him the truth. "I wish I'd had a chance to help him."

"I do, too." Kai sat up, obviously changing the subject. "So have you given any thought to dating? The last time we talked Charlotte was trying to set you up with one of the new hires."

He didn't want to be set up and he'd decided that was all right. "Everyone is trying to do that. I recently went to a family reunion and my cousin has been trying to set me up with her single friends. At least I only have to email my replies to her. Charlotte is much harder to say no to."

"But you did say no to her," Kai prompted.

"Yes. The woman she's trying to set me up with seems wonderful, but I'm still in love with Kim. It wouldn't be fair to anyone I date."

"You can't go the rest of your life without sex."

He didn't see why not. "I can take care of myself in this, Kai." He did. Often. And every single time he closed his eyes and gripped his own cock, he saw her face, felt her arms around him. "I know you think I'm punishing myself, but I've moved past that. I'm making a decision to…I don't know…hope. I'm making a conscious decision to have some faith that I'll see her again, that I'll get a third chance with her. I want to be ready for it."

"And if she's moved on?"

"If she's happy and taken care of, I'll walk away because she deserves that. But deep in my soul, I think she's still as alone as I am." They were soul mates. He was the one who'd broken the pact between them. "I can't move on until I know she doesn't need me, until I stand in front of her and apologize and tell her how much I love her. It doesn't matter what she's done in the time we've been apart. If she took a lover, I'll hope she got what she needed out of it. I just need to know I did one thing right by her."

Kai smiled. "And that is why I say you've come so far."

There was a knock on the door, and it flew open a mere second later. Kori Ferguson rushed in, followed by three of the scruffiest dogs he'd ever seen. He'd spent a lot of time sitting and petting those mutts. Kori was Kai's wife and ran the business side of the clinic they'd built up over the last decade. It had started with Kai in a single room connected to the club Sanctum. Over the years he'd added two more therapists, one who specialized in PTSD and one who ran family and marriage counseling. The Ferguson clinic worked directly with the VA to help Dallas veterans and their families get the help they needed. Kori ran the office and had a side business training therapy dogs.

"Kai, is Beck still…" She caught sight of him. "Good, you're here. Big Tag's been calling you."

"Sorry. I don't bring my cell phone into the therapy room." It was the one hour a week that was strictly for him. If he was working out and someone needed him, he dropped the weights and got to work. Sleep could be disturbed. He didn't even like days off and rarely took vacations, but this hour was sacred.

This was the hour when he felt like he was doing something that would make her proud.

"He wants you to get to the office as soon as possible. He told me to tell you that he knows you still have a couple of minutes with Kai, but he's got news." Kori was a bit breathless, her brown and gold hair in a curly halo around her head. "Do you think that means he's found something?"

He was on his feet in a heartbeat. Tag knew how important this time was. There was only one reason he would interrupt this session. "He's found her."

He ran out the door.

* * * *

Fort Saint Angelo, Malta

Kim Solomon took a deep breath and looked out over the Mediterranean. It was late afternoon and in the distance she could see travelers boarding a cruise ship. They'd likely spent the day in Valletta, looking through the quaint shops or taking historical tours and learning a bit about the history of her tiny island home. The gateway to Europe. Sicily was a hundred miles to the north while Africa was three hours south and east.

And Dallas was roughly a full day's flight away. And another world. Beck was in Dallas. She'd figured that out a year into her sojourn here. It had been a risk to go looking for him, even on the Internet, but she'd felt the need. He was working for Big Tag. Hopefully he was content.

She felt the late afternoon sun on her face as she looked down at the last of the tourists strolling over the ramparts of the fort. This was her favorite time of day because this was the time when she was reunited with the love of her life.

"You are waiting on the boy?"

She turned and smiled at the man who'd tolerated her presence for seven years. "Uncle Francis. You're back. It's good to see you again."

He'd been at the Vatican for meetings for over a week. Her uncle, known in his order as Brother Francis Bruno, was in his early seventies but had the energy of a much younger man. He was THE knight of Malta, officially tasked with keeping the base here in Malta, though the actual order had moved to Rome decades before and now formed one of the smallest principalities in the world. Despite the hefty title of knight, Brother Francis preferred Bermuda shorts, Cuban shirts, and flip-flops. He would say that he could do God's work while being comfortable. He leaned in and gave her a kiss on each cheek. "And you, darling girl. I'm glad to be back and away from all those Italian fuddy-duddies."

He was Italian. He was actually a second cousin, but he was so much older she'd always called him uncle. He liked to complain about pretty much all nationalities. For a humanitarian who had worked across the globe, he could be a bit dour. "That's what you always say. Well, I'm glad I made a double batch of pasta."

Uncle Francis patted his belly. "You've gotten so good at it. What kind of sauce are you making?"

"Bolognese," she replied, hooking her arm through his as they began to move across the plaza. To her left was St. Anne's Chapel, a small, deeply peaceful space. She liked to sit there in the afternoons. Somehow no matter how hot it got outside, the chapel always felt cool.

"Ah, Roman's favorite. Mine as well, though I must admit that I've grown fond of your alfredo sauce. Have you been into the shop this week? Anything new I would like?"

Four years before she'd taken another chance and bought a small bookshop that specialized in antique books. Her uncle was always interested in historical texts about his order. "I've got a line on the journal of a knight I think you'll love. Seventeenth century. It was recently found in the archives of a privately held castle in Germany. I managed to snatch it up at auction."

"Yes, I would like to study it." He stopped in front of the gates that led from the tourist section of the fort into their residence. It was another one of those places she loved to sit because it was a short tunnel with a couple of stairs that led from the stark, military architecture of the fort into her own personal sanctuary. Well, not merely hers. Ezra lived here, and there were daily workers who kept up the grounds.

"Hey, Mom!"

And then there was the light of her whole life. Her son. He bounded through the gate Ezra opened, his backpack falling to the ground. He looked precious in his school uniform, and her heart clenched as she got to one knee and opened her arms. "Hey, baby."

She hugged her son and felt that sweetness she always got when she held him pierce through her. He'd started school two years before and every day Ezra walked him to school before either heading to the hospital he served at as a chaplain or coming back to the fort to work with her uncle. Sometimes he spent weeks in Africa with the church on various charities. She always missed him when he was gone. Ezra was good company and a positive influence on her son, who looked more and more like his father as he grew up.

He already had his father's intelligence.

"I'm so glad to see you," she whispered.

"Brother, could you take Roman inside and get him his tea?" Ezra asked. "I think Kim made cookies earlier. I smelled something delicious. And I brought some fresh milk in this morning."

Normally they would all go in and have high tea together. Malta had been owned by the British in the fairly recent past, and the country still held on to some British traditions. She stood up, a little nervous because sending them in alone meant Ezra wanted to talk to her. She ruffled her baby boy's hair and looked down into Roman's blue eyes. They were so much like Beck's staring back at her. "Your uncle is right. There are snickerdoodles waiting for you in the courtyard. I've got tea set up there since it's such a nice day."

"Well, then yes, I will certainly take him," her uncle offered because he was never one to turn down a treat. "Come along, young Roman. I will tell you all about my meeting with the pope and you can tell me about your school day. We will speak Italian."

"*Non è l'italiano il problema,*" Roman said with a sigh.

"Well, you can't expect me to help you with Maltese," Uncle Francis said as they began to walk toward the domicile. "Such an odd language. Better to speak Italian. *Tutti capiscono l'italiano.*"

Ezra shook his head as he watched them disappear behind the gate. "Not everyone understands Italian, and honestly, Roman's

Maltese is getting better. He's the single smartest kid I've ever met. I talked to his teacher and they want to give him more challenging work. They're not talking about promoting him early, but they don't want him to get bored. He was working on an algebra problem earlier today and didn't want to be bothered with physical activities."

She frowned his way. "Whose fault is that?"

Ezra grinned, a youthful expression. "Math is fun. And you're the one who had him reading at the age of three."

"Like I could stop him." Her son was a force of nature. "Is that why you wanted to talk?"

He moved to a bench among the gorgeous beds of Sicilian marigolds the gardeners had planted earlier in the season. They were in full bloom now, a lovely sea of yellow blossoms. Roman had been out here during his school break, helping the workers plant and learning all he could. He was a sponge, and living with two men dedicated to study hadn't hurt either.

"No, I wanted to talk to you about something else. I went by the bookstore," he said, settling down and leaving room for her. "You've been in a couple of times this week."

She had a small staff who worked the retail portion of the business. Her shop was within walking distance of the fort, with beautiful views of the marina and all the boats coming in and out of the bay. She loved walking down the winding path to the marina, the sun on her face and the wind in her hair. Only one other place in the world had ever called to her like this one, and she would never see Bliss, Colorado, again.

But she had her bookshop, and her son was thriving. She oddly didn't miss the adrenaline of working as an operative. Now she used her investigative skills tracking down books. She'd gotten damn good at being the last one standing when a particularly old text went to auction. She'd often tangled with some dude who owned a store in Copenhagen, but she usually came out on top.

"I went in because Anna was sick, and I didn't want to have to close up," she admitted. "It was a cruise ship day and you know how the tourists love the front of the shop."

The front of the shop was filled with touristy knickknacks and postcards and books about Malta and the Knights. And Roman's favorite part of the shop—the chest she kept filled with sodas and water and ice cream treats for hot days.

"I had some time to kill before I picked up Roman," Ezra said. "I went by the shop to grab a water and Anna told me a man came in and asked about you."

A chill went up her spine. "He asked for me by name? My real name?"

Naturally the shop was held in a corporate name that she was fairly certain couldn't be traced back to her. Even her employees didn't know her real last name.

"No, he asked about the tall blonde."

She breathed a sigh of pure relief. "Good. I'm sure it's nothing. Like I said, I went in last week for a few hours and talked to some of the customers. A couple of the guys hit on me. It's kind of nice to know I still have it."

Ezra's eyes rolled. "You're a gorgeous woman and you know it. If you weren't so cautious, you could have had many relationships by now."

"I have the only one I need," she replied with a sense of satisfaction.

"You're not just a mother. You're going to need more."

"Oh, you thought I meant Roman. No. I was talking about my body wand," she replied with a grin. "I've got a great relationship with that. Give me a glass of wine and that wand and I'm in for a good night."

Ezra's head dropped back and he groaned. "I do not need to hear about that."

She enjoyed teasing her brother-in-law. She still thought of him that way. But she sobered slightly. "Do you miss it?"

"Sex?" Ezra sighed and sat back. "Sometimes. But what I do now fills me in a way sex never could. I know you worry I'm punishing myself or doing some sort of penance for my crimes, but I'm more settled than I've ever been. We make choices in our life and I'm content with this one. You sending me to your uncle saved my life."

And ruined a part of hers, but she'd come to peace with that. "Well, I'm glad you're here. I wouldn't worry about the man at the shop, but I can go through the CCTV feed tomorrow. I'm going in to inspect a couple of books that came in this afternoon. Anna said this was yesterday?"

"Earlier today. I would feel better if you did. I don't know. I've been feeling antsy lately."

She cocked a brow his way because he should know why. The anniversary of his "death" was rapidly approaching. It was the one time she worried that he might fall back into his old habits. She always made sure she spent time with him during this week.

"It's not about that," Ezra countered. "Or maybe it is. I'm feeling guilty. I should never have brought you into this. It should have been between me and my brother."

She reached out and took his hand. He and her uncle had been a good family for her. Ezra had become her closest friend, the brother she'd never had. It had been Ezra's hand in hers when she'd given birth to Roman. "You had your reasons and honestly, I think it would have been one thing or another between me and Beck. We weren't meant to be."

"I don't know about that. When you were with him you glowed."

"And I don't now?"

He smiled, a wistful expression. "You know you do. You glow every time you look at Roman. You glow when you're in love."

"I'm not in love with Beck anymore," she admitted. "I didn't run from him because I hoped he would find me. I ran because I couldn't live like that another day. I need you to understand that I genuinely hope he's found someone. I hope he's found the right woman for him, the one who can bring him some peace. I'm like you, Ezra. I've found my peace. It's not perfect, but I'll take it."

"For now, I hope." He squeezed her hand and then let go. "I hate the thought of you being alone. At some point your uncle will retire and we'll have to move on from this place. I'll be reassigned, though I suppose I could always leave the church."

She didn't want that for him. He found peace and satisfaction in his job. "I bought the building my store is in. If it comes to it, Roman and I will move into one of the apartments."

"I'm worried he's still out there. The man who was coming after you, that is."

"It's been seven years." She'd kept track of Levi for a while. At least once a year she did a deep dive on the man who'd burned her whole life down. It was a little sad that she no longer kept up with the man she'd been married to, but she kept an eye on the one she hated. "He's gotten pretty much everything he wanted."

"He wanted you."

That was where Ezra was confused. He didn't understand the nature of Levi Green. "He wanted power more. He's getting married, you know. He's marrying a highly connected woman. She's the daughter of the vice president, who will likely be the president when the next election cycle is over. He's left operative status. He doesn't need to go into the field anymore. He has whole teams at his command. That's the kind of power he thought being married to me would get him. Or rather marrying into my family."

His lips kicked up in a rueful smile. When he smiled like that she saw Beck. "I'm always surprised when a mention of your family comes up. Beck never talked about how connected you are."

"Beck never cared. When we divorced he could have walked away with millions." It had oddly been one more kick in the gut. He hadn't wanted anything from her. "I didn't have him sign a pre-nup. And you of all people should be happy for all those connections."

"You can imagine how grateful I am," Ezra replied, emotion in his voice. "And then you can multiply it by ten and not come close to how much I owe you. That's why I'm going to talk to you about something that will be uncomfortable. I think you should reach out to Beck."

She sat up straighter, her spine going stiff, almost as though she felt the sudden need to physically defend herself. "Why would you say that?"

"Because Roman is starting to ask questions. Because Beck has the right to know he has a son. If Levi Green is no longer a threat, I think we should contact Beck and invite him to come out here. Beck has the right to know I'm alive." He stared at the flowers that surrounded them. "He has the right to face me and accuse me and hate me."

Her fear deflated a bit. "Is that what this is really about? I know you think you need to face him, but that's more about you than him. Do you really want to uproot whatever life he's made for himself because you need closure? He's got it."

"If it was only about me, I would say you're right and that seeking him out again is a selfish act," Ezra replied. "I will admit that I miss my brother. But this is not merely about me. It's about Roman."

The fear was back, and it mingled with an anger she thought she'd gotten over a long time ago. She stood up. "He told me flat out he didn't want a child of mine. He was happy we'd never had kids."

"Beck says a lot in anger that he doesn't mean."

"Another reason to keep my son away from him."

Sometimes it was easy to forget Ezra Fain was an ordained priest and that he was serious about his faith. Often he was merely her friend and brother-in-law. This was not one of those times. He gave her the same look he gave people who didn't behave around mourning families in the hospital where he worked. "Becoming a parent is one of the life events that can change a person, that can allow growth. He didn't have that chance. I agreed with you in the beginning. You were in danger and reaching out to him would have put you in more danger at a perilous time."

It had been such an odd time. She'd made it to Malta a few weeks before travel had been shut down due to the pandemic that raged across the globe for more than a year. Sometimes she was sure the pandemic and all the chaos it had wrought was the very reason no one had managed to find her. She'd given birth during that time, in a country that was a short distance from one of the epicenters. "He couldn't have come here anyway. No one could."

"The world is healthy again," he prodded. "It has been for years. There's no reason to not gently reach out. Carefully, of course. I'll be with you. I'm not going to let you go through this alone, but I think it might be time."

She couldn't. She couldn't even think about Beck. She was happy. Her life was peaceful, and injecting him back into it would spark a fire she couldn't put out. "I am a different person, Ezra. He brings out the worst in me. I do the same for him. I can't put my son through that. I don't know how he'll react to Roman. He could have his own kids by now."

"He doesn't."

"How would you know?"

"Because our cousins don't keep a lock on their social media and I monitor their pages," he admitted. "Beck was at a family reunion recently and he was alone. One of our cousin's friends asked about him in the comments and was told that Beck is the family hermit. He's living in Dallas and working with McKay-Taggart. From what my cousin said he doesn't date at all. He's going by his own name again."

She hated the fact that her first impulse was to go to the computer and look him up, see his pictures, stare at them and see if she could pick out the changes the years had brought. She'd known he was in Dallas, but she'd imagined he'd moved on.

How would he react? Just because he wasn't dating didn't mean he was still thinking about her with anything but anger. He might blame her for his lack of a love life. He'd blamed her for everything else.

She shook her head. "It doesn't matter. I'm not giving him a chance to savage me again. He made himself plain that night."

Ezra stood and gave her what she liked to think of as his "peaceful, but I'm disappointed" look. "All right. I'll let you sit with the thought for a while. I'll help Roman with his Maltese this evening. He's got a quiz coming up. Will you let me go with you to his teacher conference next week?"

He was asking her if she would punish him for bringing up Beck's name. "I would love it if you would come with me. You know they're always nicer when I bring a priest in."

He nodded. "Then let's enjoy tea. I'm sure Brother Francis brought back some treats from his trip. I heard from Anna that we have a shipment coming in soon. Let me know when and I'll try to make sure I can be there to help."

It was what he did. He helped, and he was only trying to do that now. But she wasn't ready. "Thank you. I will think about what you said."

She started down the path that led from the gardens to home at the top of the fort. They walked through the arched doors that once would have kept potential invaders from the inner sanctum, a gentle breeze caressing her skin as she heard her son laughing in the courtyard at something her uncle had said.

Life was peaceful. It was good. She couldn't risk that.

"And don't forget to check the CCTV," Ezra reminded her. "I know it's probably nothing, but I would like to make sure. I think you still have very good instincts about people."

She forced herself to smile as they started toward the big covered patio. It was one of her favorite spaces because almost no one was allowed behind those gates. The gardens were open from time to time for special tourist groups, but the residence was private. Occasionally they would have guests from the Vatican, but she'd found they mostly ignored her.

"Of course."

"Kim, I'm sorry if I upset you. I genuinely thought you were in a place where we could talk about him," Ezra said as they approached the shaded space where her uncle and son were already enjoying tea and snacks.

Her son ran out, speaking in rapid Italian about the science kit his great uncle had found for him in Rome.

She let him lead her under the shade and tried to forget that the minute she'd found out his father was still single, something in her heart had leapt at the thought.

She squashed it ruthlessly and joined her family because she was over Beckett Kent.

She really was.

Chapter Eight

Beck forced himself to walk when all he wanted to do was run in like a crazy person, force Tag to tell him where Kim was, and go get her.

It was more complicated than that. He had to think about what was best for Kim. Levi was still out there, and that fucker played a long game. Beck didn't care that Levi was engaged. He knew the man would still want Kim. They had to be careful.

He strode to the office and stopped at the door because he realized he'd left his keycard in his truck. He glanced through the heavy glass doors and frowned because the normal receptionist was not at the desk. It was Yasmin's lunch hour. Normally that meant one of the guys took over. Instead there was a thirteen-year-old girl sitting at the front desk, staring at her overly bedazzled phone. The Taggart kids had been coming into the office all week because it was summer break and their camps hadn't started yet. Tag believed in his kids learning the business. Or he believed in free labor. She grinned at something and he realized which Tag twin he was dealing with. At least it was the reasonable one.

He knocked on the door. "Kenz, buzz me in."

Kenzie Taggart looked up and waved. "Sure thing, Mr. Kent."

"Hold that." Kala Taggart came into view, staring at him with her

146

blue eyes. The shape resembled her mother's eyes, but that stare was all Ian. She was dressed in black, from her T-shirt down to a pair of combat boots. "How do I know you're the real Beckett Kent?"

He did not need this. "Kala, let me in this office right now. Your father called me in."

"Which is exactly what you would say if you were some bad guy who wanted in the office," Kala replied.

He wasn't sure how her parents were going to survive her teen years. "You know what I look like."

She shrugged. "Surgery is a real thing. You wouldn't be the first dude to have a whole bunch of surgery done so he could pass for someone else. You think I haven't read those files Dad thinks are secure? Uncle Li's own brother did it and then nearly killed him and Aunt Avery. It's not happening to me. I learn from ancient history. I'm going to need DNA."

He was going to have such a talk with Tag about putting his barely teenaged menaces in charge of the reception desk.

Kenzie stepped up beside her sister. She was dressed in bright colors, her strawberry blonde hair in a high ponytail. She was the lighter of the two, like she'd gotten all of her mother's joy. "He looks like Mr. Kent and he's wearing the same clothes he was earlier today. But then he had his keycard this morning."

Kala was her sister's mirror, but she was all her dad. "His clothes are super basic. I don't think I would even notice if they changed. Like how hard is it to get khakis and a collared shirt?"

"I am going to talk to your dad if you don't let me in," he said, his patience running out.

The door buzzed open and Tasha Taggart was shaking her head from behind the receptionist desk. "Dad told me to make sure Mr. Kent got in all right. Sorry, Mr. Kent. Kala takes things way too seriously, and Kenz not at all. Come with me. Did you lose your badge? I know how to make a new one."

Tasha Taggart had recently turned fourteen and had only the barest hint of her former accent, though it was thick when she spoke her native language. The girls liked to go into Russian when they didn't want anyone to know what they were saying. Tasha seemed constantly amused by her younger siblings.

"I still think we should make him take a DNA test. He's changed his name a couple of times," Kala said under her breath.

"I think you're cool." Kenzie gave him a wave. "And khakis aren't bad. Lots of dads wear them."

By *dad* she meant old dude. He wasn't a fool. But then he probably looked ancient to those babies.

The phone rang and the girls started to argue about who should answer it. Tasha opened the door to the inner office. "Don't mind Kala. She's in a bad mood because Cooper is at baseball camp and he's not replying to her texts. I've tried to tell her if she wants a boy to reply to her she shouldn't punch him on a regular basis."

The ways of those kids were a mystery, and he liked it that way. The big group of kids contained cliques within cliques, and as they got older they seemed to be pairing off. He preferred the youngsters who wanted to treat every surface of a space like their own private jungle gym. "Are they in the big conference room? And my keycard is in my truck. I ran up here and forgot it."

"They're in Dad's office," she said. "I'm sitting in for Genny. She's in New York with Wade this week. It's pretty cool. They're with Remy and Lisa. The guys are working as bodyguards for this reality star who's been accused of murdering another reality star. I hope we get to meet her. The alive one, I mean."

Despite the fact that the man had a whole business in another state, Remy still honored the pledge he'd made to Tag many years before. He came in on some of the higher profile cases. He particularly liked the ones where the company paid for travel.

Up ahead the door to one of the four largest offices on this floor came open and Charlotte stepped out. "Beck, excellent. Come on in. We've got something to show you. Adam's on his way up, and Hutch is already in there." She smiled at her oldest daughter. "Everything okay out here? Are the twins all right? Yasmin should be back any minute."

"Kenzie's answering the phone. Mostly. We shouldn't lose too many clients," Tasha promised. "I'll go check on Seth and Travis and make sure the nursery is still standing."

Charlotte watched her walk away with a smile on her face. "I have no idea what I would do without that child."

"Where is Kim?" He wanted to get straight to the point.

Charlotte turned serious. "You should come in."

He walked into Big Tag's office. It was bigger than Beck's apartment and had a glorious view of Dallas. Taggart was standing over his chair, which was occupied by Greg Hutchins. Hutch was the head of cyber investigations and security. He was in his early thirties, but then he'd been one of the youngest CIA employees in history. Recruited by Tennessee Smith for his hacking skills, Hutch had been Big Tag's man for over a decade.

"Beck, I'm sorry to interrupt you," Tag said. "You have to know I wouldn't unless it was important."

"Where is she?" Only one thing mattered.

"It's complicated." Taggart had his hands on his hips.

Hutch looked up from his laptop. "Nah. It's not really. She's in Malta. Did you know there was a country called Malta? I didn't. It's apparently some weird island in the Mediterranean. It's super tiny."

Tag frowned down at Hutch. "What about *let me handle this* did you not understand?"

Hutch shrugged. "He wasn't going to listen to a lecture, boss. He's been looking for Solo for seven years. I spend way more time with him than you do. Now that he knows we actually have a location, he'll chill."

"Or he'll take off after her, and the situation is complex," Tag insisted.

Malta. She was in Malta. "He's right. I wouldn't have stopped until you gave me a location, but I'm not going to immediately run off after her. Unless she's in some kind of danger."

"We've got some feelers out," Charlotte explained. "Chelsea is on it."

"How did you find her?" His heart was racing. Kim was in Europe and she was alive. "What do you know about her?"

"Very little." Tag came around his desk. "This intel is literally an hour old. I called as soon as we got the report."

"You know I've been tracking Solo's history for years now. By history, I really mean her family's business and social connections," Hutch explained. "It's this big weird puzzle because the Solomons have family across the globe. Did you realize Solo's connected to three different heads of state?"

"She didn't talk about her family much." It had been a point of contention with her. "I know she trusted a couple of cousins, but she wasn't close to any of them."

"From what I've been able to gather, she traveled a lot as a kid. She spent a whole lot of time in boarding schools," Hutch continued.

"Yes. Her parents didn't pay a lot of attention to her."

"After I realized that studying her super-classified time at the Agency wasn't yielding anything, I thought I would go deeper. I looked at her childhood. Sometimes when things are rough we go back to basics. She spent a few years at a boarding school in Austria," Hutch said. "She had very few visitors, but according to the records I acquired…"

"He hacked," Tag interjected with an eye roll.

"You say tomato," Hutch replied.

"Interpol says violation of international law," Tag shot back.

"Who visited her?" He didn't care what Hutch had done or how he'd done it. If Hutch got his smart ass taken to jail, Beck would break him out.

Hutch turned his way and seemed to get serious. "According to the records, a man named Francis Bruno came to visit her six times over the course of the four semesters she spent there. He visited on both of her birthdays."

He thought he might have heard the name. "Was he Italian?"

"Yes," Hutch replied. "He's got an Italian passport, but his official residence is in Malta."

"She mentioned an uncle in Rome." She'd so seldom wanted to talk about her family. "He was a physician of some kind."

"Francis Bruno is technically a cousin, but he's old enough that I could see where she might call him uncle in familial situations. He was a surgeon." Charlotte leaned against the desk, looking down at her notes. "When he was in his fifties, he developed a tremor in his hands after a car accident. He was the passenger. His wife was driving and she didn't survive. He came from a very wealthy family himself, but his wife had an even greater fortune and they did not have children. He couldn't work as a surgeon anymore, so he dedicated himself to charitable work. A few years later, he joined the Order of the Knights of Malta."

Hutch sat back. "It's not as cool as the thrillers make it out to be. They used to be warrior priests, but now it's pretty much a bunch of doctors and medical professionals who do charity work around the globe. But this dude, he's the knight. Like the head dude."

"What Hutch is trying to say is Francis Bruno took the same vows a priest would," Tag explained. "He lives in the one place the knights still own property in Malta. It's called Fort Saint Angelo. The actual fort is a tourist attraction, but at the top is a residence."

"They filmed *Game of Thrones* there," Hutch said with a geeked-out smile.

"You think Kim is at Fort Saint Angelo?" Beck asked.

The door to Tag's office came open and Adam Miles strode in. "I've got it. The report doesn't lie. It's one hundred percent her. That was an amazing call, Hutch. Are you sure you don't want to come work downstairs?"

Tag growled Adam's way. "Do not poach my employees. Unless it's one of the kids. You can't have Tash, but the twins are ready to work."

Adam rolled his eyes. "Not on your life." He turned Beck's way. "Hey, man. You ready for this?"

He'd been ready for years. He nodded.

Adam handed him a folder. "These were taken by CCTV in the town of Birgu, Malta. She's walking on the road that leads to the wharf and up to the fort."

He stared at the series of shots. Her head was down in almost all of them, but he would recognize that blonde hair anywhere, and the set of her shoulders. She wore a long sundress with spaghetti straps, and he could easily see the scar she'd gotten in Colorado.

But then he got to one photo where her head came up and a smile lit her face like she'd seen someone she cared about. That smile kicked him right in the gut.

She was still so beautiful it hurt.

"Is she happy?"

"Dude, we just figured out she's alive," Tag said. "We do not know the state of her joy."

"Ian." Charlotte knew exactly how to make her husband's name a warning. "Beck, this intel is so new, I haven't seen those pictures yet. You're sure it's her?"

He stared down at that photo. It was the first tangible evidence he'd seen that she was alive. He'd always believed it, but here she was. "Yes."

"You have to know I've been looking for years," Adam said. "Ian put me on this, and he's been on my ass all this time. He doesn't understand that I can't hack into every single CCTV system in the world. It's like looking for a needle in a haystack. Usually when I'm looking for a missing person, I at least have some clue where he or she's gone. My starting point was Paris. Also, I'm not usually tracking down highly trained operatives."

He'd known Adam's group had been working on the problem, but he'd thought that they considered it a cold case. "I thank you for this."

Adam gave him a nod. "Once Hutch told me to look into this particular section of Malta, I came up with those pictures pretty fast. Phoebe immediately looked into property around the area and she thinks Solo bought a building near the marina around four years ago. It's not in her name, but Phoebe pulled a couple of strings and it led back to a holding company Solo used to purchase the property we found she owned in Sydney. This street she's walking on is the same as where the building is located. There's a bookstore on the ground floor. We've got some of our people working on getting more data. Hopefully within twenty-four hours we'll know more."

"I want to be on a plane by then." He couldn't take his eyes off her. What had she been through in the last seven years? When she thought of him, did she still hear the last angry words out of his stupid, selfish mouth? "I don't have to make contact if you think it's for the best, but I need to check the situation out."

"I thought you would feel that way. I called Damon and let him know I need to borrow Robert to work out the logistics." Tag moved in and looked down at the pictures. "She looks good. Healthy. Not under Levi Green's thumb."

It was what they'd all worried about. It kept him up at night, the fear that somehow Levi had found her and had her hidden. "Do we have eyes on him?"

Tag nodded. "I've also got a call in to my contact there. Drake still keeps up with Levi. He's on an assignment, but he usually replies within twenty-four hours or so. Levi is in Europe. He's in Berlin meeting with some senior intelligence officers."

He didn't like the fact that they were on the same continent. "How long has he been there and when is he supposed to come back?"

"He's scheduled to be in meetings for the next three days," Charlotte replied. "After that, Levi has a flight scheduled for the night the conference ends. He's supposed to be back in DC ten hours later."

"I want to make sure he's on that flight." This was a delicate time. If he watched Levi, he was fairly certain Levi still watched him. Levi definitely watched McKay-Taggart. "If we send a team over, he's going to know it. I might be able to get there on my own if I'm careful."

"You are not going over there alone," Tag commanded in that he-will-not-be-moved way of his. "Tash is putting in a call for the company jet."

Adam frowned. "Uhm, I've got some meetings in Seattle."

The two companies shared a single jet. Ian and Adam had made the purchase only the year before, and now they bickered about it constantly.

"I can't hide where he's going if I put him on a commercial jet," Tag pointed out. "Do you want to be the reason Solo gets caught by Levi?"

Adam's eyes rolled. "Of course not, but I also don't want to fly commercial. It's horrible."

They started to argue. Charlotte took him to the side. "I'll have you in Malta by tomorrow afternoon. But Ian's right. You can't go alone."

"If half the team here suddenly goes missing, Levi will know something's up." He didn't want to go without a team either, but he wasn't going to put her at risk. "Maybe I can take Hutch."

"I need him here," Charlotte replied. "But I think I might have a team for you. Some of them are out of practice, but I know they won't let you go alone."

The door came open again and there was another Taggart in the doorway. Theo looked like he'd run down from the gym they kept on the second floor of MT. He was in a T-shirt, sweats, and sneakers. "Hey, I got the text. We found her?"

He hadn't expected Theo to be so excited. "Yes. Were you in on this?"

Theo stepped inside and took a look at the photos. "Not the investigation, though I've kept up with it. But the plan on how we'll work this op is one I've been thinking about for years." He grinned. "It's time to get the band back together, brother. Come on. We've got some calls to make."

He felt his heartrate tick up.

It was time to face his wife and find out if there was any way to earn her forgiveness.

* * * *

Bliss, CO

Jax Seaborne watched his kids running after Buster on the lawn in front of their cabin. They giggled madly and chased the big mutt who'd been his constant companion for almost eight years. Buster was slower than he'd been back then, but he could keep up with two rambunctious boys.

Sometimes better than their dad.

"Caden, don't hit your brother," a feminine voice called out, and then the center of his world was stepping out onto the porch.

He smiled and looked her over. No matter how many years he'd been married to River, he still took in every inch of that beautiful body as often as he could. "Hey, gorgeous."

She moved next to him, wrapping her arm around his waist. "Are you packed? Henry should be here soon."

He hugged her close. "Yeah. You know I don't want to leave you, right?"

She tipped her head up and wrinkled her nose. "You never leave me, babe. You've barely left Bliss for seven years. Come on and tell me there's not a part of you that's excited."

He couldn't lie to the love of his life. "I love Bliss, but I wouldn't hate one last mission."

"Especially since it's Solo." River laid her head against his chest. "Please tell her I miss her."

Over the years, his wife had come to forgive the woman who'd lied to her. Solo had been River's friend in a time when she'd needed one. Forgiveness had always been his wife's default position. She'd even forgiven him. "Are you sure you're okay with me going? Hiking season is in full swing."

They'd built up Mountain Adventures over the last seven years, and now they had twenty employees and offered everything from guided camping to a weeklong kids' camp they were debuting this summer. He still wasn't sure that hadn't been a mistake because Max Harper had gleefully signed up all four of his kids the week before and then run out of the office yelling "no take backs." He was absolutely certain the Harper kids combined with the Hollister-Wright brood would make the summer interesting.

Could he make this mission last until fall?

"We'll be fine as long as you're home before summer camp. You're not leaving me alone with those hooligans." She stepped back and grinned up at him as though she'd known exactly what he'd been thinking. Which she probably had. "If it helps, Laura came in and signed up Sierra. She'll keep the Harper boys in line."

"The boys? The boys are easy. I'm worried about Paige." He heard the sound of gravel crunching and realized it was almost time to go. He held a hand out and pulled her close again. "God, I'm going to miss you."

She hugged him tight as Henry Flanders's truck pulled up. Henry was driving him into Alamosa where Beck was picking him up in a jet. Henry was probably going to give him an hour-long lecture on how to survive this op.

"I will miss you, too, babe," she replied. "But have fun and take care of Solo. I can't imagine having to hide for seven whole years. I hope she's had some company. I wish she'd called me."

"It's not your fault." He knew she felt guilty.

"I wasn't nice to her. I didn't give her a real second chance," River admitted. "If I had, she would have felt welcome, and we could have given her a place to stay. She could have hidden here. If you can't resolve her case…"

"I'll let her know she has a place waiting for her here," he promised his wife as Henry put the truck in park.

River went on her toes and brushed her lips against his. "Be careful. Remember how much we love you when you're out there in the great big world."

He breathed her in and held her close a moment more. He didn't need the great big world. He only needed the one he'd built with this woman. "I love you. Take care of our boys."

Henry was chuckling as Caden and Rio and Buster basically tackled the former operative. He simply opened his arms and let in all the love. "Hey, River! I've got some bread from Nell and the girls. She wants you to know we're happy to help at the office if you need it."

Of course they would. It was what the Flanders family did, what everyone in Bliss did. They helped.

"I hope you're still saying that by the time summer camp rolls around," Jax said, kissing his wife one last time. "Boys, come say good-bye to your old dad."

In a heartbeat he was covered in giggling little boys and a dog who thought he was a giggling boy.

His life was so full, and it was time to pay back two of the people who'd helped make it all happen.

* * * *

Solna, Sweden
Outside of Stockholm

Owen Shaw ran the last few hallways that led to his wife's lab. He prayed she hadn't been called to the hospital. She rarely performed surgery anymore, but she did assist with some of the neurosurgeons in the city to keep her skills up.

The Karolinska Institute was all modern angles and smooth lines, and it made it easy for him to find his way to Rebecca's offices, though they hadn't been in Sweden for long. She'd finally found the research project she couldn't pass up, and because she'd once given up her whole hard-fought life to be with him, he'd felt good about doing the same for her. Being a stay-at-home dad wasn't a dream job, but he found it utterly satisfying to spend so much time with his children.

He hoped she wouldn't see what he had to do now as a betrayal of the pact they'd made when they'd agreed to move to Sweden.

"Mr. Shaw," the assistant said as he rushed inside. He was a young Swede, still in medical school, hoping to study the mysteries of the brain with the best. "We weren't expecting you. Is everything all right?"

His wife was the best. "Is Rebecca around?"

Please let her be around. He wasn't sure he could wait, and he didn't want to call her from the airport to tell her he'd left their son and daughter with friends.

"Hey." Rebecca walked out of her office, her eyes wide with alarm. "Has something happened? Where are the kids?"

"They're fine." He moved to her, taking her hand in his. He had a hastily packed duffel slung over one shoulder, and her eyes went to it. "I got a call from Dallas. The one we've been waiting for."

She led him into her office, shutting the door behind her. "They found Solo?"

She asked the question in a hushed tone that let him know she still remembered those days when they'd been on the run, hiding and praying they wouldn't be found.

"Aye, and she's here in Europe," he replied quietly. "Love, I…"

She put her hands on his chest and tilted her head up. "You have to go help your team. Are Hannah and Arran at Lilly's?"

Their next-door neighbor was a retired physician who'd taken to their kids. Hannah was six and Arran only eighteen months. Lilly and her husband had no grandchildren yet and seemed more than happy to offer the new couple some babysitting from time to time. "Yes. I didn't want to bring them up here. I hope it's all right. She said they would be fine there until you get home."

"Good. I'll call her and let her know I'll try to leave a bit early." She wrapped her arms around him. "It's okay for you to go. I know it's hard. I hate it when I have to go to a conference. I'm always scared I'll miss something with them, but you can't skip this one.

They're your brothers. They need you."

He thanked god every day for this woman. "I promise I'll be back as soon as I can. I'm heading to the airport. Rob got me on a flight to London. I'll stay at The Garden tonight and then fly down with him tomorrow morning. Beck and Theo are picking up Jax and Tucker and meeting us in Malta. I'm not sure if we're extracting her or merely doing some surveillance."

It didn't matter. He would go when his brothers called. They might be spread across the globe, but they were still a family. Once a year they got together and had a reunion—usually at The Garden, but they'd all gone out to Colorado one year and had a lovely time catching up. This wouldn't be a fun reunion. This would be the chance they'd been waiting for—the chance to pay back the man who'd helped them all those years ago. None of them survived without the help of Beckett Kent.

"I assure you there's zero chance Beck leaves without her." She looked up at him, her eyes getting that steely, stubborn look he shouldn't find so sexy. "Do not let Levi Green get the jump on you."

"I promise. And I promise I'll take the fucker out if I get the chance." He kissed her and wished they had more time. "I've got to make the train if I'm going to get to the airport. I'm so sorry, love."

She stepped back and slipped out of the white coat she wore at work. "I'll drive you. I can take the afternoon off." She grabbed her purse and keys. "Now tell me everything."

He followed her out of the office, already missing his children.

But there was an energy to his step he couldn't deny. He'd missed this, too.

"All right, love. According to Rob, she's been living in this fort," he began as they made their way to the parking lot.

* * * *

London, England

Robert hung up the phone and tossed it on the bed. It had been a hell of a night, and it wasn't over yet. Owen had gotten in, and they flew out to Malta in the morning where he'd already found a base of operations close to Fort Saint Angelo, and a secondary site where they would be comfortable staying while they were on the island. But they needed more than that. "Believe it or not I got us a helicopter if we need it. I don't think we will, but it's there. Turns out the king of Loa Mali had a meeting in Italy on the second wave of his green energy project and he bought one because he doesn't like rentals. He's sending it our way. The rich are really different."

Ariel sat in the middle of the big bed they shared. For years it had been just the two of them, and they'd been content to be everyone's favorite aunt and uncle. And then their princess had come along. "They are, love. Come to bed. Owen's already asleep. He called home and now he's snoring away. You've got an early flight."

"I wonder if we shouldn't have gone tonight."

"The apartments aren't available until tomorrow afternoon. You've been legendary today. You put this whole op together in a few hours. You have a house, an apartment, equipment, a helicopter."

"And a boat." They were right on the water, after all. He wanted the team to have every chance they could to do this right.

She wore a white silk gown that came down to mid-thigh, showing off those gorgeous legs of hers. She'd already put up her hair for the night, wrapping it in silk. It left the lovely graceful line of her neck on display. "You did good work. Now come to bed and make love to me while the beast is sleeping."

He shook his head. "She's a princess."

Ariel's lips turned up as she moved off the bed and came to stand next to him. "She's a raging beast when she wants to be. Just like her mother."

She still took his breath away. He let his hands find her hips and brought her close. "You're a queen, baby. I'm the lucky pauper who managed to catch your eye." He leaned over and brushed their lips together. "I'm still so fucking crazy about you."

Her arms drifted up to his shoulders. "Back at you, love. You have no idea how much I wish I could go with you."

The funny thing was they'd both stepped back from the field in the last few years. He'd taken on the role of Damon's logistics lead, and Ariel was on maternity leave but she planned to go back to her job as a profiler and therapist working with McKay-Taggart and

Knight, and occasionally Scotland Yard. "I don't think taking our princess on this particular op is what I meant when I said I was eager to start our adventures. I was thinking more along the lines of walks in the park, maybe Disney World one day. Definitely not into the line of fire."

"I'm hoping there's no fire at all."

He stared down into those gorgeous deep brown eyes of hers. "What's your read on Levi? Is he still interested after all these years? Beck believes so. Charlotte is more hopeful. She thinks he might have moved on since he's engaged now. She hopes he might not care anymore since he's found a way to get what he wants without Solo."

Ariel went back down on her heels. "You're asking me if Levi is still a problem? If he's still obsessing over Solo?"

"Yes." Her opinion was the one that would inform how he operated, how careful he was.

"He will not have forgotten for a single second. Whoever he's marrying means nothing to him because there's only Solo. It's odd when you think about it. He's a dark mirror for Beck. Beck can't get over her and neither can Levi. You will have to kill Levi for Solo to be safe."

He took a deep breath. "And that's why I got a boat and a chopper."

She smiled brilliantly. "You are always prepared, love. Now kiss me and take me to bed because I don't think this is the easy in and out op Beck was talking about."

"He only wants to get in and get a lay of the land before he makes contact with her." Rob had his doubts, too. Things always got complex between those two.

"He won't be able to let go." Her hands moved up to caress his chest, pressing under the cotton of his shirt. "When he sees her, he'll have to protect her. He won't let her be alone."

"That's kind of what I'm afraid of," Rob admitted. "Solo ran. She didn't want to be found."

"All you can do is make sure your team has everything they need." She brushed her lips against his. "And tell my friend I miss her and I want her to meet our daughter."

Their baby girl. Daraja. She was as beautiful as her name, as lovely as her mother.

"I will," he promised. His wife was right. He had some time, and he knew exactly how he wanted to spend it. With Dara sleeping peacefully, he had a chance to show her mother how much he would miss her. He picked up his wife and carried her back to bed.

* * * *

Laramie, Wyoming

Tucker watched the plane land and turned to his wife. "It's time. Are you sure you can handle the clinic, because we can call in some friends to help cover my patients."

Roni rolled her eyes. "I can handle your patients and my patients. We don't have that many patients. It's a small town. Now go and play hero. I would say one last time, but we all know it won't be. I'm surprised it took this long."

"Because this isn't my life anymore," he countered. He needed to make her understand how much he loved their life together. He wouldn't trade it for anything. Their rural clinic was all he needed. "You are. Our kids are."

He had three. Violet. Gavin. Aurora. They were back in Jennings with his mom and Roni's. Sandra had moved from Dallas after Aurora had been born and opened a new business.

"I know," she said with a smile. They were standing outside the private terminal, the stars all around them, but nothing was as bright as his wife's smile. "But this is family. Rob is going to be there. I'm glad you get to spend some time with him. It's been months since you saw him, and they have a baby now. He's going to need you."

He hadn't even had a chance to meet his niece. Life had been so busy, and the distance had taken its toll. He couldn't help but be excited to see his brothers. Talking on the phone wasn't the same. "I hope I remember how to do this."

He wished he'd kept up his training at the shooting range, but he rather thought when the time came he wouldn't have trouble shooting Levi Green. He would never forget how to do that.

The plane had come to a stop and the door came open, then Jax was standing on the stairs.

"Tucker! My brother! Let's get going. We've got beer, and Theo brought board games. Hey, Roni!"

He had to laugh because his brothers never changed. When they got together they were all dumb kids enjoying each other's company.

Roni waved to Jax. "Don't let him drink too much beer. I want him back in the same physically fit condition I sent him off in." She turned to him and went up on her toes to kiss him. "Be safe. I love you."

"I love you, too." He held her close. "I'll be home soon."

He prayed he could keep that promise.

Chapter Nine

Kim stepped out into the sunlight with a sigh and immediately caught sight of her uncle sitting on the patio sipping his midmorning tea.

"Good morning, dear girl. How are our patients?" Her uncle gave her a wave and gestured for her to join him.

It had been a rough couple of days. "Better, thanks to you. I think Roman could probably have gone to school today, but I would feel better if he had more rest."

She moved down the steps and crossed to join her uncle. She set her bag down and took a seat as her uncle poured her a coffee.

"It was just a little bug," he said, handing her the delicate cup. "I told you it would pass. I don't expect that you will get it. You have what we physicians like to call Mommy immunity."

She was glad for it because apparently Ezra didn't have it. He'd been every bit as sick as Roman. She'd been pushing fluids and bringing down fevers for days. "Well, I'm happy for it. I talked to one of the teachers at the school and it's going around. She said half the class is out with it. It's almost certainly where Ezra picked it up, too."

"He's a baby." Uncle Francis passed her the milk and sugar tray. "He needs to build up more fortitude. Are you going into the store?"

"Only if you don't mind." Her uncle had many things to do in a day, and he'd put a lot of them off so he could help her. "I need to go through the shipment we got in, and I promised Ezra earlier this week that I would go through some of the security feed."

"I'm staying home for the rest of the week. I can certainly look in on our patients," her uncle assured her. "I've got some research I would like to do. Is my book in the shipment?"

At least she had something to offer him. "I hope so. Anna told me we got some mail from Germany. If it's here, I'll bring it back for you."

"Why does Ezra want you to go through the tapes? Are you having problems at the shop?"

She shook her head and picked up one of the croissants on the breakfast tray. She filled a small plate with cheese and fruit. "Someone asked about me a few days back. Not by name. I think it's nothing more than a tourist looking for a date. Ezra's being overly cautious, so I had Anna save the files from earlier in the week."

Her uncle had gone all kinds of serious. "Kimberly, you can't take these things lightly."

"I'm not. I meant to go in the day after he asked me to, but then we were dealing with two sick boys." Ezra wasn't really a baby, but he had needed a bit of nursing to get through the stomach bug he and Roman had picked up. "However, I seriously doubt anyone's found me after all these years. I'm almost certain they've stopped trying."

He stared at her for a moment. "And that is when they will get you, my darling girl. Perhaps it's time for you to reach out to Beckett."

She sat back, her appetite fleeing in a second. "Have you been talking to Ezra?"

"You know I've always thought Ezra should face his brother. He's done much good work in the years since he walked away from his old life. But he can't fully embrace his new life without facing his brother. He's merely putting off the inevitable, and you are, too."

She intended to be entirely stubborn on this front. "There's nothing inevitable about me seeing Beck again."

"Are you truly willing to spend the rest of your life in danger? Beck is the one who might be able to help you clear your name. He's connected to that group, right?"

"McKay-Taggart. He works for them. But if he hasn't been able to find the information that will exonerate me by now, he likely won't." She took a sip of her coffee and put it back down. "He doesn't owe me anything."

"I beg to differ, and I suspect your son will, too, one day."

"That's not fair."

"Life isn't fair, and you know that," her uncle replied with a frown. "If you are in danger, then Roman is, too. I don't want you to have a false sense of security. It's not easy to live with your guard up. It is inevitable that you will let it down because it's impossible to live your life constantly in fear. But the way to quell those fears is to be proactive. If you won't talk to Roman's father, perhaps we can bring in a lawyer."

She stood suddenly. "I don't want to talk about this." Her life was nice. She didn't understand why her uncle and Ezra felt the need to try to rattle things now. "If we're bothering you, Roman and I can move out."

Her uncle seemed to deflate. "That's not at all what I want. You and the boy have been the light of my life. I love you, niece. My Rosa and I were not blessed with children, but we were blessed with you. Sometimes when you love someone, you have to risk the relationship in order to save the loved one."

She sighed and let go of her anger. This man had been everything she'd needed him to be. Even when she'd been a child her aunt and uncle had been the bright spots in her life. "I'm sorry. I'm happy here, and I don't want to think about what could happen in the future."

"The future always finds us." He settled back in his seat. "It's about more than merely your safety. It's about your ex-husband. I don't think you've gotten over him."

She actually laughed at that thought. "I assure you I was over Beck the moment he threw my childhood in my face." That had been the hardest thing to deal with. She'd talked to him about her fears because she'd trusted him, because he'd been her safe place. With all the fights they'd had, he'd never broken her trust in that way. "He'd always been angry, and I was used to dealing with it. But he turned cruel over the years. I don't know what he would have done if I'd stayed."

"Have you considered that he might have apologized? That if you had talked to him, he might have come to understand how much that hurt you?"

That felt like victim blaming. "It's not my responsibility to make Beck see reason. He divorced me without a real talk. I figured I could take charge of my life without begging him to see my side of things. You don't know Beck. Once he has a grudge, he never lets go. He always loved his outrage far more than me."

"Well, you did hide his brother from him," her uncle pointed out. "You lied to him."

"I did that to protect Ezra. Maybe Beck and I were always doomed."

Her uncle sighed. "All I know is I lost my Rosa far too early."

She felt a soft spot in her heart when she thought about her aunt. "Beck and I were never you and Aunt Rosa."

"Oh, your aunt and I fought a lot in the beginning. I think it was only our religion that kept us together for some of those early, volatile years. Even with our profound belief, we talked about separating more than once in the first six years of our marriage."

She felt her eyes go wide. "What did you do?"

He chuckled. "Your aunt wasn't a saint. She instigated many of our fights. You only knew us when we were solid. And your parents were a terrible example of a good marriage. I worry that you were caught between what seemed to be a perfect marriage and your parents web of lies and neglect. I wish I'd been able to advise you when you and Beckett were having trouble. Do you know what turned your aunt and I around?"

"What?" Kim asked.

Her uncle leaned closer. "We learned how to talk to each other. I know it sounds odd, but women and men speak different languages."

She wished it was that simple. "It was more than that."

"And I worry it still is. I worry you'll spend the rest of your life alone because no one will ever move you the way he did."

"You should talk," she replied pointedly. "You took actual vows of celibacy, uncle."

"I did that because I won't ever love another woman. I'll be true to my wife until I die, and the vows show both my love for her and my love for God," he explained. "It's the same for Ezra, though he didn't have an earthly love. Some men and women don't, and there's nothing wrong with that if they're fulfilled by something else."

"I'm happy with my son. He's the love of my life."

"Then why do you dream of his father at night? Why do you call out for him?"

She felt her skin flush. "I do not." Except she knew she dreamed about Beck. Almost every night. "I'm sorry. It's a subconscious thing. It doesn't mean I'm still hung up on Beck."

"All right."

She could practically feel the disappointment coming off her uncle, and she hated it. Had he and Ezra decided to push her? She stood again, grabbing the crossover bag and slinging it over her torso. "I should go. I'll try to be back before dinner. There's chicken salad in the fridge in case I'm late."

She strode away because her uncle could be stubborn.

He wasn't right any more than Ezra was right.

What was she going to tell Roman when he asked about his dad? She made quick work of the walk from the residence to the battlement, passing from the cool confines of the garden into the open sun and tourists who stopped and stared as though trying to figure out why she'd come out of the highly secured area. Most simply shrugged and figured she was some kind of curator, but she'd had a few pushy tourists question her and try to get a tour of the area.

She breezed past them, not even giving them a chance to ask. She didn't want to pretend today.

Her uncle's questions were making her restless. Seven years before she'd decided to live in the now, to let the future take care of itself.

How long could she do that? It had been easy when Roman was a baby. She'd spent the first few years of his life doing nothing more than taking care of him, hiding away from the tumult of the world outside. When the world had started to heal, she'd stayed here, playing with her son and making him the center of the world.

That was fine for her, but Roman would want more.

He would want to see more of the world than this tiny island, and she wasn't sure how he would do it. She couldn't go with him unless she truly believed they weren't at risk. Was she safe now that Levi was marrying into a powerful family?

McKay-Taggart could help with that. They could talk about ways to neutralize her as a threat to Levi and maybe work out a deal where she could come out of hiding and give her son a more free life.

But then she would have to admit that her son existed, and she would finally know what Beck thought.

She moved past the unmarked guva that had served for years as Fort Saint Angelo's prison. It looked like nothing more than an ancient manhole, and likely most tourists thought it was access to some kind of system, but she knew it for what it was. It was an oubliette. The prisoner would be thrown down the narrow entrance into the bulblike bottom of the prison. It was impossible to get out without help because the walls were curved and couldn't be climbed.

That was where she was. Stuck. She could see the light, but she couldn't reach it. She would never get out of that prison without someone throwing her a line and lifting her out. If she stayed, she would spend the rest of her life hoping someone threw her scraps.

And Roman would be there with her.

She practically jogged down the steep embankment, moving past the tourists on their way up to the battlement. She barely saw the boats in the marina or the happy visitors sitting outside and eating their brunch al fresco. It was a stunning day, but she didn't feel the sun the way she normally did. Her uncle's questions were ringing in her ears.

They were still there a few moments later when she got to the front of her shop. The door was open, along with the big windows that allowed the breeze from the bay in.

Anna was at the cash register, handing over a small bag that likely held something other than books from the shape of it. Most likely one of the snow globes featuring the knights.

Was this the life she wanted for her son? Selling cheap souvenirs to tourists? There wasn't anything wrong with the life, but she didn't want Roman limited by his mother's mistakes.

"Hello." Anna greeted her as she walked toward the backrooms. "I put the box from Germany on your desk."

"Thanks." She liked Anna, but she needed some alone time. The last few days had been hard with Roman and Ezra being sick. That was why she was so restless. It wasn't thinking of Beck. It wasn't the dreams she'd been having lately, the ones where he held her in his arms and took charge. Where he saved her, and she didn't have to worry about the future because they would face it all together. "Let me know if you need anything."

She was relieved when she closed the door to her office. It wasn't much. She'd certainly had much bigger offices in her time, but this place had become a calm space for her. While the fort was large and the gardens plentiful, the actual residence wasn't huge, and there were four of them living there. This was the place she could come to when she needed to be alone.

She really needed to be alone today.

There was a box of books on her desk. Work was good.

She carefully opened the box from Germany and settled in.

Hours later she was satisfied the small leather-bound tome was the real thing, and her uncle would be thrilled to add its knowledge to the order's library. He would pay her handsomely for finding it and then she could buy more books.

It might be time to think about renovating one of the apartments above.

Or maybe it was time to talk to a lawyer the way her uncle had suggested. One who could be trusted.

She glanced up at the clock and realized it was far later than she'd imagined. She'd worked on authenticating her latest purchase and had only stopped to briefly eat a sandwich. She'd taken over the cash register so Anna could have lunch. The day had flown by and soon she had to make the walk back home to face her uncle and Ezra.

Maybe she would stop and grab some pizza. Ezra had texted her with updates on her son's rapid recovery. They'd both been eating today, and perhaps if she fed them they wouldn't have to talk too much.

She needed time to figure out what she wanted to do.

She wished she could call Ariel.

Why shouldn't she? She could buy a burner phone, call up The

Garden, and hope Ari was still living there. Or she could use a computer and bounce the signal around. There were programs that could mask her location.

Did Ariel ever think about her? Or was Ari glad she didn't have to deal with all the crazy that came with being friends with her.

There was a knock on her office door and then Anna was standing there, a harried look on her face.

"I'm so sorry. I got a call from the school and Leni is sick," Anna said. "She threw up in the middle of class."

It really was going around. "No problem. Go on and I'll close up when it's time."

"We only have a few customers." Anna already had her purse in hand. "I'm so sorry."

"Don't worry about it. Roman is getting over it. It's only bad for about twenty-four hours. Lots of fluids and she'll be fine in a couple of days," Kim advised.

"Thanks so much." Anna started out the door. "A courier delivered a letter, but I think it was a mistake. I didn't recognize the name. I'll check into it tomorrow."

Anna thanked her again and Kim walked out to the front register. The shop was quiet, but she could hear the murmurs of customers wandering through the back shelves. At least it wasn't a cruise ship day where she would be bombarded with tourists. She glanced out and it looked like a storm was moving in. The afternoon had turned cloudy.

Did she have an umbrella?

She sold a couple some postcards and a book on the underground tunnels of Valletta and then opened her laptop. She could check the CCTV files from here.

A package caught her eye. It was in one of the courier services flat-rate envelopes and covered in plastic. The markings were in German and claimed it was an overnight guaranteed envelope.

She sighed. It was likely legal papers, and someone was going to be pissed. It wouldn't be the first time they'd gotten someone else's mail. She turned it over and then the room seemed to go cold.

K. Solomon

The reason Anna hadn't recognized the name was because Kim

had never told the woman her real name. She went by Kay Bruno.

No one outside of her family knew what her real name was.

Her heart started to race, and she had to force herself to breathe.

Seven years. She'd been all right for seven years. How had they found her?

She tore the letter open and inside was a single slip of paper.

Remember, remember the fifth of November. The People know Reva. Find her.

What the hell did that mean? It didn't matter because someone knew her real name.

She shoved the letter and packaging in her bag and dragged it over her head, securing the crossbody against her hip. She couldn't stay. "I'm sorry. I need to close the shop. My son is ill, and I have to pick him up."

The few patrons in the front of the store walked out without an argument, though she heard a few curse as the rain started.

It didn't matter. The CCTV tapes didn't matter either. The letter was all that mattered. That and getting to her son. Her mind raced as she walked the store to make sure she wasn't about to lock anyone in.

She would need two new passports, but she would take the ferry to Sicily tonight. She would pack up Roman and they could be in Rome by tomorrow. They would rent a room and figure out how to make their way to Australia. Yes. That would be a good start. She had a small flat in Sydney no one should know about.

But then no one was supposed to know she was here in Malta.

She turned down the last aisle and there was a man in a black trench coat, his back turned as he looked up at the books in her biography and memoir section. "Sir, I'm sorry. I've got to close the store. I have to pick up my son."

It wasn't a lie. She was probably going to pick up her son and take him to an entirely different continent.

God, she wanted Beck. It was right there. She wanted to call him and ask him to help her and not be in this all alone. She wanted him to care about Roman, to know Roman's dad would do anything to save him.

"Your son?" That voice sent a chill down her spine. The man turned and he was staring at her, his gaze burning every bit as much

171

as it had seven years before. "I hope you're lying because there's no room for a child in my plans. Hello, Solo. Long time no see."

Levi Green started to walk down the aisle, and she knew her life was over.

* * * *

"The storm's coming in," Jax said over the headset. "I looked it up and it's a doozy. We might want to pull up stakes and get back to base before it really hits."

"She hasn't come out of the store yet." Beck sat in the building across the street from the bookstore Kim owned. "I want to follow her home to make sure she gets in all right."

Three days. They'd been in Malta for three days, and this was the closest he'd gotten to her. She'd been holed up in her tower. He knew it was a fort, but he'd come to think of her as a princess in a tower, hiding away from the big bad wolf.

He'd torn her apart once. Did he have any right to ask her to risk it again?

"All right, boss. I'll send Tucker out in a car to get you. I think the boat would be risky," Jax replied. "I'll let Rob know you're coming in."

Robert was on a boat in the marina. It was a small yacht that included a bedroom and everything a person needed to hang out for days peeping up at the princess in the tower. "I'll let Rob go back to base. I'm going to stay here in Birgu. Now that she's left the fort I want to track her movements. Hopefully she leaves more often than she has this week."

"Seriously?" Theo Taggart was in the flat with him. They'd been taking shifts going between Birgu and an isolated farm on the south side of the island where no one would question six Americans coming in and out with tons of equipment. And a chopper. Robert had outdone himself. "You're going to stay in town again? How much sleep have you gotten?"

Not nearly enough, but that didn't matter. "I'll sleep on the boat. I'll be fine. I would rather stay close to her."

Theo moved in beside him. "She looks good."

She'd looked gorgeous when she'd walked down the narrow road and strode into her little bookshop. Her hair had shone in the sunlight, but she'd had a frown on her face. "She's worried about something."

Even after all these years he knew her tells. She walked fast when she was worried. When she was happy, she took in the sights around her, even when they were familiar. It had been a beautiful morning and she'd been focused. He'd followed her, waiting down at the marina until she'd come through the gates that led to the fort. He now knew this area of Malta better than he knew his own Dallas neighborhood. He'd spent days studying that fort of hers, walking along the battlements and hoping he caught sight of her.

"Well, she is in hiding," Theo pointed out. "But she's gotten sloppy. She wasn't even wearing a hat, and that hair of hers is a giveaway. She should have dyed it and cut it."

He couldn't stand the thought of her doing that. Her hair was glorious, like the woman herself. "I can't imagine keeping up that level of security for seven years. She probably needs something that feels familiar. Did you get the report on her employee?"

"Yes," Theo replied. "Anna Rossi. Her husband's, too. Hutch ran them both through all our databases and they came back clean. I would bet she knows nothing about Solo's true identity. She's been working for the bookstore since it opened a few years back. Before then, from what we can tell, Solo didn't have a job. Now there is one record of a Kay Bruno spending two nights in a local hospital six years ago."

"What happened?" Even though it was years before and he knew she was safe now, his stomach still clenched at the thought of her being in a hospital.

"I don't know. Jax is looking into it. It could also be another Kay Bruno. It's not an uncommon name here." Theo leaned against the wall, staring down at Beck. "Have you thought about what you're going to say to her?"

He'd gone over and over it in his head. It kept him up at night. Even before he'd known where she was, that he might have a chance to say anything to her at all, he'd envisioned what he would say.

I'm sorry.

I love you.

173

"I don't know that I'm going to say anything at all," he replied.

Theo huffed, a disbelieving sound. "Sure. You brought us all halfway around the world so you could look in on her."

The impulse to tell him that if he didn't want to be here, he could leave, was right there. But he knew now that his defensiveness had everything to do with his own insecurity and likely nothing with Theo's willingness to help. "I worry I could do more harm than good if I approach her."

Honesty. That was what he was going for now. If honesty made him vulnerable, then he had to deal with it because being dishonest with himself had led to hurting the people he loved the most.

"Do you think she would run again?" Theo asked.

"Yes."

"Have you considered the fact that if we figured out where she is, Levi Green might be able to as well? It might be time for her to move."

If that was the case, then he would have to be the bad guy again. "What if she's happy here? She's got a shop. She's got some family. Telling her she has to drop everything again because I haven't been able to exonerate her feels like another blow."

"Ian can be over here in a day and a half. Or I can be the one to talk to her," Theo offered. "If you feel like she wouldn't take it well from you, we can find someone she won't mind talking to. Ariel would do it. She would have to call since she's got a baby now."

"We do not need to bring a baby into this." He didn't like to think about babies. Or kids. Even though he was surrounded by them. It wasn't that he desperately wanted them. It was that he'd kind of always thought Kim would drag him into the whole family thing. He'd heard it was something a guy got used to. "But I understand that this place might be dangerous for her now. I worry she'll blame me for that."

He stared at the front of the shop and watched a man in a dark trench coat enter. He had a hat on his head and didn't look like the normal tourists who walked in and out of the shops along the street. He touched his earpiece. "Rob, did you catch the guy in the trench coat?"

Rob was watching the CCTVs coming from the marina toward

the shop.

"I don't have anyone like that. I've got a ton of people in shorts," Rob replied. "Sounds like your guy actually watched the weather report."

A light drizzle had started, and the wind was beginning to pick up. He should have checked the weather. The few days they'd been here had been sunny and calm. He'd wondered if his sun-loving wife was sitting at the top of her tower soaking it all up. He liked to think about her wearing a bikini, drinking a fruity drink, and reading some romance novel. He liked to think she'd been enjoying as much of her life as she could.

There was a buzzing sound and Theo walked off to answer his cell.

"Yeah, Ian, I'm with him. Go on," Theo said.

He didn't like Trench Coat. Even the locals tended to wear light colors given the climate. Someone in all black stood out here. He brought up the cameras around the shop and tried to catch a glimpse of the guy's face.

The man kept his head down. All he gave to the camera was the top of his covered head.

Damn it. He did not like that. "Rob, I want you to call Owen and tell him to be on standby."

"Shit. You think someone's going for her?" Rob asked, but then he could hear Rob contact their base in the background.

"I want to be ready if we need to extract her."

"Tucker's on his way," Rob relayed. "I'll keep an eye on the fort and anyone coming this way."

"I want you to look at any single men or men in groups. You know what to look for." Agency guys. If they were smart they would send in women, but Levi didn't work with a lot of women. He didn't have a single one on his team with the exception of admins.

"Will do," Rob replied. "Tucker's approximately two minutes away. Are you confirming we're going to make contact?"

"No." He might be completely paranoid. "I want to monitor the situation. I've got eyes on both ways out of the building." There was a small CCTV camera on the back entrance. He moved to pull it up.

The screen was dark.

"Hey," Theo said, "Ian's got some intel that puts Levi Green leaving Germany on time, but the plane didn't return to the States."

Beck got to his feet. "He's here. He came for her. We need to move in and extract her now. Contact Owen."

Theo frowned. "Uhm, there's not a lot of places for a chopper to land here."

He wasn't thinking. "We don't need to land. That chopper is fully equipped for a rescue, and we've got a good, solid high place to extract from. We get her to the top of the fort and go from there. But I don't know how many men Levi has with him."

"I don't think the local government is working with the Agency." Theo checked his SIG. "I'll call the cops and get them out here. If they show, we know they haven't been given instructions to let Levi take her."

"The top of that fort belongs to the Order. The residence she's been staying in is its own tiny principality." It wasn't exactly free from Malta's government, but he would use any loops he could get through. Levi wouldn't be able to storm that particular castle easily. "I'll try to get her to Rob and get away by boat but if we can't, the fort is our last extraction point. Do you see another way?"

Theo huffed. "No. Let's hope we're about to scare the fuck out of her and all this is for nothing."

It wouldn't be. He was going to have to completely upend her life because even if that wasn't Levi in her store right now, he would be there soon. He was coming for Kim. "You take the back. I'll go in the front."

He picked up his own gun and slid it into the holster at the small of his back, covering it with his T-shirt. He had to hope they could make it to the wharf without gunfire. He was counting on the fact that Levi didn't want a scene either. Otherwise he would have brought the police with him.

He was still trying to do this under the radar. He didn't want anyone to know he had her. Beck could use that to his advantage. Levi would come in with a smaller team than usual.

Theo followed him down the stairs. He got to the ground level in time to see Anna jogging down the street toward where her car was parked.

Good. Now they needed to hope Levi was in there alone.

Theo motioned to the back of the building and then made his way around to the alley that would lead to the rear entrance.

"I'm here." Tucker ran up the narrow, cobblestone street and leaned over, taking a deep breath. "Sorry. I don't run as much anymore. Rob's right. I'm soft."

He was glad to have Tucker around. He might not be the fastest runner, but if anyone got hurt, he wouldn't want anyone except Tucker to put his men back together.

Except Ezra.

He shook off the thought of his brother. It was only the week that was making him think of the brother he'd lost. That and the fact that he was surrounded by men who'd treated him like a brother. He prayed if any of these men ever got in trouble, they could come to him because he would not let them down.

"Theo's taking the back," he said quietly as they approached the front door of the small shop. The glass door was propped open and a man and a woman stepped out holding hands and talking about where they could get coffee. They ran down the street as the rain started in earnest. "I don't know how many we're dealing with."

"Unless someone else came in after that couple left, it's the worker, a couple, two young women, Trench Coat, who might be the evil overlord of our lives, and one other man."

Tucker was also incredibly observant. Beck touched the device in his ear. "Anna left while you were on your way. There goes the couple and the two women. So it's two men. Theo, do you copy?"

"I do." Theo's voice was steady over the line. "There's a van parked here, and I've taken out the driver. It's obvious to me they intended to smuggle her out the back. I believe this was a three-man job. I'll see you inside."

He trusted Theo's instincts. His gut knotted but he needed to go cold. Kim didn't need him to run in screaming her name.

And there was a reason they called her Solo. She was a deadly operative in her own right. Kim wouldn't panic. She would go to that place where there was nothing but the fight.

The rain had started to come down pretty hard and he moved under the awning.

There was no one in the front of the store. A laptop lay next to the cash register, but there was no gorgeous blonde standing there.

He stepped inside and pulled his gun, Tucker moving in beside him.

He gestured for Tucker to take the left and he would take the right.

As silently as he could, he started to move across the floor. It was a nightmare, a freaking labyrinth of bookshelves. He couldn't get a clean line of sight to save his life, but at least he was certain Theo would be making his way from the back.

"Hello, Solo. Long time no see."

He stopped at the sound of those words. Levi. He would know that fucking voice anywhere. Where was she? He could barely hear Levi talking, and the sound seemed to bounce around off the shelves.

He waited for the sound of Kim laughing and spitting some serious bile. She didn't get afraid. She might save them all the trouble and kill the fucker right here. Then he would help her clean up the body and beg her to let him stay with her. He could help run a bookshop.

"Please." Her voice was barely above a whisper. "Please don't do this, Levi. If you ever cared about me for even a second, you won't do this."

What the hell? Had she gotten caught without a gun? He moved along the shelf, trying to catch sight of her.

"You weren't joking," came Levi's reply. He sounded a bit shocked. "I'll have to punish you for that."

The shelf beside him shook slightly.

"How did you find me?" It shook again and he realized she was backing up, her hand on the shelf for support.

Why the hell wasn't she fighting? Did Levi have a gun on her already? Had he caught her unaware, and she needed to play innocent to try to get him off his game?

He heard a pinging sound, and then Tucker was cursing loudly and he proved his gun didn't have a silencer.

"Fuck. I should have known that little shit would hold out on me," Levi said. "Who's out there?"

He heard the sound of a fist meeting flesh.

"Solo, don't make me hurt you," Levi growled.

Beck ran down the narrow aisle, praying he hadn't gotten Tucker killed.

"I was wrong," Theo said in his ear. "Apparently the driver wasn't the only one. I'm pinned down in the alley. I've got at least three on me. All well armed and trained."

Now he was the one cursing.

"I'm on it," Tucker replied. "I took down the one on me. Beck?"

"Go." He couldn't let Theo Taggart die again.

"I'm on my way in," Robert said. "And your extraction is five minutes out. You need to be there, Beck."

Because the chopper couldn't simply hover over the giant fort. He rounded the corner and slammed into another body. Blonde hair went everywhere, and she was slapping at him.

"Kim? Kim, it's me," he whispered urgently.

Her eyes were wild, panic clear when she should be calm. He'd never seen her lose her cool during a dangerous encounter. What had the last seven years done to her?

"Hello, Beck. I should have known you would show up earlier than planned." Levi had a gun on him, or rather on her since she was in front of him.

"I'm not alone. Kim, get behind me." He took her by the elbow and moved her so if there was a bullet coming, it would hit him first. He had to give her a chance. "Run if I go down."

But she was already running. He could feel the wood floor move as she pounded against it in her haste to get away.

Levi had a huge grin on his face. "Looks like she doesn't want to see you any more than she does me."

Beck wasn't about to have a conversation with the fucker. He fired and Levi's shoulder flew back. He turned and ran because he wasn't sure how many more men Levi had. Kim could be running into a crowd of them for all she knew. She wasn't thinking.

He felt something ping by his right arm. Levi. He'd likely been wearing a vest. It's what Beck would have done had he known he was going into a freaking firefight. He should have expected it. What he really hadn't expected was that Kim would turn and flee.

She couldn't believe he was working with Levi. Did she think he was here to turn her over?

Rain pounded on him as he made it to the street. Which way had she gone?

Robert raced up to him, his clothes soaked. "My comm's out. Was that Kim I saw?"

He heard the sound of screeching tires and then Robert was hauling him out of the way as a black van nearly ran them down.

He hit the cobblestone road hard, his body banging against it in a way that made every bone ache. The van screeched to a halt, fishtailing slightly.

"Move," a voice shouted. "Get to the fort. That's where she'll run."

Levi got into the van and it started to take off. Beck got to his feet and aimed, shooting for the tires. He heard a squeal as he made contact, but the van managed to make the turn.

Theo and Tucker came out of the store.

It was a clusterfuck, but at least he hadn't gotten anyone killed.

Rob pointed back to the wharf. "She went that way. Did she not see you?"

Oh, she'd seen him and she'd still run. She'd left him to deal with Levi. She hadn't even stayed to back him up.

They were going to have a long fucking talk when he finally chased her down.

He took off because Levi wasn't going to give up and the van—even down a tire—could still go faster than they could. Luckily they would have to turn around to get to the fort, and there were no vehicles allowed past the entrance to the marina. The waterfront was pedestrian only. He had a shot to get there before Levi did.

He ran, the wind whipping against him. Tucker and Rob took a place on either side, and Theo took their six. Up ahead, he could see Kim running past the point where Levi could get her easily in the van. They would have to drag her down. He sprinted toward her, gaining ground he shouldn't have been able to. Kim had always been fast, but it looked like she hadn't kept up her training.

Why had she run? The question was there even as he gained ground on her. He heard the van slam into the parking lot behind them.

But he heard another sound. Sirens. Theo had called the police, and that meant Levi would either have to show his hand or slink away.

Or he could try to talk them into handing over the American who didn't have real papers.

He couldn't stop. He kept running, even as he made the turn that would take him to the fort. It was a steep grade to run up, but he simply kept following her. He couldn't let her get away because if he did, he might never see her again.

His lungs ached as he kept up the pace. He ignored the glances of the tourists trying to make their way down to the ground. He lost sight of her as she made another turn and then he was at the top. The battlement.

"To your left," Theo shouted over the rain.

Kim was moving onto a narrow path that led up to a gate.

He managed to catch her as the gate came open.

Her eyes went wide as he pulled her back.

"He's still coming," he shouted to her.

She tried to pull away from. "Let me go, Beck. I'll be safe inside. They can't come inside."

She thought Levi would let her hide away?

The gate ahead of them had come open, and an elderly man in shorts and a Hawaiian shirt stood there, his eyes narrowed and what was left of his hair plastered to his forehead. "Kimberly?"

"Stay back, uncle." She turned to Beck. "Please let me go."

He hated that she was begging him the way she'd begged Levi. He wasn't the bad guy here. He tugged her under the cover of the trees that lined the path to the private part of the fort. "He's on his way. He's not going to let you go."

"I'll be safe inside."

Theo stepped in. "He's talking to the cops. I think he's trying to make a case for them arresting her and letting the government sort things out."

She shook her head. "No. They can't come in here. Past that gate isn't their jurisdiction."

"We're not completely sovereign," her uncle yelled over the storm. "It might take some time, but they will get in. I can stall them, but I have no way to get you all out of here."

Maybe he was dealing with the wrong person. He turned to her uncle, certain the rest of his crew wouldn't let Kim get away. "I do. I have a chopper coming. I can get her out and we'll be off the island by tonight. I have a jet waiting."

He shook his head. "No jet. They'll go to the airport first. Tell me where you're heading and I'll send a boat to pick you up and take you to Sicily. From there you can fly. I'm not without my own resources. Kim, it's time."

She closed her eyes and when she opened them there was a deep desperation there. "Levi knows. I have to get Roman out of here, uncle."

Who the fuck was Roman? What did Levi know that he didn't?

"Hey, Levi's coming up the hill and he's got the cops with him," Tucker shouted. "Owen's almost here."

Her uncle stepped back and allowed them in.

Kim took off again even as he heard the thud of the chopper. It would be coming from the south, hooking around to approach by sea.

He started to walk in. It looked like he would have to drag her away from whoever this Roman person was. He couldn't assure the safety of some random man. Maybe it was a dog. He would be the bad guy if he made her leave her dog behind.

Her uncle stopped him, and for a moment he worried it was all a trick to keep them on the outside.

"You will take care of them, Mr. Kent?" Francis Bruno asked.

Shit. He was going to have to take them all. "Yes."

The brother nodded and allowed them all to enter. "You must hurry. Despite what many believe, Maltese law is in force here. I can keep the police at bay for an hour at most, but they will and can come in."

"I'll have her out of here in five minutes," he promised. "We'll be in Sicily tonight."

"Ezra will know where to go," he said.

"What?" Did her uncle think he still went by Ezra's name? He'd never met the man, but he was sure Kim had talked about him.

Theo pressed through before he could ask another question. "He needs to get that gate closed. We need to go."

Tucker shook his head. "Rob and I are going to stay. We'll see what he has to say. They won't find anything on us. If we get taken in, Tag'll send someone to get us out."

Theo pulled his gun and pressed it into Rob's hand. "He's right. We'll deal with the authorities. You get her out of here. Call Ian when you get wherever you're going."

He stepped back out and Francis closed the gate.

"Hurry," Francis said. "I'll slow them down, but you must leave. And Beckett, remember that forgiveness is next to godliness."

He didn't stop to ask what the brother meant by that. He had to get Kim and apparently all her friends out of here and find a way to get to Sicily in the middle of a storm. He stepped out from under the stone roof of the tunnel and onto the large plaza. It was big, and he didn't know where Kim had gone. Fuck. Was she trying to get away again?

The chopper started a descent, and he could barely see Owen in the pilot's seat. The ladder unrolled and he hoped whoever was coming with them had a steady stomach.

"Kim!" He shouted her name because they were running out of time.

She ran from behind another set of gates, and she wasn't alone. He almost felt his heart stop. She had a child in her arms. Not a baby or a toddler. He had to be five.

Or six. Yes, that kid could be six. Six years and some change.

He felt like the breath had been knocked out of him. Then he knew it had been because a man came running behind her, carrying a bag and a backpack.

The rain didn't matter. It couldn't change his vision, couldn't make him think that he was seeing a ghost. He knew that face, knew the set of those shoulders and the grim look in the man's eyes.

His brother was running toward him. *His brother.* Her uncle hadn't been mistaken when he'd spoken before. Her uncle had been talking about Ezra Fain, who was alive.

Forgiveness. This was what he'd been talking about.

Kim stopped a mere foot away and the child in her arms stared back at him, his arms around his mother's neck. "I need to know you'll protect him. I'll explain everything, but I need you to take him.

If you can't stand to look at me, take him with you. Even if you can't forgive me, please save our son. Roman, this is your dad and he's going to make sure you're safe."

This is your dad.

Kim was talking about him. She hadn't run because she was afraid of him. She'd run because she'd been desperate to get to her son. Their son.

"It's true." Ezra came to stand beside Kim. He was standing there as the rain shifted from pouring to a drizzle. "He's your son, Beck. I know you're angry with me. I promise I'll explain everything, but I need to go with you. I can get us off the island. Hate me later. Save your wife and son now."

He forced himself to move but his limbs felt numb. He didn't have time to think. Owen couldn't stay in that position for long, even though the storm seemed to be abating. They would have to move very quickly if he didn't want to get taken in. What would Levi do to this boy? "Give him to me. I'll take him up."

The child—Roman—clung to his mother, but she whispered something to him and he let himself go into his father's arms.

His son. He wrapped an arm around his son. "Hold on tight, son. I won't let you go. I promise."

Roman clung so tightly he nearly cut off Beck's breath, but he climbed that ladder.

When the chopper took off, he was still holding his son.

Chapter Ten

Kim paced the small kitchen and wondered if Beck was going to completely ignore her. How long could he do it? The wait was making her sick, and that was saying something considering the fact that she'd spent two hours traveling by helicopter and then small ship in the middle of a storm.

She'd managed to be solid through all of it. She'd made it through Owen and Jax being utterly shocked at the sight of her. Well, she thought they were pretty prepared for her. It had been the sight of Roman and the real Ezra Fain that had thrown them. They hadn't actually known who Ezra was until Beck had introduced him.

This is my brother who's supposed to be dead. He's been living with my ex and raising my child. He can get us a boat that isn't being watched by Levi Green. Work with him.

That was all he'd said. Then he'd gone into one of the bedrooms of the safe house and changed clothes. When he'd come out, they'd immediately gotten into a van and traveled to a small marina where they'd made the passage to Sicily in rough waters, and then made their way to this small townhouse. Beck had stayed in the wheelhouse with Jax. Owen had proven that while he could fly almost anything, boats were not his thing.

Ezra had taken care of him, instructing Kim on how to hold

pressure points to alleviate Owen's nausea until he'd been able to find Dramamine.

Her son had proven he was far more tired than scared. Once he'd had a blanket wrapped around him, he'd fallen asleep, and was now tucked into the little bedroom along with his uncle.

The whole time spent crossing to Sicily she'd managed to concentrate on helping Owen and watching over Roman. Now things were quiet, and she couldn't quell the questions in her head.

Why was Beck here? How the fuck had Levi found her? Who'd found her first? Because it was too much to believe that they'd both coincidentally shown up at the same time.

She'd lost it all again. No more bookshop. No more quaint school for Roman. No more afternoon teas in the sun.

She might lose her son, too.

"Hey, you okay?" Jax stood in the doorway. "We didn't get much of a chance to talk since we had to get out of Malta so fast."

Jax. She wanted to ask about River, wanted to know how the last seven years had gone for the woman she considered to be a good friend. But they hadn't parted on great terms. By the last time she'd seen River, they were friendly, but it was obvious River hadn't forgotten her lies.

"I'm okay. How's Owen doing?"

"Better, thanks to you and Ezra. He's sleeping now. Remind me not to take him white water rafting." Jax moved in, grabbing a coffee mug. "Is there enough for me?"

She was happy he wasn't worried about her drugging it. At one point he might have. "Of course. There's sugar and some creamer. It's a powder though."

Jax grinned. "Oh, I'm not picky. I'll take what I can get. I spend a lot of time making coffee over a campfire. I'm used to instant and powdered everything." He poured himself a mug. "I suspect you won't say anything more than you personally are fine. So as one parent to another, how is your son?"

She felt tears fill her eyes. There was something else she hadn't thought about. Not that she hadn't wondered over the years, but she'd grown to believe she would never see River and Jax again. Never see Ariel. "You and River have kids?"

"Yeah," he said with a glowing smile. "Two boys. My oldest turns six next month. His name is Caden, and then Rio is four. I've got some pictures on my laptop I can show you later."

She felt her heart constrict. "I love the names. Rio for River."

"Yeah, she picked Caden. I got to pick our second son's name. She was very much against it. She thinks he's either going to be a cowboy or a male stripper." Jax chuckled. "I wanted to name him after his mom."

She was not going to cry. If she let go, she might never stop. "I think it's a beautiful name. Are you still in Bliss?"

"Yes. We're still in our cabin by the Rio Grande, though we did add on. We've now got a third bedroom and a garage." Jax set his mug down. "I know. It's impressive. Nell protested my use of materials, but we have a fully functional garage."

She wanted to ask about everyone in Bliss. "It must have changed a lot over the years. I bet I wouldn't recognize it."

Jax snorted as though that was an inconceivable thought. "Nah. Everything's pretty much the same except there's a school in town now and way more kiddos. Big Tag bought a cabin and they come up a couple of times a year. There's a few new residents, but Bliss is still Bliss." He sobered. "River told me to send you her love."

She sniffled, trying to clear her eyes. "She doesn't still hate me?"

Jax reached out and covered her hand with his big one. "She never hated you. She was tossed into a world she didn't understand, and it threw her for a loop for a while. She's home and back to being River again. She wants you to know that we would both love for you to come out and spend time with us. She misses you. She'll be more excited when she finds out about Roman. I think he would like our boys."

She nodded and couldn't help but shed one of the tears in her eyes. "He would love them. He would love Bliss. Did I see Tucker and Rob? Is he still with Ariel?"

"We're all still together, though we've spread out a bit. Owen and Rebecca are in Sweden for her work. He's staying home with their two kids. I have no idea how those kids are going to survive," he said with a sparkle in his eyes. "Tucker and Roni opened a clinic in Wyoming. They're up to three kiddos. I think he's trying to beat Big

Tag's army. Theo was there. He and Erin stopped at two. They're still in Dallas."

"And Rob?" She asked about Rob, but she was really desperate to hear that Ariel was happy.

A tender expression came over Jax's face as though he knew what she was truly asking. "Ariel and Rob are still at The Garden. She had a baby ten weeks ago or I assure you she would be here. A girl they named…"

"Daraja. She always told me she would name a daughter Daraja." Oh, she wanted to meet Ari's baby girl. She would be as gorgeous and fierce and amazing as her mother.

"That's her name. I haven't met her yet but Rob's got pictures. She's beautiful. It should tell you how much they care that Rob's here."

"Did Beck ask you to help him?"

"Yes, but this is about you, too. I assure you I wouldn't have left my wife and kids if Beck had just wanted to do a job. I'm out of that life. Many of us are, but we're back here because we care about you and Beck."

"When did he stop using Ezra's name?" She'd been surprised when Owen and Jax had called him by his real name. At first she feared he'd done it because the real Ezra was alive, but neither man had hesitated or corrected themselves. They were used to calling him by his given name.

"A long time ago. We got together after it was safe for us to. Those first couple of years were rough because of the pandemic. But we kept in touch and when it was safe, we had a reunion in London and Ezra was suddenly going by Beck. I think he'd been Beck for a year by then," Jax said, his voice low. "He's a different man. He's put in a lot of work."

"Work?"

There was a sound from the doorway, and she looked up. Beck was standing there, looking all big and manly, and she wanted to wrap her arms around him and beg his forgiveness. But forgiveness wasn't Beck's strong point, and there wouldn't be any of it for her. All her sins were laid out, and she feared his vengeance might be swift.

"Jax, I just got off the phone with Tag. He's worried he's got a leak in the office now," Beck said. "If you could reach out and let him know you'll help in any way, I would appreciate it. He might need an outsider, if you know what I mean."

"Of course. I'll call. I don't think we have Wi-Fi here." Jax pushed his chair back. "Tell me we're not staying for long."

"Theo's working on it," Beck explained.

"They didn't get arrested?" She had to know if she was the reason Rob and Tucker and Theo had been thrown into jail.

"Your uncle is a quick talker," Beck allowed. "According to Theo, once Levi realized you were gone, your uncle started in on the cops and pointed out that they were working with the CIA, who have no jurisdiction. Apparently Levi had given them some kind of story that fell apart pretty fast. So the good news is our guys are safe."

Jax sighed. "And the bad news is Levi's in the wind, and he'll be looking for us. We need to move again. Do we have a way to get her back to the States?"

"I don't think Dallas is a good idea. It's the first place Levi will look," Beck replied. "And he'll have resources there. I know he's not supposed to work in the States, but he'll have friends who can."

"I wasn't thinking of Dallas. I meant she could come back to Bliss with me," Jax replied.

Her heart leapt at the thought. And then she remembered that she would be bringing Levi down on all their heads. "No. I can't go back to Colorado. It's the second place he would look. I think he knows how much I loved it there."

Beck's jaw tightened but he moved into the kitchen. "I don't think the States are going to be safe at this point. If Levi hadn't shown up, I might have taken the risk, but he knows we're involved, and he'll have eyes out. Rob is making arrangements, but he's going to need help. I set up a satellite connection for you. I assure you it's better than Wi-Fi."

Jax's eyes lit up. "Thank god. It's been a couple of hours. I don't like being disconnected."

He winked her way and then took his coffee and went back to the front room, leaving her alone with Beck.

She'd wanted him to say something, but now that they were here, she had the greatest desire to slink away and postpone this argument forever.

"Are you in love with him?"

She frowned. "Why would I be in love with Jax?"

"My brother. Are you in love with him?" Beck walked in and poured himself a cup of the dark coffee she'd brewed after she'd put Roman in bed.

"Of course not." She should have expected this. When she looked at it logically, she could understand the question. "Roman isn't Ezra's son. I was pregnant when I went to Malta, though I didn't know about it until a couple of weeks after I got there."

Beck frowned her way. "I wasn't saying that. He's obviously mine. I thought you were on birth control."

She felt herself flush. "I was. I had an implant. I was supposed to get it changed out every four years, and my four years were up. I didn't think about it and I hadn't been home in months, so I didn't get the handy reminder. Things were kind of crazy after we found all that information. It looked like my job was on the line and I was told to stay in London. So I guess I wasn't very careful."

Beck's expression softened. "He looks a lot like my dad. Ezra and I share a mom, not a dad. But you hid Ezra from me for a very long time, and when you ran, you ran to him."

"He was with my uncle. Ezra's been with my uncle for the last ten years. Before that he was, well he should tell you that story," she replied, a bit surprised he wasn't demanding a paternity test. "Have you talked to him?"

His jaw tightened and he sat down at the table, mug in hand. "I need to calm down. I say things I don't really mean when I get angry. I'm very angry right now."

She hadn't imagined he wouldn't be, though she'd rather thought he would come in yelling and threatening to burn the world. "I'll go and try to get some sleep then."

"Kim, please sit down. I have questions. I won't lose my temper. I promise."

But he had to be really angry. Volcanically angry. Still, he was here, and she had questions too. "How did you find me?"

"Hutch and Adam found you," he replied. "Hutch connected you to Francis Bruno, which led Adam to check the CCTV cameras around Malta."

She forced herself to take a deep breath because she wasn't going to cry. She'd promised herself she wouldn't cry around him again. He wouldn't view it as anything but a manipulation. "I shouldn't have bought the shop. That was my mistake. Having any kind of a life. I didn't for a long time. I stayed in the residence. I didn't actually leave it until it came time to go to the hospital and have Roman. I guess I thought no one would care after a while. Time is funny when you're stuck in one place. It goes by slow, and then one day you look up and a year is gone."

"I understand the feeling. Sometimes it feels like that day was yesterday, and others I'm sure a hundred years have passed since Paris."

There was an ocean of time between them, but she still felt like not a moment had gone by. He looked the same except for a bit of gray at his temples. She still saw the young man she'd fallen so madly in love with. This was the danger of being anywhere close to Beckett Kent. She forgot all her good sense and longed to be the twenty-two-year-old idiot she'd been when she'd fallen for him. She needed to focus on the problem at hand. "How do you think Levi found me? Do you think he followed you? Or did you follow him? He was in the bookstore before you."

"Yeah, that's my fault. We've actually been watching you for a couple of days," he admitted. "Or rather not watching you. I was starting to think you wouldn't come into town."

"Roman was sick," she told him. When his eyes flared and she realized he was about to ask a million questions, she preempted him. "It was a stomach flu. Nothing to worry about. It's going around the school system. He's very healthy."

He nodded as though her response had settled his worry. "I'm glad to hear he's all right. And that answers why we were sitting around hoping we were in the right place for days. I was careful. It's why I brought the Lost Boys with me instead of a McKay-Taggart team. I've been looking for you for years. All this time, I never stopped."

"Why?"

He went quiet for a moment. "I can't answer that now. Not fully.

I need to process all of this before I figure out how I feel. I can only tell you that I cared about what happened to you and I was sorry for how it ended. I said things I shouldn't have said. As for Levi, I'm trying to work out how he found you. He said something about someone holding out on him. I don't think he expected we would be there. I talked to Ian earlier and told him he might have a leak. I promise you I would never have come here if I thought Levi was following me. I didn't even know if I was going to make contact."

She was confused. He was going to check her out but not make contact? "So you wanted to say you were sorry?"

"Like I said I can't talk to you about that right now." He glanced around the kitchen. "Where's my brother? Is he staying in your room?"

She rolled her eyes. "I'm not sleeping with him. He's a priest. Like a real priest, with full-on celibacy and everything. Not that I would sleep with him even if he wasn't. He's my brother-in...he's like a brother to me. He's watching over Roman. He got the same bug. Probably because most of the time he takes Roman to school."

"What grade is he in? Do they have the same grades in Malta as the US?" He stopped himself. "I don't want to overwhelm you. I'm curious. That's a stupid word. I'm beyond curious. I want to know him. He's my son."

"Ask me whatever you want. I don't think I'll sleep tonight." She wasn't sure she would ever sleep again. At least not until they'd gotten wherever they were going to go and Beck left. Until she could figure out a way to start all over. For the third time.

"Because you hate seeing me again?"

"No, Beck. Believe it or not this isn't about you. I just lost everything I worked for. Seven years I've been rebuilding my life and it's all gone again. And now I have to worry about fucking Levi Green coming after my son." She was going to be totally honest with him. Lying had never worked even though she'd done it for a good cause. "I have to worry about you coming after my son."

He sat up a little straighter. "I wouldn't hurt him."

He didn't understand what she was saying. "I don't mean that. Tell me you haven't already thought about how much safer he would be with you."

"He wouldn't be any safer since I'm right here. I'm not going anywhere, so no, he won't be safer with me."

"I'm talking about later."

"I am, too. I'm not taking him away. You're his mom. I'm his dad. I only want to know him." His eyes met hers. "I want to know if he's afraid of me."

"Afraid of you?"

"Because you're afraid of me. You ran today."

"I had to get to Roman." She would never forget that moment when she'd seen Levi, but then Beck had been there. She'd promised him honesty. "I panicked when I saw Levi. I've gotten soft. So fucking soft. I panicked and I told him I had a son because in that moment I thought it might...I don't know. I thought he might have a soul and I could get to him."

"He doesn't. I know you think he was your friend, but he was always using you. Always. He's a sociopath. He realized you had things he wanted. Money. Powerful connections. But it was always about him."

"Yeah, I get it. You would think after years of my mother trying to drill that into my head I would get it."

He shook his head. "Hey, I wasn't saying that's your only value. I'm saying that's what he sees. If you remember I didn't want your money, and I definitely could have gone my whole life without meeting your family."

"Thank god I'm attractive," she said with a hard core of bitterness she hadn't felt in years.

"I'm not saying this right," Beck said softly. "I wanted to warn you about Levi. And yeah, I was attracted to how beautiful you are, but I wouldn't have married you if that was all there was. I loved you for your spirit and how you could make me laugh. I loved you because it felt like you were half of my soul."

She couldn't handle the emotion she felt at those words. It was easier to get back to the point. "When I realized having a kid wouldn't sway Levi, that he might actually hurt Roman, I made the decision to run. Not to the fort. I was going to get out of Birgu, and then I was going to leave Malta."

"What?"

193

"I was going to leave my son behind in hopes that Levi would chase after me. I knew my uncle and Ezra would take care of Roman. In those seconds I had, I knew I had to try to protect him any way I could."

"But you ran to the fort," Beck said.

"Because then I saw you and I knew I didn't have to leave Roman because one way or another, you would deal with Levi. I ran back to the fort because you were there and I had hope again."

He stood up suddenly, and for a moment she was afraid he was going to walk, but then he held out a hand.

"What?" She stared at it. They hadn't touched. She shouldn't touch him. It was one thing to be honest with him, to lay out everything she'd done and let him judge her for it, but this was too much. Touching him would bring back every feeling she'd ever had for this man, and he couldn't want that either.

"Come here. Please. I'm asking you to come here and give me something. Not because you owe me. One of the things I've learned in all of this is I count too much. I keep score, and that shouldn't have a place in my life. Our life. I'm going to ask you one thing and then I'll let it be for now. Did you lie about my brother to hurt me?"

"No. I didn't want to keep it from you, but he was so adamant. I was…"

"Hush, that's all I need to hear." His hand was still out. "Please, Kim. It's been a rough seven years."

There was something weary and open and longing in his voice, and she found herself standing up and taking his hand. He tugged her gently against him, and then she was in his arms. It was awkward for a moment as one arm went around her waist and the other held her hand. Like they were dancing.

"I promised myself if I ever got the chance, I would dance with you again," he whispered. "I didn't dance with you enough."

What the fuck was he doing? He was holding her like she was something precious, like he'd missed her with his body and his soul. He started to move like there was music in his head. "There's no music."

"Yes, there is," he insisted. "I can hear it. That song that was playing the night we got married. I wanted to go up to the room."

He'd been horny as hell. He'd wanted to get to the honeymoon part, but they'd walked through the casino and past the postage stamp dance floor. It had been a sad thing, but she'd heard a song she'd loved. "The *Twilight* song? You hate that song."

He'd groaned and whined, but he'd danced with her. He'd swayed with her through the whole song and teased her about glitter-bomb vampires, but it hadn't mattered. Because he'd kissed her and told her he loved her and would for more than a thousand years.

In that moment, the world had been laid out in front of them. Theirs for the taking. A whole future for them.

She laid her head on his shoulder as emotion flowed through her. She'd wanted that life she'd been promised in that moment when they'd danced and the rest of the world had fallen away.

"I stop every time I hear it and I think of you," he said.

"I thought you were mad at me." She brought her head up and looked into those gorgeous eyes of his. This was absolutely not where she'd expected to be when she'd woken up this morning. Hell, it wasn't what she'd expected two minutes ago.

"I don't want to be mad. This feels so much better." His hand started to smooth up her back, and he stared at her the way he always did right before he fell on her lips like a starving man. Like he could kiss her forever and still not be satisfied.

"Mama?"

She jumped away from Beck like he was a hot stove she'd touched. Her baby boy was standing in the doorway exactly where his father had stood moments before. She couldn't help but notice they had similar expressions on their faces. "Are you all right?"

Her son was staring up at Beck somberly. "Is he really my dad?"

Her heart clenched. "Yes. He's your dad and he's Uncle Ezra's brother."

Roman frowned. "Where's he been? Because we've been in trouble and he wasn't around."

"What?" Those words coming out of Roman's mouth shocked her.

"Mom, I'm not dumb," Roman said quietly. "We're not normal. We live in a fortress, and I can barely get Uncle Ezra to stop for gelato after school. Everyone in my class goes places and sees things.

195

We don't ever go on trips. Everyone goes on trips. You don't date. And you have a bunch of passports with different names for us and guns hidden in your closet."

Now she felt sick to her stomach. "Those are in a safe."

Roman shrugged. "And the combination is my birthday."

"Are you sure he's six?" Beck was watching Roman with impressed eyes.

She kind of wished she'd had a chance to grab the stuff in that safe. She also kind of wished Roman hadn't stopped Beck from kissing her. And she was equally grateful that he had. She and Beck didn't work. It was only gratitude that made her so willing to take comfort from him. "Yes, but you should understand he's pretty much got a genius-level IQ, and he's not afraid to use it."

Was that very intelligence what had caused Roman to not ask her about Beck? They'd had one conversation about who his father was. She'd told her son that she'd loved his father very much, but that sometimes love wasn't enough. At first she'd thought he didn't ask because he had plenty of male authority in his life. Now she wondered if he'd figured out it hurt her to talk about Beck.

"I don't know that he gets that from me." Beck had a little smile on his face. It was the satisfied smile he got when things went his way. He was using that smile on Roman.

"My mom is really smart," Roman replied, a bit on the defensive side.

Beck sobered. "She is. She's the smartest woman I know. She's kept you safe for years. You see your mom and I got split up. I couldn't find her and then some things happened in the world, and for a couple of years it was really hard to travel. Then I looked for her but I still couldn't find her."

"She didn't want us to be found," Roman countered. "If she didn't want you to find us, there must have been a reason. Uncle Ezra didn't want you to find us either."

"That's not true." If she was going to be honest with Beck, she had to do the same with her son. Now that Beck was here, she knew she had to facilitate his relationship with Roman. "Your uncle asked me to reach out to him a couple of days ago. I think he's felt that way for a very long time. Did he fall asleep?"

Roman nodded. "He was snoring."

Beck chuckled. "He always did that. I had to share a room with him for years. Earplugs are the only way to go." He got down to one knee and was suddenly serious. "Roman, your mom was in danger, and she ran because at the time she didn't trust me to protect her. She didn't trust me because I was very mean to her. I had problems with anger, and I took them out on your mom."

"Did you hit her?" Roman asked, his voice going low.

"No." She couldn't let him think that. "He would never hit me."

Not in any way that wasn't incredibly pleasurable. But they weren't having that conversation now.

"I did not hit your mother, but words can hurt, too," Beck replied. "I said things to your mom that I shouldn't have. If it had just been the one time, maybe she would have asked me to apologize, but I was mean to her for a long time. Did you know that your mom and I were married once?"

Roman's eyes widened. "No." He turned her way, some accusation in his gaze. "You didn't tell me you were married."

"We're not now," Beck said. "We're not married because I broke our vows. I promised to love her no matter what, and then something bad happened, something that hurt me, and I wasn't willing to love her then. Sometimes we have bad feelings inside us, and we don't know where to put them. Often we shove those feelings at people we care about because it feels like the safest thing to do. Sometimes we don't care where those feelings go. We lash out because we don't trust that we deserve the love we're given. I hurt your mom, and I'm sure she worried I would hurt you, too. Do you know what therapy is?"

She was not going to fucking cry. He'd gone to therapy? She'd asked him to go with her, to try to save their marriage, but he wouldn't. Not that it would have worked. She'd been lying to him about the very thing he'd been angry about. "I'm not without fault here."

Beck glanced up at her. "I think we should concentrate on the simple parts of what went wrong. Roman needs to understand that I screwed up and said something I shouldn't have, and then we were separated for a long time."

She thought she understood what he was trying to do. He was giving her cover with their son and trying to make this simple for Roman. She was deeply grateful because her son was getting hit with a lot. "Your father didn't know about you until today. I haven't talked to him since before you were born. The last time I saw your dad I didn't even know I was pregnant."

"Wow. That must be weird for you," Roman said with a shake of his head. "I mean, I knew I had a dad somewhere, but you didn't even know I existed. Do you need wine? When Mom is surprised at stuff, she usually drinks wine."

A brilliant smile came over Beck's face and he laughed, a sound she loved and hadn't heard in forever. "I think I'll skip the wine tonight. I'm on guard duty now. And it's not as weird as you would think. It feels...right. But we're going to take this whole dad thing at your pace. If you don't feel good about calling me Dad, you can call me Beck."

Roman turned her way as though asking her for permission.

"It's up to you," she replied, stroking over his silky hair. "It wouldn't bother me at all if you called him Dad."

Roman turned back to Beck as though considering the problem. "Someone's after my mom. Are you going to help us? You said you were mean to her. Are you going to be mean to her again?"

"I promise that I have spent the last seven years learning how to not be mean to her ever again." There was a suspicious sheen to Beck's eyes. "I promise that I will do my best to be nice to her. And I promise you that I will protect you and your mom. I've spent the last several years working for a firm that specializes in protecting people. I'm good at it. Protecting you and your mom will be the most important job I ever do."

Roman's eyes narrowed. "Were you trying to kiss my mom?"

She felt a flush go through her system. "He was only hugging me. Like I said. We haven't seen each other in a long time."

"No, I was totally going to kiss your mom," Beck countered. "Your mom is the most beautiful woman I've ever seen, and I was a fool to push her away. Don't tell her this, but I came back because I want another chance with her."

"She probably heard that," Roman pointed out.

Beck shrugged. "Sometimes it's easier to say things when we're not directly saying them."

Roman turned his little head up. "Mom, I think Dad likes you."

Before she could say anything to that, Beck got to his feet. "He's a smart kid. You hungry, son?" When Roman nodded, Beck put a hand on his shoulder. "All right. I'm going to introduce you to the joys of MREs, and by joys I mean they are not awesome but they will fill your belly. I hope I've got some mac and cheese. Otherwise, it's all goulash. I promise when we get someplace safe, I'll make you my famous barbecue."

Roman's mouth curved down. He wasn't big on trying new food. "What's barbecue?"

Beck put a hand over his heart and tossed a horrified glance her way. "What have you done to him?"

She was so confused. "We don't have a lot of barbecue on Malta."

"Also, what's mac and cheese?" Roman asked.

"Jeez, Kim, what do you feed the kid?" Beck asked.

"Healthy things," she replied.

Beck shook his head. "That stops here." He winked her way. "Come on. Let's feed you and get you back in bed. We've got a big day tomorrow."

Father and son were chatting happily as Beck looked through his pack and found the MREs.

She sat back and wondered what he was doing. Because he hadn't come back for a second chance with her. He'd had a second chance, and she couldn't risk giving him a third.

No matter how much she wanted to.

* * * *

Beck stared at the tiny couch where Kim was asleep, her arms wrapped around their son. Roman had eaten his beef goulash with minimal wincing, and luckily Beck always kept an emergency supply of candy in his go-bag. He had a bit of a sweet tooth, and it looked like his kid did, too.

His kid. God, he had a freaking kid, and he was weird and smart and had Kim's nose and his eyes.

Those eyes were Beck's dad's eyes, too, and for most of his life that would have bothered him. His old man had been cruel. He hadn't minded using his fists on anyone who irritated him. But what he'd come to realize was DNA didn't have to be the only path a man could take. He didn't have to walk around with anger in his gut all the time. Especially not when he'd realized what the anger truly was.

Fear. Anxiety. Self-loathing put there by past events that had made him feel small.

In the beginning he'd made the choice to be better for her, for the woman he'd always loved. In the end, he'd come to realize he deserved to have a better life. He was worth more than his father had given him.

How the hell had the man not loved him? There was something deeply wrong with his dad because he'd only known Roman for a few hours and he would already give his life for the kid.

Love welled up hard and fast, an emotion that was different from what he felt for Kim. It was different but no less strong.

He should be angry with her. She'd kept their son from him for six fucking years, but he couldn't find it. There was a little ember that had flared for a few hours, but it had died as he'd stood there and talked to his son. He was lying. It had died when she'd told him why she'd changed her path, why she'd gone from running away from Roman to running to him.

I ran back to the fort because you were there and I had hope again.

She wasn't completely lost to him. Not if he could bring her hope.

He still had questions. A whole lot of them. But he remembered the words he'd said to her that last day in Paris. He'd literally told her he was happy they hadn't had kids. He'd told her she wouldn't be a good mother. He'd spent years telling her he couldn't love her, couldn't forgive her. His cruelty had sent her running every bit as much as Levi's had, and he wasn't making the same mistake again.

His brother, though... His brother was a completely different story.

He could be damn mad at his brother.

He believed Kim when she said she wasn't interested in his brother in more than a familial way, but that didn't mean Ezra wasn't. He wasn't sure what his brother was up to, but he intended to find out.

"Hey." Jax came down the stairs as quietly as a big dude possibly could. He held a cell phone in his hand—one of the burners they'd brought with them. "I've got Big Tag on the line. He and Theo have worked out our next move. Rob's getting everything lined up, but Ian wanted to talk to you."

He bet Ian wanted to talk to him. He took the cell and stepped back into the kitchen, nodding Jax's way. "Thanks, man."

"Everything go okay?" Jax asked, looking over to where Roman cuddled up to his mom.

"He's smart as a whip." Beck felt a smile cross his face. "She's done a great job with him. She's kept him safe, and he seems open to having a dad in his life."

She hadn't put her anger at him on Roman. Because despite all the shit Kim had been through as a kid, she'd never taken it out on anyone else. While he'd put up walls, she'd opened her heart to him time and time again.

Could he get her to do it one more time? One more time, forever.

"You are handling this with grace, brother. I'm proud of you," Jax said.

He didn't want to think about how much those words meant to him. If he did, he might break down. For years after Ezra had "died," he'd closed himself off. Becoming part of this weird family had softened him up for good. "She had her reasons. Watch over them for me, please."

Jax nodded and sat down on the stairs as Beck walked toward the back of the small house Ezra had guided them to. According to his brother, this place, like the boat they'd taken, were owned by wealthy members of the church Ezra worked with.

His brother was a priest? That was what he'd been told. The people who'd loaned them the boat acted like Ezra was some kind of saint, though he wasn't sure what they'd said because he didn't speak Italian. He'd definitely heard them call him *Padre*. Was that a cover? Because the last time he'd checked his brother had been a soldier, and a damn good one.

Or had that been an illusion? All their lives Beck had been the rebel and Ezra had been known for his good choices. His perfection. Ezra had been the one who did everything right, the one he was supposed to look up to.

He shoved the thoughts aside and put the phone to his ear. Contemplation would have to wait.

"Hey, Ian. How are the others? We've tried to keep our communication limited in case Levi's kissed enough ass to get someone to point a satellite this way so he can listen in on us."

"Did I or did I not tell you to use a condom?"

"What the fuck is wrong with you?" But he was laughing, trying to hold it together because he should have known that would be Tag's reaction. "And if I had I wouldn't have a super-smart kid and an excellent way to get back into his mother's good graces."

Tag was quiet for a moment. "You're really not upset about this? I was worried about your reaction. Finding out you're an instadad can be stressful."

"Upset about my son? No. Maybe it'll hit me later on that I lost all those years with him, but right now all I can think about is how much time we've got ahead of us. I'd given up hope of us having a kid. Hell, I didn't even know if I would ever see her again, much less have a chance at a family." He paced the hallway. "It's not that I'm not upset. I am, but I'm also excited at the thought of him. So I have to choose which one is going to win. I think I'm going to go with being happy to have a kid. But it's a cautious joy. Levi knows about him."

"Yeah, I was told he's on Levi's radar." There was a pause over the line that let him know Ian was being careful about what he said next. "How is your brother?"

"He's sleeping like a baby, and I might have to go fix that." He wasn't sure he was going to wait until morning to have this out.

"So he's still alive."

"I haven't killed him." The *yet* was implied.

"Can we talk about this now?" Tag asked expectantly.

He was fairly certain Tag had been waiting to have this particular conversation for years. "You investigated my brother's death."

"Of course I did. After Solo went missing, I did some checking. I think what she told you was true. I think Levi had an open investigation into one military unit that had some unsavory connections. You know as well as I do that soldiers are human beings, and that means there's a small portion of them who are bad and who use their position to evil ends. I think your brother fell in with a group of them."

He'd done some of his own poking. "And only his untimely death stopped Levi from potentially prosecuting him or using it to fuck with me."

"I don't know exactly what happened, but I think that's a safe assumption," Tag replied. "The question is why wouldn't Solo tell you. I worry about that particular answer."

"Because my brother asked her not to." He'd worked it out over the long hours in the boat. "Because my brother was ashamed, and he would rather die than let anyone know he wasn't perfect. If I'm being honest, he would rather have died than let me down. I don't know if you know this, but back then I was kind of a righteous asshole. I held him to an impossibly high standard."

"Dude, Kai deserves a medal. I told Jax he had to keep you from murdering your brother."

He sighed. "I'm not going to murder my brother. I might beat the shit out of him for putting my wife in that position, but then Kim is used to men putting her in the middle and fighting like dogs over her."

"A little beatdown between brothers never hurt anyone," Tag suggested. "Well, it hurt Sean, but he's a chef."

Beck rolled his eyes despite the fact Tag couldn't see the reaction. "Yeah, he's so delicate."

Sean Taggart was known as the Soldier Chef. He'd been the host of several television shows and had a network of restaurants across the US. Ian was a somewhat silent partner who'd made a ton of money backing his baby brother.

"You would be surprised," Tag said with a chuckle. "Jax tells me everyone's all right, and I've been in touch with some of my friends at the Agency. Apparently they are unaware that Levi took a side trip. According to my friends, Levi's scheduled to be back in DC tonight. But obviously we'll want confirmation. He's a slippery fucker. I'm sorry we didn't catch him going into Malta."

Ian couldn't have eyes on Levi at all times. "I missed him, too. I watched the fucker walk into her store and didn't realize it was him. Do we have a theory about how he found her? Does he have eyes on me?"

"Even if he did, we were careful. We covered our tracks. The only way he has eyes on you is from inside. And I don't even want to think about that. I will, but damn. Alex, Li, and I have been up here all night looking for bugs. So far we've got nothing. Hutch is going to do a deep dive on our computer systems. We'll figure out who's working with him. I trust my old guys implicitly. I've got a couple of new hires we'll have to look at."

He liked the whole crew, including the new hires. But something had gone wrong. "Are Theo, Tucker, and Rob really okay?"

How would he ever look Erin, Roni, and Ari in the eyes again if he'd gotten their husbands thrown in jail?

"Yes, they're at the safe house closing it up and getting ready to move. Apparently Solo's uncle has serious connections. The police didn't want to fuck with him, and once they called back to the station, Levi left and fast. According to Theo, he's got proof that Levi boarded a plane that's supposed to head to the States. He could turn around, but he's not welcome in Malta for now."

"You think we should go back?" They definitely couldn't stay here for long.

"No," Tag replied. "I think you should do what Theo tells you to do. He'll be there with the plane tomorrow afternoon. Hold down the fort until then. Talk to you soon." The line went dead.

He slid the phone back in his pocket and found himself standing outside his brother's room.

His brother was behind that door snoring away, and Beck was standing out here fighting the need to talk to him, or beat the crap out of him, or hug him and tell him how much he'd fucking missed him. How hard the years without him had been.

But then Ezra had known where he was for a whole lot of years. Ezra had been raising Roman with Kim. His son was sleeping on a couch while Ezra took the only bed in the place.

That didn't sit well with him. Oh, sure he'd started out watching over Roman while Kim stayed up, but that wasn't the way it ended. It wasn't the way it was going to end.

It was time to start taking back his life.

He pushed through the door. "Get up."

Ezra's eyes flew open and he sat straight up in bed. "What?" He looked around like he could find the threat. "What's happening? Where's Roman?"

The threat was standing right in front of him. He was so ready to give his brother a beatdown, but it would have to wait. "My son and wife are sleeping on a way too small for the two of them couch while you're all comfy in here. Somehow that doesn't seem fair to me."

Ezra was up on his feet in a heartbeat. He shoved his socked feet into sandals. Freaking sandals. The last time he'd seen his brother, he'd been a Marine with a perfectly kept high and tight and clean-shaven face. Now it seemed like he was trying to look like his boss, with shoulder-length hair and the beginnings of a beard. He looked older. There were lines around his eyes that hadn't been there before. Ezra's hair was starting to gray, silver shooting through the dark brown. He was thinner than he used to be, lean but not without strength.

"Kim was supposed to wake me up when she wanted to go to bed. I never meant for her to sleep on the couch. I was going to take that chair so someone would be in here with them," his brother admitted. He pointed to a small chair that would have been incredibly uncomfortable.

As much as he wouldn't mind his brother being tortured in that thing all night, he had other plans. "You can take the couch in the living room."

"Beck, we should talk."

Beck shook his head. "No. We should have talked years ago. We should have talked when you got into trouble. We should have talked when you decided to blow up your life and my marriage."

"It wasn't like that." Ezra winced. "Not exactly."

He pointed his brother's way. "Did you or did you not ask my wife to keep your secrets from me? Did you beg her? Did you tell her you wouldn't be able to live knowing I knew how low you'd gotten?"

It was the only explanation. He knew Kim. She didn't like

keeping secrets from him. She'd gotten good at it over the years, but only when it came to her job. After he'd been burned by the Agency, she'd been bound by her oath to keep some of those secrets. And even then she'd walked a razor's edge to help him.

It was funny what time and distance and a mega shit ton of therapy could do for a guy's vision. It sharpened and softened all at the same time.

Ezra got a stubborn glint in his eyes, the one he used to get when their parents would push him. Just like back then, it died and he sighed. "It wasn't that simple, but yes. Yes, I did all of that."

"And you've known where I was for all these years. You could have dropped me a line, maybe an email telling me I have a son."

"I know you're not going to believe this, but I wanted to," Ezra countered. "I've wanted to contact you for a while now. Kim thought it was a bad idea. I think she was afraid you would be angry with her."

He shook his head. That wasn't what she'd truly been afraid of. "She was afraid I wouldn't care at all. She was wrong and she understands that now. This isn't about her. It's about you and whether or not I'm going to punch you in the face."

Ezra only backed up a little. "Is that all you're thinking about doing?"

"Jax has explicit instructions to not let me kill you. I don't want to get him in trouble, and that's the only reason I haven't strangled you. Now get a move on. I'm bringing Roman and Kim in here. You can sleep on the couch and that way if anyone shows up to kill us all, they get you first and I'll have time to get my family and run. See, you're already serving a purpose."

"Beck," he began.

Beck shook his head. "I can't tonight. Not with you. We'll talk at some point, but understand that right now you're here because Kim wants you here. I have a plane coming tomorrow and if you want to take that boat right back to Malta, you should feel free."

"I'm not leaving. I know it's hard to believe but I've missed you. I can't think of why right now, but I have." Ezra yawned behind his hand. "But maybe I should stay in here and watch over them."

Beck stared at him.

"Oh, you're going to sleep in the chair. Got it. And you know you called her your wife, right?" Ezra pointed out. "She's under the firm belief that you're divorced."

He wasn't planning on sleeping in the chair at all. He was going to start winning his wife back, and he wasn't about to do it by getting a crick in his neck. He was going to show her how good it was to have a partner she could truly count on. He was going to be Roman's dad. "She'll be my wife again at the end of this if I have any kind of say in it."

"I thought you would be furious with her."

"Yeah, that's the general consensus." Well, he'd known he had a reputation. "How about I try to repair my marriage and get my family back and I be furious with you."

A ghost of a smile tugged his brother's lips up. "I can handle that. But if you're going to punch me, you need to understand that I took vows. I can't punch you back. I'll have to turn the other cheek."

He wouldn't let that stop him at all. "Good."

"Seriously? You would punch a priest."

"If he's my brother, yes. What am I supposed to call you? Father Ezra? Not happening."

"Father Kent," Ezra admitted with a shrug. "That's the name I've used. Ezra Kent."

He snorted. At least they still thought along the same lines. "That's a stupid name. You should have picked something cooler."

"Says the man who literally used my name for decades." Ezra sounded more like Ezra in that moment than he had the whole time. The whiny teen he'd been came out, and it pierced Beck through the heart that his brother was alive. Alive.

That didn't mean he had to forgive him. "I was honoring you. I thought you'd died in battle."

"I think you were trying to avoid being Mr. Black or whatever stupid color name the Agency wanted to pin on you. Mr. Vermilion or something." Ezra followed him out into the hall and stopped at the sight of Kim and Roman cuddled up on the couch. He stared at them for a moment. "He's a special kid."

And he suspected Ezra had something to do with that. "Kim said something about you walking him to school."

"Almost every day. It's on my way to the hospital where I spend most of my time. Spent. I'm not sure what I'll do now. Maybe go to jail. It's okay. I can do good work there, too."

"I'm not sending you to jail." His brother was too invested in his own drama. "But you need to understand that she's mine."

Ezra cocked a brow. "She's her own person."

"Who's going to be my wife. And I'll be her husband. Don't pull that 'I'm trying to own her' crap. She can be incredibly possessive, too."

"That wasn't the problem with our marriage." Kim's eyes opened. "Could you two keep it down? He's tired."

"Pick him up and take him to the bedroom, please," he instructed his brother.

Ezra moved in and easily lifted Roman up. He arched a brow Beck's way as though asking him why he couldn't carry his own son.

"I can get him," Kim said, starting to ease off the couch.

He couldn't pick up his son because Kim should know she was important, too. She looked adorably disheveled as he reached down and picked her up, hauling her against his chest. "You're tired, too. We're taking the bed and my brother can suck it."

Ezra groaned but disappeared into the bedroom with Roman.

"*We're* taking the bed?" Kim asked. "You know I can walk, right?"

"Why should you? And yes, I meant *we* as in you and me and Roman. I don't want the two of you alone." He walked them through the doorway as Ezra was placing Roman in the middle of the only slightly larger than a double bed. "Even in a room. Don't worry, baby. I won't try to kiss you again until you ask me to."

"Like that's going to happen." But she was relaxed in his arms as he settled her on the bed.

It would. She'd wanted him to kiss her tonight. Her head had tilted up and those gorgeous lips had parted the tiniest bit to welcome him home.

He grabbed a blanket and pulled it over Kim and Roman, making sure they would be warm and comfortable. "I promise when we get wherever we're going I'll make sure you both have proper PJs and toothbrushes and stuff."

She yawned. "I used yours. Roman was thrilled to not have to brush his teeth." She frowned. "I am tired. I wasn't going to tell you I did that."

He didn't mind at all. She'd always used his toothbrush when she'd forgotten her own, and that had happened more than once. As he'd usually spent time with his tongue on every part of her body, he hadn't seen it as a hygiene thing. They'd been married.

It was so easy to fall back into patterns when he wasn't being an asshole to her.

He reached down and touched her hair. "Go to sleep. I'll be right on the other side of our son."

"I'll apparently be outside with the computer guy waiting to be used as a human shield." Ezra was standing at the door like he was still going to try to sleep on that chair.

"Jax is good with a gun, too. He'll protect you and shit. Go to the couch." He pushed his brother out and closed the door in his face.

"That was rude," Kim said, but she was settling in, her hair spread out behind her.

He'd missed all that hair. "He should get used to it." He turned off the lamp on the nightstand and eased his body down on the bed, tucking the blanket around his son. "I promise I'm going to take care of you. I know I didn't back then, but I'm a different man now."

In the moonlight he could see her eyes close. "You're still bossy as hell. Tell Big Tag to send moisturizer. My skin's not as young as it used to be."

He couldn't tell. She looked luminous in the silky moonlight.

In seconds she was breathing deeply, slowly, as she fell asleep.

Beck laid there in bed watching them sleep, perfectly content for the first time in decades.

He would win her back. He wouldn't stop until she said yes to him again.

Chapter Eleven

"Uncle Ezra used to play football? That's weird."

Beck scooped the eggs onto his son's plate, a sense of satisfaction running through him. He didn't feel this way when he cooked for himself. He usually felt annoyed because it meant he didn't have time to stop and pick something up. He was a serviceable cook.

"It wasn't weird." Ezra pulled up a chair, ruffling Roman's hair as he sat down. "Except that we called it soccer because football means something different in the States. And you're lucky because you're getting your dad's special eggs. He used to cook them for me when our mom was too busy."

"There's not a lot special about them. A little butter and milk. That's pretty standard." He didn't want to think about the fact that he'd taken care of his brother for years while their parents had worked. It was him cooking breakfast or they ate cereal every day and then his brother whined until lunch.

"They were special to me because my brother cooked them," Ezra replied. "They were a blessing."

"I only have enough for Kim." He wasn't letting his brother con him into making him breakfast. If he'd wanted breakfast, he would have been alive all these years.

Ezra nodded. "It's fine. I'm used to fasting. It's a good way to contemplate the blessings of food."

Roman's eyes went from Ezra and then back to him, as though he was watching a fascinating tennis match. It was a good reminder that they weren't alone, and his sarcasm wasn't going to help anything at this point.

Which was sad because he had several very sarcastic responses to his brother right now.

"Sorry. Owen's already been up, and after his unfortunate seasickness incident, his appetite came back with a vengeance," Beck explained. "He was the one who went to the store down the street. There are some croissants if you want them, and a couple of pieces of fruit. Unless you're serious about fasting."

If his brother got left behind because they had to run and he was contemplating his blessings, then that was just what had to happen.

Ezra reached across and grabbed a banana. "I probably should keep my energy up."

Roman set down his small glass of milk. "Who is the man who wants to hurt my mom?"

"Don't worry about that," Ezra began.

"His name is Levi Green." Being told not to worry would likely make Roman worry more. "I'll show you a picture of him. I want you to memorize his face because if you ever see it, I want you to run and hide, and if he comes close you scream as loud as you can and get someone to help you."

"Beck, I'm trying not to scare the kid," Ezra said with a frown.

"Fear is a gift sometimes. Fear can keep you alive." He wasn't going to sugarcoat it and leave his kid in the dark. "Levi Green is a man who hates your mother. He'll tell you he cares about her, but he's lying."

"Like the devil lies?" Roman asked.

The devil's best lies were always grounded in the truth. He and Levi did have that in common. "I've thought of him that way often. But I do promise you that I'm going to take care of the situation this time."

He wasn't sure how. Levi was more untouchable than he'd ever been. He'd lain awake the night before and thought about all the ways he could assassinate the fucker. Or pay someone to since he was out of practice.

Or he could put his brain to use and find a way to nail him for every crime he'd committed. Levi might have a lot of powerful people in his corner now, but if he could find real proof, they would all back away. That was the trouble with powerful people. They often had a lot to lose.

"Are we going to stay here?" Roman asked. "Am I going to ever see my Uncle Francis again?"

His heart clenched at the fear he heard in his son's voice. He knelt down beside him. "I don't know that we'll be going back to Malta any time soon, but I do promise that your Uncle Francis is fine, and you will see him again. In fact, when we have a secure line, your mom can call him."

A look of relief crossed Roman's face. "Good, because I think he'll be lonely. So what am I going to do about school? I still have two weeks left."

"I think we're going to have to call it a year. In the States school is already out," he admitted. "I'm sorry. Are you going to miss your friends?"

Roman's face fell. "I don't have a lot of friends. They think I'm weird."

"It's because you're so smart," Ezra replied as though they'd had this conversation more than once. "They're jealous that you do so well in school and they struggle."

"No, I think it's because I'm weird. I'm not good at sports," Roman said. "But I know lots of science stuff, and I apparently talk about it too much and use big words. I can't help it that I have an expansive vocabulary."

Ezra smiled Roman's way, but his words were directed at Beck. "We do word of the day. We've done it since he was two years old. His teacher tells me he's got the most mature vocabulary of any student she's ever had."

"Not that it helps me win friends." Roman looked down at his eggs.

"You don't need to win friends," Ezra insisted.

"How many kids were you around before you started school?"

Beck had an idea of why Roman didn't fit in. Kim would have kept him close during those first years. She wouldn't have dropped him off at a daycare or arranged playdates. She would have put everything she had into protecting her son. Their son.

"I didn't really meet many kids until school," Roman admitted. "Uncle Ezra was my friend."

"Uncle Ezra was a geek. He is not the person who should be teaching you how to be cool. He was a geek in school, and when he gets the chance to pick a cover, he becomes a priest."

Ezra sent him a death stare.

Beck wasn't backing down. "You could have become anything. You chose priest."

"It's not a cover. It's a calling, asshole." Ezra frowned. "I'm sorry I cursed, Roman. Your father pushes me."

"All I'm saying is making friends can be taught," Beck explained. "The social aspects of school can be as important as the academic ones."

"Can you teach me?" Roman asked.

He hoped he had the chance. He wasn't sure how long they would be hiding. Once it was safe, he didn't know if Kim would want to take their son back to Malta to resume their lives there. He would have to move. "Of course. I would love to help out. I'm around a lot of kids. All my friends have kids. Well, most of them."

"Can I meet them?" Roman asked, his eyes bright.

"Sure. At some point. I don't think we'll be able to go back to Dallas right away. We need to make sure your mom is safe." He didn't know what Kim wanted to tell Roman about her situation. Somehow he didn't think telling Roman that his mom could be arrested at any moment would make him any less afraid.

"Where do you think we'll go?" The question had come from his brother rather than his son, but they were both looking at him like he was the authority figure in the room.

"Can we hide at the place that has all the Harry Potter stuff?" Roman asked. "We can dress like wizards and maybe Levi Green won't know we're there."

A chuckle caressed his ears and went straight to his cock. He loved that husky laugh of hers. He turned and she was standing in the doorway, all soft and tousled. She was wearing the same clothes from the day before, but she'd washed the makeup off. She was gorgeous with or without makeup, but she looked younger like this, looked so close to the young woman he'd fallen head over heels for.

"I don't think an amusement park is what your dad is thinking of," she said, moving over to their son. She leaned over and kissed his head. "Did your dad make those eggs?"

Roman grinned up at her. "Yeah, and he saved some for you. He wouldn't let Uncle Ezra have any."

Kim sent him a suspicious look. "Somehow I don't think that was all about me. I can have a croissant."

"It is absolutely all about you," Beck promised her. "You haven't eaten. You need some food, and I'm going to make sure you get it."

"Are you?" Her shoulders squared. It was her goddess warrior, I'm-not-letting-some-man-tell-me-what-to-do pose.

He placed the plate in front of an empty seat. "I'm hoping if you eat, maybe Roman will, too."

She sat down and her fork was in her hand pretty damn quick. "We should all have a good breakfast. It's going to be a long day." She turned back to Beck once she was comfortable their son was eating. "Have you heard from Theo yet? Do you know where we're going?"

Owen and Jax were in the office upstairs making all kinds of arrangements. "I think we'll either be going to England or a country called Loa Mali."

"That's where the Green King lives," Roman said around a mouthful of eggs. "He makes solar panels and green cars."

"He's also a personal friend of my boss." He'd thought about it all night and decided Ian would be looking at either moving them to Loa Mali or to somewhere Damon Knight controlled, and that would likely mean England.

He wanted to go home. It was funny because when he'd bought the three-bedroom house on the same road as Theo Taggart's, he'd done it as an investment. It had never truly felt like a home, but now he wanted to take Roman there. He wanted to show him the tree in the back that would be perfect for a treehouse, and where they could put a swing set. The yard was big enough for a dog to run around in. Did

Roman like dogs?

"I don't know that's a good idea," Kim said. "I've been following a lot of what King Kashmir and Queen Dayita have been doing lately. They're trying to get the US to join them on a couple of important initiatives. My presence could stall those talks."

"I don't intend to let anyone know about your presence." There were definite advantages to being in a country in the middle of the Indian Ocean where the government would be friendly to what they needed. If they went to England, the Brits would absolutely turn Kim over if they caught her. They'd already done it once.

"I still think it could cause serious problems," Kim argued.

"Let's not borrow trouble," Ezra said. "I think we should all take a positive attitude. Wherever we end up, that's where God wants us to go."

"I'll go where Tag tells me to go," Beck deadpanned. "He's got a god complex, after all. And what's this *we* stuff? Don't you have a church to clean or something? Confessions to hear?"

"I don't have a congregation. I'm a liaison to the Order, and I work in the hospital," Ezra replied. "I help Brother Francis whenever I can. I also do work with medical charities across Africa and the Middle East."

"Mom would be proud." Except of the whole drug-addict-had-to-fake-his-own-death part. "You should go do those things."

His brother's jaw tightened. "I'm not leaving Kim and Roman."

"What are you going to do for them? Pray? Because last I heard prayer probably won't stop bullets," he shot back.

Roman's eyes widened. "Someone's going to shoot us? He wants to shoot my mom?"

If looks could kill, he would be struck down immediately because Kim's stare was brutal. "Of course not, baby. Your father is angry with his brother and he can't help but try to twist that knife. Beck, could I have a moment?"

It would be way more than a moment. It would be a long lecture about what complete shit he was at parenting.

"Roman and I will clean up the kitchen," Ezra offered. "We can make a game out of it."

Roman didn't look like he would find anything fun at this

moment. Beck felt his son's eyes on him as Kim strode out into the living room. The minute he followed her, she turned on him, pointing a finger his way.

"How could you do that? He's very smart. Do you know what that means? He internalizes his fears, and you just gave him a huge one."

"I'm sorry. I shouldn't have said it. You're right. I was lashing out at Ezra and I did what I always do. I ended up hurting someone I didn't mean to. How do I reassure Roman?"

Kim stared at him for a moment like she hadn't understood a single word that had come from his mouth. "You can't joke about those things around Roman."

"I won't. I promise. I'm new at this. I need your help. The last thing I want to do is scare our son more than he already is, but we also have to prepare him for what might happen. He can't be in the dark about this. I want to take your lead, but I've been that little boy who knew something was terribly wrong only to have my parents tell me I was crazy." They'd sworn nothing was wrong right up to the moment they divorced and he got hauled halfway across the country. He hadn't missed his father, and it had all been for the best, but he'd come to realize that having his instincts questioned so early in life had an effect on him. "We need to talk about how we're going to handle Roman's questions during this time. It's obvious he's known something was wrong for a while."

Her arms crossed over her chest. "So this is all my fault?"

She needed to understand he wasn't fighting with her. He got it. This was how all their difficult discussions had gone before. She was merely following their old template. He got mad. She got defensive. They retreated to their corners and started all over again.

He wasn't going by their old playbook. He moved in and put his hands on her shoulders. "Not at all. He's an amazing kid and that's because he's got an amazing mom. That kid adores you. I want to earn his love, but I know what it means to have my parents gaslight me. I'm sure my mom would have said it was for my own good, but what it actually did was made me doubt everything she said to me. It made me doubt my own instincts. You should know I promised Roman I would show him a picture of Levi Green so he would know what the man who wants to hurt his mom looks like."

She relaxed and her gaze softened. "Yes, he needs to know who to look out for. I've been avoiding this talk. I should have had it when he started school."

"It's a hard talk to have."

"He's just so smart, and he can get anxious. When the school did a unit on global warming he made himself sick worrying about it. I can't imagine what this is going to do to him."

He followed his instincts now, the very ones he used to doubt. He pulled her into his arms. "We can talk about it and make some plans, and then sit down with him and discuss it as a family."

Her arms went around his chest, holding him tight. "I'd like that." Her head tilted up. "Beck, I know I didn't say it earlier, but I missed you, too."

"Beck?" Jax was walking down the stairs, followed by Owen.

He was never going to get his lips on hers. He sighed and stepped back. From the grim look on those faces, they were in for bad news.

"What's going on?" He kept his voice down. He didn't want to scare Roman more than he already had.

"Ian's on a satellite call, and he's not alone," Owen replied as Jax set up the laptop on the small coffee table. "Solo, you might want to stay out of sight."

A shiver went up Beck's spine. "What does that mean?"

"It means Levi Green just walked into McKay-Taggart and he wants to talk," Jax explained.

Kim's hand was suddenly in his. "He's in Dallas?"

"Yes, and he's been a busy boy." Owen scowled down at the laptop like he could see Levi through it. "He's doing all of this so he can get a look at her. We shouldn't give it to him."

"We shouldn't be talking to him at all." Why the hell had Ian let the fucker in?

"I can tell Ian we've got technical problems," Jax offered. "But he seemed to think this was important."

Then he wanted to get this over with. "You bounced the signal around?"

Jax rolled his eyes. "I'm not so out of practice that I would forget to do that. We're secure."

"Can you record it?" Kim asked. "I'd like to replay it. He's got some tells, if I remember correctly."

"It's already recording." Jax pressed a key on the laptop. "And we're live."

He glanced over at Kim, who was watching the back of the laptop like it was a snake that might bite her. She nodded, giving him the okay.

He took a deep breath and moved to the couch, sinking down and looking at the screen. "All right, Tag. You want to tell me why you haven't murdered him and buried his body?"

Levi was sitting in the conference room. Annoyingly enough, he was in the seat Beck usually chose. Ian sat beside him, looking like he could chew someone up and spit them out. But it was the addition of Mitchell Bradford that made Beck curious. Mitch was Big Tag's lawyer.

"You're asking me why I'm sitting my ass here at fucking three in the morning? That's what you're asking?" Tag growled out.

Levi ignored Tag and leaned forward. "Where's Solo? Don't try to lie to me, Ezra."

Tag looked Levi's way. "Catch up, asshole. He goes by his real name now. The Agency fucked him up, but I fixed him. Call him Beck or Mr. Kent or anything but Ezra. I don't want to hear that name out of your mouth."

So Levi still didn't know Ezra was alive. Excellent. Tag was telling him to stay away from that name. "How about you tell me why I'm talking to you? As for Kim, she's not here. She's someplace safe, and she's going to stay there."

"If she'd given me a second of her time, I could have told her the good news," Levi said with a frown. "You wouldn't have been forced to play out that horrible scene. Where exactly did you get that chopper? It was unexpected, and honestly, I think you're compensating for something."

"Good news?" He would ignore all the insults and get to the important part of what Levi was saying. This was all some kind of a trick.

Ian stared at the camera, his expression completely serious. "He's brought a presidential pardon with him. Solo can't be prosecuted for anything she did during her time with the Agency. She's a completely free woman."

And just like that Levi had pulled the rug out from under him.

* * * *

She was free? She didn't even think about what Beck had asked her to do. She moved in front of the camera. "What kind of game is this?"

Beck cursed under his breath while a deeply satisfied smile crossed Levi's face.

"Hello, Solo. I knew you were there. Beck wouldn't let you out of his sight. I'll be honest, I've wondered for years if he actually knew where you were. After what happened yesterday, I suspect the answer is no," Levi said. "And as for what kind of game I'm playing, I'm not playing anymore at all. The pardon is real. Your frozen accounts have been released, and while the Agency feels it would be best if you parted ways, they will not give you a bad recommendation if you choose to go back to work."

No. This was some kind of a trick. He wouldn't let her go so easily. She hadn't spent seven years of her life in hiding so Levi could simply free her.

"Solo, why do you think I got Mitch up at this unholy hour?" Tag asked. "I wanted to make sure this was on the up and up before I said a word. He's looked at it and he believes it's real. I got some of your old friends on the phone and they made some calls. They've verified this is legal."

"What he means is he called former president Hayes, who called the current president," Levi explained. "All because apparently no one here has any trust in government."

Mitch held up the piece of paper. "This is real, and you cannot be prosecuted or punished in any way legally."

"But we have to understand this fucker is likely planning something," Tag added.

Levi frowned his way.

"Yes, he was willing to do anything to get a look at you again," Beck said between clenched teeth. "Which was precisely why I didn't want you to show your face. It rewards him."

But she'd needed to see Levi to know if he was lying. "I'm sorry, but it's my freedom we're talking about here."

And Roman's. His future was on the line, and that was something she'd put off thinking about because she hadn't had the answers. Everything changed if she wasn't in hiding, if she could live out in the open.

"And I'm giving it to you," Levi said, his face softening. It was his persuasive face. It made her want to punch him, but then she pretty much always did. "Solo, if you'd given me a chance earlier, I would have told you that I'm not the same man you knew. I know I've done some things in the past that hurt you and I'm sorry. Please allow that seven years can change a man."

Like he could change. "I don't need a pardon. I didn't do any of those things you said I did."

"I never said you did anything, sweetheart. The data did," Levi corrected. "I was always going to get you out of this. Beck didn't give me the chance. Beck nearly got us all killed. And he never even thanked me for not having him locked up. I could have, you know. The truth is I stopped looking for you years ago. I even rescinded the bounty I had back then. You could have been free for a very long time."

She seriously doubted that. Every word that came out of his mouth was a lie, and he hadn't changed at all. "You told me you were going to use McDonald's drug on me. Did you think I would forget that?"

"Solo, I would never do that, and the fact that you're making up some ridiculous story makes me ache inside. How would I even have McDonald's drug?" He managed to sound truly wounded. "I know you probably told Beck that because he hates me and you needed him on your side. But it hurts. We were friends once."

"You fucking liar." She wanted to go through the screen and strangle him.

Beck put a hand on her leg. "Kim, the walls are thin."

Roman could probably hear her. She took a deep breath and forced herself to calm down, her attention still on that screen. "I know what you said to me that day."

"I said a lot of things," Levi admitted. "You know how interrogations work. I needed to get to the heart of what happened. I'll be honest—I was shocked and angry at what I saw on those reports. I felt betrayed, and if I lied to scare you, my anger was the reason. I should have calmly sat down and asked you to explain why you did it. I should have honored our friendship."

"We never had a friendship."

His lips pursed. "I'm sorry you think that way. As for why I'm doing this now, well, I think we both need closure. Nothing good can come out of prosecuting you. The Agency needs to move on from McDonald's case. I need to move on from you. At one point I thought I was in love with you. I now know what real love is. I'm getting married to a lovely young woman who understands me in a way you never could. I'm going to put this whole part of my life behind me and move on. I hope you can do the same." Levi stood up and straightened his suit. "Gentlemen, I've done everything I can. Solo, I hope you enjoy your new life with your son. Beck, I'm going to pretend like yesterday didn't happen. I wish you both the best of luck."

He stood and walked out of the camera's range.

Ian nodded to someone off screen, and she heard the swish of a door closing. "He's gone. I'm going to keep eyes on him until he leaves the city. You need to understand that I vetted that document. I really did make the former president of the United States call up the current one to ensure Levi isn't pulling a fast one. You are no longer under threat of prosecution."

She could go home? She could go back to Malta and have her bookshop and Roman could go back to school.

But there was zero way Levi let her go.

"So we need to figure out what we're going to do," Ian was saying. "Because he's planning something. I don't know what it is, but he's got something up his sleeve, and we all know he could wait a long time before he springs the trap. It could be days or months or fucking years, man. I think it's time we flat-out assassinate that fucker."

Mitch shook his head. "Dude, not in front of the lawyer. How many times do we have to go over the fact that you can't plan murders around me?"

"The only reason I didn't do it today was his entourage of soldiers," Ian admitted, ignoring the attorney the same way he apparently ignored legal advice.

"I've thought the same thing." Beck stared at the screen. "We should take him out. I'll take the fall if we get caught."

"We're not assassinating him." At one point she'd thought about doing it herself. She'd even planned it out. Then one pregnancy test had changed everything, and she wasn't going to lose Beck now that she'd just found him again. Found him for Roman. Roman would be hurt if his father went to jail. "I need some time to think."

"Think on the plane," Tag commanded in that I'm-the-boss-of-the-world way of his. "Theo should be landing soon. He's bringing you all back to Dallas. The best thing we can do is act as normally as we can while we try to figure out what Green's doing."

"Normal for me is on Malta." Though it seemed odd to think about going back. How could she resume her regular life?

"No," Beck said. "That was where you hid."

"It's where I made a home." She said the words, but she didn't really believe them. She hadn't made a home. She'd taken a room in a place that didn't belong to her, that could have gotten her uncle in trouble. She could move them over the bookshop.

She didn't want to leave Beck.

Not even one day back in his company and she didn't want to leave him. She wanted the excuse of fear to force her to stay.

That was what Levi had done. He'd taken away her need for protection. He was forcing her to make the decision to stay or leave.

"Solo, the very least you need to do is come to Dallas for the time being," Ian said. "The case against you is done, but I want to figure out why there was a case in the first place. If he did it, he had a reason, and we need to figure out why."

"Or I should take the fact that he's walked away as my cue to do the same." What if the war was over? Not that she thought Levi was telling the truth, but he did have the power he'd always wanted. What if that was enough for him? "Maybe he has what he wants, and he knows keeping this war going could cost him. You know a man with something to lose is far easier to deal with than a desperate one."

"Ian, we'll be on that plane," Beck announced. "She'll stay with me at my place until we can figure out what we're doing."

"Excellent," Ian replied. "I'll see you here tomorrow. I'll have one of the guys go out to your place and make sure your security system is working at full capacity. Send me a list of whatever else you need and someone will go shopping. I don't want Solo walking around Dallas for a little while, and I definitely want someone with the kid until we figure out how to quietly off Levi."

"Agreed. See you soon," Beck replied, and the screen went dark. "Jax, can you pull up the replay? I want to go over everything he said again."

"I'll do you one better." Jax had a remote in his hand. "I finally got the Wi-Fi working and I can throw it to the TV screen so we can all watch it. I'm going to send a copy to Eve. She's been working on a profile of him for a long time. She might catch something we miss."

"I don't need to watch it again." Something about the way Beck had simply made the decision for her rankled. "I need to figure out how to get home. I'll go and see if Ezra can get the boat again. I don't want to make you late getting to your plane."

"You can't be serious," Beck replied.

"We're going home?" Roman stood in the doorway, his eyes wide. "But what about the bad man?"

Beck put his hands on his hips and frowned as Ezra showed up behind Roman. "I thought you were watching him."

Ezra winced. "He can be slippery when he wants to. Sorry. But I'm also kind of worried about the bad guy. Could I watch the tape so I know who to look for? If we're going back to Malta, I should know who might...show up."

She knew what Ezra had been planning on saying. Who might murder us. But what the hell was she supposed to do? She couldn't simply allow Beck to walk in and take over. It had been one thing when she had no other options, but now she did.

"Set it up, Jax. Owen, see if you can get an ETA on Theo and the others," Beck said, obviously taking charge. "I'm going to have a talk with Kim, and then we'll get ready to move out. Roman, I'm not going to leave you. No matter what. Do you understand?"

Her son slowly nodded his head. "Yes. You won't let the bad guy get us."

"I won't." Beck turned her way, and she felt the weight of all his stubborn will. "Come with me. Roman, I'm going to talk to your mom and then we'll be back. Ezra, try not to lose my son."

Before she could say anything, she felt Beck's hand on her arm, leading her down the hallway. He was right. They shouldn't have this argument in front of their son.

How would she explain to Roman that yes, his dad was back, but he lived in the States and they wouldn't see him. Unless…

"What did you mean you aren't leaving? You can't promise Roman things like that." Kim turned on him as soon as they got to the small bedroom they'd spent the night before in.

He closed the door behind him, and the room seemed to get even smaller. "Why won't you come back to Dallas?"

"Because it's not my home."

"No, it's mine, and it's the safest place for you and Roman right now. So explain to me why you're fighting me on this."

"You don't know that it's safe. You don't know anywhere is safe. And don't pretend like you're the only one who can protect him. What the hell is that about?"

He pointed a finger her way. "You are out of practice. You panicked yesterday. You need me. So if I can't get you back to Dallas, then I'll uproot my life and move into the fort."

That would almost be worse. He wouldn't even have a job to go to. He would be close to her all day. He would try to take his place as Roman's father, and she wouldn't be able to hold back. And it would all go wrong because that's what happened with them. Why would she put herself through that again? Why would he want to? "I don't want you there."

He stared at her for a moment as though assessing how to proceed. "This is not you. You are a practical, logical woman. You know that going back to Malta isn't what's best for you or Roman. So what are you really afraid of?"

He was right. She wasn't being practical, but she couldn't seem to give in to him. "I don't want to be around you."

"No, that's not it either. Or maybe it is, but not because you're afraid of me."

Stubborn will rose inside her. "Do you honestly believe I've been pining after you all these years? After everything you did?"

"Baby, you lied to me about my brother's death." His voice had gone low, intimate. That deep baritone of his was a caress she could feel against her skin. "I'm really hoping you can take my lead and forgive me for some stupid, cruel words that I did not mean. Now tell me why you won't come with me."

He'd been slowly moving her back until she was against the wall with nowhere to run.

"I don't want you." The words came out awfully breathy, even to her own ears. And they were a lie. She already wanted him again. She might have spent the last few years tricking herself into the belief that he had no more power over her, but he'd so recently proven he could upend her whole world with his mere presence.

His hand came up and flattened against the wall next to her head. He gazed down at her. "Who said anything about wanting me?"

Frustration welled, and it was all with herself. "I meant I don't want you around."

"That's not what you said. You said you didn't want me, and as we're two people who created a whole other human being because we wanted each other so much, I think that's exactly what those words meant. I also think you're lying."

"You always think I'm lying."

"I'm sorry I did that to you. Although, again, you were lying about some very important things. But I know you're lying about this. Do you know how I know? Because I pushed you away all those years for the very same reasons."

"You pushed me away because you were an asshole, and I should have listened to you. You didn't want me. You didn't want us. I was wrong, Beck."

"No. You weren't wrong. I pushed you because if I'd let you close even once, we would have more than one kid now. What do you say, Kim? You want to give it another go? Roman might like a little brother. We'll make sure he's not an asshole like mine."

The idea of having another baby with Beck...she pushed at his chest. "Yeah, that's happening. I don't know if you've noticed but we're not exactly young anymore."

"All I've noticed is how gorgeous you are." He moved back, giving her the space she'd demanded. "Do you have any idea how much I've missed your face, your body? How lonely I've been without you?"

She hadn't even thought about it. The day before had been so hectic, and then she'd been weary. It was the only reason she'd let him climb into bed with her. It had nothing to do with the fact that she'd felt safe for the first time in seven years. But she hadn't asked him about the life he'd left behind when he'd come after her. "Somehow I doubt you've been lonely. If you're working in Dallas, I suspect you spend your nights at Sanctum."

A brow rose over his eyes. "Is that what you're worried about? That I've been sleeping around?"

"I don't care."

"I haven't had sex with anyone but my own trusty hand since the last time I saw you." He carefully enunciated each word, as though he wanted to make her believe them.

"Bullshit."

"No. I didn't want anyone except you. You. And honestly, the sex I had between our divorce and that night in Paris was more about trying to push you away than it was finding pleasure or happiness. I kept every relationship physical, and there weren't all that many. Three women. One of them was a one-night stand. The other two were friends with benefits that ended when they found a man they could build a future with. My future was always with you. But it is plain to me you're not ready to talk about this. So what will work?"

"Nothing." She was reeling. He wasn't one to lie to her. He almost always gave her the truth, even when it hurt like hell. "Nothing is going to work. You're right. I can't help but want you, but it's habit. It's a longing for something we never really had. An illusion."

"Our son is not an illusion," Beck said softly. "His life is at stake, too. Do you believe he'll be safer in Malta?"

She hesitated because she didn't like the honest answer to that question. "I don't want to come with you."

"Ah, so you need me to be the bad guy." He chuckled, but it wasn't an amused sound. "Somewhere in Texas Levi Green is playing out this whole scene in his head because it's exactly what he wants.

To break us up and make you vulnerable. He's counting on me not being willing to force your hand. He thinks by giving you options you'll choose the wrong one and we'll fight. It's what we always do. All right, then. I'll give him a fight."

She didn't like the sound of that. "Or you could leave him alone and hope this is all over."

He was right back to predatory. His eyes narrowed, but in a way that made her heart rate tick up.

Had he really not had sex for seven years? Somehow when she'd thought about him, she'd seen him with other women, known that he wouldn't be alone for long. How hungry would he be now?

He was probably starving. Just like her.

"That's where he'll trip us up," he said. "He'll let us think he's done playing, and we'll split up because that's what we do. Because I'll get angry and you won't take another minute of it. Throw in a kid and he'll think I'll lose my damn mind. He didn't get a look at Roman. Even if he did, Roman looks younger than he is. He could definitely be five, and that means there's a real chance Levi doesn't think he's mine. He knows how jealous I can be. He's counting on your fear and pride and my anger issues. When he's certain you're all alone in the world, he'll swoop in and he'll take you and do everything he promised."

"He's getting married."

"And he's still obsessed with you."

"How can you know that?"

"Because I know what it means to be in love with you. Wildly, crazily in love with you. And I've hurt you just like he has. The difference is I've changed and he hasn't. I'm not going to leave you alone even if that means making you hate me more than you already do." He was getting in her space again, and she couldn't move.

Not out of fear but because her body was at war with her mind. She was already thinking about the fact that he was right here, and it wouldn't hurt to let him kiss her, to touch her. Perhaps if she slept with him a couple of times, she could finally move on. She would see that sex wasn't as good as she remembered. It was all a trick. "What are you going to do?"

"I'm going to make a deal with you. If you come to Dallas with me, stay with me for a year, then I'll walk away. Not from Roman. I won't leave him, but I won't ever bother you again. I won't fight you if you want to live in Europe. I'll follow your lead on everything when it comes to Roman. I'll pay for all your security."

"And if I don't?" She already knew what she was going to do. Beck was giving her an out, and she was going to take it.

"Then I'll go to Malta, find a place close to you, and talk to a lawyer about what my rights are."

Bastard. "That's not fair."

"None of this is fair. I lost six years with him. I lost the chance to take care of you while you were pregnant. I will take this chance because I think if you spend a year with me you won't be able to leave. For one year you'll live in my house. I'll give you a separate room because I don't want to confuse Roman. You'll have your own room, but for a few hours every night after Roman goes to sleep, you'll be my sub. Every Friday night we'll go to Sanctum and you'll be mine for the evening."

Her whole body lit up at the thought. "We can't do that."

"Why? We'll be discreet. He doesn't have to know anything but that his parents are friends and will do what's best for him. Being able to stay with me, to get to know my world, will be good for him. I promise you that. He'll be surrounded by the best bodyguards, by men and women who Levi will think twice about messing with. All you have to do is give me a year."

She wouldn't last a year. Hell, she wouldn't last six months without being right back to where she was before.

Or he really changed and you might have another shot. You might be able to form a family with this man, one Roman could count on.

She shoved the idea away. It was too dangerous to consider. But she couldn't put Roman through a custody battle. "Six weeks."

"Six months," he countered.

"Three." She breathed the offer because he was so close, she could feel the heat of his body against hers.

"Three it is. And I know exactly how we should seal this pact."

Her body went liquid as he kissed her for the first time in years. Her hands went to his waist, and any thought of protest fled in the instant his lips met hers.

This. This was what she'd missed. Passion. Need. The pure fire of wanting him. This man was the only one who could make her lose her head, make her put love over logic.

No. Not the only one. They had a son now, and Roman would need his dad. Was it so wrong to indulge in this emotion? She would leave at the end. She would.

But for now, Beck had given her the gift of denial. For a little while longer.

Beck's hand cupped her breast, and she could feel his erection against her stomach. "How long has it been for you?"

"Long?"

"Since you had an orgasm," he prompted.

He wasn't asking her if she'd taken a lover, but she answered him anyway. "Same as you."

His hand moved lower. "I hate that. I hate that you haven't had that comfort. I'm going to spend three months making up for it. I promise you."

He twisted her around and she found herself with her back to his front, that marvelous cock of his rubbing against her ass. It was going too fast, but she couldn't stop it. She didn't even want to. He held her in place and there was such comfort in his strength. She could stop him if she wanted to. Hell, she wasn't even sure he would go through with the threat. Deep inside she knew he was doing this so she wouldn't have to agonize over the choice. She sank into that feeling. For years she'd had to be strong. Even though she'd had help, she'd been on her own, been responsible for a whole human being all by herself.

She let her head fall back against his chest and decided to worry about everything else later. She'd promised to be his submissive for three months, and that meant letting him take control and give her the pleasure she couldn't take for herself.

She wanted it. There had been a part of her that feared her sexuality had fled in the last few years, but that need roared back now as one of Beck's big hands slid down her body and under the waist of her slacks.

"I think you've had a rough couple of days, baby. It's my job to make sure you're relaxed," he whispered in her ear, his tongue licking the shell. "You're not going to fight me."

"We made a deal." And she was already regretting the fact that she'd got him down to three months. It was perverse, but he'd always had this effect on her.

"That's right. I get you all to myself after we put our son to bed." His fingers slipped under the waistband of her undies and closer and closer to her clitoris. "And I can't wait to get you in Sanctum."

She didn't care as long as he would keep doing what he was doing. His fingers started to rub circles around her clitoris, giving her just the right amount of pressure. "I haven't been in a club with people in it. I might not like it."

She groaned as he started building the tension, sparking waves that she knew would quickly build.

"You'll like it. You'll love it. There's no shame there. We'll fuck hard while other couples watch us and get hot at the sight. They'll all look at you and know how gorgeous my sub is. Tell me you don't get hot at the thought."

She couldn't. She couldn't find the will to breathe, much less speak, because he pressed a finger into her pussy while his thumb stroked her clitoris and the pleasure rushed over her, reminding her of everything she'd missed in the last few years. Her head buzzed with the sweet sensation of her body going over that edge. Beck held her tight as she rode the high of her first man-given orgasm in years.

"That's a preview of what I intend to do to you for the next three months," he promised. "Now take care of me. I swear, Kim, all you'll have to do is touch my cock and I'll come in your hand. I'm so close."

A thrill went through her because he didn't sound like a Dom who'd gotten what he wanted. He sounded like a man who was desperate to feel a woman's touch. Her touch. Only hers.

She still had some power.

There was a knock on the door, and she practically leapt out of his arms.

"Beck, I need to talk to you." Ezra's voice came through the thin door, and she worried she hadn't been as quiet as she'd tried to be.

Beck cursed under his breath. "I'm leaving him here. He can swim back to Malta."

She hadn't even thought about the fact that they would be leaving Ezra behind.

"Uhm, the guy on that tape, the one you call Levi Green," Ezra was saying. He stopped as though he wasn't sure how to phrase what he needed to say. "He was our contact. For our unit. You know the one I was in before I was a priest."

She looked to Beck, whose eyes had gone wide. He jerked the door open and confronted his brother.

"Are you telling me the same guy who was investigating you sent you on the fucking assignments?" Beck asked.

Ezra nodded. "I didn't know his name. He was our Agency contact."

"Damn it." Beck sighed. "Get ready, then. We're all going back to Dallas."

It looked like she had a new home.

For a few months.

Chapter Twelve

Two days later, Kim thanked the bodyguard who'd come to pick her and Roman up at Beck's house. Jamal Lewis was a massive man who looked like he should be playing linebacker instead of escorting a mom and her kid, but he'd proven himself to be a gentle giant with Roman. He'd joked around and made Roman comfortable as he'd driven through the streets of Dallas. He'd been a soothing presence with his deep baritone voice. He'd talked about his dog and how much fun the kids seemed to have at the office's daycare.

But she'd missed Beck. It was odd because they hadn't spent much time together. Between the jet lag and Roman's nightmares the night before, she hadn't played Beck's sub yet. She hadn't even managed to explore the house and yard. Still, she'd woken up to Beck kissing her forehead and telling her he had to go into work, but he had a bodyguard picking them up. He'd left all the instructions on how to set the alarm. She'd cuddled down with her son and gotten an extra hour and a half of sleep.

Beck was different and the same. He was more thoughtful, and yet that passion they'd had still sparked.

She wasn't sure what she was doing.

"Solo, welcome to McKay-Taggart." A tall, gorgeous woman with strawberry blonde hair walked in. Charlotte Taggart held out a hand. "Or do you prefer Kim?"

She kind of liked Solo when she was working. It reminded her to put up her guard. "Solo is fine." She also liked the fact that only her family and Ariel called her Kim. Beck and Ezra and her uncle used that name. Even Levi called her Solo. "I haven't come up against another chick named Solo, if you know what I mean."

"I do," Charlotte said with a smile. According to what she'd learned only Ian Taggart called her Charlie, and she liked it that way. Kim got the feeling Charlotte understood the need to compartmentalize. Charlotte turned to Jamal. "Any problems?"

Jamal shook his head. "Not at all. I made sure the house was secure before I left. I'll check in later in case Beck needs to stay late." He turned to her son. "Roman, it was good to meet you. I think you'll have a blast in the club. I'll see you later, little man."

He gave her son a high five and her a nod and strode away.

"He was definitely military." Kim had been sizing the man up. "I would bet he was Special Forces. Not ex-intelligence. He's too open for that."

"You are correct," Charlotte replied. "He was a Green Beret. Ian will try to tell you they could have worked together, but only if Jamal had joined up at the age of four. Just go with it. My husband's having some trouble with moving into his fifties. So I'm going to start your tour as soon as our other friend gets here. There he is."

Ezra walked into the foyer. He was dressed in jeans and a T-shirt and looked more casual than she'd seen him in years. He immediately dropped to one knee and held out his arms. "Roman, I've missed your face."

Roman ran and threw himself at his uncle. "I missed you, too. I miss Uncle Francis."

She'd uprooted her baby from everything he'd known.

"Don't." Charlotte stood beside her, her voice going low as Roman started to tell his uncle everything that had happened in the days they'd been separated.

"Don't what?"

"Don't feel guilty about something you couldn't have controlled," Charlotte said. "I know that look. I've seen it on my own face. Kids are resilient. Love them, give them something to hold onto, and they come out of even the worst situations well. I should know. I survived my father because I had my sister. This is a tiny bump in the road for your son."

God, she hoped so. "He likes his dad. Beck's been good to him. Good to us."

She hadn't been as good. She'd used Roman as a shield because after that first intimate encounter with Beck, she'd withdrawn. It had been too overwhelming, and they hadn't even gotten out of their clothes. She'd used jet lag and then Roman needing her to not put herself in that position again.

But tonight she had a decision to make. She'd promised Beck that she would be his sub for a few hours every night, and she couldn't keep coming up with excuses. The trouble was she knew Beck wouldn't hold her to the deal. He would protect her and their son and keep his distance if she asked him to.

She didn't want to ask him to.

"I feel bad that he wasn't able to finish his school year. He had another couple of weeks," she replied, still watching her son. "School goes through June in Malta."

"My girls would go crazy." Charlotte nodded to a woman who walked through the door after putting her keycard in and then using a thumb scanner. The security seemed very high tech. "They head for a camp for a few weeks in a couple of days, but until then they are terrorizing the office. I mean putting in some work here. They don't understand why they can't stay home by themselves. The twins are thirteen and Tasha is fourteen. Honestly, I would let Tash stay. She's never started a fire or decided to practice her knife throwing skills with my kitchen knives. But Tasha wants to come to work with me. I never got the chance to say thank you for finding her for us. Seriously, she's a light in our lives."

"The last seven years, I've done a lot of reflection on my prior career. I did a lot of things I wasn't particularly proud of. I'm glad I did one thing right."

"See, there's that guilt. I know it well." Charlotte straightened up. "Let's take a tour. I'll show you around the office and the daycare. We've expanded it in the last couple of years and share it with our downstairs neighbors."

"With MDWM?" Miles-Dean, Weston, and Murdoch had been a

start-up when she'd gone into hiding. Now it was a powerhouse of an investigative agency, and she knew the government would love to get its hands on some of Adam Miles and Chelsea Weston's software.

Charlotte started to walk through the hall on the right side of the foyer, past the receptionist desk where a young woman sat. Her name plate read Yasmin Tahan, and she gave Charlotte a wave even as she spoke into her headset. She winked up at Roman, who was now on his uncle's back, wrapped around him like they used to walk through the streets of Malta.

She followed Charlotte as she pointed out the amenities of the office. There was a lovely breakroom and several smaller conference rooms. There was a whole second floor that included the offices for the bodyguard unit and the men and women who provided home security plans and maintenance. The kids' club was huge and sported lots of kids playing in the various spaces. She'd seen Roman's eyes widen at the sight of all the books and toys.

The Taggarts had done well for themselves. She found herself walking by what Charlotte called the main conference room. It had glass walls, and she could see Beck sitting there with Ian, Alex McKay, and Liam O'Donnell. She didn't let herself stare at him, but she noticed that Roman waved at his dad.

"This is lovely, Charlotte," Ezra said. "It's a nice place to work. And I thank you for my room at the club. It's got everything I could need. And I deeply appreciate the bible. I had to leave mine behind."

Charlotte gave him a warm smile. "If you need anything else, Father, please don't hesitate to ask. I wish I could send you to church. I truly do, but it's dangerous right now."

"Don't tell anyone because I might get fired for saying this, but God doesn't need us to be in church to hear our prayers," Ezra replied.

She would have to find some time to ask him about the club later on. Her level of curiosity was high given she was due to go to Sanctum in a few days.

"Well, that's the basic tour. I'd like to talk to Solo for a couple of minutes before we join Beck in the conference room," Charlotte said. "Roman, I think they're about to have a midmorning snack in the kids' club. And then they're doing a pretty cool science experiment."

"Really?" Roman asked.

Charlotte nodded. "Yes. I told the teachers that you love science, and they thought you might help them make volcanoes today."

"I love volcanoes. Let's go." Roman dropped off his uncle's back.

Ezra took his hand. "I'll go sign him in and meet you back here."

She kissed Roman's forehead. "I'll be here all day."

Roman nodded and strode away without looking back.

"He'll be fine," Charlotte said, stepping into the hallway. "Come with me for a minute. I want to show you your office."

That was a surprise. "I have an office?"

"Well, you didn't think I was going to let you sit at home, did you? You're Solo. I can use you here. I know you haven't done Agency work in a long time, but I would bet your instincts are still good."

"I do have some work to do on Levi." It would be nice to have an office, to get out of the house every once in a while.

"Yes, I'm sure you'll do that, but I'd like your thoughts on a couple of open cases we have."

"I'm not a private eye."

"No, you're better," Charlotte insisted. She stopped in front of an office. "This is you. Beck is across the hall. I don't have an office with a window right now."

She was used to working in the shadows. "I don't need a window. Just a laptop and Internet access."

Charlotte's nose wrinkled. "Oh, we do better here. We'll talk about redecorating to your specifications later. I recently did Beck's office if you'd like to see it."

Without waiting for an answer Charlotte opened the door, and she couldn't contain her curiosity. She walked into the place where Beck had worked for the last seven years. It was funny because she'd never seen him in an office. He'd been in the field most of the time she'd known him. She would have said he would hate being stuck in an office, and any work space he had would be utilitarian because Beck liked the adrenaline of being out in the field. Even after he'd left the Agency, he'd taken the first dangerous job he could find—guarding the Lost Boys.

His home had been fairly utilitarian. Not that it wasn't nice, but it lacked the comfort of décor and plants and pictures. Not so with his office. His office was beautifully masculine, with a big dark wood desk and elegant bookshelves that contained a combination of fiction and reference books.

"When he takes a break, he tends to read," Charlotte said. "He always volunteers to work late if we need someone here at the office. I think he spends way more time here than he should, but then he's been lonely."

Charlotte could clear up something she'd been thinking about for days. "He really hasn't dated? He told me he hasn't...been in a relationship since we were last together."

Charlotte's eyes lit up like she loved to gossip, though Kim rather thought she would only do it in the kindest ways. "Beck goes to the club and he'll scene, but that scene never involves sex. I've known some Doms who won't have sex with subs, but Beck won't even get one off, if you know what I mean. Sorry. I'm not sure how into the lifestyle you are."

"I'm not completely ignorant," she admitted as she strolled around his office. There was a warmth to it she hadn't expected. As though Beck was at home here and his actual home was merely a place to sleep and eat. "And I'm sure you'll find out that he's bringing me on Friday. We have a bargain, he and I."

Those eyes lit up even brighter. "You have a sex bargain? Because those are the best bargains. It's harder when you have kids, but trust me, you can make it work."

She let her eyes roam across the books on his shelves. He still liked reading historical books and thrillers, but it looked like he'd added in a bunch of self-help books, and that didn't seem like the Beck she knew. A lot of them seemed to deal with anger. "He thinks I'll forget all the years before if I spend three months with him. But I have to do it quietly because I don't want to confuse Roman."

"Like I said, kids are resilient when they're loved," Charlotte said.

"Mom?" A teenaged girl stood in the doorway, her hair up in a high ponytail. She held a bejeweled cell phone in one hand.

Charlotte smiled at her daughter. "Hey, sweetie. Come in. I want you to meet someone. This is Kim Solomon. Do you remember I told you how she helped find you when you were a kid?"

Tasha's smile dimmed a bit, and it almost seemed like she forced herself to come into the room. She held a hand out, but it was a practiced thing, something she knew she had to do. "Hello, Ms. Solomon. It's lovely to meet you."

Any accent she'd had as a little girl was gone. There was something about the way Tasha was looking at her that made Kim's instincts flare. This girl didn't like her.

Still, she shook Tasha's hand. "I was very happy to help find you."

Tasha dropped her hand and turned back to Charlotte. "I wanted to let you know I called the bakery and they've set everything up for Dad's cake. Also, I asked them not to deliver it. I said you would pick it up. You know if we have it in the house for too long we'll find Travis's fingerprints on it."

"Smart girl," Charlotte said, her arm going around Tasha's shoulders. "My youngest has his dad's sweet tooth but none of Ian's self-control. You'll have to come to the party, Solo. It's Ian's birthday, and we have a big house party planned at the lake house we share with Sean and Grace. Adam's brother and sister-in-law run this amazing bakery in uptown and they're making all the sweets. Sean's catering the whole thing."

"And we'll get a bouncy house for the kids," Tasha said, looking happy for the first time since she'd walked in. "And Dad will decide to jump in it and then he'll complain bitterly about his back and how old he is and he'll throw us all in the pool."

"He probably will," Charlotte agreed. "Are Kenz and Kala helping in the daycare?"

Tasha started telling her mom about how the morning had gone, but Kim didn't really hear them anymore because her gaze had stopped on Beck's desk. It was neat, with pens and pencils in a mug and his paperwork stacked up.

But it was the single framed picture that caught her eye. Their wedding picture. She hadn't worn a big fluffy dress. She was in a simple emerald green sheath and a strand of Tiffany pearls, her hair around her shoulders because Beck had loved it that way. He was in a dark suit that set off his eyes. It had been taken by the Vegas chapel they'd gotten married in as part of the "package."

She picked it up and the world seemed a little misty.

"It was the only thing he brought with him when he came to Dallas." She looked up and she and Charlotte were alone again. "Besides clothes, of course."

"I can't believe he has this. This was in my condo in DC. I never thought I would see it again." She'd kept it all those years. Even after the divorce and selling the place that had been their home, she'd kept this picture on her mantle. "I don't even know what happened to my place in DC. I owned it but I didn't pay my property taxes."

"I think you'll find Beck did," Charlotte said. "He worked with a lawyer to make sure you still had a home if you wanted it. I'm surprised he didn't tell you."

He hadn't told her a lot of things.

He'd brought their wedding picture here. It had been sitting on this desk for years.

She took a deep breath and put the picture back down. She wasn't staying here any longer than the three months she promised Beck. It would give him time to get to know his son and for them to work out how they would parent together.

She might even fuck him out of her system. But she wasn't falling for this. Not again. "We should get to the meeting. I want to run by the daycare and make sure Roman's settling in."

She also needed a moment. She wouldn't do anything more than look through the big windows and maybe wave his way, but the walk through the building might calm her down.

Charlotte looked her over as though assessing her. "You're going to be a tough one, aren't you?"

"I plan on being impossible." She had to protect herself. Beck was an indulgence her heart couldn't afford. At some point he would get mad and they would start their cycle all over again. It wouldn't be only her who got hurt. This time Roman would be involved.

"That's okay. Ian did, too." Charlotte stepped out into the hallway. "He lasted three days. I'll go let Eve know we're ready, and I'll meet you in the big conference room."

She followed Charlotte and prayed she was stronger than Ian.

* * * *

"But I just got used to not using that name. I don't understand why people don't stay dead. It's way easier than this constant 'he's dead and some overly emotional asshole is using his name. Then overly emotional asshole gets some much needed therapy and reclaims his own name only to find out the dude he was honoring has been happily quarantining with overly emotional asshole's ex and the son he didn't know he had.' It could have been he's just dead. See how that's easier?"

Beck wasn't in the mood for Tag's shenanigans. Not in any way. He was horny as hell, and it had been two full days since he'd gotten his hands on his wife. And seven years since she'd put her hands on him. That was probably the part that was really getting to him. "Well, Ezra's not dead and I need to figure out what Levi was doing with his unit."

"His Marine unit. They're all dead, right?" Alex McKay asked.

"Or are they?" Tag offered, a brow climbing over his eyes.

Alex gave him a one shouldered shrug. "Hey, if they're in hiding after faking their own deaths, I'm all for finding them. It would be easier if we could ask them what they were doing."

He'd known this wouldn't be an easy conference, but they were testing his limits. "I'm pretty sure they're all freaking dead, Tag. So unless you have a medium hanging around the office, you're going to have to do some actual investigative work."

The third person in the conference room leaned over toward Taggart, his voice going low. "He's in a bad mood. Do you think it's jet lag, now? Because I'm thinking his purity is finally taking a toll on him. You said his brother was a priest, but Beck's the one who's been living like a monk."

The Americans weren't the only ones well acquainted with the art of sarcasm. Liam O'Donnell's Irish accent had softened a bit over the years, but he could lay it on thick when he wanted to.

When he'd gotten Kim to agree to his devil's bargain, he'd expected the sex to come hot and heavy. Hell, he'd thought he'd be able to revisit the mile-high club with her. What he hadn't counted on was how many damn people had been on the plane and how tired she'd been. He'd spent the majority of the ridiculously long flight watching her and Roman sleep. Then he'd had jet lag and he'd slept.

He didn't want to live like a monk anymore. He wanted to sin and hard.

The object of his affection took that moment to walk in front of the conference room. Through the glass, he could see that she wore a simple pair of slacks and a chic silk blouse, and those sky-high heels she seemed to have been born to wear. Her long blonde hair was down, and she tucked a wave behind her ear, revealing a half smile she was giving the other woman she walked with. Charlotte was showing her around the office.

Then he saw his brother walking behind the two women. He hadn't seen Ezra since they'd landed in Dallas and Tag had whisked him away to a secret site where Levi hopefully wouldn't figure out he was alive.

He watched as Ezra walked by with Kim and Roman and Charlotte for their tour of the office. Roman was on Ezra's back, treating his uncle like the free ride he was.

Then Roman looked Beck's way and a big grin came over his face and he waved like this was the greatest adventure in the world.

He waved to his son as Ezra started toward the back of the office, following after Kim.

"And then vampires attacked and took back the world from the evil werebunnies," Tag was saying.

"What?" Beck forced himself to focus.

Tag's eyes rolled. "I was repeating the end of the bedtime story I heard Kala telling her youngest brother. She's not a good babysitter. But she is cheap."

"Only until you get the therapy bill for Seth and Travis." Li sat back with a frown.

Tag waved that off. "The boys don't need therapy. They're going to shoot things and then they'll feel better. That's manly therapy."

Tag was such a fucking liar since Beck happened to know a whole lot of men who'd gotten the help they needed because Tag eased them into therapy. He'd literally funded Kai Ferguson's practice for years. "Sure. I'll get them both BB guns for their next birthday."

Tag actually paled. "I was joking. Dear god. Don't arm my children. They're too good at it themselves. I keep the gun locker double locked because once Kala started..." Tag winced. "Once she started with the hormones and stuff, my house got way more dangerous."

Li chuckled. "Ah, sweet, sweet karma. Tag's girls got their periods and Kenzie uses it like a baseball bat. If she wants to get out of anything, she announces she's got her period and Tag goes and hides. It's funny. Daisy is never doing that, by the way."

Alex rolled his eyes. "Sure. You stay in that sweet delusion, my friend. But he's right about Kenz. Does she have to announce that? It's disturbing."

"It's nothing compared to what Kala can do," Tag said with a shudder. "What were we talking about?"

He was really happy Roman had a penis.

"I believe you were pointing out that Beck's distracted," Alex explained. "Not that you shouldn't be. When Tag's wife came back from the dead he was all sorts of distracted."

Tag snorted. "Was not. I was focused and clear because I never really thought she was dead. Deep down I knew she was alive."

The door had come open and Charlotte and Eve McKay were standing in the doorway. Charlotte frowned at her husband. "Oh, really? You want to explain all those subs then?"

"I completely believed she was dead and lost to me forever, and I indulged myself in meaningless sex to cover up the fact that my heart was broken utterly," Tag said with absolutely no sarcasm.

Eve simply shook her head and took the seat next to Alex.

Charlotte's eyes rolled but she leaned over and kissed her husband. Her voice went low, but not so low he couldn't hear her. "Obnoxious man. And according to Solo, Beck's a saint compared to you."

"Well, we all know that," Tag said with a grin.

So Kim had been talking. It was one of those things he used to get mad about. Anything about their private life should have been private. Except Kim needed a friend to talk to. She so often in her life had no one. She'd been isolated and it had cost her. It had been one of the things that had gone wrong the first time around. He hadn't realized he needed someone to talk to so he'd put all of his emotional needs on her. Since he didn't need anyone else, she shouldn't have needed anyone else. The trouble had been he was shitty at handling her emotional needs.

He looked to Charlotte as she took a seat across from Tag. "Thank you for showing her around. I appreciate it. And I also appreciate everything you've done to make her feel welcome."

"I like her," Charlotte said with a smile. "And I always love shopping. I brought some of Travis's clothes. I think they'll fit Roman. The girls and I did a Target run and bought him all of the basics. Also, if you noticed, there's now food in your kitchen. I know many men are confused about where food comes from, so I made it easy for you."

He chuckled because she was right. He ate sad takeout far too often. "I promise I'll take them both shopping. From what Kim's told me she's become quite good at cooking. I'm looking forward to some home-cooked meals." He saw Charlotte's eyes narrow and immediately moved to block the inevitable lecture on household duties and emotional work. "And the dishes and cleanup that I will do after our lovely meal."

"Well played, Kent," Eve said. "You want to keep those meals coming, you have a bottle of wine chilling for your lady after dinner and you let her relax while you deal with the dishes and the kiddos."

Li huffed. "Kiddos? He's got it easy. His is six. He missed all those terrible toddler years. Not that mine were bad. Daisy takes after her mother, and she's practically a saint."

"Sure she is," Tag said while shaking his head. "All our kids are."

"Mine aren't," Alex admitted with a sigh. "How did I go from we probably can't have kids to having three? And don't let Li overemphasize the toddler years. Yes, they suck, but I would take all the stinky diapers in the world to not have to answer questions about what is lube and why is there so much of it in your bathroom, Dad?"

Eve groaned. "I have to admit, I ran. I left him standing there to answer that one."

"You don't hide it well enough," Tag replied.

"I hide it fine. Who do you think put Coop up to asking that question? I'll give you three chances, and the first two don't count," Alex shot back.

"See, my Daisy doesn't know anything about that. An angel of a girl that one is." Li looked perfectly satisfied with his self-delusion.

"Not if she's around Tag's monster she's not. You need to talk to Kala about…everything," Alex said. "Just everything."

"I'll get right on that," Tag replied in a way that said he wouldn't do that any time soon.

"Is Kim coming back?" He was waiting for the moment when she walked in the room.

"She wanted to run by the kids' club," Charlotte explained. "We have to call it that now or I can't get Travis to go. It's not a nursery anymore. It's a very cool club that only kids get to go to. It's important that it be elite."

"It's important that his dad is banned," Tag groused. "I really thought that slide would hold my weight."

The conference room door opened and Kim walked in. Beck shot to his feet and pulled out a chair for her. "Hey, I got you some coffee."

He'd even put it in one of those little thermoses so it would stay hot.

She smiled as she sank into the seat he'd saved for her. "Thank you. I could use it."

"Did you get me coffee?" Ezra asked, taking the seat across from Beck.

Beck simply stared at him.

"All right then." Ezra settled in. "I've been meaning to cut back. Discipline is good for the soul."

"It's good for a lot of things." Tag winked his wife's way.

Beck wouldn't know. He hadn't been able to discipline his sexy sub at all. And now he had some questions because he was fairly certain they'd agreed it was dangerous for Ezra to be out and about. "Why is Ezra here? I thought we were keeping my brother in a bunker somewhere."

"Nah, they're keeping me in a sex club," Ezra replied. "Mr. McKay tried to tell me it was some sort of a gym given the large hamster wheel that lights up, but I didn't think that bench thing was for weights."

"You stashed the priest at Sanctum?" Li was suddenly sitting up straight.

"Well, it was good enough for Jesus," Tag replied.

Beck couldn't help but laugh, which earned him a stare from Kim. He saw church in his future.

"I'm serious," Tag continued. "Contrary to what most people think, Jesus liked to hang with a rough crowd. Also, there's nothing wrong with sex. What consenting adults do is a beautiful thing. I personally am very grateful for sex."

Beck would be grateful for sex. So freaking grateful. When he looked at it, this situation was really his brother's fault. Had his brother not decided to get involved in some very unsavory activities years before, he wouldn't have faked his death, and then there would have been no divorce and he would have been fucking his wife for years.

Yeah, not even he could fool himself about that. They'd been on thin ice before the divorce, and it had been all about his own anger and jealousy.

"Father, you don't have to stay at Sanctum," Li said. "You can come stay with me and my family. My daughter is a saint of a girl, but my boy could use a little religion, if you know what I mean."

A smile tugged at his brother's lips. "I'm fine where I am. I find it amusing, and I agree with Mr. Taggart. Sex is a gift."

"One you do not partake of," Beck pointed out.

"Well of course he doesn't." Li looked at him like he'd lost his mind. "He's a priest."

"It's all right. I'm also his brother," Ezra said. "Beck is having to adjust to a lot of hard truths he didn't understand. I think he's doing a good job of it so far."

"Like I need your praise. And of course I don't think of you as a priest. I remember when you used to take hour-long showers after you discovered girls," he grumbled. "I had to choose to be late to school or go without a shower."

"The father is fine where he is. Sanctum is the best place for him. He's got everything he needs, and we can move him around without eyes on him. We can smuggle him in and out easily from there." Tag sat back, obviously getting down to business. "Theo's working with Jax and Hutch on trying to track Green. Green's in DC, but according to what we've learned he's supposed to head out to the Hamptons this weekend where his fiancée's family is holding a campaign event for her father."

"Who is the vice president of the United States, looking to be president," Charlotte explained. "Levi has thrived under the current president, and we expect he'll continue if his father-in-law wins. He's moved into the upper echelons of the CIA. I wouldn't be surprised if he ends up heading the Agency."

Eve had a notepad out, a pen in her well-manicured hand. "Solo, do you have thoughts about Levi's past? I've got a full dossier on him, but you've known him for a long time."

"Yes. Most of my adult life. We met when we were both in training. Power has always been very important to Levi." Kim had her hands around the mug like she needed the warmth. "He grew up in a wealthy family, but his parents weren't all that interested in him. I think they were a bit like mine. Unfortunately, his father's wealth was wiped out during a financial crisis. Levi was in college at the time, studying political science. He wanted to go into politics, but without cash it wasn't going to happen. Levi didn't want to be a mayor or a state representative. He wanted to go to the top and fast. He still had a lot of connections, including some at the Agency."

"He was never really an operative." It was one of the many things that rankled Beck. "They never put him in the field, but he quickly was given the lead to use operatives and teams. In this case, it was my brother's Force Recon team."

"I know we did a deep dive on this back in the day, but I need a refresher," Li admitted. "It's been years, and I don't think we had much to go on back then."

"Well, in my defense, the whole team was supposed to have died." Tag started passing around folders with the original report in them. "Solo, did you hide the other team members around the globe somewhere?"

Kim's grip tightened. "No, they died in a firefight."

"I wouldn't call it that. It was more like an ambush." Ezra's eyes were on the table in front of him. "Most of us didn't get a shot off."

"What was the purpose of the op?" Tag asked. "And why was Solo in charge?"

"Beck, I think we should talk about this in private first," Ezra said quietly.

"There's no need to." He'd avoided his brother's *mea culpa* for days. He intended to do this on his time. "Everyone's read the reports."

"Okay." Ezra sat up and folded his hands together on the table in front of him. "In order to understand that particular mission, you need to understand how I got there."

"No, we don't." Frustration welled. He didn't want to hear his brother's sad story. "You liked drugs and you got recruited by a guy who liked to make money off drugs. We got it."

Kim sighed. "And that reaction is exactly why he couldn't come to you. You were always so judgmental. It's why I couldn't tell you. Ezra, there's no point in going over this. I'll explain the op."

Shit. The last thing he needed was for Kim to decide he hadn't changed. "I'm sorry. I'm angry with him and I'm not being reasonable. Ezra, if you want to talk about this privately, we can go to my office."

"You were right. He has a leash now." Li had leaned over and whispered to Tag.

"No, it's fine. It's best I get it all out there," Ezra said. "I had a minor injury after a mission. I was my team's medic. The truth was I wasn't all that brilliant in battle with a gun, but I was excellent at saving soldiers. I often think if I hadn't found my way into medic training, I would have left the Navy pretty early on."

"I thought he was a Marine." Liam opened the folder in front of him.

Tag tried to pass him a pair of reading glasses. "The Marines get their medics from the Navy. Avery says you have to wear these or you get a headache."

"Fuck you, Tag." But Li took the glasses. "I'm only wearing them because my darling thinks I look good in them."

"Avery's the one who needs glasses." That quip earned Tag a wifely smack against his big bicep. "So while Ezra would have started out in the Navy, and technically wasn't ever a Marine, he served with a Marine unit."

"He was an honorary Marine. He passed his test and got his pin." Somehow he felt the need to defend Ezra. Not that he didn't like the Navy. He didn't care either way, but it had meant something that his brother got that pin.

"He's talking about my Fleet Marine Force pin," Ezra explained. "It's a test you take to prove you know what you need to know about the Marine Corps. I was my unit's corpsman, what you call a medic. What that means is I was a Marine right until someone got hurt and then I was a doc. And I loved that. I thought about going to medical school after I got out, but that was pretty unrealistic for me."

"Why?" He'd never once heard that Ezra wanted to do anything but be in the military. He'd gone in because their parents hadn't had the money to send him to college, but he'd seemed happy there. How much had he missed? How much had Ezra hidden down deep?

"It costs a lot to get through medical school even with the military aid, and honestly, I don't know that I'm smart enough. I certainly didn't believe it back then."

"You were always smart."

"Not compared to my brother," Ezra said. "Anyway, to make a long story short, I got hooked on pain meds after my injury. I think it was a combination of things that included a deep depression I went into after my father died."

Beck had to shake his head. "You never seemed depressed."

"The drugs will do that to you," Ezra allowed. "Uhm, I'm pretty sure during that last year you never saw me when I wasn't high. I was excellent at hiding it, though I know some of the guys in the unit I was in at the time suspected I had a problem. I got called in by my CO one day and I thought I was going to get in serious trouble. Instead that man on the tape was there and he offered me a place in what he called a special unit."

"Just so we're clear," Eve began, "you're talking about Levi Green. He was the man who recruited you onto the unit you were in when the incident took place."

"Yes. I saw him the once and then one other time during the six months I was with that unit. I didn't talk to him much. He talked to my CO much more. I also wasn't given his name. That alone let me know we were working for the Agency," Ezra explained. "But I trusted them. My two favorite people in the world were agents."

Beck didn't want to think about what his brother's words were doing to him. He wasn't going to forgive Ezra. He didn't have to. He didn't have to forgive the people who had done him wrong. He could understand it in Kim's case, but he would still be married if Ezra hadn't played his games.

Wouldn't he? Then there was the issue of Levi Green picking Ezra Fain for his "special" unit. "He picked you specifically?"

Ezra nodded. "Yes. He said he'd been looking for the right corpsman to fill the last spot. I took it because I thought I might be able to hide my problems. I got on that team and realized I didn't have to hide at all."

"Because they were all corrupt in one way or another." Tag was looking down at the file in front of him. "Levi put together a group he could manipulate if he had to. Every man on the team had issues. Did Levi supply you with drugs?"

His brother's jaw tightened. "Someone did. I think we can probably bet it was him."

"I've got Theo working on finding out if Levi had any other special teams," Tag explained.

"I think he did." Kim glanced Tag's way, a serious expression on her face. "I think he had one in each branch of the military. He bragged about it to me once and told me his units would take him far. Most of us work with whoever is in the area, but Levi would move his own teams around the globe if he had to."

She'd never told him that. Suspicion was an old friend, and he felt it brush up his spine. Why wouldn't she have told him?

She turned his way as though she could read his mind. "I wasn't aware of this until after our divorce." She went back to speaking to Tag. "And obviously, we were working for the same agency during the time with the Lost Boys."

"You were a good agent." Tag looked almost sympathetic. "I truly understand the walls you had to put up. You were walking a very fine line, and I appreciate everything you did for us during that time. Charlie told you about the office, right?"

"Yes." Her face went a careful blank. "It looks nice."

"It's yours for as long as you want it," Tag offered. "I know you don't need the paycheck, but you do need the work. This isn't some sympathy offer. I'm not trying to placate your ex-husband. I think you've got excellent instincts, and I can't buy your experience. I want you to take the next couple of months and think about staying here with us."

"I appreciate it." The smile was back on her face. "I especially appreciate having a safe place for Roman for the rest of the summer."

"We're going to make sure you're all safe," Tag promised. "Now this seems to be getting emotional and that is icky. Do y'all need to sort this out and then Beck can write up a report?"

"I think that would be best," Eve said quietly. "I wasn't aware they hadn't talked. This is not the place for family history to be revealed. Why don't we leave you the conference room?"

"No," Kim said. "It's all right. It's better to get it out here and now so I can answer your questions. The truth of the matter is Ezra didn't understand the whys behind the missions he was sent on. We've all read the report Levi wrote?"

He should have taken Ezra up on his chance to make this private because it was obvious that his offer of coffee hadn't made a dent in Kim's walls. He wasn't sure why, but they were all up again this morning. She was sitting feet away but further than ever.

"The one that he never actually turned in? Yes." Charlotte sat back. "In it he accuses Ezra Fain of being the ringleader in delivering several packages of contraband materials to rebel groups in Southeast Asia. These materials include guns and other weapons of war. And they could go in under the radar because recon is what MARSOC does."

"Yes, I got the feeling it was Levi's version of Iran-Contra," Alex said. "So this was his way of covering his tracks. How did Solo get involved?"

"He wasn't just covering his tracks." The enormity of what Levi had done hit Beck forcibly. "He set Kim up to take the fall. Who handed the op over to you?"

"The director came into my office the day before it was going down and said he needed me to oversee a recon op because the original handler was dealing with something else. I asked who it was. I was told that was classified and all I had to do was give them a go and make sure I watched for anything that might halt the op. I didn't even know it was my brother-in-law's unit until Beck asked me to call it off."

"I talked to him the night before." Ezra stared at the conference table. "I called him because our mom was in bad shape and I wanted him to look in on her."

Beck shook his head. "That wasn't what it sounded like to me." He remembered how scared he'd been. His brother had been on another continent, walking into a dangerous mission, and he'd sounded suicidal. "You were upset that night."

"I was high that night," Ezra said quietly. "I was upset and high, and I don't even remember what I said to you, but I remember that you told me I better get my shit together or you would have me pulled from my unit."

"Because I didn't think you should be going on dangerous ops when you were that emotional. I wasn't trying to fuck up your career." How could he think that? Except apparently he sounded like a judgmental asshole a lot of the time.

"See, this is the family dynamic stuff that probably should be dealt with in therapy," Alex said.

Ezra shook his head. "I want to get this over with so I can head back to Sanctum. I'm still tired."

Weary. His brother looked weary. "That night I went to my wife and told her how upset I was and that I was going to talk to whoever was handling the op. Ezra was talking about a classified op to a person who didn't have clearance on it. Namely me. That meant I could likely get him pulled."

"And wreck his military career," Tag added. "Though I'll be honest, I can't think of anything worse than going into a dangerous op with an unstable team member. I don't think it was unfair of Beck to try to pull you."

"I wish he had. An addict doesn't care about right or wrong. That particular demon is selfish. He doesn't care who gets hurt. All that matters is his own comfort." Ezra's eyes found Beck's. "I'm so sorry for putting you in that position. And for everything that came after."

Yes, he definitely should have done this in private because he was going to look like such an asshole. He felt frozen. He didn't want to let go of this anger he had. He shouldn't have to. Years. Ezra cost him years with her. Still, Kim was sitting next to him. "I appreciate that. So as to that day, what were you there to do? I know what you were supposed to be doing. According to the records, you were supposed to do recon for a rescue mission. What was your true mission?"

He'd spent years thinking his brother had died trying to save a group of young women from their jihadist kidnappers. He'd made his brother a saint in his head, and he was having trouble remembering Ezra had been human and flawed.

Ezra sat up straighter, as though the soldier was still in there somewhere. "We were supposed to pass off a package to a rebel leader in the area. I don't know what was in it. It was odd, though. When we actually got there, the man we met with looked like an American. I didn't hear him talk because I was standing in the back. I wasn't feeling great."

Because he'd been coming down off a high. Because his brother had been using drugs.

How would he have reacted back then?

"Solo, what had you been told about the op?" Alex asked.

"Not much. I'd been told it was highly classified and I wasn't allowed to discuss it. I did not know who the original handler was. It was odd but not unheard of. It was stranger that Beck knew about the op. I should have gone straight to my boss and made a report, but I didn't want to get my brother-in-law in trouble. That was my fault. If I had, we likely wouldn't be in this position."

"No recriminations are necessary," Tag announced. "I think we can all agree that putting Solo on that headset was part of Levi's plan at the time. He had to have known what was going to happen."

"Like I said before, it was an ambush. He had to have planned it," Ezra agreed. "I know at one point he argued with our CO. I think Green was worried we were about to turn on him. That's the trouble with mutually assured destruction. It only works as long as one party isn't willing to actually kill the other and set himself free of that worry."

"According to Solo's report, the communication system malfunctioned. How much did you actually see of that op?" Charlotte asked.

He hadn't gone into the office with her that day. He'd spent the night at a cheap motel because of the fight they'd gotten into when she'd refused to call off the next day's op. He hadn't seen her again until he'd come home that night and she'd given him the news that Ezra was dead. He'd walked out and hadn't seen her again for months. He'd shipped her divorce papers and refused to take her calls.

He hadn't even considered her feelings. She'd cared about Ezra, too. She'd loved his whole family and he'd barred her from his mother's funeral.

He'd been so fucking selfish, and he didn't know if he could ever make it up to her.

"Did you know that day that Ezra was alive?" Liam asked.

"It doesn't matter when she knew," Beck said quickly.

A gentle smile turned the corners of Eve's mouth up. "It does for our investigation."

"I didn't know until he called me two days later," Kim admitted. "By then there had been a fire, supposedly set by the jihadist group that ambushed the unit. The whole area was considered too dangerous to go into for a week."

"I got hit, but I managed to hide." Ezra continued his story. "Like I said, I'd been a bit away from the group. There was a lot of confusion at the time. We really were in a bad area. One controlled by rebels. We were in unfamiliar terrain and when the shooting started, everything was confusing. I was hit and dragged myself behind a rock. I passed out at one point and it was all over when I woke up. Someone must have come out later and set the fires to cover what happened. I was found by some local who took me in, patched me up and hid me for days until Kim sent someone to get me out."

His brother had come so close to death. "And who was that?"

"Brother Francis Bruno," Ezra said, his eyes shining in the lights from overhead. "He was with a group of surgeons risking their lives in the area to help people. So many people risked their lives and their careers to help me. The brother got me through rehab. He helped me learn Italian. Between him and Kim, they got me the documents I needed to stay in Italy and go to seminary. Turned out, I was really good at that. I'm a better priest than I ever was a soldier. And that is all I know about what happened that day. I beg forgiveness every day for my cowardice, and I'm ready to stand up now."

But if he did, he would lose everything. "You would likely go to prison."

His brother nodded. "And there is good work to be done there, too."

Emotion threatened to choke him because it was overwhelming. His brother was sitting right in front of him. Was he putting on some kind of act?

He suddenly couldn't stay there a second longer. He pushed back his chair and stood. "I need to make a phone call."

He strode out of the room without another word because he wasn't sure what he would say.

Self-loathing was an old friend, and it bubbled up inside him. He'd been the cause of a whole lot of this. While he'd been telling himself he was righteous, he'd left his wife to deal with problems that should have been his, problems that he couldn't deal with because he hadn't been kind.

He slammed the door shut to his office and sank down onto his chair, his eyes catching on the picture on his desk.

"Liar." Kim had quietly opened the door.

"I needed a moment. That was a lot to take in. I'm sorry I didn't do it privately." He'd been warned and he'd arrogantly walked right into it and forced them all down the path with him. "I'll apologize to my brother later. I promise."

She sighed and closed the door behind her. "Hush. We don't do well when we talk." She closed the space between them and eased herself onto his lap. "I promised myself I wouldn't do this. But just hush and hold me. You had a rough morning."

She offered him comfort, and it made his eyes water. He wrapped his arms around her and let his head find her shoulder.

"Was he serious?" Beck asked.

"Ezra Fain is the kindest man I've ever met. If he says he'll go to prison and find meaning there, I believe him. And I believe he loves you."

He sat there, accepting her kindness, and something eased inside him, something that had been tight and uncomfortable for a very long time.

"I love you, Kim."

She was silent but she didn't leave.

He would say it until she believed him again.

Chapter Thirteen

Two hours later Kim found herself standing in front of the desk outside of Ian Taggart's big office. The name plate stated that the desk belonged to Geneva Rycroft and there was a picture of a woman with dark hair holding a toddler girl with a big bow in her hair, a smiling young man, and a dude with a beard who had to be the dad standing behind them gleaming with pride.

But it was a frowning Tasha sitting at the desk. She looked up from her phone. It must have been a different one because this one was smaller and had no bling on it at all. She slid the phone into her backpack and her spine straightened. "Hello, Ms. Solomon. How can I help you?"

There was definitely an iciness coming off the Taggart's eldest. She was starting to wonder if the teen didn't have a thing for Beck. She couldn't blame her. Beck was still hot and looked younger than his years. And he seemed kinder than he'd been before.

"I've got a meeting with your dad. I think your mom was coming, too."

The door came open and Charlotte waved her in. "We're here. Adam's coming up in a minute."

She walked through the door and into Tag's office, which was a monstrosity compared to Beck's. She'd thought his was nice, but Tag's was larger than her Paris flat and Manhattan apartment combined. He had a whole sitting area and a wall covered in pictures of his family.

"Is Beck all right?" Charlotte asked.

Big Tag was sitting on the couch, the remains of their lunch in front of him. "I would like to point out that I was not all for the family group therapy session we went through. I have enough of that with my own family. The boys have PTSD after the pranks Kala pulled last Halloween. We had a couple of sessions after that and now the boys have stopped trying to kill every clown they see."

"It made kids' parties very interesting for a while there," Charlotte admitted. "We were banned from one neighborhood entirely. I'm not joking. The watch group had our faces on posters and everything."

She was so glad Roman was a calm child. "Beck's all right. He needed a minute to process, that was all."

Why had she followed him? When Ezra had admitted he was all right with going to prison, that he was ready to pay any price he had to pay, she'd noticed how pale Beck had gone and she'd realized it had just become real for him. What had happened to his brother, how he'd changed and the years between them, had hit Beck with the force of a locomotive.

That wasn't true. She knew exactly why she'd followed him. She'd expected to catch him putting his fist through a wall. She'd wanted to see it, wanted to know that anger was still Beck's fuel of choice, that he was talking a bunch of bullshit about changing.

All she'd seen was regret on his face, a terrible sorrow as he'd sat there, and she hadn't been able to walk away from him. After what Charlotte had told her this morning, she'd wondered how long it had been since he'd had any comfort at all. Beck had always been a physical creature. When they'd been together, he'd loved holding hands and sitting with his arms around her. He could hold her for hours.

She'd had their child to hold, had someone to pour all her love into. Who had Beck had? A sad, single photograph? So she'd dropped herself onto his lap and waited for him to kiss her or let his hand find her breast. She'd been willing to give him that comfort and honestly, to take it for herself.

But he'd simply held her and breathed like he had to concentrate to do it. He'd laid his head on her shoulder and they'd sat there for the longest time.

I love you, Kim.

The words had damn near broken her heart because she couldn't say them back. Not because she didn't feel them. There would always be love between them. They had a son and she was eternally grateful.

She couldn't say them because she'd wanted nothing more than to surrender everything to Beck and tell him they could be a family. She'd wanted to lay right down and pretend nothing had happened, but she'd just relived the worst part of her life. While they'd talked, that time had played out in her head and she could still hear him cursing her.

She could still hear him saying she'd killed his brother and he would never forgive her.

When he'd decided to drive Ezra back to Sanctum himself, she'd been relieved.

"I'm glad you could be there for him," Charlotte replied as Ian handed her the plastic containers she packed in a tote bag she'd carried their lunch in. "I'm sorry to put you through that but it's important we have an idea of what happened then."

Ian sat back, crossing one leg over his knee as a big arm relaxed along the edge of the couch. "Tell me something, Solo. Are you going to be happy letting Levi ride off into the sunset?"

"I don't know that I'd put it that way." A bit of guilt bubbled inside her. She wasn't the only one Levi had hurt. He'd affected them all in ways, and giving him more power wouldn't make him less dangerous. "I guess I want it to be over, and I could pretend when I was in Malta. I could sink into being nothing more than Roman's mom, and now I have to think about a hundred different things."

"You would always have had to come out of that cocoon," Charlotte said with a sympathetic smile. "Roman would have started asking questions. He's a smart boy. Kenzie and Kala told me he knew more about the volcano experiment than the teacher, and he explained to my youngest in no uncertain terms why he shouldn't eat the magma even though it was nontoxic."

"That boy doesn't have a brain in his head," Taggart said. "But yours does, and at some point he's going to want to do something that requires real ID. Have you and Beck talked about changing his last name? Right now his paperwork is all under Roman Bruno. You can go back to your real name. Are you changing Roman's to Solomon?"

She knew what Beck would want, and it wasn't like she was deeply attached to her last name. It had so often brought her trouble. "I don't know. I suppose we need to talk about it."

It was odd how numb she felt today. Even as she'd sat in Beck's lap and let him hold her there had been a distance she wasn't sure he'd felt. She had. She'd held herself apart from him.

She felt like she was walking through her life but looking at herself from the outside.

"You probably have a lot to talk about." Charlotte sat down on the couch, and her husband's arm moved around her shoulders.

What would it be like to know the man she loved was a couple of doors down and that she could get a hug whenever she needed it?

There was a brisk knock and Adam Miles entered wearing a slick suit, his hair cut in the latest style. He was a stunning man and he'd kept himself very fit. She knew him only by reputation. And his wife's books. She'd loved his wife's romantic books all those years ago. Now she only read nonfiction and children's books.

She'd given up on everything but Roman seven years before. Did she want to live that way the rest of her life?

"Hey, you said you needed me?" Adam strode in. "Tell me it's not about Tris. What did he do? Because the last time he was showing off for Carys he broke his damn arm."

"That's because he was trying to show up Aidan on a skateboard, and he's nowhere near as coordinated," Charlotte said. "He needs to stop trying to be Aidan and start playing up his strengths."

"His strengths include hacking computer systems, so I'm going to challenge you on that." Adam sighed. "The last thing I need is the feds to show up on my doorstep."

"They're always on your doorstep," Ian pointed out. "You work with them constantly."

Adam pointed his way. "Yes, so they will probably be watching my young, wanna-be anarchist. I long for the days when I didn't have to worry about hormones. So what do you need?"

"I need you to keep track of Levi Green for me."

Adam groaned. "Damn it. You're going to get me arrested, aren't you?"

"If I do, I'll go in with you," Ian promised.

Adam snorted. "At least you'll protect me."

Ian grinned. "Nah, I'd sell you for cigarettes, buddy. I don't smoke. Ramen noodles. I've heard those are premium items in the joint."

Adam's eyes rolled. "So you want me to use my incredibly superior surveillance techniques on a CIA operative? I'm only saying yes because he's such a fucking asshole."

"I'm only asking because right now Jax and Hutch are working on it, and Jax needs to go back to Colorado soon. I've got an assignment for Hutch coming up in a couple of days," Ian explained. "I would put it on someone else and keep him here, but it's for an old friend of mine."

"Anything I can help with?" Adam asked.

"I think Hutch is the best person for this particular job," Charlotte replied.

"She's plotting." Ian slid his wife a sidelong glance. "The client is a friend's daughter, and she's adorably dorky. And single."

"And she would look so cute with Hutch. They're both a little nerdy and sweet, and I heard she's into baking." Charlotte's eyes sparkled as she played matchmaker. "Hutch has a big old sweet tooth. I think it's going to work out. I can feel it."

If only it were that simple. "I've actually got something I wanted to ask you all about. I meant to talk to you about this earlier, but I got sidetracked."

"That's what we call it, too," Tag snarked.

She ignored him. She wasn't about to tell him nothing had gone nasty between her and Beck in his office. It had been sweet. It had been emotional. It had been so fucking scary. "The day Levi showed up at my store I got this weird package. It was sent via courier, but it was nothing more than a single piece of paper. *Remember, remember the fifth of November,* and then a line that told me to look for Reva. Honestly, I didn't think about looking into it with everything that's gone on, but it had my name on it. K. Solomon. Maybe I'm being paranoid, but it seems a little coincidental to me that I would receive a message sent to my store the same day Levi showed up."

Tag was on his feet. "It's not a coincidence, and I think that message should have been sent here."

Adam was groaning. "I don't think Hutch is going to make it to his assignment."

"What's going on?" Kim watched as Tag threw open his door. "Hutch! Don't you hide. I see you. You cannot get away from me. I know all your hidey holes. Get in here, now."

Greg Hutchins walked into the room, a grimace on his face. He was a stunning man in his early thirties, with golden brown hair and a lean, muscular body that he somehow kept even though the rumor was the man loved candy. "Hide? I would never hide, boss."

"Who is Reva?" Tag asked.

Hutch started to turn. "I take back what I said. I'm hiding."

Charlotte intervened, catching Hutch's arm. "Come on, Hutch. We know you're not active."

"Do we?" Tag asked, looking every bit like a dad who would get his kid to talk. "Do we?"

Kim turned to Adam. "I have no idea what's going on."

"I think Hutch's past is coming back to haunt him," Adam said. "When Hutch was a kid, he got involved in a group called the People's Revolution. They were a bit like Anonymous back in the day, and they were way too invested in a comic book series called *V for Vendetta*."

"Which centered around an anarchist in a Guy Fawkes mask." She knew that much. "I think I remember a bit about them. They were a hacktivist group, right?"

"We were trying to do good things." Hutch seemed to be resigned to his fate, and he took a seat.

"You were releasing private paperwork and hacking citizens' computers." Tag stared at Hutch.

"Only to point out hypocrisy and to catch criminals." Hutch turned his blue eyes Kim's way.

Tag patted his shoulder. "Hutch, are you still working with them?"

Some of the tension left the room as Hutch rolled his eyes. "No.

But I do check in on them from time to time. Especially Reva."

"So this Reva is a real person?" Kim asked.

"Yeah, I've known her since we were kids. And by know, I mean online," Hutch admitted. "But she's not in the business anymore. She hasn't worked with the People's Revolution for years. She's married with two kids."

"She told you she's no longer working with the group?" Adam asked.

"I believe her. Look, I haven't actually messaged her in a couple of months. Some of the old crew checks in every now and then." Hutch pulled out his cell phone and offered it up to Adam. "Here. I'll let you go through everything I have."

Tag shook his head. "I believe you. I wasn't really upset. I think I have resting dad face now. I called you in because Solo got a message a couple of days ago to look for Reva."

Hutch's eyes widened. "Shit. That's not good. Why would anyone look for her? Like I said, she hasn't done anything for years."

"Did Reva specialize in anything?" Charlotte asked.

Hutch nodded. "She was an animal activist. She liked to prove that some of the makeup companies who said they weren't testing on animals were merely allowing third parties to do it for them."

"So she used to hack corporations?" Kim started to put some things together. "Here in the US?"

"Nah, she was somewhere in Europe at the time. She was from the States, but she was living over in Germany when I knew her. We bonded because we both came from military families and had knocked around the globe a lot," Hutch explained.

All of her alarms were starting to go off. "Did she ever do side projects? Hire out her skills?"

"We all did. I stopped when I went to work for Ten. But the rest of the People all had side hustles. Most of them worked in IT, but they weren't necessarily above doing some shady shit for cash." Hutch's eyes brightened. "Hey, you know it was about ten years ago that Reva got out. She told me she had a big job and she was cutting all her ties and doing the family thing."

Tag stared down, his dad face definitely on display. "And she was in Europe and she liked to hack corporations like pharmaceutical companies."

Hutch nodded again. "Yep."

"And she got a big job ten years ago and someone magically put her name in front of Solo." Tag seemed determined to lead his puppy to water.

"Yeah, it's weird, huh?" Hutch asked.

It was a good thing Hutch was cute. "All right. We need to find her and figure out what she knows about the original Kronberg job. I can tell you right now that Levi would have had to go outside the Agency to fake those records."

"We're talking about the records Tucker stole from Kronberg? The ones we found in Paris seven years ago?" Adam had his tablet out and he was using a pen to write some notes on it.

Charlotte had perked up, too. "The ones that supposedly proved Solo was working with Hope McDonald? Yeah, I always wondered how he managed that. He was good with a computer, but he wasn't that good."

"Levi always hired out his IT work. Normally he would have used someone like Hutch when he was working for the Agency. But he wouldn't want anyone to know about this. And he's a smooth talker. A hacktivist looking to make some cash would be perfect because he would have something over her." When she thought about it, using someone connected to the People's Revolution would be perfect. Anyone working for a group like that would be vulnerable.

Hutch's jaw dropped slightly. "Hey, do you guys think Reva might have done that job for Levi?"

Tag groaned and looked to his wife. "Are you sure about sending him?"

Charlotte waved him off. "Noelle is smart enough for both of them. Now, let's talk about why and who would have sent this to you. How did you get the note and do you still have it?"

"Of course. It's one of the only things I brought with me from Malta. It showed up the same day Levi did." When she wasn't going over all the ways living with Beck for three months was a mistake, she was thinking about this.

"How was it delivered?" Tag asked.

"Courier. I've got the envelope. It's in my purse in the office

Charlotte showed me." She'd dropped it off at the desk she'd been assigned. "I'll go grab it. I assume you can try to hunt down who sent it to me."

Adam nodded. "And I'll also try to figure out where Reva is hanging her hat these days. Hutch, I know you're supposed to protect the identities of your former friends."

Hutch had stood, and he was focused now. "If she worked for Levi and someone knows it, she's in danger. She's got a family. We need to find her and move her somewhere safe."

"Good, then we have a plan." Kim wished she was more eager to get on the case. At one point in her life she would have felt adrenaline running through her veins, but now she worried. "I'll go grab it."

She opened the door and stopped because Jax was standing at Tag's assistant's desk.

"Can you let Solo know I was looking for her?" Jax asked Tasha.

Tasha simply gestured behind her. "She's out."

Jax turned and smiled. "Hey, uhm, I hope you don't mind but Beck thought you might like some company."

She turned and tears filled her eyes because Ariel and River were walking down the hallway. River was laughing at something Ariel had said.

The two true friends she'd made in all her life. Her feet felt rooted to the floor. Why were they here?

Ariel's head turned and she caught sight of Kim and stopped, her hand going over her heart for a second before she jogged down the hall and held her arms out. "Oh, Kim, I missed you. I missed you so much."

It took a moment for her to bring her arms up and hug Ariel back.

"River's nervous. She's worried you won't want to see her," Ariel whispered. "She forgave you years ago and we talk about you all the time."

Kim glanced back at River, who was standing there looking like she wasn't sure what to do. Now Kim let the tears flow. She held out a hand, offering River a place in their circle.

River ran and joined them, her arms going around them.

"I missed you both so much," Kim said.

For a moment, she was content.

* * * *

Beck turned down Pearl Street and started making his way to Woodall Rodgers. From there it was five minutes to Sanctum and Kai's office.

That was the only reason he'd offered to drive his brother back. It was simply easier for him to do it since he had a session with Kai. It had nothing to do with the fact that he hadn't been able to stop thinking about what had been said in that conference room.

"Roman seemed to like the kids' club." Ezra was lying in the back seat, staring up at the roof of the car. "He didn't even notice when I left."

The words were said with a forlorn sigh.

"He didn't notice me, either. He was having too much fun with the Taggart boys and Jesse's youngest." It had been good to see Roman laughing. Jesse and Phoebe's youngest was Roman's age, a cute kid with a ready smile named Jeremy. They were fast friends, and Roman seemed to be fitting in.

"It's nice to see him with other kids. He always seemed lonely back home." Ezra was the one who sounded lonely.

"When do you think you'll go back? I mean, you work for the church, right?"

"Unless they figure out I lied about my name and all the other stuff, and then I'll probably get kicked out." Ezra sighed. "Obviously there are some people who know, but it's one of those things that only works if it's not out in the open. If it gets out, then the press runs with the story and they'll have to let me go. I don't know what I'll do if I don't have the church. Prison at least would give me purpose."

He wasn't sure how all of this had worked. "Aren't you supposed to confess your sins? Did you forget about that part?"

"I confessed. I confessed to a priest in Italy. Every single one of my sins. This was after rehab. I'd decided I wanted to give seminary a try. The father told me that sometimes the path God leads us down is winding, but we get where we need to go. He said a name isn't as important as what was in my heart if serving God and my fellow man in this way is what I wanted to do."

Beck was quiet for a moment as he made the turn that led to the freeway. "Is this what you want to do? It's possible I might be able to get your name back. I think we should talk to a lawyer about the possibility of immunity if you testify about what really happened with your team."

"To what end? Do you honestly think I would make it to a courtroom? Or that there would even be a trial?"

He'd thought a lot about this since the moment he'd realized his brother was alive. "I think Congress would be interested in what the Agency was doing. They're likely still doing it, and they got a bunch of Marines killed."

"Ah, but they picked us carefully, didn't they?" Ezra pointed out the main problem. "It's exactly why we were selected for the team. Because once the secrets come out, we wouldn't be credible witnesses. I gave up on justice long ago, and honestly, some of the men who died had families. Let their children believe they were heroes."

He made the turn and accelerated to enter the highway. "You think I should let sleeping dogs lie, don't you?"

He wasn't sure he could. Levi Green had cost him so much, but it was about more than vengeance. It was about safety. No matter what Levi said, he would come after them again. And who knew how many others Levi had hurt in his never-ending quest to climb to the top of the ladder.

"Not at all. I think you should do what you need to do to protect Kim and your son." Through the rearview mirror he could see that Ezra had turned and gone up on one elbow, resting his head there. "I think you should take down Levi Green. Then you'll confess to me and I'll offer you penance."

"You're supposed to tell me to turn myself in," he pointed out.

Ezra merely sighed. "I'll confess, too. I've found my European brothers are very understanding. Especially the Italians. I've listened to mafia confessions. You cannot unhear those."

He really wanted to ask about it. It was easy to slip back into their roles. Ezra could tell a great story. He'd been the go-to guy at all sleepovers to make up something scary. And he could embellish a wild night out with style. The desire to find a bar, order a beer and some wings, and ask his brother to spill about the last few years of his life tempted him, but he forced the thought aside. This wasn't some game they were playing. Ezra was a different person. He'd lived a whole life in the time they'd been apart, and he didn't recognize parts of the man. If things had been normal, perhaps he would have watched his brother change over time.

Or Ezra would have died of a drug overdose and his brother would have been lost forever.

He couldn't possibly know what would have happened. That's what Kai would tell him. He would say a bunch of crap about forces that shaped a person, but the truth was his brother was here and he had a decision to make.

He could simply hope that Ezra went back to Malta, and half a world's distance would do its work. Ezra would have his world and Beck could have his. They didn't have to truly be brothers. They would be two guys who'd once shared a mom.

The truth was he didn't need Ezra anymore. Ezra had always been the fun brother. People flocked to be around him because he was brighter than the rest of the world. Beck had gone with him, had rolled with Ezra's friends. Now he had friends of his own. Now he had his own family, one he'd cobbled together over the years, formed despite the pain of losing Ezra and Kim.

Ezra had Kim and Roman, and Beck was taking them back because they were his. Because Ezra had stolen them from him.

He wasn't going to feel guilty about shipping his brother back to Europe. Ezra had made his bed and he would lie in it.

"Do you want me to tell you about what Roman was like as a baby?" Ezra asked the question softly, as though he wasn't sure he'd wanted to make the offer at all.

He was about to point out that he wouldn't have to be told stories about his son if Ezra hadn't helped Kim keep him hidden when he noticed the blue and red lights come on behind him.

He glanced down at his speedometer. He wasn't speeding. He turned on his blinker and moved over to let the police car speed by.

"What's going on?" Ezra asked.

The cruiser didn't speed by. It followed him.

Fuck. "We're getting pulled over by the police. Is there any way you can hide in the floorboard?"

"Do you know how tall I am?" Ezra asked. "Also, I still think he could see if he looked through the back windows. That might cause some questions."

He started to move to the side of the highway. "All right. I need you to ease up and try to get your seat belt on. I'm not sure why he's pulling me over, but I'm going to take whatever ticket he gives me and then we'll get to Sanctum as quickly as possible."

He had zero idea what he'd done to catch the officer's attention, and he was paranoid enough to have his mind go a thousand different places.

But Levi didn't know Ezra was alive. He couldn't. Beck took a deep breath and came to a stop as Ezra eased up in the back and gingerly reached up to pull his seat belt down and click it into place.

"Follow my lead and don't talk if you don't have to." Beck rolled the window down and put his hands on the steering wheel.

The officer stepped up. He wore mirrored aviators over his eyes. Beck made careful note of his badge number. "Sir, are you all right?"

"Of course," he replied, sending the officer a surprised look. "Why would you ask? I wasn't speeding. Why was I pulled over?"

"You were driving erratically." The officer stared into the back seat, his hand on the gun at his side. "You swerved in your lane. And I didn't notice you had a passenger. Are you in danger?"

"He's a friend of mine," Beck said quickly. "He had too much to drink at lunch and I'm giving him a ride home. I made him sit in the back because I didn't want him to throw up in the front."

"I feel so bad," Ezra said in a way that didn't make it sound like he was either drunk or feeling bad. "I need to get home and lie down."

"You need to stay in your seat belt." The officer relaxed slightly and took a step back. "All right then. I'll let you off with a warning since I can see you've got a lot on your hands. You keep focused on the road. Stay safe."

Beck didn't move for a moment, watching the officer through the rearview mirror.

"That was okay," Ezra said, letting out a long breath. "It could have gone way worse."

His brother was out of practice, or perhaps he'd never had these particular instincts. "No. That went far worse than I expected. He didn't have a reason to pull me over."

"You can't know that."

The cruiser pulled away and Beck put the car in drive again. "I know I wasn't driving erratically. I was perfectly steady. He had no reason to pull me over except he wanted to look in the car."

"Maybe he caught sight of something odd in the back seat," Ezra offered. "Why else would he want to look in the back?"

He touched the button on his dashboard that connected his phone. "Call Ian Taggart." While it rang he replied to his brother. "Because he wanted to see if I'm driving you around."

"Beck, no one knows I'm alive."

The line picked up. "This is Taggart."

"Ian, we have a problem." He took the next exit and headed back to the office.

His session was going to have to wait.

Chapter Fourteen

Kim stood in the doorway watching her son sleep. He wasn't twisting or turning. He'd pretty much dropped right off after she'd kissed his forehead and turned the lights out.

But then he'd had a big day. He'd been brimming with excitement when she'd picked him up at the kids' club. He'd introduced her to a bunch of kids that he'd called his new friends, and she'd talked to Kenzie Taggart, who'd told her all about Roman's day and explained that he'd really liked peanut butter and jelly sandwiches, and how could he be six and not know what they are?

Dinner had been more of Roman talking about his new friends and the teachers and how some of the kids were going to a camp soon, and didn't that sound like fun? Beck had listened intently and then asked about how her reunion with Ariel and River had gone. He'd been patient and attentive. After dinner he'd explained that he and Rob and Jax had made plans for the three ladies to have a spa and lunch day at a swanky hotel where they could spend their entire Sunday catching up and the men would handle all the childcare. The only reason they weren't going on Saturday was Big Tag's party, which he'd asked her to attend with him.

It was incredibly thoughtful and yet she could sense something simmering inside him, something dark and needy.

She turned, ready to go to the bedroom he'd assigned her to. It was comfortable, larger than her room in Malta, and it felt incredibly empty.

She wasn't sure how long she would be able to hold out. How long would it be before she was the one knocking on his door looking for comfort?

She stopped because he was standing at the end of the hall. He'd changed out of the khaki slacks and button-down he'd worn to work. It was obvious he'd taken a shower because his hair was still wet, and all he was wearing was a pair of pajama bottoms.

One of the things she'd always found so fascinating about this man was how he morphed from blandly attractive office guy into the kind of alpha male that would make any woman's heart skip a beat. It was like the khakis and loafers were some sort of armor he wore, and every layer he peeled back exposed the hard masculinity underneath.

"Is he asleep?"

She wasn't sure if she wanted to answer that question. If she did, then she owed him time, time that would lead to his bed. Time that would lead to his hands on her and his mouth on her. His body against hers.

God, she wanted him. "Yes. Did you hear anything back from Tag?"

"He's got a call in to his friend at the DPD." Those pajama bottoms rode low, exposing his six pack and the notches at his hips. "Hopefully we'll know something tomorrow. Also I talked to Rob and Jax. We'll all be together on Saturday at the party. But we're sending a bodyguard with y'all on Sunday."

She nodded. She wasn't going to fight him on protection, despite the fact that she and Ari could take care of themselves and River. At least Ari probably could. She needed to start training again. "All right. Thank you for the spa day. And for bringing Ari and River here. I loved seeing them again. I loved meeting their kids. Roman seemed to get along with Caden and Rio. They're darling. And Dara is adorable."

She'd sat and held Ariel's baby while she slept, and it had reminded her so much of how she'd felt holding Roman.

She wanted another baby. She shouldn't. She was too old, right?

Her life wasn't exactly settled.

"She is. Luckily she takes after her mom," he said wistfully. His gaze hardened. "Are you going to the club with me tomorrow?"

"Yes."

"Then there's no reason to stay away from me tonight. Come to my bedroom."

She hesitated.

He stared for a moment and then took a step back. "All right. I'll see you in the morning."

This was what had been bubbling under his surface. He'd had a day and he needed sex. He needed the control that came with his kind of sex. He needed her to submit to him and let him know she trusted him.

She might have been able to turn him away if he'd simply needed it from any woman, but he needed her. Only her. He'd been faithful even when he'd had no idea where she was or what she was doing.

They had a horrible past, but through it all this desperate need had always been between them.

Because she needed him, too.

At least now she knew how long she could hold out.

She crossed the distance between them and let her hands find his chest, glorying in the warmth of his skin. "I don't want to be alone tonight either. I'm sorry. I'm nervous. It's been a long time for me."

His fingers sank into her hair. "Exactly the same time for me. Except you had a nice man who touched you and caressed you and brought you to orgasm a couple of days ago."

He was staring at her like she was the most beautiful thing in the world, and she started to relax. It would be good. Sex between them had always been good, and she needed the release. She could hold herself apart. She could get what she needed and not give too much up.

"It wasn't enough." Those few moments in Sicily hadn't even been close to enough. "It was good, but I wanted more."

His fingers tightened, pulling lightly at her scalp. "I can give you more. Do you remember the rules?"

She liked the rules. The rules reminded her that they were different now. They weren't the same dumb kids who'd fallen into bed and never wanted to get out. "Yes. I obey you for as long as I like, and I can stop you at any moment."

It was true. She was in control, but what the exchange did was give Beck permission to put everything on the table. He didn't have to hesitate to ask for what he wanted because they'd agreed to talk about all of it.

The kids they'd been certainly hadn't done that.

"Yes, but let's emphasize the 'you obey me' part and just know the rest of it is there if you need it." He stopped short of putting his mouth on hers. "You might need it. I feel restless today."

She felt certain it wasn't only today. "I'll let you know if it's too much. But seriously, Beck, I hadn't even kissed anyone until I kissed you a couple of days ago. I don't know...I've had a baby since you saw me last. I've changed."

Her body had scars she didn't have before, and he was still the gorgeous man she'd dreamed of at night.

She was older, a little heavier.

He tugged on her hair. "You're still the most gorgeous woman I've ever known. You still make me crazy just thinking about getting my hands on you. I want you to walk into that room and take your clothes off for me because I'm going to think you're sexy as hell. I want to look at you. I want to study you and memorize you all over again. I want to touch and kiss and lick every inch of you, and when I'm done I want to fuck you until I forget we were ever apart."

It would be dangerous to forget, but she wanted everything else he'd promised. She especially wanted to feel sexy again. Her skin was already starting to heat, to tingle wherever he touched her. "Yes."

"And then tomorrow night we're going to drop Roman off with my friend Kai and his wife, and we're going to a club where we'll check everything at the door. All that will matter for four hours is that we are Dom and sub. We'll spend the whole time indulging in everything we can't all week long."

Sex. Intimacy. Each other.

It scared the hell out of her, but she couldn't tell him no. She'd agreed to this deal. It wasn't fair to back out.

She might be out of practice when it came to the spy stuff, but damn, she was up to date on self-deception.

He finally brought his lips to hers and brushed them in the sweetest kiss. It was over altogether too soon, and he stepped back, releasing her. "Go to my bedroom and take off your clothes."

It would be so much easier if he ripped her clothes off. She wasn't even fond of the blouse she was wearing.

He turned and walked down the hall, the opposite direction of his bedroom. She glanced back and he stopped at Roman's bedroom, looking in on their son the same way she had.

It made her heart feel too tight. She forced herself to walk away, to move down the hall and into Beck's bedroom with its king-sized bed and carpet her feet sank into. She'd only been in this room once when he'd given her the tour of the house. It was a comfortable room, but there was very little of Beck in it. There was a small dish on the dresser where he could put his wallet and a charger for his cell. Other than that, it was utilitarian, and that was a shame because there was so much room.

It needed a comfy chair for reading and something other than the one sad lamp on a plain nightstand.

She glanced in the mirror and caught sight of herself. She wasn't bad. Her cheeks had taken on a rosy glow and her hair was mussed. She looked like a woman who'd recently been kissed.

She didn't look like a woman who'd uprooted her whole life and her son's and who might still be in danger.

"I want you to take a deep breath," Beck said from the doorway. "I want you to acknowledge a couple of things for me starting with the fact that our son is all right."

She turned back to him. "I know. I'm sorry. I was looking around and I didn't follow orders."

His eyes narrowed. "I understand. I can completely forgive you not being naked. Now I want you to obey me and take me seriously. I want you to close your eyes and take a deep breath."

This was stupid, but she got the feeling if she told him so, she might be in actual trouble. She let her eyes close and forced her shoulders down from around her ears. She filled her lungs and held the breath there for a moment before letting it out.

"And another." He sounded like he was closer to the big bathroom now.

She forced another breath, though she felt herself relax slightly.

"This time I want you to know that our son is sleeping and he's happy and he's eager for tomorrow. He's not afraid. He's not in pain. He's a resilient kid and he knows he's loved."

He was not going to make her cry. She took a deep breath. "Okay. Roman's okay."

"This time I want you to know that Ezra is safe. He's got two bodyguards staying the night with him, and Sanctum has a lot of security. He's okay."

She knew how much it took for him to add his brother in what was essentially nighttime prayers. "Ezra's okay."

This time the breath felt cleansing.

"And you're okay. Whatever happens between us, you are okay, and I will ensure your safety and comfort. I'll take care of you."

She opened her eyes and looked at him. He was standing there, his gaze on her. "I'm okay. You're okay, too, Beck." How did he do this to her? Two minutes before she wasn't going to acknowledge anything but the sex. "I'll make sure that you're okay."

The sexiest smile crossed his face. "How are you going to do that, baby?"

She could think of exactly how she wanted to do that. He was good. Far better than he used to be. He'd settled her fears so she could focus on herself for once. On them. On him.

It would be so good to focus on him.

But first she was going to prove that she could obey when she wanted to. She started to slowly unbutton her blouse. "I seem to remember you asked me to touch you. I could start there."

He'd put something on the nightstand while her eyes had been closed. It was a tray, and she couldn't see what was on it. "That would be an excellent place to start. Where will you go from there?"

She set the blouse on the dresser and went to work on her slacks. "I'll take you in my hand and I'll stroke that big cock of yours until it's hard and thick and long. I'll think about what it's going to feel like to have you inside me."

His eyes closed briefly, and a low groan came from his mouth. "You don't need to touch me to get me hard. I'm hard as hell right now, baby."

275

She could tell. His flannel pajama bottoms had tented admirably, and she hadn't lied at all. She truly was thinking about what it would feel like to have that big cock penetrating her. Her nipples had peaked, and it had nothing to do with the air conditioner. She folded her slacks and reached behind to undo the hooks of her bra, deeply grateful that Charlotte Taggart apparently didn't believe in plain cotton undies. There had been a week's worth of outfits hanging in the closet, and several bags of underwear, bras, socks, and pajamas, all in her size.

The undies were a pearly color with lace adorning the sides, and suddenly she felt sexier than she had in forever.

"After I finish stroking you, I'm going to get on my knees and I'm going to lick your cock, Beck. It's been so long. I want to taste you again."

He grimaced. "Baby, it's been so long that if you keep spitting those dirty words out of that sweet mouth of yours, I'm going to show you how good my imagination is. I'm close right now. I'm close because we're in the same room and I can see your beautiful body. There were nights I sat up and wondered if I would ever see you again."

She shook her head. She couldn't do this part. "Please. Can we stay in the moment?"

"We can for now, but my whole past is wrapped up in loving you. I want a future, too, but I took that from us and I have to earn it back. So we'll stay in the present for now. Take those panties off. I want to see every inch of you, and I want everything you promised me."

She could give it to him. This was exactly what she needed—to sink into what they could give each other in the moment. In this room there was no future to worry about and no past to drag them down. They were Kim and Beck—a sub and her Dom.

She hooked her thumbs under the waistband of her lacy panties and shoved them off. Then she took every bit of knowledge she'd gleaned from romance novels years before and sank to her knees, spreading her legs wide. It was a vulnerable position, but it did something for her. It made her feel incredibly sexy to open herself physically to him.

He moved in front of her and his hand came down to tip her chin up. "I dreamed about this every single night."

"Beck," she started.

He shook his head. "Sorry. That was the last of it. You are gorgeous and I'm going to be so proud to show you off tomorrow. Are you going to have a problem walking around the club showing off how gorgeous you are?"

"I would have said yes, but I feel pretty good right now."

"I intend to make you feel fabulous." His hands went to his hips. "I think you should undress your Dom."

There was nothing she wanted more than to see him in all his glory. She felt a deep sense of power as she reached up and began to slowly drag the pajama bottoms down. He wasn't wearing boxers so his cock sprung free quickly, and she was reminded how thick it was, how it barely fit in her hand, and how it would make her jaw ache the tiniest bit when she deep throated him. She helped him out of the pajamas and settled back. "You're still gorgeous, Beck."

"Touch me. God, I'm going to die if you don't touch me," he said, his voice deep.

She sighed and reached for his cock. He smelled like soap and that delicious musky scent that let her know he hadn't lied. He really was ready to go off, and she hadn't touched him yet. It wouldn't matter. They had these hours to do whatever they liked, and she intended to spend them with her hands on him. He'd said he wanted to relearn her? She would do the same. She would caress every inch of his skin, kiss every scar, make memories for when they were apart again.

His cock was still lovely and the moment she touched him, a thousand memories shot through her of all the nights they'd lain together. She'd missed this so much, and yet she hadn't been able to bring herself to have this level of intimacy with anyone else. He was the only one for her.

"You're going to kill me, aren't you? You know I won't rush you so you're going to make me ache for it." He said it with a smile on his face.

But hadn't they both ached enough? She took him in one hand and gave him a long, slow stroke. Breath rattled out of his body, and she watched a shudder run through him. Pleasure? Or relief? He looked like a man whose longing had finally been realized. Like he knew he would finally get what he needed.

Her.

His hand found the top of her head, and slowly he tangled his fingers in her hair, getting a gentle grip. "You know I can come and still take care of you a few minutes later. I promise."

She knew. He would take care of her one way or another, and there was nothing she wanted more than for Beck to use his hands and mouth to throw her over the edge before he sank his cock inside. "You should tell me what you want me to do in great detail. Like I said, it's been a while for me, and I might not remember clearly."

It was a lie, but a playful one. She remembered every moment with him, knew exactly how he liked to have his cock sucked, but she wanted to hear him.

His eyes were narrowed as he tugged on her hair, urging her forward. "I want you to put that gorgeous mouth of yours on my cock. I want you to use your tongue to make me crazy. I want you to cup my balls and suck my dick until I can't see straight, until the only thing in the world that matters is how soft and hot your mouth is around me."

She leaned forward and licked at his cock, thrilling in the way it jumped at her touch. She sucked him lightly behind her lips, giving the head of his cock a brief twirl of her tongue before releasing him again.

"Oh, that's good. That's so freaking good," Beck breathed.

She gripped the base of his cock and leaned forward again, giving him exactly what he wanted. She licked every inch of his cock, paying particular attention to the super sensitive underside of the cockhead. There she flattened her tongue and caressed that bit of skin while sucking gently.

"I knew you were going to kill me." Every word out of his mouth was accompanied with a panting breath.

She settled in to the job at hand, sucking and stroking and reveling in the power she had over him. She might be in the submissive position, but she had the power right now. It would be an exchange because she got the idea once he'd come in her mouth, once she'd swallowed him down and he could breathe again, he would take the power right back and she would be the one shaking and begging.

"That's it. Just a little more," he said as his hips started to pump.

She sucked him deeper with each pass of her mouth, rolling her tongue around him as best she could. When she gave him the barest hint of her teeth, he hissed, and she felt his balls draw up tight against him as he began to fill her mouth.

She drank him down, her heart thrumming in her chest and every inch of her skin feeling alive as he softened in her mouth.

She sat back, licking her lips as she looked up at him.

It wasn't more than a second before he was lifting her up and lightly tossing her on the bed.

"I make this mistake with you every single time. I know we need to work through things, but I can't stop myself." He gripped her ankles and tugged her down until she was in the perfect position for him to drop to his knees and get his face right in her pussy.

She was about to point out that they were living in the moment, but the first swipe of his tongue took her breath away. He didn't play around. He started eating her pussy like the starving man he was.

His tongue plunged deep as he parted the petals of her pussy and his thumb found her clit.

She clutched the soft comforter and bit back a cry, spreading herself open so he didn't miss an inch of her pussy. She didn't think about the fact that she was wetter than she'd been in forever, that she could smell her own arousal. All that mattered was Beck groaning against her sensitive flesh and the long luxurious licks of his tongue.

Her eyes closed as pure sensation took over, rushing across her skin and making the blood thrum through her as she moved closer and closer to orgasm.

He pressed down and pleasure washed over her, sweeping away all her cares and worries. They were gone in a wave of heat and satisfaction, the thrill heightening her senses.

Beck rose to his feet, staring down at her. "Now I think we can really get started."

She caught the gleam in his eyes and knew he was far from done for the night.

* * * *

Beck stared down at the woman who'd always been the center of his universe, and a feeling far more satisfying than any orgasm flowed through him.

He had another shot with her. She was here. She wasn't running. Oh, he knew he would have to deal with some bullshit about how much better they would be apart in a couple of months if he didn't prove to her how they'd changed, but he had no intention of failing at that.

He reached to the small tray he'd place on the edge of the bed before she'd gotten naked. While he'd been leading her through a personal inventory, he'd brought this little kit out and set it where he could reach it easily.

What he hadn't told her was he'd gone through the same exercise while he'd taken a shower. He'd closed his eyes and told himself that Kim was safe, that Roman was safe.

That his brother was safe.

The day had been rough. He knew the cop could have been honest in his reasoning for pulling them over, but he doubted it. He didn't believe in coincidence anymore. He had to think that Levi now knew Ezra was alive. And then there was that mysterious note Kim hadn't mentioned to him. She'd brought it to Tag. He'd had to let that go, too.

He had to earn her trust back.

But she was here, and he left behind the worry of the day because he'd promised her they would spend this time in the now.

And the now included making her scream for him again.

"I want you to kneel on the bed for me."

Her eyes came open. "What? Beck, come on. I'm good. You can go for it."

How quickly she forgot. It was time to show her that he meant business. He gripped her ankles and easily flipped her over so he had access to her gorgeous ass. She'd barely gotten out a minor shriek before his hand came down in a short arc. It wasn't more than a light crack against her cheek, but it made her gasp.

"I said I want you to get on your knees for me."

"I already did that," she shot back like the brat she was.

He'd only ever dealt with perfectly submissive partners for the simple fact that he wasn't going to touch one of them sexually. He was strictly a service top at Sanctum. He spanked subs and whipped them when they wanted. He always used a chair and St. Andrew's Crosses. He rarely ever used his hand during a spanking.

Because it was all for her. All for this mouthy brat who'd held his heart in her hands more years than he cared to admit.

He slapped her ass again. "You remember your safe word?"

Her head turned slightly, and she wrinkled her nose his way. "You think I need a safe word for that baby tap, Beck? You forget who I am."

He wasn't the one who'd forgotten she was a Valkyrie glorious bitch goddess he worshipped with his whole heart. He gave her a harder smack, one that got her skin pink. "I know exactly who you are." He spanked her again. "Do you know who I am? Because I can spank you all night."

He gave her another three, each slightly harder than the last, and she was breathless when he finished, but she got up to her knees.

"Happier?" she asked, apparently unwilling to stop the saucy replies.

"Yes, because you've given me new ways to punish you." He grabbed her from behind, dragging her back against his chest and getting his hands on those magnificent breasts of hers. He cupped them and let his fingers find her nipples. He gave her a hard tweak that made her wriggle against him. "See. I can pull and pinch all your sweet parts like this."

Her head fell back against his shoulder. "I'm sorry, Beck."

He should tell her to call him Sir, but he didn't want that. He liked his name coming from her mouth. For so long he'd denied himself the name he'd grown up with. Hearing her say it with that breathy plea in her voice brought him right back to the moment when he knew they were meant to be together.

She'd believed it even when the world had fallen apart. She'd had faith.

It was time to repay her.

His cock was coming back to life rapidly. He rubbed himself

against the seam of her ass, nestling himself lightly there. "I love you."

She stiffened in his arms. "No. You told me we would stay in the moment."

"I love you in the moment," he whispered in her ear. "Right here. Right now. I love you."

He didn't mention that he'd loved her in the past. He would love her in the future. He would love her long after they'd passed from this earth and their son lived on.

"That's not fair."

He tweaked her nipples again. He'd never promised to play fair. "It's true. As true as this is." He flexed his pelvis and slid his cock along her backside. "Are you going to be good for me now or do we need to continue with the spanking?"

"I like the spanking, but I want you inside me."

At least she could be honest with him in this space. He planned for a lot more honesty tomorrow night. Tonight he was going to give her what she wanted. As much pleasure as she could handle.

"I want you to come for me again." Because he likely needed to sleep with her a couple of times before he would last as long as he wanted to. But he'd planned tonight's session out carefully. He wasn't getting them in trouble the way he had the last time. If she got pregnant, it would be because she wanted to.

Because she trusted him enough to share a pregnancy with him, to share their kid's childhood.

He reached over and picked up the small wand he'd bought earlier in the day. It was sterilized and ready for her. He flicked the *on* button and a low, unmistakable hum started.

A breathy moan escaped from Kim and she rubbed back against him. "Seriously?"

He nipped at her earlobe. "Seriously. You're going to come for me and then I'll get my turn. But I want to hear you, want to feel you come."

Her hands came back to cup his hips as though she knew she would need something to hold on to. His left arm was around her, just below her breasts. He had no intention of letting her fall.

He brought the vibrator against her pussy. "Tell me when I hit the right place."

He didn't need words. Her whole body started to move against the wand in his hand.

"That's it. It feels so good," she whispered. Her hips moved, bumping her ass against his cock and getting him harder than he'd been before she'd used that sweet mouth of hers to swallow him down.

He moved with her, cupping her breast and holding the wand against her so she could find the perfect spot to send her into bliss. It wasn't long before she shuddered against him, and he felt every muscle in her body relax.

He eased her down on the bed and set the wand on the tray. There was the sweetest smile on her face. He remembered that dreamy expression. It meant he'd done his job well.

He reached for the second item he'd put on the tray. He watched her as he rolled the condom over his cock. Her blonde hair was spread across the comforter and she looked so fuckable it hurt. She'd been worried about the changes in her body, but she'd only gotten more gorgeous. He'd loved her body when it was in peak physical condition, when she'd been a weapon. He loved her body like this, too. Softer.

He accepted that he would love her no matter what. Her body was beautiful because it housed the soul that completed his own.

"Beck?" She was staring up at him, a bit of the dreaminess fleeing.

He was pushing her too hard, too fast, but he couldn't help the way he felt. He needed to keep some of it to himself. "I was thinking of how beautiful you are." He moved between her legs, spreading them wide. She needed this to be hot. She wasn't ready for his emotion yet. He hooked her knees over his elbows, making her utterly vulnerable to him. "I was thinking about how much I want to fuck you."

Her pussy was still wet from the orgasms he'd given her. She was slick and hot, and he couldn't wait a second longer. He surged inside her and his eyes rolled from the pure pleasure of her tightening around him.

He thrust in and pulled out, letting himself off the leash for the first time that night. All day this was where he'd needed to be. He needed to end every night inside her and wake up with her in his arms.

He let her legs slide down and pressed his body to hers, kissing her in long passes as he fucked her hard. Her arms and legs wound around him, surrounding him with her silky heat.

It was more than pleasure that struck him as he came. It was the feeling of being home and safe. It infused him with a vibrant joy as he started to come down from the high of his orgasm. He let himself drop down on top of her, sighing at how good it felt to be close. He would have to get up in a moment, have to deal with the condom he didn't want to wear, deal with the fact that they were only really together in these moments.

But for now he was going to revel in her.

She hugged him close. "We're in the now, right? Just right this moment."

He was going to spend the rest of his life trying to convince her they had a future. "Yes, baby."

She was quiet for a moment. "I love you, too. Just for now."

He kissed her again. He would take it.

Just for now.

Two hours later it was almost midnight and he watched as Kim slipped out of the bed and grabbed one of his T-shirts.

"You could stay, you know," he said quietly. He'd made love to her twice more and they'd rolled around in the bed like they were young and just learning each other's bodies. But when she'd started to get tired, the mood had changed.

She was back to being wary.

Their time—for tonight—was done. He watched as she gathered her clothes.

"I don't want to confuse Roman." She turned back to him. "This is how it has to be right now. I understand if you don't want it."

He managed to not roll his eyes. Instead, he got out of bed and walked to her. He stopped in front of her and cupped her cheeks. "I told you I'll take what I can. Tomorrow I'll get you in Sanctum and we'll play for a couple of hours. Then we'll get our son and come home and I'll tuck you both in bed. I'm looking forward to it, and Roman is definitely looking forward to the party on Saturday."

A smile crossed her face. "Yeah, a party will be fun. I'm eager to see what Big Tag thinks a family celebration looks like." The smile faltered. "I should go to bed."

She needed to run away but she wasn't going far, so he leaned over and kissed her forehead. "Good night, Kim."

She stepped back. "Good night."

She practically ran out of the room and he realized he wasn't going to be able to sleep. He took a quick shower, grabbed fresh pajama bottoms and his phone.

It wasn't fair but he couldn't sleep, and his brother was part of the reason.

He'd thought about Ezra all afternoon. Since they'd been pulled over it had run through his head a thousand times. He could lose his brother again.

He dialed the number and in seconds a groggy voice came on the line.

"What? Is something wrong?" Ezra asked.

"What was Roman like as a baby?"

Ezra had offered earlier in the day. Now Beck found he needed to listen.

If Ezra was upset it was after midnight, it didn't show in the tone of his voice. "He had the fiercest cry. When he was hungry everyone knew it."

Ezra started to weave his tales and Beck started to forgive his brother.

Chapter Fifteen

Kim took her seat at the conference table and tried not to think about how nice the morning had been. She'd woken up to the smell of bacon cooking and the sound of her son giggling. Then she'd heard Ezra's voice, and for a single moment she'd feared she would open her eyes and be back at the fort, back in her tiny room looking out over the Mediterranean, and it had all been a dream. Finding Beck, coming to the States, being free.

For that moment, she'd felt a panic that still echoed through her brain hours later.

And that wasn't good.

"Hey." Charlotte slid into the seat across from her, a mug of coffee in her hand. "I heard Beck had one of the bodyguards pick up Ezra and drive him over to your place for breakfast. At first Ian was worried Beck was going to murder Ezra and bury him in the backyard, but I saw him earlier and he looked alive."

Ezra had been sitting at the breakfast table laughing with Roman when she'd walked out, and Beck had placed a mug of coffee in her hand. He'd been standing at the stove, turning bacon and looking so handsome in the early morning light that her heart had done a stupid flip-floppy thing.

She was in serious trouble. "Apparently they talked last night, and they seem a little better. I don't know. Part of me doesn't trust it. Beck's always been so angry. It has to be somewhere in there waiting."

"I don't know. He's done a whole lot of therapy in the last seven years," Charlotte countered. "Almost all of it centered around dealing with his anger. Men are weird. Women are taught to handle their anger from a young age. Men are taught to punch things."

"Punching things used to work for me."

"Shooting things used to work for me," Charlotte replied with a chuckle. "I think Beck is into breathing now. I drink a lot of wine. And it helps to not be so angry. How are you dealing?"

"Well, I'm hoping we find something that leads to Levi dying in prison." She'd thought about the mysterious Reva when she wasn't thinking of how much better it would have been to sleep wrapped around her husband. And he wasn't her freaking husband anymore, which was precisely why she was in trouble. "And not like he dies of old age, if you know what I mean. I'd like for him to be hard-core shanked and die in a puddle of his own piss."

"We all want that. Though I suspect Ian would like to do the shanking." Charlotte glanced back at the door as though trying to make sure they were alone. "I wasn't talking about being angry with Levi. That's easy. The anger you must feel toward Beck has to be harder."

"Why would I be angry with Beck? He's apologized. He's been good with Roman. What more should I ask for?"

Charlotte's eyes went wide. "Kim, he upended your life not once, but twice. Some might even argue it was three times. He divorced you."

She shrugged and shoved the emotions that threatened to well down deep. That was where it all belonged. "Yeah, well, I was lying to him. I hid his brother from him for years."

"According to Ezra that was the only reason he didn't hurt himself," Charlotte pointed out. "He didn't want his brother to know what had happened. You saved him. You got him in touch with people who could help him and put him on a path he seems to genuinely love."

"Well, he helped me out later. I wouldn't have gotten through my pregnancy without him." Any anger she'd felt at Ezra, she'd dealt with a long time ago. She'd made her choices and she lived with them.

"I doubt that seriously. I think you're one of the most capable women I've ever met. But that's another point. He left you alone to raise a child."

Kim wasn't sure why Charlotte felt the need to grill her, but it made her antsy. The night before and this morning weighed on her. Not because they'd been bad, but because of how comfortable she'd been. The truth of the matter was she was waiting for it all to fall apart, and there was a piece of her that wanted it to, wanted to get it all over with so she could move on. "I left him. I didn't give him the chance to be Roman's dad."

"Yes. You fled in the middle of the night while a psychopath was looking for you. That's not the actions of a pragmatic operative. That tells me he did something awful that night."

"He said some words. He was angry." Those words still echoed in her mind. She heard them every single time she worried she wasn't a good mom.

"Words can hurt way more than punches sometimes. Especially when they come from someone we love. I should know. I did a lot of things to Ian I'm not proud of. In the beginning, that is. I hurt him quite badly. I thank the universe that my husband is actually pretty good at expressing himself and processing his emotions. Oh, he'll tell you it makes him vomit, but he's good at it. We had a shot because he let us work it out, and not just in bed, though there was a lot of that. He let me apologize."

"I told you, Beck apologized. We both did bad shit. Some marriages aren't supposed to work out." That was precisely why she was so antsy. She believed that. They'd been through too much to start over. She was done being angry with him, had let go of that emotion altogether, and it was good to feel…numb. God, was that what she was afraid of giving up? The safety of the cocoon she'd woven around herself? She wanted to get up and walk out and not talk about this another second. Instead, she forced herself to smile. "There's no need to worry. I'm good. Beck and I are in a good place. And I'm glad he's talking to Ezra again. Now if we could solve our

Levi problems, I think we could all get on with our lives."

"What does that involve? I ask because if you're planning on staying here, I can give you information on the best schools," Charlotte offered and sat back. "The elementary school close to your house is fabulous."

An image of her and Beck walking Roman to school whispered across her brain. "I'll keep that in mind if I decide to move here. I'm pretty established in Europe."

"Ah, so I should start thinking about who can take Beck's place," Charlotte mused. "It's been nice having him around. He doesn't mind traveling and he doesn't mind working with different partners. You wouldn't believe how rigid some of our guys have become. And by guys, I mean Erin."

"Why would Beck quit?" It was a dumb question. He'd already said he would, but she felt the need to ask it, to force an answer from someone else. It was illogical for him to uproot his life since they weren't going to be together.

"He's going to want to be with his son," Charlotte replied. "He can't do that from here if you're back in Malta. I was hoping offering you a job here would tempt you to stay, but if you're taking Roman back, I know Beck will go, too."

"It's not as easy as that. He can't simply move to Europe. There are a lot of hoops to go through." She knew Beck had said he would move if she forced the situation, but she hadn't truly believed it. Except he seemed to want to be a dad.

If he wanted to be a dad, then he shouldn't have pushed her away. He didn't get to waltz back in seven years later and dictate what happened in her life.

Damn it. Maybe there was some anger down deep.

Charlotte was looking at her like she wasn't sure what to say. "I don't think a bunch of red tape will deter him. He's been searching for you for seven years. He's not going to let his lack of proper paperwork keep him away from his son."

The door opened behind her and Charlotte's face lit up as her girls strode into the room. Tasha was carrying a couple of packets of creamer in her hand. She placed them in front of Charlotte. "I found some in the storage room, Mom. I refilled the break room, but I knew you would miss it."

"Thanks, sweetie," Charlotte said, patting her oldest daughter's hand.

"Mom, there's something wrong with Mr. Kent's brother," one of the twins said with a frown on her face. "He's weird."

For a second she'd been scared, but Ezra *was* weird. "What did he do?"

The girl with strawberry blonde hair turned toward her, one brow arched over her eyes in an amazing imitation of her father. "He overheard me talking to Kenzie about this girl in camp last year who was mean to me and how I'm not taking it this year."

"You didn't take it last year," Charlotte pointed out. "You punched her."

"She punched me first," the girl who was definitely Kala announced. "And Mr. Kent's brother told me I should turn the other cheek. Why would I do that, Mom? Do I want her to hit my other cheek?"

"I believe he's talking about the Christian principle of nonviolence." Charlotte winced. "We need to go to church more often. You see Mr. Kent's brother is a priest."

"I thought that was his cover," Tasha said, her arms folding over her chest. "I heard he was a criminal on the run."

Charlotte was the one arching a brow now. "Where did you hear that?"

Tasha flushed slightly. "I've just heard rumors around the office. I wasn't eavesdropping. Uhm, Uncle Alex is loud."

"Your Uncle Alex said Father Ezra was a criminal?" Charlotte asked.

"I didn't hear him say that," Kenzie replied. "I heard him say that it was good we had a priest around now because someone should make Kala exercise."

Kala's eyes rolled. "He said he wanted someone to exorcise me."

"What did you do?" Charlotte asked.

It didn't get by Kim that Tasha had retreated to the door.

Kala shrugged. "I put a couple of bugs in Cooper's lunch box. Or I thought it was Coop's box. Turned out Aunt Eve used it, and she does not get a joke. They weren't real or anything. They were plastic."

Charlotte leaned over and put her hands on Kala's shoulders. "You are never going to get Cooper to like you by playing practical jokes on him, baby."

Kala made a gagging sound and backed away. "Like I want him to like me. I don't even like boys."

"You keep that up, baby girl. Boys are stinky and gross and bad for you." Ian Taggart walked in and winked Tasha's way. "Any chance I can get you on the no boys train?"

"Sure, Dad." Tasha gave her dad a hug. "After all, you smell stinky lots of the time."

Ian simply chuckled and kissed the top of her head. "True. And that's what you're in for. Now go, my daughters. I'm paying you. You gotta work before you go to camp."

The girls all rushed out.

Ian raised an arm and gave himself a sniff. "I'm not stinky. I took a shower and everything."

"I don't think your daughter likes me very much." It was good to have something to distract her from her previous thoughts. Not that it was a problem for her. She'd had lots of people not like her, but she usually had to do something to them first.

Tag waved a hand and took a seat by his wife. "I wouldn't worry about it. Kala doesn't like anyone."

"Except Cooper," Charlotte said.

Tag flinched. "I reject that notion."

"I was talking about Tasha." There was something going on with that girl. "Does she have a thing for Beck?"

Ian's whole body shuddered. "No. Ewww. That is a sweet baby girl we are talking about, and she doesn't like boys much less super-old dudes who haven't smiled in seven years."

Charlotte frowned and glanced out the conference room windows. "She did seem a little off. I'll talk to her. I've never noticed her paying Beck any attention. Not more than she pays any of the adults. I would be less surprised if she had a crush on the younger guys. We've got some attractive bodyguards."

"And they're smart, too, because none of them would be interested in fourteen-year-old girls," Tag said and then seemed to get serious. "Has Tash been rude? That's not like her. She's the sweetest of my kids. Probably because she doesn't actually have any of my DNA. I swear Kala got a double shot."

"I wouldn't say she's rude exactly." Kim shook her head. "Or I'm being paranoid. It's been a long time since I hung out in an office. Forget I said anything."

"She's a teen. They're all on the moody side." Charlotte nodded as the door came open again. "And honestly, she gets a bit emotional any time the fact that she's adopted comes up. It's why we don't talk about her dad often."

Tag sobered. "When she's ready, we'll tell her everything."

"God, don't." Beck had a grin on his face as he held the door open for his brother. "Sasha could be on the wild side."

Beck was smiling like nothing was wrong. Like everything was going right in his world. The man who hadn't smiled for seven years.

Well, she hadn't been the one who pushed him away. She hated that she was suddenly having these thoughts. They'd crept up on her. Or perhaps they were leaking. Perhaps last night had exposed some cracks in the walls she'd built, and years of pain were beginning to seep out.

She needed to patch those up and quick.

"Hey, you need anything?" Beck asked as he set a folder on the table, claiming the seat beside her. "Coffee?"

She shook her head. "No, I'm good. Thank you."

He settled in as Ezra took his other side. "So, Tag, what's the word? Did you hear back from your DPD contacts?"

"It was Beck's bad driving, right?" Ezra asked.

It was odd to sit here with them. She hadn't thought about it before, but it had been so very long since she'd been with the both of them. Even back when she and Beck had been married, Ezra had been deployed or on assignment, or Beck had been out of the country. They hadn't spent much time together as a family. They hadn't all sat around the breakfast table making jokes and enjoying the morning.

Had she ever truly had that? What would it be like to have it and lose it?

Was that what she was setting Roman up for? Even back in Malta her uncle had spent a lot of time traveling. It was usually her and

Roman and Ezra in the mornings.

"I wish I could agree with you." Tag sat back. "Adam did a deep dive on your officer yesterday. I don't like the situation. Derek Brighton is our police department contact and he told me that Officer Gates has been bragging that he's going to get a job with the feds. According to Adam, he's been in DC recently."

"Any overt ties to Levi?" Beck asked.

For her the fact that he was applying for a federal job was all the ties she needed. "He wanted to get a look at you. I would bet he had his body cam on the whole time. We have to assume Levi now knows Ezra is alive. The question is how did he even know to look? We know for a fact he didn't see Ezra in Malta."

"Do we?" Beck asked. "I know if I'd been Levi I would have had someone use their phone to tape the helicopter rescue."

"It was rainy and Owen got pretty low." The walls to the upper fort were high. "I don't think that's where he saw Ezra."

What she didn't say was how worrying it was.

"It's possible that Levi was trying to figure out if you're staying with Beck," Charlotte mused.

"Why pull me over?" Beck slid a look her way like he was coming around to her way of thinking. Or trusting her instincts. "It would be far easier to put someone on surveillance. We've been coming and going. We're not hiding. Ezra is, and we need to consider that Levi won't be happy he's alive."

"But why would he even think to check if I'm alive?" Ezra asked. "Unless he saw me or someone told him. I've been in Europe for years and not once have I thought someone was looking for me."

"I can assure you he thought you were dead," Kim said. "If he hadn't, he would have moved heaven and earth to kill you. You're a loose end, and Levi doesn't like those. You could potentially testify against him."

"Ezra and I talked about this." Beck sat back, looking thoughtful. "We decided he shouldn't try to testify. He isn't the best witness because of what he was doing back then."

Ezra held up a hand. "Drugs. I was doing drugs. I'm betting there aren't many people who would listen to me. There's also the fact that I didn't really interact with him. I remember his face, but he talked to my CO and my CO relayed his orders."

"That sounds like Levi." She needed to start thinking like an operative again. "I want to do some homework on the missions you went on back then."

"That'll be hard," Ian pointed out. "I'm going to assume most of them were classified."

"Yes, but I think if Ezra can tell us where he was and what he was doing, Kim and I might be able to piece some things together," Beck offered.

"It was a lot of running guns, especially in North Africa, but I suspect those guns found their way to the Middle East." Ezra fiddled with the mug of coffee in front of him. "There were a couple of rebel forces the Agency wanted to support."

She knew the play. "Yeah, they'll arm everyone to see who comes out on top. They do it quietly because Congress almost always has a problem with us fucking around in other countries. Levi's bosses loved to do that. The question is can we get enough proof?"

"We would need something that made everyone above him nervous." Ian proved he knew how to play this game.

All they needed to do was get the higher-ups scared enough that they threw Levi Green to the wolves. It was a sad fact of their world.

Which was why she didn't want to have anything to do with that world again. Even McKay-Taggart felt too close. One good thing about having those seven years away had been not being worried every day that she was doing the right thing, that she was being part of the solution instead of the problem. She'd forgotten that knot in her stomach that she'd been forced to live with.

"If there's anything we've learned from history it's that the big dogs will let someone like Levi take the fall." Beck seemed to be thinking the same thing she was. "If we can prove he was involved with evading Congress's oversight, they'll either quietly ship him to prison or take care of the situation."

"You mean they'll kill him," Ezra said solemnly.

Beck turned to his brother. "I'm trying to save you and make sure that asshole never comes after my...after Kim and Roman. Make no doubt. He'll use Roman someday. He'll find a way to put him in a bad position. Just like he did with you."

Ezra held his hands up as though conceding the point. "I get it. Hey, I'm all for this plan. I'm a priest. Not a saint. I wish there was another way though. Are we sure I shouldn't go to the press? I know it'll cost me a lot, but if it helps…"

"Not a saint? You're looking to be a martyr, Father." Tag shook his head.

"I'm not." Ezra took a long breath. "I don't want to go to jail, and I definitely have no interest in being assassinated, and those are likely my two options. But I cannot sit by if I can help. I wouldn't do it to a stranger. I'm certainly not going to do it to the most important people in my life. Kim saved me. In so many ways. Roman gave me purpose and hope. My brother was the single most influential person in my life. I cannot fail them."

Beck stared at the conference table before reaching out and patting his brother's arm. "I don't think we've exhausted our possibilities, and even when we do we'll need to really think about our chances that it could work. Levi is in a different place than he was back then. He's on far more solid ground."

"After President Hayes left office, a more Agency-friendly administration took over," Charlotte explained.

"Helped along by Levi, who used intel he found in the documents Tucker smuggled out of Kronberg," Ian continued. "I saw those papers. That same year we had a candidate drop out six weeks before the election citing health reasons, despite there being no rumors before or after about his health. That candidate had ties to Kronberg."

"I'm absolutely certain Levi used the information from Kronberg against him." She could still remember that day in the limo. "He told me he was going to do it. So he's responsible for this president being in office, and he's marrying the VP's daughter. I think he's made himself bulletproof."

"Unless we find a specialized bullet," Beck mused. "No one is untouchable, and Levi's made mistakes. It's all about finding the right mistake. Have we figured out who sent the message Kim got in Malta? I find the timing interesting."

"I've tracked the package back to Berlin." Charlotte had her cell in hand as though she was waiting for something to come through. "Now the interesting thing is Levi himself was in Berlin up until that very day. I think we're dealing with someone inside the Agency."

"My contacts aren't so great there anymore," Ian admitted. "I backed the losing side."

The losing side being her and Beck.

"I thought you still had some contact with Drake," Beck prompted.

"A bit, but usually when he needs help from us," Ian explained. "When Levi moved into a more powerful role, he brought Drake with him. Look, Drake's been helpful, but he's also close to Levi. If he for some reason sent this note to Kim, we can't count on him to follow up. If he did it, this is all the help we should expect from him."

Charlotte slid a glance his way. "We could have Sandra call him. He's still got a soft spot for her."

A slow smile spread across Ian's face. "Well, she did teach him everything he knows. Damn, I miss her."

Beck leaned over. "He's talking about Roni's mom. She worked here for a couple of years, but then left to be closer to her grandkids."

"She now owns the rowdiest bar in Wyoming," Charlotte said with a chuckle. "But at one point she was pretty close to Drake. He might listen to her."

"We'll hold that in our back pocket." Ian made a note on his phone. "We don't even know Drake was in Berlin. I need a list of everyone in that group. If he was there, then I'd like to reach out to him."

"Why would Drake put himself at risk now?" She wasn't sure it mattered who'd sent the note. And that proved she was out of practice, too. In the past she would have obsessed over the hows and whys of that tip. Now she just wanted it all to be over so she could concentrate on what was important.

Roman. Putting her life back together. Figuring out where to go from here.

"No idea," Ian admitted. "He's always been a bit of a mystery to me. But I think whoever sent us the lead was on to something. Hutch is downstairs with Adam and Jax and the other Lost Boys right now. They've been up all night working on finding this Reva person. He's supposed to come up and fill us in."

"He found Reva?" She should have been the one searching for

the mystery lady, but no, she'd been playing around in Beck's bed instead of doing her damn job.

And that right there was another reason she'd found some peace when she no longer was working. She was a control freak, slightly paranoid about anyone else doing what she thought she should be responsible for. It was one more reason they called her Solo.

She liked to work alone, be alone, be on her own.

She didn't want that life anymore.

"I think there was definitely movement on that front." Charlotte glanced down at her phone and then she was sitting up straighter. "They're on their way up."

She leaned toward her husband and they started to whisper.

Beck did the same toward her. "Hey, are you all right? You've been quiet all morning. I'm worried I was rough with you last night."

She rolled her eyes his way. "Yes, you were so rough."

His eyes narrowed. "I can be rougher tonight."

She wished that didn't send a shiver of anticipation down her spine. "I'm fine."

"I doubt that." He frowned. "I want to hold your hand, but I don't think you want that right now."

The desire to sit in his lap and wrap her arms around him was almost overwhelming. But she forced herself to sit in her own chair. They had specific parameters, and that was all she could be comfortable with right now. Any feelings she had for him could only be indulged during those hours they'd agreed on. Anything else and she would drown. If she let herself, she would end up marrying him all over again and living the life he wanted to live.

Or you could figure out what you want and ask him to go with you. You knew all those years ago you should get out and try something else. You knew it would make you miserable. You stayed because he was there and then you stayed because that damn job was the only thing that connected you to him. Let him make the sacrifice this time.

"I'm fine. Just worried, but I think I have every right to be." She kept her tone calm and it was an effort because she found herself restless. Things were happening fast. Faster than she was ready for.

"You've got that look," Beck said. "The one that lets me know

297

you think it's all about to go to hell."

The conference door opened, and Hutch had the brightest grin on his face. He held up a thick stack of papers. "We got him."

Yep, all the pieces were falling into place, and that was when everything exploded.

* * * *

The conference room was full of smiling faces, with the exception of one. It was the grim expression of Kim's that made Beck wary.

"Okay, explain this again with actual words people outside of the computer world use and slower," Ian instructed Hutch. He glanced Adam's way. "How much sugar did you feed him?"

Adam grinned. "A lot. I had to keep him going."

Hutch was practically vibrating. "So it took me a couple of hours, but I managed to get in contact with Reva. She's in hiding. Changed her name and everything."

"Is she hiding from Levi?" Kim asked with a weariness that made his heart ache because he didn't think she was tired from lack of sleep.

She was tired from all the intrigue, exhausted from people pulling her one way or another. She'd been Levi's chew toy for years.

And he himself had done a lot of damage, too.

"She didn't know his real name, of course, and everything they did was online." Hutch seemed to force himself to go slower. "But after the job was done some scary stuff started to happen, and lucky for us like many hackers, Reva's completely paranoid. So to put it plainly, Levi hired a hacker to get into Kronberg's systems and upload material he wanted there. At the time Reva needed the cash, and it didn't seem to be such a crazy thing to put a couple of names in a pharmaceutical company's backlog of investors. She admitted she didn't read a lot of it. She knew what she was doing was wrong, but she considered it to be rich people fucking each other over."

"When did she figure out it was something more?" Ezra asked.

"Is she safe?" Kim asked at the same time. "You said she had kids."

"Answer Kim first, please." Hutch would likely answer the question that interested him first, but Beck wanted Kim to be comfortable.

Hutch stopped and looked Kim's way. "Reva's good. I don't even know where she is. She's changed her name, moved, and she told me she feels comfortable that whoever hired her back then doesn't know where she is."

"Then why is she willing to come forward?" Kim asked. "She would have to testify."

"Ah, but she won't," Hutch said. "Because she's got this, and she's still got the original."

"And what is that?" Beck was pretty good with computers, but even he didn't quite understand all the tech stuff Hutch and Jax and Adam had spewed in the first frenzied moments after they'd walked into the conference room.

"She basically took a snapshot of Kronberg's systems before she touched them. She's got everything. It's a beautiful job," Hutch said with excitement. "She didn't leave anything behind. It proves what she put in and what was real. This was as much a cover-up as it was a reveal."

Damn, he'd worried about that. "If he could prove some of it was true, he could slip the lies in and no one would question it. That's what he was trying to do with Kim. The question is how we use it."

"We use it to fuck Levi over," Tag announced with a shit-eating grin. "This is what our Berlin guy was telling us. Do you understand how close we are to another election? How this could bring down his soon-to-be father-in-law? He's running and he's probably going to be his party's candidate. If the Agency has to pick between a potential president and a man who could bring them all down, I know who they'll choose."

They would choose the candidate who was ahead in the polls, and then hold it over his head and serve themselves.

"Or we could expose them all," Kim said.

"If we expose them all, we expose McDonald's drug." Charlotte got to the point of the problem. "If we do that, none of us is safe. I understand the impulse. In a perfect world we could do it and justice would be done."

"In the world we live in, it puts targets on the Lost Boys." He had to be honest. There was a reason they hadn't taken the whole thing to the press in the beginning. McDonald's work had to stay in the dark. "There would be agencies who would think experimentation might lead to discovery."

He didn't want to state it blatantly since Jax was sitting right there. There might be people out there who would take a chance that the Lost Boys themselves held the secrets of McDonald's drugs. And those experiments would be painful and lead to the death of the patient. He couldn't let it happen.

"I think I can speak for all of us when I say we would prefer our names didn't get leaked," Jax said solemnly. "We've talked about this over the years. It might be braver to put it all out there, but it would also open doors none of us could close again."

Kim's eyes had gone wide. "We can't let anyone know. They could come after their families, too."

Now he did what came naturally. He reached out and offered his hand. She clutched it like a lifeline.

"But we can send this intel to someone in the Agency. We can let them know someone has to be held accountable," Ian explained. "I have a friend who handles oversight at a very high level. He'll take care of it. They'll do one of two things."

Beck knew exactly what Tag was talking about. "They'll take care of the problem or they'll interrogate him, find out everything he's ever done, and then they'll take care of the problem. Either way, they won't put McDonald's research out there and we'll be safe."

Kim's hand came out of his and she sat back. "All right. We do this and then we hope they arrest Levi in order to cover their own crimes, and then we all go back to our corners and the mutually assured destruction sets the balance again."

He understood her frustration, but this wasn't an easy situation. This wasn't something they could simply shine a light on and the problem would burn away in the sun. Unfortunately this problem would burn a lot of people they cared about if it was put in the light.

It would lurk in the background. It would be something they would all have to live with the rest of their lives. He missed the comfort of her hand in his.

"All right. I'd like to take a look at the data." Kim seemed to pull herself together and Solo was back in the house. He'd come to think of her as essentially two people—his Kim and the Agency's Solo.

She'd had to compartmentalize to do her job, to survive in the harsh world they'd lived in for so long. Even here at McKay-Taggart there were hard calls to make.

Had she found a softness in Malta that she missed? This was the first time since he'd seen her again that Solo had come out. How hard was it to bring back her cast-iron persona?

"I can walk you through it all," Jax promised. "It really is good news, Solo. If Levi's out of power, there's not much he can do to you. Given the fact that we can prove he manipulated this data, I can't imagine a scenario where he keeps his job. Not only did he threaten to point a finger at some people who did support McDonald, he implicated people who didn't. And he hid the actions of people who could help him, including his future father-in-law. The current VP not only had stock in Kronberg, he met several times with McDonald herself and had a close relationship with McDonald's father. He'll dump Levi like a hot potato."

Kim got quiet. "He'll dump Levi and move on with his life. In the end, Levi was nothing to him."

"He made his choices," Ian said softly.

"Of course he did. He deserves every fucking thing he gets. And more. When you think about it, he's getting off easy." A bit of his old anger bubbled up. They were still here. She still had some kind of feelings for the bastard even after all this fucking time. His old insecurities welled inside. "Do you even want to pursue this? I guess I should have asked. Maybe you want…" Fuck. He wasn't doing this. He wasn't falling back into this pattern. "I'm sorry. I didn't mean to say that."

She stood. "Oh, but you did. I assume what you were going to say was maybe I want it. Maybe I want Levi to continue to come after me. Maybe I'll miss having a sick stalker coming after me. Who knows? Maybe I'm some pathetic creature who craves his attention." She sighed and turned to Jax. "Can we do this downstairs?"

"Kim, I'm sorry." He knew he'd been an ass, but he didn't understand what she'd meant. She'd looked like she felt sorry for the bastard. "Let's go to my office and talk. Please."

She was already at the door. "No need. I'll see you later. After all, we're still going to Sanctum tonight. Or maybe I should ask Levi."

Damn it. He'd fucked up. "We're still going unless you want out. I won't make you do anything you don't want to do."

"I made a deal. I keep my deals. I don't break them when I get my feelings hurt," she said and strode out the door.

Every word felt like a kick.

Jax gathered up his papers. "I'll go and show Solo what we found. Adam, you can handle walking the rest of them through it, right?"

"Sure," Adam offered. "Though if I'd known I was getting a show, I would have popped some corn."

"Why don't we take a break before Adam starts his presentation?" Charlotte stood up and sent her husband a look.

Ian sighed. "Yeah, let's do that."

Adam shook his head, but he was already out of his chair. "You guys are no fun. Anyway, I should go and make sure we've got eyes on Levi if we're doing this today."

"As long as Solo and Beck are good, we're a go," Tag replied. "I say the sooner we get Operation Summer's Eve underway, the better."

"We're not calling it that," Charlotte said with a groan.

"It's because he's a douche, baby," Tag replied.

Ezra stood up and moved close to him. "You want to take a walk?"

He stared up at his brother. So much had gone wrong, but it might have started with him. "I'm sorry I made you feel like you couldn't come to me. I don't know how I would have reacted back then, but I know I would have still loved you."

"I'm sorry I didn't trust you, and then I let too much time pass. I'm sorry I had a part in what happened between you and Kim," Ezra said softly. "She doesn't care about Levi. She loves you. She always has. Maybe you should go downstairs and try to talk to her."

Before he could answer, Ian was leaning forward. "I need a word with Beck, Father. If you don't mind."

Ezra put a hand on Beck's shoulder and nodded Tag's way.

"Sure. I'll go check on Roman."

It had felt good to say those things to his brother. Why couldn't he and Kim do the same?

They all filed out and he was left with Tag. He knew exactly what was coming. "I didn't mean to hurt her."

"And yet you did. I thought you were past this."

He felt sick but he forced himself to breathe. "I did, too."

Tag sat back with a sigh. "Thank god you're not, man. For a while there I'd thought you'd become some weird perfect therapy patient. Kai was walking around like he's some guru because he fixed you. I always knew deep down that you were as fucked up as the rest of us. All you needed was one specific trigger."

He didn't like the sound of that. "Kim is not a trigger."

"She is totally a trigger for all that anger festering inside you," Tag insisted. "See, you have to fix that. Me, I got a million triggers for my rage. Assholes who don't drive the speed limit. Assholes who go way over the speed limit. Assholes on skateboards, unless they're falling off their skateboards and then I think they're hilarious. Asshole hipsters who say they won't listen to anything but vinyl. Asshole…"

He held up a hand. "You don't like assholes. Got it."

Tag sobered. "The point is I'm angry all the time."

Beck knew how that felt. "I've learned to control mine. It was a slip."

"No, it was a trigger, and she needs to be the opposite of a trigger," Tag countered. "She needs to be the button you push when you need to calm down. She needs to be the one thing in the world that can wash away all the bad shit. She and your son."

He would have said she was, but once again their relationship had proven to be complex. "You know it's not that simple."

"It's not simple for her either. She's at a serious crossroads, and you need to help her make a choice that's good for her and Roman and not that's simply a reaction to you being an asshole."

He didn't want to push her away again, but he hadn't imagined what had happened. "She was feeling sympathy for that bastard."

Ian's head shook. "No, she was feeling empathy because she could easily have become Levi Green. Any of us could. Why do you think I got out? I got out because I met my Charlie and even though I thought she was dead, I knew I couldn't become the raging pit of darkness that I would become if I stayed in. Some people can do it. Some people can compartmentalize so well they can have a family and feel love and compassion and still walk into that office and move people around like chess pieces. I couldn't. But if I hadn't met Charlie, I think I would have. It's so tempting to be in control every second of the day, to know you don't have to be afraid because you're the monster."

"You're saying you feel bad for Green?" It was hard to comprehend.

"My ability to see the hows and whys of Green won't make me gut him with any less enthusiasm," Tag promised. "Do I understand him? Yes. Do I understand that he had no one growing up, that he was a pawn to his parents? They threw money at him, and then there wasn't any more money and he was totally on his own. With the exception of the money being gone, who does that sound like?"

He sighed because he knew where Tag was going with this. "I know it sounds like Kim."

"She knows damn straight that she could be in Levi Green's place," Tag replied.

"That's bullshit." She wasn't like that. Yes, she'd made some hard calls, but she wouldn't have sold her soul.

"No, it's not." Tag obviously wasn't backing down. "In this, I understand her far better than you can. You're one of those people who can't be moved. It's not in you to do the wrong thing. You've proven that time and time again."

"I'm not freaking Captain America. I've got blood on my hands, too."

"When killing a person meant saving others, yes, you did," Tag agreed. "You put your job on the line to take out someone who was killing his own people when you were ordered to work with him because it was in the best interests of the United States. You're the guy who can't stand by when someone is being hurt. Not for any reason. It's why you should always have been on the civilian side."

He sat back, a lot of what Tag was saying settling in. Had he not spent so much time with Kai, he might have dismissed it all and hung on to his anger. "So what you're saying is Kim sees herself in what's going on with Levi. There's a part of her that understands why he did the things he did. He wanted to belong. He wanted to be important. He did everything his bosses wanted him to and more, and they are going to ruin him for it. But she wouldn't have done any of it."

Tag pointed his way. "That's your righteous self doing the talking. You don't know that. She's chosen her job over you before."

"Because I pushed her away."

Tag sat back. "I do think you're the difference, but Solo knows she could have gone down that path given the right circumstances. And just for a second, she felt bad for him. It doesn't mean she loves the asshole. It means she knows what it feels like to be left adrift. And the part at the end about going to Sanctum was about you being a whiny man bitch who didn't honor your marriage vows."

"I never cheated on her." He hadn't even thought of another woman when he'd been with Kim. Hell, even when he wasn't with her, he barely seemed to think of anyone but her.

"No, but you left her," Tag pointed out. "For better or worse, my man. If you can't honor that, let her go and find someone who can because that woman could have found you with a gun in your hand standing over a dead body, and all she would have asked was how she could help. Maybe you need someone a little less dark than Solo." Tag started to stand.

He didn't want to leave things like this, and if there was one person who knew how to handle some darkness it was Tag. "I love her. She's the only woman I'll ever love, and I worry that the minute she's safe, she's going to leave me again. I'm worried she won't let me back in and the only connection we're going to have for the rest of our lives will be Roman. I love my son. I didn't even know I could love someone the way I love that kid, but I want to be a family. I want my wife back. What do I do to get her back? How do I prove to her that I've changed and I won't leave her alone again?"

It had been the worst thing he'd done in his life. He'd abandoned her when she'd needed him. Maybe if he'd stayed with her she would have trusted him enough to tell him about his brother. Maybe they wouldn't have wasted all those years.

Tag stopped. "You really want her? You have to stop the bullshit with Levi. He's the bad guy. He's on the other side and she's not in the middle, man. She never was. For years you treated this like a love triangle. She can't be in a love triangle with her fucking stalker, and she can't trust anyone who thinks she would. So let that go."

He felt a bit weary. Why had he opened his stupid mouth? He knew her deep down. "I have. I know I had a moment of weakness, but I see it now. I can be dumb."

"It's good that you acknowledge that. The second thing you have to do is all about anger."

Beck shook his head. "I'm not mad at her."

"No, but she's furious with you. I don't think she knows how angry she is with you. She won't acknowledge it."

"I know." He felt it every day. The only time she'd truly softened had been when they'd made love the night before. "She needs to let it out. She needs to yell at me and call me every name in the book and tell me how much I fucked up."

Tag nodded. "Yeah. Until she does, it's going to eat her up inside."

"She doesn't want to talk about it." Every time he tried to gently broach the subject, she shut him down.

"She doesn't feel safe talking about it. So make her feel safe. Give her what she needs to let it out." Tag tapped the desk with the folders in his hands. "Sanctum is the sight of many a primal scream, my man. If you need to game plan, I'll be in my office this afternoon."

If he could get her to open up, they might have a chance. He sat back and played out the possibilities in his head.

Chapter Sixteen

The mood in the ladies' locker room at Sanctum was jubilant. It was a stark contrast to the quiet that had fallen over her the minute they'd dropped off Roman in the building next door. She'd been told it was owned by Beck's therapist, Kai Ferguson, who allowed a couple of conference rooms to be used as kids' care when Sanctum was open. This evening Kai and his wife Kori had been there to greet them along with two women and a man who were working as caregivers that night. It had been explained to her that Doms and subs who couldn't afford the cost of a Sanctum membership could still gain access by working one night a week.

Though it didn't look like work. It looked like holding babies and playing games with kids.

Roman had immediately found Jeremy and the young Taggarts and had barely waved good-bye.

Then had come the nearly silent walk to the club where Beck had dropped her at the ladies' locker room door and told her he would see her in twenty minutes. She'd walked in and been faced with some kind of party complete with champagne, bouncy music, and someone had brought cupcakes.

What the hell was she doing here? She wasn't in a party mood.

Charlotte Taggart was sitting in what appeared to be the lounge portion of the large locker room. There were several comfy-looking sofas and a large ottoman covered in a gold tray that held the aforementioned champagne and cupcakes. Charlotte was wearing a silky robe, her hair up in a loose bun and a gorgeous diamond collar around her throat. She flashed a brilliant smile as Kim walked in. "Solo, it's so good to see you. Welcome to Sanctum. Come in and meet the girls."

"Thanks." She kind of wanted to run. The "girls" were all gorgeous women, every one of them happily married for long periods of time. They were all friends who had barbecues and supported each other. They were a family.

She didn't belong here.

Charlotte quickly introduced her to Avery O'Donnell, Serena Dean-Miles, Grace Taggart, and Erin Taggart. She already knew Eve, who sat to Charlotte's left. There were other women moving around the locker room chatting, but these six women seemed to be their own club. "Thanks for having me. Do you know where my locker is? Beck told me there would be one for me."

He'd also told her he'd arranged for her clothes for the evening. She was supposed to wear what he wanted her to wear, do what he wanted her to do, be who he wanted her to be.

Did she want to do that?

Charlotte stopped and Kim could practically see the wheels in her head turning. "Why don't you sit for a minute and have a glass of champagne with us? Just one though. Club rules and everything. Ariel and River aren't here yet. We can keep you company. Was Roman okay with the babysitting arrangements? Sorry you had to leave him in another building, but I promise it's secure. We used to have on site care."

Erin wrinkled her nose. She was a lovely redhead. "Then a couple of twins got way too nosey for anyone's good."

"Hey, TJ helped them get into the air vents," Charlotte pointed out.

Serena set her glass down. "It was only a matter of time. When the kids got older they were bound to get curious."

"The boys can be distracted with video games." Avery O'Donnell wore an emerald green corset that peeked out of her robe. "But the girls are terrible. Daisy is the worst. She looks so sweet but she's sneaky. The twins call her their secret weapon because Daisy turns on those doe eyes of hers and suddenly her dad lets her get away with anything. She's going to be a menace, my girl."

"Carys wants to start dating," Grace announced. "She's fifteen. I don't think she should date until she can drive herself out of a bad date. Sean's heart seizes every time she mentions it. I'm genuinely worried about him. And anyone Carys tries to date."

"*Start* dating?" Serena said, her eyes wide. "Grace, you do know Tris has been paying for her movie tickets for years."

"And Aidan pays for her snacks. All those times we dropped them off at the theater or the mall? They're basically dates," Avery affirmed.

Grace went a little pale. "Dear god, don't tell Sean."

"Sorry." Charlotte turned her way and patted the seat beside her. "Our teens have a whole lot of drama. Tasha's the only one who doesn't seem to create tidal waves of angst. It actually worries me."

Eve shifted to form a conversation group away from the main one. The others were talking about how hard it was to have teens. Eve glanced Charlotte's way. "You know I think she's well adjusted."

"I'm worried she still thinks she's going to be kicked out if she misbehaves," Charlotte admitted. "I worry I praise her so much for being helpful that she's decided it's the only way to keep her place. But that's trouble for another day. Solo, I need to tell you something and I don't know how you're going to react."

She could guess what had happened and why they were drinking champagne. The thought made her lips curl up despite her weird mood. She'd spent most of the day studying the information they'd gotten from the woman named Reva. Kim admired her. Reva had managed to avoid Levi Green for years, and she'd held on to the one card guaranteed to take him down. Hutch had talked her into giving it to them. "Did they arrest him?"

Arrest wasn't the right word. There wouldn't be a fair trial for Levi Green. There would be pain and interrogation, and he might be allowed to live in a prison cell, but it was far more likely the Agency would put him down like a rabid dog.

She liked dogs way more than she liked Levi. Even rabid ones.

She'd sat on the back porch before dinner and thought about Roman playing with a dog. But it hadn't been Beck's backyard she'd seen in that happy vision. However, it had been Beck sitting beside her, watching their son play.

It was one more reason she shouldn't be here. She was getting in way too deep.

Charlotte nodded. "We got word that he was taken into custody about an hour ago. And you got a bunch of flowers after you left work. I put them on your desk. But I brought the card."

She reached into her pocket and handed her a note.

Glad you picked up the trail, Solo. Hope your second act is happier than your first.

"It isn't signed." She stared down at it. It was a typed note. "Do we have any idea where it came from?"

"Turns out the woman Levi was going to marry has a cousin named Drake," Eve explained. "According to him, she's one of the only people he can stand in his family."

"He was in Germany at those meetings with Levi." Charlotte set her champagne down. "Apparently he's been looking for a way to take him down without doing it himself. He'd found the Reva connection, but couldn't locate her. He managed to get a message out, but she refused to take his bait. He was hoping you would have more luck. I think he was also hoping sending you that note would let you know you had a problem on the way."

Kim frowned. "He could have picked up the freaking phone and called Beck. He could have said hey, heads up, a psycho's about to take out your ex."

"I don't think that's how spies work," Eve said. "Also, we can't know he was certain Levi was coming after you. I wonder if the Agency found you. Alex was on the conference call with Drake. He says he has no idea how Levi found you."

"I'm worried he's got eyes on us," Charlotte admitted. "Ian had the boys do another search, but we couldn't find anything. Not here. Not at home. I'm going to be nervous until we figure out how he knew where you were."

"And to look for Ezra. I'm with Beck. There's no way he simply got pulled over by a cop who has ties to DC. That wasn't a coincidence." There were still things to figure out, but if Levi had been taken into custody, she could breathe easier. She also had decisions to make. That office at McKay-Taggart was sitting there waiting for her. She didn't have to live with Beck after their agreement was up. It was only smart to do it for a while, to let Roman get to know his dad. At some point she would explain that it was time to find their own way.

Would she go back to Malta? Stay here in Dallas? Or start all over again somewhere else? She had the money to do it now that she could get back into her accounts.

The vastness of her options was overwhelming. She had to shove it all down or she would lose it. Quite frankly, it had been easier when she'd had one choice—to stay with Beck and stay alive.

"Are you okay?" Eve asked quietly. "I know you were close to him once. Even if he hurt you later on, he was your friend at one point."

Did they all think she cared about him? "He was never my friend. I know that now. He was always trying to use me in one way or another. Seven years ago he was willing to take all of my memories to serve his own purpose. He's a sociopath who doesn't understand love. He's only capable of obsession. I hope his corpse is already rotting. What I was feeling earlier was about how hard the job was. I was remembering how it felt to be all alone because I'd gotten burned. I was thinking about how that job that seemed so important to me had almost taken my soul."

"Which is why it's awesome you don't have to go back," Charlotte said brightly. "You can stay here. No one gets burned here."

"Charlotte," Eve said, and they exchanged a look.

Charlotte put a hand up, obviously conceding the lead to her friend. "I should go and finish getting ready. Again, Solo, it's awesome to have you here. I hope you enjoy yourself. If you've got any questions, please don't hesitate to ask."

Charlotte stood and started for her locker.

"Thanks." Despite her wariness, she was excited to see Sanctum.

She was also excited to forget about everything for a little while and sink into the role of the submissive. She could enjoy Beck in those moments because they weren't Beck and Kim. They were other sides of themselves, sides that existed only in this time and in the spaces they chose.

She would "play" with him until it was time for her to go. She would have to think about how to handle it if she decided to stay in Dallas.

If she stayed in Dallas, how long would it be before she was right back where she was in the beginning? Working cases, getting dragged into subterfuge. Falling madly in love with Beck again, and this time when he left her he would be leaving Roman, too.

"Do you have any questions?" Eve asked.

"How did you forgive him?" The question was out of her mouth before she could think better than to ask it. That hadn't been the knowledge Eve had offered to share. Eve had been following up on Charlotte. She'd been asking her if she had questions about BDSM and the club.

But Eve McKay and her husband, Alex, had divorced at one point and then figured their shit out, and they seemed solid this time around.

Kim held a hand out. "Forget I asked that. It was rude. I'm sorry. I think I'll…"

Eve reached for her hand. "It was hard. I didn't want to for a long time. I was punishing him in a way, but the worst part was all the years I punished myself."

Kim hesitated. This might not be a road she wanted to go down. It might be better to let it lie and move on. Wasn't that what she'd been trying to do all along? She'd chased after Beck for years. She didn't need to do it anymore. They could be over.

Eve leaned in. "I'm glad you're talking about it. It's healthy to talk about it, Kim."

"You're the only one who calls me Kim. Everyone else calls me Solo."

"You're only Solo if you choose to be," Eve said softly. "I think you hide behind that nickname more than you want to. I think it feels like a shield here."

Eve was good at her job. Which was precisely why Kim should stop talking, but she couldn't seem to help herself.

"It was always armor. It was a stupid nickname I got in training, but it came to mean something to me. I needed it when I worked with the Agency." She shook her head because she wasn't being honest, and there was zero reason to lie. Being open felt…better. "I think I've always had some kind of armor. Whether it was a nickname or a blustery attitude, I've always hid behind something. I learned early on how much other people could hurt me. I learned that from my parents, from the kids of people who hated my parents. The world I grew up in sucked."

Eve cocked a brow. "Did you ever wonder why you didn't get out when you could?"

"I did get out. That's why I joined the Agency when I did."

"But the Agency is full of intrigue and backstabbing," Eve pointed out. "Don't get me wrong. There are great people at the Agency, but when you work as an operative, you're always lying to someone. Beck was in that world, too, but I don't think he was as ready for it as you were."

"He was excellent at his job." For some reason she always felt like she needed to defend him.

"No, he wasn't. He wasn't able to follow orders in the end," Eve argued. "There were several cases of his where he went against what he was asked to do."

"An operative isn't a soldier. Beck made the best decisions he could."

"Would you have made the same?"

"No, and I probably would have been wrong." She sighed. "I don't know. Sometimes I wonder what would have happened between us if we'd met in a regular office. If he'd been an accountant and I'd been the chick who made copies."

"See, that's interesting. You put yourself in an inferior position."

"I'm not here for a session, Eve."

Eve shrugged. "But you kind of are. It's what D/s is for a lot of us. It doesn't have to be some therapy where you process your emotions. Think of it as a session where you attempt to get what you need, whether that be a particular type of stress relief or being able to communicate more intimately with your partner. This kind of play often reveals parts of ourselves we don't give much consideration to. I find it interesting that you put yourself in a position where Beck is over you even in your fantasies. Is that because you think he needs it?"

The whole conversation was making her uncomfortable. But didn't she need to figure out why she did this to herself time and time again? Was it comfortable behind her walls? What would she teach her son if she kept this up? She didn't want Roman to learn to live the way she did. "Maybe it's because he was teaching a class when I met him."

"I don't think so. Did you ever work together?" Eve asked.

She shook her head. "No. He mostly worked alone, and so did I."

"So once you completed your training, you were equals."

"Yes."

"Were you submissive in your marriage?"

She snorted at the thought.

A knowing smile crossed Eve's face. "I didn't think so." She sobered. "So why do you think you imagine yourself as his subordinate?"

When she really looked deep, she knew the answer. "I lied to him. I did it for reasons I thought were good, but I lied. I suppose I feel like I need to make it up to him."

Eve nodded as though she'd come to the same conclusion. "He's forgiven you. I don't believe he wants to punish you in any way, but that doesn't mean you can't punish yourself. I've found humans are excellent at finding ways to hurt themselves."

"I can accept that." She had been in such a bad place. "But I wasn't punishing myself when I walked away from him in Paris."

"Weren't you?"

"Eve, you don't know the things he said to me. He ripped me apart."

"And there was a man waiting in shadows to do worse," Eve argued. "You could have called Ian. You could have told him you wouldn't spend another minute with Beck."

She hadn't even considered making a call. "Ian wasn't my friend. He was Beck's."

"Yes, but Ian understands how people can tear each other apart. He would have sent someone else to be with you. You left for two reasons. You left because you didn't trust anyone else in the world to

314

help you once Beck had lashed out."

That was true. "And the other reason?"

Eve reached out and put a hand on hers. "Because everyone who should have loved and protected you in your life betrayed your trust. Your parents. The man you thought was your friend. The man you loved. Because life taught you that you were not worth saving. You walked out because deep down you didn't care if Levi caught you."

Kim went quiet. The need to cry was there inside her, but there was a wall between her and that emotional well. A wall she'd erected so many years before. A wall she wasn't sure she could live without. "Maybe. But I don't feel that way now. My life changed the minute I found out I was pregnant. I love my son. I can't live the same way. But I don't know how to handle having Beck back in my life."

Eve shifted, sitting back and giving her some space. "The question is can you forgive him. You lied but he walked away. You have to acknowledge that his was the greater infraction. He caused the greater harm. It's not a contest, but you get to be angry with him."

"Beck has high standards."

"I think you'll find Beck has relaxed a bit over the years. He's done a lot of work on his anger issues."

There was far more to the problem. "I guess I don't understand what he was so angry about. I know his bio dad was a piece of shit, but he spent the majority of his childhood with Ezra's dad. He was a good guy. His parents loved him. He had a brother who looked up to him like he was some kind of a superhero."

"Some men don't need a reason to be angry," Eve replied. "They're born with it. It fuels them in a way. But it can eat them up if they don't figure out how to control it. My husband took something that happened to me and made it about him."

Kim nodded. "Yeah. I think it's safe to say Beck did that, too. What he doesn't want to acknowledge is that Levi would have done this to anyone I fell for. He was incidental."

"Harsh, but potentially true," Eve agreed. "Some men struggle to understand anything they can't control. It was easier for Beck to understand someone coming after him. The same way it was easier for Alex to think about revenge instead of taking care of me. I was the one who'd been assaulted, but Alex focused on punishing my attacker instead of helping me piece myself back together. It took years for me to forgive him, but I did because I love him and I'm happier with him than I ever was without him. Our marriage is far stronger today than it was then."

"What if it happened again?" It was why she really couldn't wrap her head around reconciling with him fully.

Eve was silent for a moment. "I believe deep in my heart that Alex would let Ian handle any investigation and he would concentrate on his family. I believe Beck has changed, too."

Could she love the new Beck? It was a foolish question because she already loved him. She simply wasn't sure she could trust him. "Charlotte thinks I should move here and pretend like nothing happened."

"You don't want to do that, do you?"

"I've changed so much. I worry if I stay here, I'll fall back into the same patterns I used to follow. I didn't like who I became in the end. I learned to treat it all as a game. I don't want to be that person again. I know a lot of people would say *then don't be.*"

Eve shook her head. "It's difficult to change your nature. It's much easier to understand what kind of pressure you can handle and what you can't. Kim, you need to do what fulfills you. Not what you thought you should do or what would shock your parents. You're past that, and now you don't have to worry about Levi. You need to ask yourself what you want."

"And if it isn't Beck?" It was a question she wasn't sure she wanted to answer.

"Then you two need to sit down and figure out how to move forward as parents," Eve advised. "Before that, I want you to think about giving him the chance to confront how he treated you, to truly see what it did to you. To take that into himself and apologize with his whole heart. You might not want to be his wife again, but he'll always be Roman's father. You understand that you don't owe anyone forgiveness, right? People who transgress against you are not owed your grace. You decide who deserves it. But I think Beck is important enough to you that you do owe him your honest emotion."

That wasn't what she'd been expecting from Eve. "I would think the psychologist would tell me forgiveness is important."

Eve seemed to consider what she said next. "It is, but it's also important to know that forgiveness is like submission in D/s. You're in control of it. It comes from you, and you make the decision whether or not to give it. Our society puts pressure on people to forgive even when the transgression cuts so deeply the injured party will never be the same. You can live without forgiving. You can let go of what he did to you without forgiving him. It's up to you."

She was sure of one thing. "I'll never forgive Levi."

"But the question we've been dancing around is the one I had to deal with before I could move on."

"What's that?"

"Can you forgive yourself? And that, my friend, is the one forgiveness you might truly owe. I know it sounds crazy but tonight might help you figure out how you want to move forward with Beck if you let it."

She shook her head. "We agreed this would be a place where we don't worry about those things."

Eve went quiet for a moment. "All right. Well, if you want to talk more, my door is open. Beck has Kai. You should have someone to talk to as well. If you don't feel comfortable with me, I know some great people you could talk to."

Therapists. Eve thought she needed a therapist. Someone she would pay to be her "friend."

The door came open and Ariel walked in with River right behind her.

The joy she might have felt at seeing her friends was dimmed by her conversation with Eve. Were they really her friends? Or were they Beck's, trying to get her to do what Beck wanted?

God, she hated this. She hated not trusting anyone. It was an anchor keeping her in the dark, cold water.

"Just think about it," Eve said, standing and welcoming the newcomers.

Ariel briefly said hello to everyone, but her focus was on Kim. She came and sat down beside her, reaching for her hand. "Hey, I heard they took Levi into custody. Are you okay?"

She had a choice to make with the woman in front of her.

River was on her other side. "I've been thinking about you all day."

And the one beside her. Trust. It came so easily to some people. It didn't to her, but if she never trusted anyone again, how empty would her life be?

Did she want to live in a world where Ariel and River tricked her?

She held Ariel's hand and leaned her head against River's shoulder. "I'm okay. I'm relieved it's over. Now tell me how the trip to the aquarium went."

River had spent the day showing her sons around Dallas.

She wanted to think about pleasant things.

Because she feared if she let the darkness in, it would swallow her up.

* * * *

Beck glanced down at Kim. She was doing and saying all the right things, but there was a distance that worried him. They were standing in front of Sanctum's main stage, watching a scene play out in front of them. Simon Weston was flogging his wife. The big Brit was graceful as he moved the heavy flogger over Chelsea's back and legs.

"She started with BDSM because she found it helped her deal with the chronic pain in her legs," he whispered. "Maybe we should try it. One of the things that kept me up at night the last seven years was wondering who was taking care of your leg."

She didn't look at him but kept her voice low in deference to the scene in front of them. "Ezra recommended a TENS unit. I use it a couple of times a week. I probably need to buy another one, but I'm fine. I can handle it."

He moved behind the crowd, gently taking her hand and urging her to come with him. When they were far enough away, he stopped. "I don't want you to be in pain."

"I told you. It's fine."

"I can get a TENS." He was actually pretty sure there were several right here in the building.

A blank smile came over her. "Sure. That would be great."

God, she was so fucking far from him. And all because he'd fucked up this afternoon.

No. It went so much deeper, but they couldn't get through it if she wouldn't talk about it. And it was obvious that she didn't want to talk.

"Let's go up to a privacy room."

She simply nodded and followed when he started for the stairs.

She was so fucking gorgeous in the sapphire-colored corset and boy shorts he'd picked for her. Her legs looked a mile long in the stilettos he'd chosen. She loved shoes, and he hated that she'd had to leave them all behind. She walked gracefully in them, like she'd been born wearing the damn things though he knew it was likely something she'd had to learn.

Kim had to learn lots of things. She'd had to learn that she couldn't depend on anyone but herself. He'd had a hand in teaching her that lesson, and it was up to him to teach her something else.

That he would never leave her. That he would always love her.

Tag nodded his way as they made it to the stairs that would lead them up to the privacy rooms. It was a gesture that let him know Tag understood how hard this was going to be on both of them.

Did he have any right to push her the way he was going to? Should he simply follow her around until she figured out he wasn't going anywhere and let him back in her heart?

The trouble was he wasn't sure she would. He wasn't sure she wouldn't run the first chance she got, and then he would be out. He knew she wouldn't keep Roman from him, and her moving back to Europe wouldn't be about making things hard on him. All those moves would be about protecting herself.

He needed her to understand that she needed no protection from him. Not anymore.

He led her upstairs. The dungeon monitor let them onto the floor where the privacy rooms were located. He was a big guy who manned the floor that held five privacy rooms. Beck hadn't been up here to play. This afternoon had been his first visit since he'd taken the original tour. He'd been struck by the sign on the monitor's desk.

Carpe Noctem.

Seize the Night.

That was what he was planning on doing. Seize the night so he and Kim could have all their days together.

It was quieter on the third floor, the thud of the music now a distant thing. The minute the door closed on the room he'd selected, he felt the heavy weight of being alone with her.

This would either work or she would hate him more than she did now.

He didn't want to live in a world where she hated him.

"Did you like the scenes we watched?" Beck checked the tray he'd prepped earlier, making sure he hadn't missed anything.

"I did. The rope was pretty. I don't know that my arms could be in that position for long though." She walked around the room, running her hand over the wood of the St. Andrew's Cross. This particular room was decorated for heavier scenes. "Are all the rooms the same?"

"No," he replied. "They're all different. They serve different functions. There's one room that's nothing more than a big bedroom."

"Is that the one Ezra's staying in?"

He'd almost managed to forget his brother was hanging around somewhere. "Maybe. I hope Tag hid the butt plugs or the good father is going to be shocked."

She sent him a look that let him know he was on thin ice. "He's not a prude."

Unfortunately, she was just going to have to get used to how he and his brother communicated. "I thought that was part of his job now."

"And I thought you were getting along."

He had to grin at that. "You forget how we were before he died. We're brothers. We give each other shit. We are better. I promise. But I hope he's not right next door to us. It would be weird to walk out in my leathers and see my brother trying to get ice or something."

He got his first smile out of her. "It's not a motel."

"No, it's way kinkier than any motel. But there is an ice machine on this floor. There's a tiny pantry because a couple of members are into food play. Also, as we've seen with Ezra, Tag often stashes people he wants to hide here."

"It seems to be a theme," Kim replied. "Does Big Tag have a

thing about multiuse spaces? He seems to think all BDSM clubs should also be safe houses. Maybe he thinks the bad guys will be scared off by all the leather."

He loved joking with her, but tonight it was a way to distance herself. He could see it in the blandness of her expression. "Or he knows how to use lube as a weapon, and there's plenty of that here." He had everything he needed. He couldn't put it off anymore, but he could give her one last chance. "Do you want to change rooms? We can sit and talk in one of the bedrooms."

A stubborn look crossed her face. "I'm fine with this one. It looks like fun."

She was going to fight him until the end. "Excellent. Then take off your clothes."

"I don't know that I would call them clothes," she snarked.

He wasn't having that tonight. It all started here and now. He picked up the paddle he'd bought for her. "Turn around and lean over. We'll start with five."

Her eyes widened. "Why?"

"Now it's ten."

She huffed but turned around and reached for her ankles. It gave him the most gorgeous view of her ass. "I'm going to take it this is about sarcasm."

"It's mostly about wanting to spank your pretty ass and make it red." He put a hand on the small of her back and gave her ten rapid smacks. He wasn't playing around. He wanted her to feel it.

Physical pain to release the emotional pain. And he would be the bad guy.

But then wasn't he always the bad guy with her?

"Watch your mouth while we're playing. I'm due respect in this place." He knew he sounded like an asshole, but that was the point.

She stood up straight. "Respect. Got it."

Oh, she was on the edge, and he prayed they got through this. He knew exactly what had pushed her to this point. He'd reverted to form earlier in the day, and she suspected that was the truth about him— that the asshole who'd torn her up was still there just waiting to be set free by a single misstep.

He saw the moment she decided to play a part with him. Her

expression softened as she turned around and offered him her back. She looked over her shoulder, her hair tumbling down. "Is it all right to ask you to help me? Or should I do it all on my own?"

She wanted the sex and she meant to get it without any of the scary emotions he wanted between them. He moved in and put his hands on her shoulders, easing her hair to one side so he could kiss the nape of her neck. It wasn't fair. What he was going to do to her wasn't fair. It wasn't what they'd agreed on, but if he didn't try, he would lose her. Maybe he deserved to lose her, but he worried that he was the last stop on the road her heart had been on since she was a child. If he failed to get to her, she might never open herself up again, and he couldn't live knowing Kim was alone.

"You deserve the whole world, you know," he whispered.

He felt her muscles go tight. "Sure, Beck."

He took a deep breath and hardened himself. He quickly got her out of the corset, setting it aside. "Take off the panties. If you have a comment about them, keep it to yourself. And take off the shoes."

They were one more bit of armor, and he wasn't leaving her with any tonight.

"But I…" She stopped as though realizing saying anything more would put off getting to the place she wanted to be. She stepped out of the shoes and handed them to him.

With the four-inch heels, they were almost eye to eye. Without them, he could loom over her.

When she handed him the underwear he'd selected for her, she stood in front of him naked, and her eyes had gone soft again. She was like a caged cat, testing every inch of the fence she found herself in for weaknesses.

"Back up to the St. Andrew's Cross. We'll start there," he said, paying no attention at all to the sex she was exuding.

He wanted her more than he could say, but her soul was more important than her body.

He started to tie her to the cross and prayed they came out of this night whole.

Chapter Seventeen

Frustration was starting to get to her. She gently pulled against the ties that bound her to the X-like cross. She'd thought she would be facing the cross like Chelsea had during her scene with her husband, but Beck had turned her around.

She didn't like it this way. She'd been excited when she'd thought he would flog her back and legs like the scene. But he'd proven that he didn't like gentle suggestions tonight.

He was so freaking sexy in those leather pants with ties that would make it super easy for him to release his cock when it was time for him to fuck her. He'd worn a leather vest that showed off his chest and abs, but he'd just taken it off. He was dressed for sex, a decadent walking sex toy, but he seemed determined to make her wait.

But then this was all a game, and she had to play it if she wanted mind-blowing orgasms. That was the goal.

Life was transactional. That was what she'd reminded herself of all afternoon. You had to pay for anything in life, and playing Beck's mind games were the price of her pleasure.

He stared at her for a moment, looking her up and down, his eyes hot on her body.

Maybe he wouldn't take so long after all.

He stepped up and came so close she could practically feel the heat coming off his skin. "I'm going to introduce you to some toys."

She bit back a groan. She wanted him to touch her.

A brow cocked over his eyes. "Unless there's something you want to talk about."

He seemed to want to push her tonight. She knew why. He wanted to talk about what had happened this afternoon, but there was nothing to talk about. He was the same old Beck.

Except the same old Beck would have been more than happy with her ignoring what he'd done. In fact, the same old Beck would have never apologized. He would have thought he was right and been stubborn as hell about her agreeing with him.

"All right." She was here to explore her sexuality. That included more than mere orgasms.

"I wonder how long you'll be this agreeable," he murmured. His fingertips came up and brushed against her nipples. A shiver raced across her skin.

"I thought that was the point." She wished he would blindfold her. Then she could concentrate on nothing more than the sensations he could pull from her body.

"The point of D/s for most couples is to find greater intimacy. To learn to communicate better. I wouldn't know because you're my first submissive. So far my only experience has been to give my partners what they need."

He'd given her an excellent opening. "I need sex."

His fingertips twisted her nipple, sending a delicious sensation through her. "And you'll get it. Do you know what your job is?"

"To do what you tell me to do."

He sighed and stepped back, turning away from her and walking over to the tray he'd checked out when they'd entered the room.

She wasn't sure how much she liked this room. It was on the cold side. There were none of the romantic trappings they'd had when they'd been in the dungeon of The Velvet Collar. Even earlier downstairs, there had been a softness to the place. Perhaps because she'd been surrounded by all those happy couples and singles who were perfectly comfortable with themselves. There had been a joy that had surrounded her.

Once again the idea of family played through her brain. It was a weird kinky family, but it was a family all the same. Beck's family.

Beck got everything. Beck fucked her over and still managed to find a place in the world while she was left all alone.

That was not what she was thinking about tonight. She wasn't thinking at all.

It would be so much easier if he would get on with it.

When he turned around he had what looked like earrings in his hands. "That's because you don't understand D/s. And maybe because neither one of us truly understood marriage."

"I don't want to talk about our marriage."

If that bothered him, he didn't show it. "D/s only works if it's a two-way street. Now that two-way street might look different to a lot of people, but at the end of the day, an intimate, long-term D/s relationship has to be about both parties getting what they need and communicating about what those needs are. The Dominant works hard to meet the sub's needs, and the sub does the same for the Dom. It's not enough for the Dom to worship the sub. All that does is put the sub on a pedestal, and those tend to topple over. These are nipple clamps."

She wanted to argue that she knew what he was trying to do, but he was holding up the earrings, and they were not meant for her ears. He showed her the clamp that would hold the jewelry in place. They would bite into her nipples. They would hurt.

She kind of craved them. "You're going to put them on me to sensitize my nipples?"

She would ignore all the stuff she didn't want to hear.

His frown told her he knew what she was doing, but he moved on anyway. "I'm going to put them on you so you'll be very aware of your breasts. They'll go numb at some point, but when I take them off, you'll get a hard rush of pain that I think is going to do something for you. You've got a masochistic streak. It's okay to indulge it. To a point."

"Yes, I think I can look back and say my masochism has gotten me in trouble many times. It's certainly kept me hanging around when I shouldn't." *Fuck.* She hadn't meant to say that.

He cupped her breast with that big palm of his. She didn't have petite breasts, but Beck could hold her in one hand. "Good. That's honest. I think you'll find I reward honesty."

He dropped to one knee and leaned over, sucking her nipple in between his lips.

She gasped and felt heat curl through her system, making her hold on to the rope that bound her wrists. It was over all too soon and he was straightening up.

He gently pinched her nipple again, twisting it before he slipped the clamp on. It bit into her flesh and made her grit her teeth, but there was something about the pain that made her hot, too. She could feel it in her pussy, feel herself getting slick and wet.

"I've got a bit of a sadistic streak when it comes to you, my love," Beck admitted. "But I promise I'm going to keep it to the dungeon from now on."

"What are you talking about?"

He cupped her other breast, giving it the same treatment. "I'm talking about taking my anger out on the one person I should protect above all others. Except Roman. He's up there with you. I'm saying I don't ever want to hurt you the way I did. I've worked hard for seven years to make sure I don't. You're safe with me."

Safe? She'd thought she was safe with him and the minute she'd proven inconvenient he'd tossed her aside like a piece of fucking garbage. His words made her stop.

His actions made her body go liquid. He was kissing her breast, biting it softly and getting her ready for the clamp.

She hissed when the teeth bit into her nipple. She wanted to sink into the feeling, to float along, but he was being every bit the sadist he claimed to be. "Fuck you, Beck."

His eyes were on her breasts, as though studying his work. "I didn't think I got the clamps too tight. Did I?"

He was such a bastard. "Stop talking about the past."

His eyes came up, holding hers. "Fine. Let's talk about your clit."

That was better. It was certainly a safer subject. And it was good to know he wasn't serious. If Beck was serious about something, he rarely let himself be sidetracked. "My clit wouldn't mind some attention."

He turned and she was treated to a delicious view of his back. His strong back. When they'd been married she would wrap her arms around him and feel the muscles of his back, the long line of his spine, and she had felt safe with him.

She wanted to feel that way, but how stupid would she be if she walked back into that fire again?

You're playing around the edges. You know you'll fall in and you'll burn up this time.

Beck had gone to the mystery tray again, and this time he came back with a chain in his hands. "This is for you, too."

She gasped as he gently pulled on the ring of her clamp and attached one end of the chain. When he attached the second part of the chain, he released it and she felt the drag against her nipples. She bit her lip against the ache the weight caused.

It brought her right back to that nice place where she didn't worry about anything but how good it felt to have Beck touch her. She still had hours before she would have to even think about the future again.

"I thought we were supposed to talk about my clit." Every word made the chain move slightly, and she felt it in her nipples.

He moved in, his left hand disappearing while his right came up around her throat. "I would never forget your clit."

Her whole body reacted to the buzzing sensation that simulated her clit when he ran his finger across her pussy. "What the hell?"

"It's a small vibe that fits on my finger. But what it lacks in size, it makes up in power."

Her breasts bounced and she was trapped between the pleasure from the vibe and the bite at her nipples.

"Oh, you like that, don't you?" He was looking right into her eyes, that gaze of his piercing her.

She liked how close he was, that she could almost kiss him. She loved how she was on the edge, caught between pleasure and a pain that defined the pleasure in a way she'd never felt before.

God, she could get in so deep with this. If they could have this…maybe they could keep a small connection. Maybe.

"You won't let me talk about the past, so let's talk about the future," he whispered. "I want you to stay with me in Dallas."

She shook her head to clear it because that wasn't what she'd expected. "What?"

She shuddered as he stroked her with the vibe.

"I want to throw out the three-month thing. We don't need it. We need to acknowledge that we were always supposed to be together."

"Again with the fuck you." What was he trying to do?

He sighed and stepped back, taking away the pleasure part of her torture. His hand came up and he gently pulled on the chain, making pain flare through her nipples. "No cursing. Not unless the *fuck* is used kindly. Like fuck me Beck, or I need to fuck you. Those fucks are acceptable. Anything else will get you punished."

"You said we only live in the moment here. We're not supposed to talk about anything but sex."

He was gorgeous when he frowned. "I think that was our problem in the first place. We didn't talk enough. Kim, I love you, but beyond that I know you. I know what you're planning. You want to take this time with me so you can tell yourself and Roman that you tried, but you've already checked out."

That was too close to the truth. "I'm here, asshole. What more do you want?"

He winced and suddenly he was pulling the chain again. "We only talk about pretty assholes and how fun it would be to fuck yours."

She was thinking he wouldn't ever see her pussy again, much less her asshole. "Are you into that now?"

He moved in and touched his forehead to hers. "I'm into everything about you. I want us to be together in any way that brings us both pleasure. But I can't do that if you won't open up to me."

This wasn't going how she'd thought it would and everything she'd talked to Eve about threatened to bubble over. She couldn't do this with him. "Maybe you should untie me. You said you wouldn't use this time to rehash our relationship."

Without the vibe, her nipples ached with nothing to balance them, but that reminded her what life with Beck had been like. Pleasure and pain. Mostly pain.

Except the last few days had felt like a new beginning.

He kissed her forehead. "I can't treat this like sex. I know I said I would, but it's too important. I love you. You're in my soul and I'm empty without you. If you don't want to talk here, let's go to therapy and talk it all out there."

He was pushing her every button. "You want to relive some past history, Beck? You're such a hypocrite, and you don't even realize it.

You get me all hot and bothered and then think I'll do anything to please you?"

"No," he replied. "It's the attempt of a desperate man. Say you'll go with me and I'll do my best to get this scene back on track."

He wanted to bargain? When he'd just broken their last one? "Or it's proof that you never change. Not ever."

His eyes were oddly soft as he stepped back. "How do I not change?"

Apparently she had to say it. Maybe it would feel good to say it. She was naked and clamped, and he'd done it all to her. "You're always a bastard. You're the one who tells someone you want them and then it turns out to be a trick."

"That's not all I did."

Was she falling right into his trap? "No."

"Say it, Kimberly," he said quietly. "Say what I did to you."

She wasn't going to do anything he told her to. "Fuck you."

He stepped in and lowered his head to her forehead, cupping her cheeks and whispering to her. "You can't heal until you acknowledge the wound."

Had he been talking to Eve? Was this one big conspiracy to force her into fucking therapy? "Let me out."

He didn't move, simply kept stroking her hair. "Baby, you can walk away from me. Maybe I don't deserve a second chance, but you do. You deserve a chance to find a man who doesn't hurt you, who stands by you no matter what. I want to be that man, but more than that, I need to know if that man shows up, you'll give him a chance."

She was not doing this with him. No. He was being a manipulative fucker and she wasn't doing this. He didn't get to put her in a damn corner. "Let me out. This is over. Get these stupid things off me and untie me and I am leaving. Do you understand? Roman and I are going to be on a plane tomorrow and you can fuck yourself."

"I don't want that. I'm trying so hard to avoid that." There was a stubborn gleam in his eyes. "If you get on a plane, I'll be behind you. You need to understand that. I won't leave you again. Even if you never let yourself love me again, I'll be your friend."

"You were never my friend. You wanted to use me until I proved

I wasn't worthy of you."

"I was cruel to you."

She wanted him to fight, wanted him to argue that he'd been justified. The fact that he was agreeing with her made her even madder. "Get me out of these ties, Beck. I'm not playing with you this way one second longer."

But the thought of not getting one last night out of him threatened to break her.

He looked like he wanted to argue. "Please talk to me. We can't go on this way. We have to find a way through this."

"I told you what I wanted. Or was this one more trick? Beck gets what he wants. Beck gets to do whatever he wants and everyone forgives him. Beck fucks me over and still comes out of it with a family. I do everything I can to save his brother and do you know what I get?"

"Left alone. You get left alone." He smoothed back her hair. "If I'd reacted differently you might have trusted me enough to tell me the secret."

She struggled against the bonds, needing desperately to fight something because he was so close to the truth. "If you'd shown one moment of love to me, I would have told you. I would have broken my promise to Ezra. Do you know how alone I felt? Do you think I wanted all that responsibility? I had to smuggle him out of a foreign country. I had to keep the fact that he was alive a secret or he would have been killed. Do you think I wanted to fucking do it alone?"

"No." He was staring down at her, a stark look on his face. "No. You didn't. You saved my brother and I never thanked you. All I did was tear you apart. I made you the bad guy because I didn't know how to handle my grief. I didn't know how to deal with it. I'd lost most of my family by that point. My stepdad. My brother. My mom was sick. It was good to be angry with you. It was good to lose you, Kim, because if I went ahead and broke off that piece of myself, I could get on with my life. If I could cut you out of my heart, I didn't have to mourn you, too."

"You fucking coward." The world had gone watery and she couldn't even feel her nipples anymore. "I'm doing it. I'm saying my safe word. You let me out of here right now."

A hollow look came into his eyes. "Kim, please…"

She was going to have to use his language. "Red. That's my safe word. Get me out of these bindings or I'll make sure Tag never lets you in this club again."

"I won't come here without you," he said, but his hands were working the ties that held her to the cross. "I won't be here without you. Baby, we need to talk."

Naturally now he wanted to talk. And Beck always got his way. Always. "I tried it for years after our divorce. You didn't want to talk to me then. You could have turned to me. I loved you so much I would have moved heaven and earth to help you. But you didn't. You were scared? That's your excuse?"

He moved to her other hand. "It's not an excuse. There is no excuse. And at the time I didn't think I was scared. I was angry at the world, and I took it out on you. I truly believed you made the mistake that cost my brother his life. I should have talked to you. I should have given you a chance."

She was free, but she didn't feel that way. Rage poured through her. He'd ruined it all again. She felt so stupid. "We could have had this, Beck. We could have had this one connection, but you can't accept anything less than full submission, can you? This has all been bullshit. This has all been a way to get what you want."

"Let me help you out of the clamps, baby."

She wasn't letting him do anything for her. She reached up and released the clamps, wincing as the pain hit her. It pulsed through her, oddly reminding her of everything she'd wanted out of the evening, everything he'd denied her.

"Damn it," Beck said. "That had to hurt. I didn't mean to hurt you."

She threw the clamps at him, hitting him in the shoulder with one and narrowly missing his head with the other. "You should have been the one wearing them. I don't have to submit to you."

He stared for a moment. "Okay. You can put them on me if you want. You can tie me to that cross and use every toy in this room on me. There's some cock and ball torture toys in the closet."

Her nipples ached and she knew she should take her clothes and leave, but she watched as he kicked off his boots and worked the ties of his leathers. He shoved them off and tossed them to the side. She heard something ping against the tray, but she was staring at him as he moved around her.

He went to the cross and laid his arms against the ties. "Do it. You do whatever you want to me. I deserve it and I want it. If you want me to submit to you every night for the rest of my life, I'll do it."

She laughed, but it wasn't because she was amused. It was because the entire thought was ridiculous. "You want me to torture your balls?"

"If that's what it takes to get you to forgive me. Yes. It'll hurt so much less than losing you again, than losing this chance we have at making a family together."

They'd lost that chance years before. "You threw that away. You threw me away."

He nodded. "I did. I did all of it and more, and I am begging you to not be as cruel as I was. I'm begging you to do what I couldn't. Be brave. Be Kim. Be the best part of us."

Us. For so many years she'd wanted to be a part of an us. No. Not any us. She'd wanted to be part of Kim and Beck.

Why did it have to be this man? Why?

"Please, Kim. I'll do anything. I've spent seven years working to figure out how to be the man you need."

He was naked and vulnerable. He had tears in his eyes.

"Are you doing this for Roman?" It would be okay. She could handle it.

"I didn't know Roman even existed." He brought his hands down, his shoulders slumping. "I went into therapy for you. Because I wanted to be ready if I got another shot. Let's try couple's therapy. We don't have to do anything but talk."

Talking was where he would get her.

"I meant what I said. If it's not me, then I want there to be someone for you. You deserve it. I fucked up. I fucked up my life. I fucked up your life. God, I fucked up the life we could have had, but I promise I will dedicate the rest of my life to making sure you're happy."

It was everything she'd longed to hear from him. It was all she'd ever wanted out of life—to have someone who loved her and she could love back.

But they'd missed their chance. Hadn't they?

She shook her head and backed up. And pain flared across her foot. She bent down and picked up what she'd stepped on. A ring. She knew that ring. She held it in her palm. "I thought you threw it away."

His wedding ring.

"I couldn't. I've carried it with me pretty much everywhere I've gone. At first to remind me of what went wrong, and later to remind me you were still out there in the world and we still had a chance. Kim, I love you. I've always loved you."

She stared down at that ring and remembered the vows he'd made, the promises he hadn't kept.

She'd never loved anyone the way she did Beck. Roman had opened her heart to a different kind of love, but it had been Beck who'd haunted her dreams.

She tossed the ring aside. She would have her one last night with him.

She walked right up to him and kissed him, pressing her aching nipples against his chest. She wanted the pain, wanted it to balance out the pleasure, to remind her that there would always be pain with this man.

Who gets out of this life without pain? Even as his arms encircled her and he held her with a desperation she could feel, her mind was working.

She didn't owe Beck anything. Not forgiveness. Not another chance. She didn't owe Roman anything but to be civil to his father and accommodate their relationship.

"God, I'll never get used to having you in my arms again." Beck's hands moved across her back and down to her ass where he cupped her and pressed her against his body. "It's like I was missing a piece of myself."

He kissed her again, his tongue going deep, sliding against hers and bringing her right back to aroused as hell, though this time it was tinged with deep emotion. There had been something so good about telling him how she'd felt all these years.

She could feel his cock, long and hard against her belly.

What did she owe to herself?

Did she owe herself one last chance at happiness? Should she simply take every chance she had, never giving up on finding what she needed? Never shutting herself off?

Never giving in and truly becoming the Solo she'd been on track to be when she'd found Beck. The Solo who needed no one, cared for nothing but her own ambition. She'd joined the Agency because she'd wanted the cold precision it offered, wanted to numb herself out, and hadn't it been irony that she'd found the one man who could tear down all her walls.

Did she really want to live behind walls for the rest of her life?

She let her arms wrap around him and she surrendered to the inevitable. She loved him. She didn't want to stop loving him. Maybe if she could have stayed away from him... No, if he hadn't come back into her life, she'd been ready to live it strictly for Roman. She hadn't even wanted another man, hadn't wanted this connection with anyone but Beck.

But she owed herself more. If she was going to try, she was going to do it her way. "I'm not living here in Dallas. There's some place else I want to be."

He backed her up against the wall, right next to the cross where he'd bound her, trying to force her to break.

Because sometimes a person had to break down to build back up again. To be stronger. To want more.

"Anywhere," he vowed. "I'll go anywhere with you."

She felt the wall against her back as he pressed her there. He positioned her so his cock was rubbing against her clit, and she was so aware he wasn't wearing that piece of latex that he usually would. "You can't work for McKay-Taggart if you're not in one of their cities."

He pulled her leg up, urging her to wind herself around him. "I'll get another job. Or I'll become a stay-at-home dad. I don't care. My job will be loving you, building a future with you. I love you so much."

She couldn't say it back. "I don't know if I can ever fully love you again."

"I'll make you believe. I'll make you believe in me again, in us.

All I need is a chance. Give us a chance. I won't let you down this time." He winced and started to pull away. "I've got to…"

She lightly dug her nails in, holding him tight. "I want more kids. I want Roman to have a brother or a sister."

If she was in, she was going all in. She wanted everything they should have had the first time. She waited for him to argue with her, to tell her they needed time to adjust. It was what the old Beck would have done. It was precisely why they hadn't had a kid back then. She'd wanted to step back from work, and he'd wanted to give it a little time.

She'd learned time was the one thing she couldn't get back.

"I know I should argue, but I won't ever make you wait again," he promised. "Hold on to me."

She wrapped her arms around him and gasped as he entered her in one powerful thrust.

The little pains in her nipples and on her ass were incidental now. All that mattered was how good it was to have Beck inside her once again.

She would try. She would give them another chance. If he would really let her decide where they lived, where they worked, then he'd changed.

"You can't leave me again," she said as the pleasure started to build inside her.

"Never. We'll fight it out. No matter what, we'll stay together," he promised and then he kissed her again, letting his mouth take hers, drinking down the shout that came as she went over the edge.

He ground out his own orgasm and held her tight.

They were still for a moment. She breathed him in.

"I'm still mad at you," she said quietly. "But I'm not going anywhere."

He nuzzled her neck. "I'll take it because I am so in love with you."

She kissed him, content with her choice. They would see where they went from here.

Chapter Eighteen

Beck looked around the party and felt a deep satisfaction invading his bones. It hadn't even been a day since Kim had chosen to give him another chance, but he felt like his whole world had changed from black and white to glorious color.

He'd gotten to take his family home the night before. All of them, since Kim was moving into his room—where she belonged—and that freed up a bed for his brother. They'd woken up this morning and had breakfast as a family. They'd gotten ready for the party and he and his brother had argued over the best Scotch to get for Ian's birthday, and Kim had finally rolled her eyes and told him she was rethinking her position on more kids if they all fought like he and Ezra.

Then he'd pinned her to the bed and made her rethink her position all over again.

"Your kid looks like he's fitting in nicely." A hand patted his shoulder. Theo Taggart was wearing a pair of board shorts and a tank top, sunglasses over his eyes. He was ready for some fun in the sun. The lake house's massive yard was filled with people eating and laughing and talking. There were a bunch of kids in the pool, and the bouncy house Tag had set up was rocking.

He was going to miss this family he'd made for himself, but he had to follow his heart and she wasn't going to be happy here. He could be happy anywhere as long as they were together. "I think Roman is learning to make friends quite well. But I'm afraid he's going to have to take that new talent and put it to use someplace else."

Theo set his beer on the table as one of the kids giggled while going down the slide and hitting the water with a splash. "You're not staying? Solo wants you to go back to Europe?"

"She's Kim. Solo was her Agency name, and she's not with the Agency anymore." Across the pool, he saw his brother talking to Avery and Li. He was sitting on a chaise lounge. He had his brother back. He never thought he would see him again, but there he was with a smile on his face.

"Kim." Theo nodded. "It suits her."

"I wish you all would pick one name and stick to it." Owen joined them. Rob and Ariel and their daughter had been staying at Theo and Erin's place, Owen and Tucker at the Dean-Miles house, and Jax, River, and the kids were staying with Ian and Charlotte.

But now they were all at this gorgeous lake house Ian and Sean had purchased a few years before. It had become a regular weekend hangout for the whole crew. He came out a few times a year, and he'd always wanted to take Kim hiking. They weren't far from the city here, but they were surrounded by nature, and she'd always loved to get away.

"I promise this is the last name change. We're all going to stick to the ones we've got." Although he intended to talk to Kim about Roman's last name. Technically Roman shared a last name with her uncle. But he wanted them all to have the same last name. His. Hers. It didn't matter as long as it was theirs.

Rob and Tucker walked up, Rob cradling his tiny baby girl in his arms. Jax was right behind them, and he was carrying a tray of what looked like shots.

"I heard you might be turning in your notice soon," Rob said. "Tell me you're coming to Europe. Come on, man. London is a great place to live."

Tucker frowned his way. "You're looking to buy a country house."

Rob shrugged slightly. "Yeah, but only for the weekends. I could never get Ari out of the city. She likes to shop way too much. But I wouldn't mind having another friend around. I'm the last one of us left in London."

"I'm going to let Kim decide," he admitted. "I'll go wherever she wants, but she likes to travel and she hasn't been able to for a couple of years, so I suspect we'll see everyone from time to time."

Jax set his tray down on the table. "You better show at family reunions. We're going to Wyoming this year."

"I already rented out our only decent hotel," Tucker admitted. "All six rooms. I'm going to warn you. It used to be a whorehouse, and like way more recently than you would think."

Beck laughed. "Kim will love it."

Despite her money, his love never complained about something not being five star. She had a never-ending curiosity and thirst for life that made her open to new experiences. He liked to see the world through her eyes because she was so willing to try new things.

They could show their son the world. This time they would do it right. This time they would be tourists, learning for the love of learning and not because they wanted to know how to take advantage of a situation.

It felt like he was starting his life all over again.

But there was one problem.

"Do we know where Levi is being held?"

He watched as the men he'd worked with all those years ago went from play to work mode. Every expression went taut.

"Ian's on it," Theo replied. "He's been trying to get in touch with Drake. He's a slippery guy. He works with us when he wants to and ignores us when it serves his purposes."

"Sounds like every Agency arsehole I've ever worked with." Owen shook his head. "I was wondering if we were going to let it lie."

Rob patted his daughter's back and bounced slightly. He smiled his wife's way as she walked up. "I don't think we can. He's too dangerous."

Ariel was dressed in a pretty orange and yellow sundress. She held her hands out and Rob transferred the baby to her. "Are we talking about Levi?"

Beck glanced around, looking for Kim. She'd been with Ariel earlier.

A brow rose over Ariel's eyes as she settled her daughter into her arms. "She's taking a walk. I saw her down by the lake with some of the kids. Is this something you want to keep from her?"

"Yes. I'm going to kill Levi," Beck admitted.

Ariel's expression changed to a sunny smile. "Oh, is that all? Of course you are. We can't allow the bastard to live. He has a terrible habit of popping back up when you least expect him. Carry on, then. Let me know if you need a sniper."

She gave him a wink and walked out to the pool where River waited to welcome her.

"God, I love that woman." Rob had the goofiest look on his face.

But then they all understood that look. They were all still madly in love with their wives.

Theo took one of the shot glasses and held it up. "So one last mission?"

Owen held up his. "I doubt it will be our last. At some point we all know our kids will get in trouble."

Tucker selected his. "Of that I have no doubt. The next generation is already giving us hell."

Jax picked up the last two shots, handing one to Beck. "I've tried to keep my boys away from the Tag twins, but they're practically in love. They already like dangerous women. I'm doomed. How about a toast? To making the best of a really bad thing."

"To making the most of our second chances," Theo said.

Owen lifted his glass. "To forgiveness and acceptance."

"To finding family we didn't even know we'd lost," Tucker offered.

Rob put a hand on his brother's shoulder. "To all the brothers who aren't here. Who we did lose. May we remember them."

Emotion welled up hard and fast as Beck raised his glass. "To Sasha."

They all drank down the vodka Jax had brought. He'd likely had a choice of many liquors, but they always chose vodka in honor of the Lost Boy who wasn't here to share it.

He'd fought and bled with these men. They were part of his family now, and standing here with them he realized he always held himself slightly apart. And he realized why. Because that part of his heart that could truly open up had been halfway around the world.

"I love you guys." It was good to say it.

Owen's eyes went wide. "Oh, he loves us now, does he? I wonder what caused this amazing turn of events."

Jax snorted as he put his shot glass back on the tray. "We all know what did it."

"Guys, come on. He's had a breakthrough." Rob was always the reasonable one.

"He had an orgasm." And Tucker still said too much. Or what everyone else was thinking.

Beck laughed because these were his brothers. They'd been through something terrible and come out the other side. If there was one thing in the world he'd done right, it was helping these men. "Hey, I can take it. And he's right. It's been a long dry spell waiting for that woman to come back to me."

The door to the house came open and Sean Taggart was suddenly there. "Hey, Beck. I think we're going to need you in here."

A chill went through him. He glanced back and Roman was being helped out of the pool by Ezra. Jamal Lewis was standing at one end of the pool and Charlotte at the other as all the kids seemed to be getting out.

Fuck. They were locking down the kids. That could only mean one thing. "Levi escaped, didn't he?"

Sean held the door open. "Come inside. Ian has news."

"I need to find Kim." His heart had started to race. If Levi had gotten out or been freed by his friends, he would go straight for Kim. Levi was always going to come after her. No matter what he'd said.

"I think you should come in here first," Sean said. "We've got some of the bodyguards bringing everyone inside. If she's not already in the house, she should be here soon."

"Come on." Owen gestured to the door. "Let's see what's happening. I might need to call back home and have Rebecca lock down our house."

"Dad?" Roman had a towel wrapped around him and his hair was still wet. "Is there something wrong?"

His son. He wasn't sure he would ever get used to the emotion that threatened to take over every time he looked down at his son. "I don't know, kiddo, but I'm going to take care of it, and Uncle Ezra is going to stay with you."

Ezra nodded. "Yeah, buddy. Let's go get you dressed, and I bet we can find some games to play."

Roman wasn't fooled. "Is Mom okay? Is the bad man here?"

Beck got to one knee. "I'm going to find out. I need to know you'll stay close to your uncle." Who was a priest and might not remember how to fight. He looked up and Jamal was a reassuring presence.

"I'll watch out for them both, Beck," Jamal assured him. "You do what you need to do. I'm going to take the kids inside, and we'll keep them all together."

He trusted Jamal and the bodyguards. He was certain Charlotte would stay behind and help guard the kids, too. And she would be surrounded by women who knew how to take care of themselves.

"Go on," Rob said. "We'll make sure everyone gets in all right. Go talk to Tag and we'll figure out where to go from there."

He kissed his son's forehead and followed Sean Taggart inside.

"Ian got a message from Drake," Sean was saying. "Apparently at some point during the night, Levi slipped away. Obviously he had someone on the inside because they didn't report he was missing until this morning. Drake didn't find out until an hour ago. However, Adam's already tracked him using one of his aliases. We believe he was on his way to DFW."

It was bad, but they had a couple of things in their favor. "He'll likely go to my house. I'll give Adam my password so he can monitor my security system."

Sean snorted. "Adam's already in, man. He doesn't need a password."

Well, he should have expected that. "Levi will think I'm home on a Saturday. If we don't catch him there, I'll take my family to a safe house."

"I don't know. According to Ian he's got an uncanny ability to figure out where you are at all times." Sean opened the door to the large room they used as an office when they were up here at the lake.

"Where's your sister?" Ian was standing in front of four of his kids. They were lined up by size, as though Ian had taught them exactly how to present themselves.

Kenzie and Kala stood next to Seth, and then Travis at the end. The boys were wrapped in towels while the girls were still in the clothes they'd come here in. Only Tasha was missing.

Kenzie shrugged. "Don't know. She didn't want to watch the movie with us."

Kala stayed silent.

Big Tag stared down at his kids with a look that would have made most hardened soldiers think twice. "Do you honestly believe I don't know when you're hiding something from me? What don't I know? I'm not joking. This is a dangerous situation and your sister could get hurt."

Kenzie opened her mouth but shut it again when Kala glanced her way.

Tag turned his gaze on the boys. They both stared at their fathers.

Travis shook his head. "Daddy, I don't know. The girls are mean and me and Seth stay away."

"No, you don't." Tag's focus lasered in on Seth Taggart, a lanky ten-year-old with his father's sandy hair and mom's smile. Tag stared through his oldest son. "I also know who can handle a month-long grounding from all screens and who can't."

"Tasha's got a secret phone and we're not supposed to talk about it, and I overheard her tell Kenzie that she was going to fix everything and save Mom and Dad from Roman's mom because she's here to hurt them." Seth couldn't talk fast enough.

Kala rolled her eyes. "We are never telling you anything again."

"What do you mean she's going to fix everything? Why would Tasha think Kim is here to hurt your mom and dad?" Kim had told him she felt like Tag's eldest daughter had something against her. "Where did they go?"

Kala's arms went over her chest.

But Kenzie had obviously had enough. "She's been talking to a kid whose dad knows her bio dad. He used to work with him in Russia, and he has proof that Kim is the one who gave her dad over to the same crazy lady who nearly killed Uncle Theo."

He couldn't believe the kids had this drama going on for months and no one had heard about it. "Kim didn't have anything to do with that."

"She's the only reason we found Tasha in the first place." Tag stood up and he had his hands on his hips as he loomed over his kids. "She's our friend, which I would have explained to Tasha if any one of you had done the right thing and told me what was going on."

"She's our sister," Kala shot back. "We have to protect her."

"And you have to know when to turn her in to protect everyone," Tag said, his jaw tight. "The man who has been catfishing your sister is the man who killed her father. He might not have pulled the trigger, but he primed it and let it go off. Now he's going to kill your sister because he won't leave her behind to tell the truth."

Kenzie started crying and even Kala looked shaken.

"Ian!" Charlotte strode into the room.

Ian took a long breath. "I'm sorry. But this is a dangerous situation and honestly, they've been acting like they're ready to take on adult decisions, so they should damn well understand what could potentially be the outcome."

"Someone's going to kill Tasha?" Travis looked to his mom as tears started to stream down his face.

Charlotte wrapped her arms around her youngest child and sent Ian a death stare.

Seth stood beside his brother. "Dad will take care of it. I knew we should have talked to him."

"Tasha's been talking to Levi Green?" His gut clenched.

"She wanted to know more about her dad in the beginning," Kenzie said through her tears. "It started about a year ago. She met him online playing this game we all play."

"She didn't want you to know because she thought you would be mad she was trying to find out about him—her dad." Even Kala looked shaken now. She stared up at her dad. "She thought you would think she didn't love you. We just wanted to protect our family."

"Where would she take Kim?" There was no question in his mind that Kim was out there with Tasha, and that Levi had set it all up.

Was he already too late?

Kala finally started talking and Beck got ready. He was going to finish this. No matter what it took.

* * * *

Kim looked out over the water and had to admit, the kid had a point. It was a spectacular view. "It's lovely."

"It's my favorite place out here. I like being in the boat, but the pier is my favorite." Tasha's long dark hair was up in a ponytail and she was dressed in cutoffs and a T-shirt, sneakers on her feet. "It's usually peaceful here. Dad and Uncle Sean bought three lots so we would have some distance from the other houses. I love my family, but there's not a lot of quiet. Kala's quiet, but that's usually a bad sign."

She'd been surprised when Tasha had asked if she would help her grab some stuff from her dad's boat. She'd explained that she wanted to take some of the younger kids fishing, and the equipment was still on the boat from the last time they'd gone out.

But it also gave her a chance to talk to the girl. She'd been awfully nice to Roman, but there was still a chill coming off her.

"I was hoping we could talk, Tasha." They were standing within the shade of the trees. It was a bit of a hike to the lake from the house, but it was worth it for the view.

Tasha turned her way and her mouth firmed. "Yes, I think we should. I want to know why you hated my dad so much."

She hadn't expected that. "I don't hate your dad. He's sarcastic, but I actually think he's pretty funny. I owe Ian a lot. Why would you think I hate your father?"

"I'm talking about Oleg Federov."

Kim went still. "I didn't hate him either. I didn't know him very well. I only met him a couple of times. Who told you I hated him?"

"A friend of mine."

"A friend from school? How long have you known this person?" She glanced around because she was starting to get the feeling that this was a setup.

This was starting to feel like something Levi would do.

But he was in custody. He wouldn't survive long if Big Tag found out he'd catfished his daughter. It explained why Tasha had a problem with her. If Levi had been feeding Tasha a line of crap about how Kim had hurt her father, of course Tasha would hate her.

The teen's shoulders straightened, and Kim wondered if Tasha knew where she'd gotten that stubborn stance. That stance was pure Ian Taggart going into general mode. "His name is Lev. He's Russian. He's the son of a man who used to work with my dad. He reached out to me online last year."

Well, at least Levi remembered their training. Try to pick a name that's easy to answer to when going undercover. "Sweetie, I know this is going to be hard for you to believe, but the kid you think you're talking to is actually a CIA operative. His name is Levi Green."

She shook her head. "No. He's a kid. I've seen a picture of him, and I've talked to him on the phone. He speaks Russian. He's not American."

"He's good at his job. He can fake a lot, and he does speak Russian. He speaks Russian and Mandarin. Most of the top operatives speak a couple of different languages." This would also explain how Levi seemed to know the things he did. Tasha had been working at McKay-Taggart during the early weeks of summer. She was an observant kid, and she likely would have known something was going on with Beck. "Did he ask you to tell him if they found me?"

Tasha frowned. "He showed me documentation that you handed over Oleg Federov to Dr. Hope McDonald. He got it from his dad."

"I never met Hope McDonald," Kim said, trying to keep her tone calm. "But Levi Green once faked evidence that I did. I would never have turned anyone over to that monster. I'm so sorry he's made you think I would. Let's go talk to your dad—to Ian."

She shook her head. "Ian is my dad. That's why I didn't take this to him. I don't talk about my bio parents because I don't want my dad to think I don't love him. He would feel betrayed if he knew."

"He'll understand." Tag would understand that Levi was a monster who used a little girl's insecurity against her. She also couldn't see Ian keeping knowledge about Oleg Federov away from Tasha. "If there's one thing I know it's that your dad loves you. So does your mom. Did you ever ask Beck or Rob about the man they knew as Sasha?"

Her dark eyes had gone watery. "I told you. I didn't want my parents to think I didn't love them."

Sympathy welled for the baby standing in front of her. She'd been through so much, and all she wanted were some answers.

"Wanting to know your roots doesn't mean you don't love them. The drugs that McDonald gave to your dad, they took his memory."

"I know that."

"Yes, but did you know that sometimes a memory would be so precious that it still got through? Like your Uncle Theo would remember your Aunt Erin."

"Yes," Tasha replied. "I read that. He would get punished for remembering."

Oh, she was going to have a talk with Tag about locking his files down. She shouldn't have to process that as a child. But Kim could give her one bit of peace. "Yes. Sasha only ever remembered one thing."

Tears made Tasha's eyes shine, and she looked so young and vulnerable. "What was that? Did he remember my mom?"

"You. He remembered holding you right after you were born." Ariel had told her the story that she'd gotten from Rob. "He couldn't remember anything else, but he remembered he loved you. Tasha, let's go talk to Beck and the others. They would love to tell you about him. When I was looking for you, I learned a lot about your mom. I can tell you what I know about her. She fought to find your dad. She loved you. She was trying to bring you all back together. Charlotte and Ian Taggart would never keep that information from you. Ever. You are their daughter. It doesn't matter that you had two other parents who loved you. They will share you because they know love isn't something finite. There's more than enough to go around."

If she let it. If she let herself, she could love Beck and Roman and any other kids they were blessed with. If she let herself, she had a real shot at the family she'd always dreamed of. She just had to be brave enough to take the risk. The risk was that she would get hurt again. Oh, but the reward would be everything.

She'd told Beck she would give them a shot the night before and she'd meant it, but she also acknowledged that she'd meant to hold a piece of herself back, to keep a part of her soul that he could never touch again.

She didn't owe Beck forgiveness, but she did owe it to herself.

Sasha had held on to that one memory of a daughter he would never meet again. Theo had endured torture to keep a single vision of the woman he'd loved. Rob and Tucker had remembered their mother, the feeling of brotherhood that brought them close even when they hadn't been able to recall the other's name. Owen had spent years talking to relatives, having them tell stories of the family erased from his mind. And Jax had forged ahead.

She and Beck could remember every moment, and they'd been the ones stuck because they'd held on to the bitter times. She'd been angry at that dumb girl who'd wanted nothing more than to be Beck's wife.

But that girl had been brave. She'd been rejected time and time again and still opened herself to the possibility of love.

"Be brave, Tasha," Kim said. Tasha was crying freely now, and Kim felt her own tears. "Let's go talk to your mom and dad. Let's sit down and figure this out. They won't be angry. They'll protect you."

Tasha sniffled. "I'm confused."

Kim nodded. "I know you are. It's okay. You don't have to believe me. You only have to know that your parents love you and want to protect you. The man you're talking to is very dangerous. But it's okay because right now he's in jail and he can't hurt us."

Tasha's eyes widened. "See. You're wrong about him. He's not in jail. His dad is coming here in a couple of hours. I'm supposed to bring you down here so he can arrest you and take you back to Russia." She went a bit pale. "I'm sorry. I thought I was being like Dad. Me and Kenzie and Kala, we just wanted to be like our mom and dad and show them we could take care of a situation like they do."

They were babies trying to play spy games, and Levi should die horribly for taking advantage of them. But first they needed to get to safety because something had gone wrong. Maybe Levi had someone on the outside working for him.

Or someone on the inside and he'd gotten away.

Either way she needed to get herself and Tasha to safety. "Come on. We need to go back to the main house."

Tasha nodded and then her eyes widened in pure terror.

"Too late for that, Solo. You should have known I would do anything to win."

She turned and Levi moved from behind a tree, a gun in his hand.

Chapter Nineteen

Kim's heart threatened to stop, and she knew she had mere seconds to avoid a tragedy. She hadn't spent months trying to find this kid all those years ago only to watch Levi Green kill her today.

She stepped in front of Tasha. "Stay behind me."

"But I told him where you were." Tasha's voice shook as she whispered the words.

"It doesn't matter. Stay behind me. If I tell you to run, go for the house and I'll try to keep him off you." Kim never took her eyes off Levi.

"Ah, there's my Solo." He looked worse for the wear. He was dressed down, in all black, wearing a hoodie despite the heat. He likely had more weapons than that gun on his person. "You look good. Seven years hasn't aged you at all, sweetheart. You're a sight for sore eyes."

"What are you doing here?" She knew but she had a game to play, one that was hampered by the fact that she couldn't let Levi kill anyone else. She didn't even know where all the kids were. What would happen if they ran up?

"You remember when I told you about my wedding?"

"Yes. Is it this weekend or something? I thought you would be getting ready." She had to stay calm. Levi was between them and the trail to the house, though she had to hope Tasha knew these woods. She'd been coming up here with her family for years.

"Well, turns out my lovely bride has changed her mind. I bet I know who helped her." Levi had a dark gleam in his eyes. "You know, baby, if you'd told me you objected, I would have left her in a heartbeat. It was always you."

"What are you talking about?" She hated this man. It was a churning fire in her gut, but spitting bile wouldn't solve the problem. She had to keep him calm until someone came looking for them.

His eyes rolled. "Like you don't know. I bet Beck threw a party when he found out. My question is who found her? Reva, that is."

"Do you honestly think Beck tells me anything? He doesn't trust me." She could play off Levi's desire to see them fractured.

"Reva was a dirty little whore hacker I hired and paid good money to. She wasn't supposed to keep her Wayback Machine version of my crimes. I'd really like to pay her a visit," he admitted. "I've been looking for her for a long time. So long it makes me wonder who knew about it. Me thinks there's a spy in our midst." He laughed, a slightly maniacal sound. "Spies within spies. But you should know all about that, right?"

"I've been out of the game for a long time," she admitted. Was he alone? If he was alone, she might have a shot if he got much closer.

Levi shook his head. "I wasn't talking about you. Hi, Tasha. Like father like daughter, I see. You know I got your father to betray his friends, too. They'll all lie to you and tell you stories about Sasha, but he was willing to sell every one of them out to buy himself some safety. Like you sold out the Taggarts. You'll never be one of them now."

"Don't talk to her that way." He was a monster. How had he ever tricked her into believing he was a human being? She'd genuinely cared about him once, and now all she could see was the selfish sadist he was.

A real sadist. She'd thought of Beck that way, but it wasn't true. Levi enjoyed ripping people apart, but Beck had been hurt and angry and he hadn't known how to deal with it.

Seven years. He'd spent seven years in therapy to make himself a better man, to have a chance to solve their problems because somewhere along the way he'd grown up.

God, would she ever see Beck again?

He would take care of Roman. They all would. This weird family had stuck together over the years through all kinds of hardship. They'd seen each other through it all, and they would take care of her son.

They would take care of her husband.

"Why not?" Levi shrugged a shoulder. That was when she realized there were two men coming up to flank her. They were dressed like Levi and both held guns. One had a pair of handcuffs peeking out of his pocket.

Only one pair.

She had to work him if she was going to get Tasha out of this alive. "Because she's a kid. Give her a break. You've been working her over for how long now?"

"Eighteen months. Ever since I realized I was going to have to change plans and marry that cypher I found. She was dumb as dirt but well connected, and her father owed me. I had to make sure Beck didn't know where you were. I had to make sure there wasn't any way we could still be together. And as for Tasha, we were all kids once." Levi moved in. "It's better to understand the world is shit now and that Mommy and Daddy only love you while you're perfect. Tasha gets that. She knows the world is shit and she can't trust anyone now."

"My dad is going to kill you," Tasha said with a quavering breath.

Levi sneered her way. "Your dad is dead. Taggart isn't your father. All you are to Ian Taggart is an obligation. He took you in because he fucked up and got your real dad killed. He was a prick, too. The stories I could tell you about Sasha, the traitor."

She took a deep breath. It made her sick, but she had to do it. She had to convince him she wanted to go with him. "Levi, let Tasha go and I'll be a good girl."

He studied her for a moment, his eyes going up and down her body. "I don't think you have a weapon on you. You're out of practice."

"I haven't run an op in years, but I know when to quit, and you were right about Beck. He's never going to care about me." She glanced over to the two men edging closer and closer and really wished a little of the old Solo had come back. He was right. She wasn't carrying a weapon. "He hasn't forgiven me. All he cares about is his son."

A brow cocked over Levi's eyes. "I'm supposed to believe you don't care about your son."

She prayed Roman never had to know what she was about to say. "He's a good kid, but do you honestly think I'm cut out to be a mommy? Do you have any idea how boring the last seven years have been?"

They hadn't. She'd needed them to prove to her what she wanted. A quiet life filled with love and family and people who did the right thing because the world was good for them. Because they worked hard to make it good. People who didn't hide behind patriotism to fuel the greed of a few. There were good people working in intelligence, but she couldn't do it anymore because they always had to fight the faction the Levis of the world aligned themselves with.

"I don't know if I believe you." But there was a hesitation in his tone. He wanted to believe her. His sick mind wanted to believe he would get everything he desired.

"Let Tasha go and I'll prove it to you." She used her husky voice, the one she dragged out when she needed to pretend she wanted some dumbass so he would give her information.

Yeah, she hated that part, too.

"So I'm supposed to believe that you want me now."

"I want out, Levi. Beck has it in his head that I should be his housewife. I'm supposed to take some desk job at McKay-Taggart and hand over everything to him. So if getting out of that means going with you, then I'll give it a try. He's holding Ezra over my head."

"Yes, that wasn't well done of you." Levi nodded. "Boys, take the kid out."

"No!"

She tried to shield Tasha but the man on the left was a good shot. He managed to avoid Kim altogether. He struck Tasha in the right thigh.

With a dart.

Tasha slumped to the ground. God, she hoped they had the dosage right.

"I'm not stupid. Killing Tag's daughter would irritate him. She'll take a nap and maybe she'll learn a lesson," Levi said, looking down at the teen. "Maybe Tag will be too busy dealing with his fucked-up adopted mess to look for me. Now, I believe you said something about wanting to come along."

Could she get close enough to fight him for the gun?

"Come on. We've got a car waiting about half a mile from here. I want to get on the road before they find the girl. She'll cost them some time." Levi gripped her elbow and pulled her close.

"Where are we going?" She forced herself to stumble a bit to slow them down.

Levi merely pulled her along. "I've got a safe house in the Philippines no one knows about. And luckily, now I have your money. We're going to clear your accounts out so we have some working capital. I have to pay these guys. I don't get to call up a Special Ops teams anymore. You know I'm really going to miss the perks."

How slow could she go? "I was surprised you didn't clear out my accounts when you had the chance."

"Beck blocked me. I'm sure he was planning on finding you and getting his hands on it. He went to your banks with a couple of lawyers and made sure the government wasn't able to access the funds. But now I've lifted the freeze on your accounts, and we can march right down to the bank and transfer the funds. We're going to need them for our new life."

"In the Philippines." The grip on her arm was starting to hurt. She wished she knew the land better. They were surrounded by trees. She was certain they were heading southeast, away from the lake. They couldn't be far from the house. It hadn't taken them more than ten minutes to walk down to the pier.

If she ran, would he kill her? She'd been perfectly willing to die seven years before when he'd had her in that limo. There had been a part of her that had been disappointed Beck had stopped her from finishing it. Her life had seemed like such a misery at the time.

She didn't want to finish anything. She wanted to watch her son grow up, wanted her second or third or fourth chance with Beck.

"In the beginning we'll stay there." Levi stopped and forced her to look up at him. "I've got plans. Don't think I can't take care of you."

"It sounds like I'll be taking care of you." She couldn't let him get her in the car. She had to time this so they wouldn't go back for Tasha, wouldn't be close enough to the house to catch one of the kids. But she wanted her shot at surviving, and that meant delaying the moment when they got her to the road.

"I don't think you'll mind." He actually had the balls—or the insanity—to brush her hair back. "I think we're going to get along quite well this time around. This time Beck won't be between us, and you won't lie to me about anything."

"Because you're going to drug me and turn me into some kind of zombie?"

One side of his mouth kicked up in an arrogant grin. "Not at first. Remember when I said I wasn't going to torture you? I changed my mind. You kept Ezra Fain from me for years. You hid that fucker when he was mine to deal with."

"Ezra wasn't a bad man. He was in trouble and you manipulated him." It was what Levi did. He saw a weakness and used it to his own advantage.

"He chose to do the things he did, and I need you to understand that I can't let him live." He started walking again, his grip tightening. "You won't mourn him. Like you won't mourn Beck. Or that brat of a kid. I'm not stupid. I know you're playing me for time. You've run out of it. I'm taking you back to my safe house where I'll properly punish you for your infractions and then we'll start our new life. You think I haven't had to start over again? I've done it more than once and I always come out on top, Solo."

"Don't call her Solo," a deep voice said. A familiar voice. A heavenly voice. Beck stepped out from behind a big oak, his SIG in his hand. "She's not alone."

Her breath caught as she realized she wasn't. Beck hadn't come alone. Somehow they'd moved in behind them. Rob and Tucker. Owen and Jax. Theo. They all moved out of the woods, surrounding Levi and the two mercenaries he'd brought with them.

"Lay it down and walk away." Theo had his gun trained on the man flanking her right. "You should understand my brother is back at the lake holding his daughter. The only reason I'm letting you go is he'll kill you, and the last thing he needs is more blood on his hands. You better be fucking happy you used a tranquilizer on her, and I would suggest you watch your back for the rest of your life."

"And you," Beck ordered. "My friends will escort you out of here and I better not see your faces again. That was my wife your boss was kidnapping."

Both the mercenaries dropped their guns and held their hands up.

"Tell Taggart it was a job and we didn't know it was him." The man Owen was guarding had gone pale.

"We can tell him. Doesn't mean he'll believe it," Owen replied. "Only reason you're not going down is it's harder to bury three bodies than one."

Levi had pulled her close, putting his gun to her head. "I don't think you're burying anyone. Unless you want to put Solo in the ground with me. It would be fitting. You should know that I'll have her in the afterlife, too, Beck. She was always meant for me."

She was so sick of one asshole wrecking her life. Maybe she and Beck would have imploded the first time around no matter what happened, but Levi had been the match. Levi Green had decided she belonged to him like she was some piece of property he could occupy. He treated the whole world like it was his and no one else mattered.

She was not going down with him.

She could be Solo one last time. Just once, because Beck was right. She was never going to be alone again.

"Baby, what do you want me to do?" Beck asked, and that was when she noticed the fine tremor in his hold. He wasn't the cold "Ezra Fain" he'd become when they'd been apart.

They'd played roles for so many years. Maybe the whole time they'd known each other. But it was time to be Beck and Kim. Solo and Ezra—sexy operatives—had been a toxic combination. But she thought maybe Beck and Kim—parents, partners, madly in love— might be able to make it.

But Solo could do one last mission.

"Follow my lead," she said.

He nodded and no one else moved. Owen and Theo had escorted their guests off, and she heard the squeal of tires as the car left.

"Well, it looks like I'm going to need..." Levi began.

God that fucker could talk. She brought her arm up and back, breaking his hold and forcing the hand with the gun in it to drop. She kicked back, sending him to his ass. In seconds, she had his gun in her hand and she was in the superior position.

He always did underestimate her.

She held the gun on him. "I'm going to suspect Tag wants a word."

"Yes," Beck said, moving in beside her. "I would, too."

That was the moment she noticed Levi had something in his hand.

"You always were magnificent," Levi said softly. "And you were always fair. I'm going to have to use that against you, my love." He had a hypodermic needle in his hand, and he plunged it into his own arm. "You won't get any answers out of me. That was the last of the formula. In a few minutes, I'll start all over again."

Kim Solomon shot him without hesitation. She watched as the light faded from Levi's eyes and he slumped back.

She turned to Beck. "He's right. I wouldn't have been able to kill him if the drug took effect. But it hadn't. He was still the same son of a bitch he's always been. He doesn't get to start over."

Theo Taggart walked up to the body and solemnly put another bullet in him. "Just in case."

Jax was next. "Can't be too sure."

Owen and Tucker took their turns as though they all needed a hand in finally putting down the man who'd caused them so much trouble.

Rob stepped up and another crack sounded. He looked to Beck. "Your turn, man."

Beck shook his head. "No. I have everything I need. You got this?"

Rob nodded. "We've been ready to clean this particular mess up for a long time, boss. Take Kim back to the house. They're all worried about her."

He left the guns on the ground, obviously trusting the Lost Boys to deal with the situation.

He hadn't even looked Levi's way. Every bit of his attention had been on her. "Beck, it's okay if you need to stay."

He shook his head and cupped her cheeks, bringing his forehead down to meet hers. "He's incidental in our love story. He's nothing but a blip, and now we move on. Together."

"I love you, Beck. Wholly and without holding anything back. I love you. I trust you." Tears fell on her cheeks because she did. She let go of all her anger. They could start over. They could take all that passion they'd had in the beginning, pair it with the abiding love and patience they'd found, and have the marriage they'd always wanted.

"I love you. More than anything." He kissed her forehead and then leaned over to pick her up and hold her against his chest. "Let's get our son. And my brother. And a drink because I need one. My hands are still shaking."

She laid her head on his shoulder and held on to him.

* * * *

Beck sat back as the CIA operative known as Drake lowered himself into the seat at the big conference table. Drake had been with the Agency for years, but he still looked like a baby to Beck.

He and Kim had been babies when they'd started. So many years had passed, and yet he felt far younger than he had back then. He reached over and brought her hand to his lips.

She gave him a smile that rocked his world. And she winked his way before turning slightly. The movement made her blouse gape a bit, and he caught a hint of the ring looped on her necklace. Her uncle had sent it to her from Malta along with a letter for Beck. He'd promised severe retribution if Beck screwed up again. The man had explained that he had a good relationship with the almighty, and he wouldn't hesitate to use it.

Beck liked her uncle.

That ring was going back on her finger this weekend.

"I need you to understand that I had no idea what Levi was doing." Drake looked like a man trying to placate a predator who wanted to rip him apart.

But then Ian Taggart was still angry.

Beck would never forget how pale Tag had gone when he'd seen

Tasha on the ground. He'd never once seen that man cry, but the tears had fallen as he'd gone to his knees and held his daughter to his heart. He'd managed to send the rest of them on when he'd realized she was alive. But he'd still been holding her an hour later when she'd woken up. The fact that they'd had a doctor and a few nurses there who had been able to monitor her hadn't meant anything to the Taggarts. They'd held vigil around Tasha and only breathed again when she'd woken.

"The Agency didn't know one of their top men was using an innocent teenage girl as an asset?" The question came out of Tag's mouth like a bomb waiting to go off.

"I assure you I didn't know." Drake seemed determined to defuse it. "Tag, you have to believe me. I would never have let him hurt Tasha. I would have gone against any orders I was given. I did go against orders to get Solo that package."

"Kim," he insisted.

"I'm only Solo now when Beck there wants to get some role play in," Kim replied, giving the man too much information.

But it was true. Sometimes it was fun to have the badass Solo interrogate him.

Tag ignored it entirely, focusing all his attention on the Agency liaison. "Let your bosses know that I won't forget. And I won't forgive."

"I think they are aware," Drake said cautiously. "They wanted to let you know that as far as they're concerned Ezra Fain died during the operation that took out his team. There will be no repercussions, and you'll find no one is concerned with a priest."

His brother could return to the life he'd built for himself. He could go back to doing good. After he'd spent some time with his family. "Thank you."

"I'm happy to have been able to make that happen," Drake replied as though relieved at least one thing had gone right. His jaw tightened as he looked to Taggart. "I was hoping you could give me a debrief on what happened that day. The Agency is interested in bringing Mr. Green's body back to Langley."

A humorless smile crossed Taggart's face. "You'll have to find him first."

Drake frowned. "Are you trying to say you didn't kill him?"

"I was far too busy being concerned with my daughter's life, Drake," Tag shot back. "And then I was concerned with what that fucker did to her. The things he said, they will haunt her for the rest of her life. So no, I did not bother to kill Levi Green."

Before the Lost Boys had left to return home, they'd spent an evening at Tag's place, sitting around the fire pit in the backyard with Tasha. They'd told her stories about her father and how he'd given his life to save Owen's.

Charlotte had stuck close to her oldest daughter the last weeks. So had the other kids, though that hadn't been hard since they were all grounded. According to Tag that might last forever.

Beck didn't think so. The Taggarts would pull together and get through this as a family. The way the Kents would.

Drake looked Kim's way. "Come on, So…Kim. You can't expect me to believe Levi got away. If he had, you would have a bodyguard on you twenty-four seven."

Kim merely smiled. "Beck totally trusts me to take out the bad guys. That's what we've decided our jobs are. I'm the muscle and he's the beauty."

He had to laugh at that because his almost wife was so gorgeous it hurt. "Yep. I just make myself pretty for her. I'm strictly arm candy from here on out."

"And I'm supposed to believe that the Lost Boys just up and left and went back to their lives with Levi on the run?" Drake asked.

"Jax and River are opening their summer camp next week." He knew that schedule far too well since his wife had announced her plans for future employment. "They can't keep the kiddos waiting. And the rest of them wanted to get home."

Ari and Rob were the only ones hanging out. Ari was helping Kim get ready for the big move. Mostly that included the duo shopping like there was no tomorrow. It was so good to see Kim smiling and relaxed and happy.

They were walking away from everything they knew, and it felt good. It felt like the adventure he'd been waiting for all his life.

Drake sighed. "You know this means we'll have to use Agency resources to look for him. And there are a whole lot of bosses at the top of the ladder who will likely be looking over their shoulder…and that's why you're doing it. Damn it, Tag. It's going to look bad on me if I can't find a body."

"You're young. You'll do fine. I have no idea where Levi Green is," Tag said flatly. "I can't help you."

"All right. I get it. I even understand it." Drake pushed his chair back and faced Kim. "Ms. Solomon, I've been given the go-ahead to offer you any position you want at the Agency."

So she would tell them what happened to Levi Green? He snorted.

Kim looked back his way. "You're not worried I'm tempted?"

Not for a second. "You have a job."

Kim stood and offered Drake a hand. "I'm afraid my fiancé is right. I've found a much better position."

Drake shook her hand. "Here? McKay-Taggart is taking a lot of our talent."

Taggart finally flashed something like a real smile. "Nope. She turned me down flat, and she's taking Beck with her. But she's going to another place that seems to suck a whole lot of talent up. They won't be the only ex-Agency employees there. And I've heard there are aliens."

Drake's expression turned distinctly horrified. "Are you talking about that weird place John Bishop ended up in? You know most feds avoid it like the plague. What the hell are you going to do in Colorado?"

"I'm a nature guide with the best tour agency in Southern Colorado. Mountain Adventures," Kim announced. "And Beck has a job with a group Adam Miles works with from time to time. The Kincaid-Briggs Group. They're private investigators who work specifically with small law enforcement offices and cold case files."

He'd talked to the former FBI agents and found himself excited to focus his talents on solving mysteries, on giving families peace. "The pay is crap, but moneybags here already bought us a gorgeous piece of land on the Rio Grande."

"They're staying at my cabin until theirs is built," Tag acknowledged. "We usually go up for a month before school starts, but not this year. My family is keeping close to home for a while.

Drake, you need to let your bosses know I won't handle any further interference in my business or my family life well."

Drake picked up the bag he'd carried in. "I will. And Tag, if you do need anything, call me. I know you don't like who I work for, but I owe you." He stopped. "I need to know if my cousin should worry. She's a good kid. She got taken in by Levi, too. I just want her to feel safe."

"Your cousin shouldn't worry." Tag gave him a nod. "And thank you, Drake."

The CIA agent breathed a sigh of relief and walked out.

Tag stood. "You leaving this afternoon?"

Beck held out a hand. "We're all packed up. The paperwork on the sale of the house should go through in a couple of weeks, but I told Hutch he can move in whenever he likes. I'm glad he's taking the place."

"I'm glad he's getting out of that apartment he's been in for years. We'll miss you around here, but I think you'll like Bliss. Well, except for Max Harper. He's annoying," Tag admitted. "And all the protests. You should get used to listening to Nell Flanders sing protest songs through a bullhorn."

"I can handle it." He hoped. He'd only been there once, and it hadn't seemed so weird to him. When he thought about it, his life had started again in that tiny Colorado town where he'd met up with his wife after years apart.

"And the beets. There are so many beets." Tag shook his head. "And the nudists. Whole lot of junk on display on the mountain, if you know what I mean."

It was starting to come back to him. Maybe he should rethink this.

Kim's hand found his. "Stop scaring him. We're going to love it there. And thank you for everything." She went on her toes and kissed him. "Let's get our son and pick up Ezra. He only has a couple of weeks before he's got to get back to Malta."

He was road tripping with his wife and son and brother. It would be bliss.

He followed his wife out and into their new lives.

Epilogue

Later that afternoon

Hutch sank into the chair in front of Ian's desk. "Hey, boss. How is the family?"

The office had been oddly hushed the last week out of respect for what the Taggarts were going through.

"We're good," Tag said solemnly. "I find myself walking the edge a lot of parents do. I have to find a way to keep my kids safe while not breaking everything that's good about them. They were being loyal. They were trying to be brave. They were being stupid because they're kids and not spies. But they were emulating me and their mom. I thought I would be more angry. I just find myself...I don't even know. Wear a condom, man."

He wasn't used to contemplative Tag. "I do, boss. Every single time."

He wasn't even close to being ready for kids. He'd barely had a real girlfriend. He'd lived with a waitress from Top for a couple of months, but it hadn't worked out. He wasn't sure there was some mystical one for him out there. He'd managed to be good friends with some of the women he'd shared a bed with, but he'd never felt that spark his friends with wives talked about.

But he was about to be an actual homeowner. It was a first step in trying to move into real adulthood.

"I called you in because I want you to work on a case for me." Tag handed over a file. "It's probably nothing, but I got a call from an old friend and I promised him I would look into it."

"I'm going in the field?" He almost never went in the field. He was a desk jockey. He was the computer nerd.

"Sort of," Tag replied. "Though you won't be going far. The client is here in Dallas. She works for a biotech firm, and she's worried there's some corporate espionage going on."

He opened the folder and found a picture of a pretty woman, likely in her early to mid-twenties. She had brown hair and glasses, a ready smile on her face. She wore a white lab coat that hid her figure. But there was something odd in her hands. "Are those crutches? Did she get hurt?"

"She was in a car accident when she was a teenager," Tag explained. "She can walk, but she typically uses a cane or braces. She's a chemist and the daughter of a sheriff friend of mine. He's worried about her. Says since she started working on this project some weird things have been happening. I want you to study up for the meeting tomorrow."

He closed the folder. "Will do, boss."

Likely it was nothing. He would look through some computers, make sure her house was secure, and then he would be right back at his desk. Right back to his life of playing video games and being everyone's fun uncle.

It was starting to feel a little hollow. He was starting to crave responsibility.

It was weird.

He stood.

"And Hutch," Tag began. "I'm sending someone out with you. I need you to take care of him."

"You're sending a bodyguard?" Sometimes he got paired with one of the guards. He could get deep into an investigation and focus so much on a screen that it was good to have someone watching his back.

"I want you to walk Kyle Hawthorne through his first time in the field." Tag's expression had gone distinctly serious.

Hutch stared at him for a moment. "You want me to take your brother's stepson out in the field? Maybe you should pair him with Erin or Michael. Boomer isn't doing anything this week."

Kyle Hawthorne was Grace Hawthorne's baby boy. Baby? Hell, Kyle was slightly older than Hutch and had recently gotten out of the Navy. He had a ready smile, but Hutch saw a bit of darkness in the man that made him worry. He knew all about darkness and the things it could make a man do.

"He can take care of himself." Tag's lips kicked up in an amused grin. "Mostly. But I do want you to look out for him."

And if he got Kyle killed, Sean Taggart would fillet him.

Still, like Tag had said. It was probably nothing. "Sure thing."

Famous last words. He hoped Noelle LaVigne was worth it.

He walked back out to his office and read through her file. Tomorrow he would go to work.

Hutch, Noelle, and the McKay-Taggart crew will return in *Submission Impossible.*

Author's Note

I'm often asked by generous readers how they can help get the word out about a book they enjoyed. There are so many ways to help an author you like. Leave a review. If your e-reader allows you to lend a book to a friend, please share it. Go to Goodreads and connect with others. Recommend the books you love because stories are meant to be shared. Thank you so much for reading this book and for supporting all the authors you love!

Submission Impossible

Masters and Mercenaries: Reloaded, Book 1
By Lexi Blake

He loves the sweet life

Greg Hutchins is reluctantly adulting these days. He's settled in his job, recently bought his first house, and has a network of friends he can call family. But there's something missing in his life, and he can't quite put his finger on it. When he's assigned to a case that involves investigating a biochemical company, he meets a woman who's sweeter than any candy. Maybe she's just the thing to make him feel complete.

She's ready for the future

Noelle LaVigne has faced plenty of tragedy in her life, but she's on the right path now. Between her new job and settling into a new city, she's got no time for dating or relationships. She's worked hard to get where she is, and no man is going to push her off track. Except the minute Hutch crosses her path she can't seem to think about anything but the handsome security expert. He's there to find a corporate spy, but late-night work sessions make her think they've both found something much more meaningful.

A twist they never saw coming

When the case becomes dangerous, both of their futures are on the line. And when the bullets start flying, they will have to learn to trust in each other if they hope to survive.

Treasured
Masters and Mercenaries, Book 21.5
By Lexi Blake
Coming June 29, 2021

David Hawthorne has a great life. His job as a professor at a prestigious Dallas college is everything he hoped for. Now that his brother is back from the Navy, life seems to be settling down. All he needs to do is finish the book he's working on and his tenure will be assured. When he gets invited to interview a reclusive expert, he knows he's gotten lucky. But being the stepson of Sean Taggart comes with its drawbacks, including an overprotective mom who sends a security detail to keep him safe. He doesn't need a bodyguard, but when Tessa Santiago shows up on his doorstep, the idea of her giving him close cover doesn't seem so bad.

Tessa has always excelled at most anything she tried, except romance. The whole relationship thing just didn't work out for her. She's not looking for love, and she's certainly not looking for it with an academic who happens to be connected to her boss's family. The last thing she wants is to escort an overly pampered pretentious man-child around South America to ensure he doesn't get into trouble. Still, there's something about David that calls to her. In addition to watching his back, she will have to avoid falling into the trap of soulful eyes and a deep voice that gets her heart racing.

But when the seemingly simple mission turns into a treacherous race for a hidden artifact, David and Tess know this assignment could cost them far more than their jobs. If they can overcome the odds, the lost treasure might not be their most valuable reward.

About Lexi Blake

New York Times bestselling author Lexi Blake lives in North Texas with her husband and three kids. Since starting her publishing journey in 2010, she's sold over three million copies of her books. She began writing at a young age, concentrating on plays and journalism. It wasn't until she started writing romance that she found success. She likes to find humor in the strangest places and believes in happy endings.

Connect with Lexi online:

Facebook: Lexi Blake
Twitter: authorlexiblake
Website: www.LexiBlake.net
Instagram: https://www.instagram.com/lexiblakeauthor

Sign up for Lexi's free newsletter!

Printed in the USA
CPSIA information can be obtained
at www.ICGtesting.com
LVHW020308080324
773861LV00002B/61